# not my
# daughter

D0804233

KATE HEWITT

# not my daughter

FOREVER

New York   Boston

This book is a work of fiction. Names, characters, places, and incidents are the product of the author's imagination or are used fictitiously. Any resemblance to actual events, locales, or persons, living or dead, is coincidental.

Copyright © 2019 by Kate Hewitt

Cover design by Alice Moore.
Cover copyright © 2019 by Hachette Book Group, Inc.

Hachette Book Group supports the right to free expression and the value of copyright. The purpose of copyright is to encourage writers and artists to produce the creative works that enrich our culture.

The scanning, uploading, and distribution of this book without permission is a theft of the author's intellectual property. If you would like permission to use material from the book (other than for review purposes), please contact permissions@hbgusa.com. Thank you for your support of the author's rights.

Forever
Hachette Book Group
1290 Avenue of the Americas, New York, NY 10104
read-forever.com
twitter.com/readforeverpub

Originally published in paperback by Bookouture, an imprint of StonyFire Ltd.
Carmelite House, 50 Victoria Embankment, London EC4Y 0DZ.
First Forever Trade Paperback Edition: November 2019

Forever is an imprint of Grand Central Publishing. The Forever name and logo are trademarks of Hachette Book Group, Inc.

The publisher is not responsible for websites (or their content) that are not owned by the publisher.

The Hachette Speakers Bureau provides a wide range of authors for speaking events. To find out more, go to www.hachettespeakersbureau.com or call (866) 376-6591.

Library of Congress Cataloging-in-Publication Data has been applied for.

ISBN: 978-1-5387-1744-8

Printed in the United States of America

LSC-H

10  9  8  7  6  5  4  3  2  1

Dedicated to my wonderful mom, Margot Berry. Thank you for always supporting my writing endeavours from *The Christmas Rose* till now. I love you! Love, Katie

# PROLOGUE

The room is softly lit by the luminous stars on the ceiling, a present for your fifth birthday, and a sliver of moonlight from the window that slants in silver bars across your bedroom floor.

You lie so still, your lashes fanning your cheeks, your golden hair spread across your pillow. You're so beautiful, and just looking at you makes my heart ache and ache.

Your breath is so soft I can barely hear it, but at least I can see the steady rise and fall of your chest, every breath a promise. *You're still here. I've still got you.* For now.

I've been reconciling myself to your diagnosis for months now, trying out the words, testing the reality like a toe dipped in ice water, but in moments like this it is still a shock, realisation slamming into my chest, leaving me breathless and reeling. *How did we get here? How can this be?*

And, worst of all, the question I've seen clouding your eyes too often: *why is this happening to me?*

I rise from the side of your bed, too restless to sit still. I pick up your toy rabbit with the silk-lined ears that has fallen on the floor and tuck it safely under your arm. You smile in your sleep and snuggle closer.

In the quiet stillness of a long, lonely night, I let myself look back over the years—all the choices, all the mistakes, all the longings and losses, everything leading to this.

It is a form of torture, this futile second-guessing, agonising in every detail because of the questions I must ask myself. What if

I'd been different? What if I'd done things differently? What if I'd been smarter, stronger, more selfless, right from the start? *What if?*

You wouldn't be here. You wouldn't be here at all. And in this moment, poised on tragedy, overwhelmed by love, I don't know the answer to that terrible, desperate question—if I could go back and do things differently, would I?

# PART ONE

PART ONE

# CHAPTER ONE

## MILLY

It's bad news. I can tell from the doctor's face, and I clench my fists in my lap as I wait for it.

"I'm sorry." Dr. Finlay, or Meghan as she asked us to call her a while back when we started this laborious journey towards having a baby, makes a little moue of sympathy, causing my stomach to clench along with my fists. *That bad?*

Silently, Matt reaches over to hold my hand, threading his fingers through mine. My palm is icy and damp, my heart starting to thump. I was hoping for good news today, news about how there was nothing to keep me from being pregnant, from us being a family, after months of consultations and charts and tests and *waiting*. So much waiting.

"After looking at the results of Milly's pelvic scan," Meghan begins, her gaze moving between the two of us, "I think I can make a certain diagnosis." She turns to focus on me, her mouth turned down at the corners. "I'm sorry, Milly, but based on what I've seen in the scan as well as the hormone levels we've been monitoring over the last few months, I can now confirm you have Premature Ovarian Insufficiency."

"Pre...what?" I stare at her blankly. We've talked about monitoring my ovulation, and trying to relax, and maybe, just maybe, starting a prescription for Clomifene. Dr. Finlay—Meghan—has assured me that at thirty-four I'm still on the youngish side to conceive, and I have every chance—her words—that it will happen. And now she's telling me something else, something *worse*? The dread that was swirling around in my stomach coalesces into a cold, hard ball.

"Essentially it's premature menopause, although we don't like to call it that because menopause is its own natural process, and this, of course, is something else."

I swallow, clinging to Matt's hand, my only anchor in all this uncertainty and ignorance. "So what does this mean? I go on Clomifene?" I ask, hearing the hopeful note in my voice and inwardly cringing at it.

"No, I'm afraid that's not a possibility now, with the level of deterioration already present."

Which sounds *awful* as well as final, and that is even worse. "So what happens now?" I ask, although I'm not sure I want to know.

Meghan hesitates, and in that tiny pause I hear all I don't want to know. She's breaking the bad news to me. I can see it on her face, in the way she places her hands flat on the table, as if she has to brace herself, when I'm the one who is going to need to absorb the hit.

I slip my hand from Matt's and clench my fists in my lap once more. I've been so determined, doing everything right, whether its prenatal vitamins or avoiding caffeine, making time to relax or meditate, or whatever else the latest expert says will help, but in this moment I know none of it's going to matter. It's not going to count the way I thought it would.

"In terms of your own pregnancy," Meghan says in that careful voice a medical specialist uses when the news isn't good, "I would suggest using an egg from a donor." She turns to Matt. "If you feel that is the way you want to go forward. Obviously, you'll need to take some time to consider, but there are other options as well…" She continues on about egg donation, and IVF, and then surrogacy and even adoption, all the alternatives no one wants to consider, but at some point in her recitation my mind blurs and blanks. All I'm hearing is that I will *never* be pregnant. I will never have my own biological child, born of my body, sharing my blood.

Twenty minutes later, Matt and I are both standing outside the clinic, an icy, unforgiving winter's wind off the Bristol Channel buffeting us.

"Do you want to go home?" Matt asks after a moment, as we simply stand there. "Or we could go out for a coffee...?"

"I don't want to go out for a *coffee*." The words burst out of me in a snarl, surprising us both. I'm not angry at Matt, though; I'm just *angry*. "I'm sorry." I take a deep breath, willing back the tidal wave of emotion. "Sorry," I say again.

"It's okay," he says gently, even though it isn't, and then he takes me by the arm as if I'm an invalid or an old lady. I'm not—it's just my eggs that are old.

We drive in silence back to the three-bedroom semi-detached house in Redland, one of Bristol's family-friendly neighbourhoods, that we'd bought two years ago, when we'd started thinking about families and babies and all those optimistic next steps.

We'd sold our one-bedroom flat in Temple Meads and bought the kind of house you had kids in, on a leafy street, with a garden, in walking distance of the local primary, in the catchment area of a good secondary. There's a village hall where they do toddler groups and Girl Guiding, and a playpark right around the corner. It was all the way I'd imagined my life as a little girl, and now none of it matters.

"Do you want to talk about it, Mills?" Matt asks after a few minutes.

I stare out the window as I shake my head, my mind numb and frozen, refusing to move past the dead-end diagnosis we've just been given.

"No. Not yet."

"Do you want to ring Anna?"

Anna, my best friend since year seven, the only person in the whole world besides Matt who has always had my back, who has never let me down. I know she will hug me, cry with me, and pour me more wine, but all that understanding might break me right now. I feel fragile, everything in me brittle, ready to shatter, but I know I'll need her. I nod, sniffing. "Yes. I'll ring her soon."

Back at home I get out of the car first and walk quickly inside, flinging my keys on the hall table as I breathe in the scent of lavender cleaner—organic, of course—and lemon furniture polish. *Home.* Except everything feels changed now; everything feels like a horrible mockery…the garden perfect for playing, with space for a swing and a sandpit, the shallow stairs safe for children, the third bedroom we intended to be a nursery. I haven't been so foolish as to paint the walls or buy a cot, not when I haven't even been able to get pregnant yet. But I've dreamed. Oh, how I've dreamed. And that's all it's ever been—dreams.

Matt comes in behind me and heads for our open-plan kitchen and dining area, with plenty of light and room for a high chair, a playpen, a rattan basket for soft toys. I'd pictured it all in my mind so perfectly.

The French windows that overlook our tiny terrace were another plus, and we talked about sitting out there on sunny Saturday mornings with our coffee, our child on a swing in the horse chestnut tree at the bottom of the garden. Now the house I've loved so much has become a cruel reminder, taunting me with all the what-ifs that have suddenly turned into nevers.

I draw a quick breath, and it hitches like a sob. Matt turns from the kettle he's been filling at the sink.

"Milly…"

"No. I can't. Not yet. I'm sorry." I'm not ready to talk. I'm not ready to dismantle my dreams in a pragmatic conversation as we discuss a forward plan the way I normally like to do, complete with bullet points. Someday, but not yet.

I go upstairs, to the room we planned on being a nursery. There is nothing baby-friendly about it now; it just has some plastic storage bins, a few empty suitcases, and Matt's saxophone stand gathering dust.

I stare at the empty room for a moment and then slowly slide down onto the floor, my back against the wall, my knees drawn up to my chest. Outside, bare branches tap against the window as the wintry gusts of wind rattle the pane. I rest my chin on my knees, drawing another breath. This one doesn't hitch.

I'm not going to cry. I know if I cry I'll have given up, and I'm not ready to do that yet. Not after everything. Not even if I will have to eventually.

*I've been so good.* I want to shout the words, but at whom? Who will listen? Who will care? I know life isn't fair, not for me, not for anyone. I've seen too much suffering in the news, too much casual cruelty in the world around me, to think otherwise, but I realise now that some small part of me believed if I played by the rules, if I did everything right, if I was kind and loving and respectful and all the rest, I'd get the deep desire of my heart. I believed there was some overarching justice I could appeal to, that I could count on, some cosmic jury that would decide in my favour. But today tells me there isn't. There can't be.

I'm in menopause, no matter that *Meghan* didn't want to use that word. I'm thirty-four and my eggs are withered up, dried out. Useless. So useless, in fact, that there is less than one percent chance of me conceiving naturally. I remember Meghan telling me *that.*

The door creaks open and then Matt is there, crouching next to me with a cup of tea. As I take it, tears sting my eyes.

"I wasn't ready for that news," I say, my hands cradled around the warmth. I blink hard, because I'm still not ready.

"I know."

"I won't be able to get pregnant." I say the words as if I'm trying on an outfit to see if it fits. It doesn't. It's tight and scratchy and I want to rip it off right now.

"Dr. Finlay didn't say that exactly." Matt has never called her Meghan. "She discussed other options…"

"But it won't be my baby." I wasn't able to take in all the details that Meghan outlined, but I understood at least that much.

Matt rests his hand on my knee, warm and solid. "It would be," he says gently. "You of all people should know that."

Yes, I should, because I'm adopted myself. I don't know who my birth parents are. I chose not to find out. And my adoptive parents, my *real* parents, are wonderful. They always have been, strong and supportive and loving. So, yes, I of all people should not have a problem with the idea of adoption.

Except I do.

But I don't expect Matt to understand that, and I'm not sure I could articulate it even to myself. Not now. Not yet.

"We don't have to rush into anything," Matt says, and somehow that hurts too. We don't have to rush, because it's already too late for me.

I rest my head against the wall and close my eyes. I feel exhausted, my body aching, my eyes gritty.

"Do you want me to call the school?" Matt asks. I only took the morning off for the appointment; I'm due back after lunch to take my Year One class, a prospect that now fills me with dread. I'm not ready to face twenty-eight five- and six-year-olds with their constant chatter and piping questions, but I can't afford to take off the whole day. And while curling up under my duvet is very tempting, I know it would just make me marinate in self-pity. I don't need that.

"No, it's okay. I'll go in."

"What about Anna?"

"I'll ring her soon." She knew about the appointment today, of course; my phone has already pinged with a text from her asking how it went. Over the last year and a half, I've kept her informed of every torturous step on this journey, all the hope, all the disappointment, and she's cheered and sympathised in turns. I know she will be there for me now, but her unwavering sympathy might send me over the edge, into the abyss of grief I sense is waiting for me.

I finish my tea and make to get up; Matt holds out his hand. As I take it, I realise with a painful jolt that this affects him too. He won't be able to have a child, his wife's child. Infertility isn't just my problem, even if it's my fault.

"I'm sorry," I say, and he looks at me in surprise, his hand still holding mine.

"For what?"

"For not...for not being able to..." I can't finish the words; suddenly I'm crying, all sobs and snot, my shoulders shaking as Matt pulls me towards him and I collapse into him gratefully. I wasn't able to keep it together for that long, after all, and I need this hug, his arms around me, holding me together.

"This isn't your problem, Milly. It's ours. We're in this together. And we'll find a way through, whatever happens, together. It's all going to be okay, I promise."

I press my face against his shoulder, willing myself to stop crying, determined to take comfort from his words. Because I believe him. Stupid me, I believe every word he says.

# CHAPTER TWO

## ANNA

When Milly finally sends me a text, hours after her appointment, I know it must be bad news. I can tell, just by the three bleak words, with no added detail: *Meet up later?*

*Of course,* I type. *What time?*

*Five?* comes the quick reply. I usually finish work later, but I can leave a bit early.

*Sure,* I text. *Do you want to talk about it now?*

Several minutes pass before Milly replies. *No. Later.*

It must be really bad, then. *Oh, Milly.* All she's ever wanted is a baby, a family. She talked about it even when were in year seven—how she wanted three children, because two didn't seem like quite enough. Because she's never had siblings. Because she's wanted to see what someone related to her looks like. Would they have her wild hair, her slightly crooked front tooth? Every time she talked about it, her eyes would light up and her expression would turn wistful. *I can't wait.*

What if it can't happen now? What will she do? I've had a front row seat to Milly and Matt's fertility issues over the last two years; I've known how anxious she's been, and how hard she's been trying to relax. I've even known when she's ovulating.

Most of all I know how much Milly has wanted a baby, what a great mum she would be, and if this news is really bad, I know how devastated she will feel.

I also know how much I will need to be there for her, as I always have been, as I always will be, because Milly is my best friend and she's been there for me time and time again, starting when I showed up to the first day of secondary school looking as overwhelmed and lost as I felt, and Milly marched right up to me and declared that we were going to be friends. I stared into her small, determined face, and felt a wave of relief break over me. It was going to be okay now, I thought. Finally something in my life was going to be okay. And it was.

That evening, I weave through the tables in Harveys Cellars, the underground wine bar in Bristol's old city that Milly and I have always used as our regular. I find her in the back, legs wound around a high stool, sipping a large glass of red wine. Her expression is closed and shadowed, her wild, dark hair tamed into a neat ponytail. When she looks up at me, I see a terrible depth of grief in her eyes, and wordlessly I pull her into a quick hug.

She returns it tightly, burrowing into me for a second, before she pulls away, dabbing at her eyes. "I don't want to fall apart completely," she explains in a shaky voice, and I ache for her.

"What are you drinking?" I ask.

She shrugs. "The house red, whatever it is. I wasn't too bothered."

Matt's the foodie of the two of them, insisting on pairing a proper wine with whatever meal they're having. I've eaten enough happy suppers at their kitchen table to know how he likes to talk about bouquets and hidden notes and all the rest of it. "All right," I say, trying to pitch my tone somewhere between cheerful and sympathetic. "I'll get one, and a refill for you."

Milly shakes her head. "No, I'm driving. I can't get drunk, as much as I want to."

When I return to the table with a glass of wine, Milly has nearly finished hers, and she sits with her chin in her hands, her expression resigned yet determined. She almost looks angry.

"So the news wasn't good?" I knew she'd gone in for a discussion about the scan she'd had a week ago, along with a battery of other tests. Milly had been buoyant, determined to get some answers and finally be able to deal with the situation, but I'd felt more cautious. I always do. Milly can get carried away on a tide of resolute optimism, while I tend to hang back. Wait. Observe. I think that's why we've worked as friends; we balance each other out.

"No, it was just about the worst news I could get." She glugs the last of her wine and then looks up, her face bleak. "I can't get pregnant, Anna. There isn't even the smallest chance."

"What?" In shock, I listen as Milly tells me all the details—even I, in my cautious, over-worrying way, hadn't thought it would be as bad as *that*. "Milly, I'm so, so sorry."

"I feel selfish, being so sad about this," she says as she rotates her wine glass between her palms, her gaze lowered. "I mean, this is a first-world problem, you know? So I can't get pregnant; there are other solutions, and having a baby isn't everything. I *know* that. I do."

"But it's still your problem. Your grief."

"Yes." She presses her lips together. "It's just...it's so hard to let go of that dream, you know? A baby that's like me and Matt. Someone who is actually *related* to me. It's never going to happen now." She sighs, a shuddering sound. "But I'll get over it. I have to."

She straightens her shoulders, determined, as always, to be brave. I reach over and squeeze her hand, and she gives me a quick, trembling smile.

"So what are you going to do?" I ask after a few minutes of heavy silence. "Have you thought ahead yet?" Milly is a determined planner, marching towards some shining destination or other—a

promotion, a bigger house, an exotic holiday, a marathon. Whatever it is, she has always gone after it with resolute optimism,
taking Matt along with her, and often me. When I would have
just wavered or wobbled or simply stood still, Milly has pulled
me along. I don't think I would have survived secondary school
without her. I almost didn't.

"I don't know. Dr. Finlay mentioned some options, but I can
barely get my head around them."

"Adoption?" I suggest, and her expression tenses a little.

"I don't want to adopt." For someone who is adopted herself,
she sounds surprisingly firm. She holds up one hand as if to
forestall any protests I might make, although I wouldn't. "Look,
I'm very glad I was adopted, of course I am, and my parents are
wonderful. I love them to pieces. But it still has its complications,
you know?"

"Yes, it must," I say after a moment. Milly's adoption has not
been something we've discussed very much in our two and a half
decades of friendship. She told me quite matter-of-factly that
she was adopted that first day of year seven, and that seemed to
have been both the beginning and end of the subject, a fact that
had to be got out of the way before we could move on to other,
better things.

"It's just..." Milly blows out a breath. "Mum and Dad never
wanted me to look up my birth mother, and so I never did."

"Did you want to?"

"Yes, when I was a teenager, I became curious, but I could see
that it would devastate them." She purses her lips. "And it's not just
about that. It's always been such a *thing*. I can't explain it exactly, but
I've always felt this...this weight. The fact of my adoption always
has to be trotted out at various events, in schools, with friends.
'These are my parents but I'm adopted.' It's the hashtag to my life."

"I didn't realise." I'm surprised Milly has never told me this
before; she has always acted as if her adoption didn't matter, and I

genuinely believed it didn't. I love Milly's parents. They practically became my own in my turbulent teenager years, when my parents were constantly battling each other and then me. They're low-key and loving, warm without being effusive. Her mum sends me a birthday card every year, and always hugs me when she sees me, a *real* hug, the kind where you know the person means it. The kind I never got from my own parents.

"I don't talk about it that much because I feel guilty for feeling that way, even just a little. And it is only a little, really." Milly lets out a sigh. "My parents have never been anything but completely loving and generous to me, and I know that if I did adopt…" She pauses, her forehead furrowing, her voice catching. "It's just, I really wanted to feel that connection. My child kicking inside me… knowing they were and always will be a part of me." She swipes at her eyes, the gesture impatient. "If we adopt, I'll never have that. I won't have it anyway. I can't now." Her voice breaks and she covers her face with her hands. "Sorry," she gulps between her fingers. "I really didn't want to fall apart. I'm trying not to. It just keeps hitting me, over and over, a shock every time."

"You don't have to be strong all the time," I tell her gently, and Milly does not reply. I reach over and touch her arm. I want to make this better for her; I want to solve it, the way Milly does so often with me. How many times has she brainstormed with me, found solutions? *You want to meet more people? Let's join the gym. You don't like your boss? Let's look into changing jobs.* The gym worked out, the job change didn't, but Milly is always about answers. Without her, I'd just stay in stasis. "There must be some way forward," I tell her, injecting a Milly-like note of determined optimism into my voice. "Some kind of IVF… there are so many fertility treatments these days…"

Milly shrugs, dropping her hands from her face. "Dr. Finlay mentioned the possibility of IVF with an egg donor, but that seems a bit weird, you know? I just place my order for an egg, from someone I'll never even know? Besides, the waiting list is something like two years minimum, and it's incredibly expensive if you do it privately."

I try to dredge up everything I know about egg donation, which is very little. "Still, you'd get to carry your own child."

"Someone else's child," Milly interjects, and I shake my head.

"It would feel like yours. You'd be the one growing a baby, giving birth. Really, donating an egg? It's practically like giving blood."

Milly gives a small smile. "Not really, Anna. It's quite invasive, from what Meghan said. I can't imagine doing it myself, knowing there was a child out there that looked like me, that was mine in some way . . . not that it's a possibility now. Obviously."

"Still, I don't think it's like that." I'm not sure why I'm being so stubborn. I don't know the first thing about egg donation.

"Perhaps not, but with the waiting list and the expense . . . I'm not sure it's really viable for us." Milly shrugs, and I sip my wine.

An idea is forming in my head, taking shape like an elegant sculpture emerging from the mess of damp, wet clay, but I know I need to think about it. I certainly shouldn't blab it out to Milly right now, when she's feeling so raw and I don't have all the facts.

But this is *Milly*, my best friend, the one person in the world who has been there for me, time and again. I picture her in year seven, shouting at some mean girls poised to bully me. I remember her in year nine, when someone wrote something rude about me in the boys' toilet—completely unwarranted at the time—and she marched in there and covered it with Tipp-Ex. And then I recall how she found me at my absolutely lowest point, how she rescued me from the depths of my own despair, and never asked any questions, because I couldn't bear to give her the answers.

"What if you didn't have to go on the waiting list?" I blurt, knowing I should think through this first, but unable to stop myself.

She stares at me blankly for a second, before her eyes narrow. "What do you mean?"

I hesitate, knowing I shouldn't be suggesting such a thing so soon, without doing any research, without thinking about how it might affect me or Milly, but I feel in the depths of my being that this is the right thing to do. For Milly. And maybe even for me. "You said you can go privately with these things, right?" A cautious shrug is her assent. I can tell she still doesn't know where I am going with this, and I wonder if I do, really. And yet I keep talking, because for once I can make it right for Milly. For once I can be the one who rescues. "If you have someone who is willing to donate an egg, you don't have to wait—or pay. Right?"

Milly stares at me for a long moment, and I know she is starting to realise what I am getting at. She is beginning to see the sculpture. "Right," she says slowly. "In theory."

"Well, that would be something, wouldn't it? I mean, if you wanted to go down that route...?"

Milly leans forward, a new urgency lighting her eyes. "What exactly are you suggesting, Anna?"

"I could give you...an egg." It makes me sound ridiculous, like a chicken. "If you wanted."

Milly stares at me hard, her expression almost fierce. "Do you really mean that?"

*Do I?* I'm not even sure what it might entail, how I would feel, and yet... "Yes. Of course I do, Milly."

"But..." She shakes her head slowly. "It's an invasive procedure, Anna—weeks of hormone injections, monitoring, all sorts. I understood that much from what Dr. Finlay said."

"I can manage that." I feel as if I've just catapulted myself into the deep end, the water closing in over my head, but I don't regret it.

Milly's eyes fill with tears and she shakes her head again. "That's so, so kind of you, Anna. I mean it. But it's not something we should decide right this second. I'd be asking a lot of you, and I don't mean the injections. It's such a big thing, for both of us. A really big thing. Bigger even than, I don't know, a kidney or something."

"Technically," I joke, "a kidney is bigger than an egg by quite a bit."

"Yes, but...you know what I mean. DNA. A *baby*." She bites her lip. "That's big. It would have...repercussions. Emotionally, I mean. It's not something to jump into."

*A baby.* The words reverberate through me and I have to look away. Yes, that's big. I know that more than Milly will ever realise, and it's another reason to say yes. One that Milly will never understand, and I will never explain it to her.

So I just smile and squeeze her hand. "You're right, of course. We should both think about it, do some research. Know what we're getting into. But the offer is there. I'd be honoured to do this for you, Milly."

She smiles back at me, tremulously, and I push away any niggling doubts as I realise I mean every word. I want this. For Milly...and for me.

# CHAPTER THREE

## MILLY

My mind is racing as I drive home from being with Anna, and I feel a surprising rush of something close to elation, so unexpected after the despair and grief of earlier.

I hadn't got my head around the various options yet; I hadn't even begun to think of a way forward for our wanted family... and now, when everything had felt closed off and impossible, Anna has just thrown open a door. All I need to do is walk through it. It can be that simple... can't it?

Matt is sprawled on the sofa, watching something mindless on Channel Four, when I come in, dropping my bag by the door. I still have some lesson planning to do for tomorrow, but I push it aside for now. This can't wait, although part of me knows that it probably should, at least until I've done some research, *thought* about it a little. But I am buoyant with hope, alive with possibility, and I need to share that with Matt.

He glances up as I come into the sitting room. "How was Anna?"

"Good." Although we didn't actually talk about anything in her life. A pinprick of guilt needles me; I should have asked her about her job. I usually do, and Anna offers up a few details with some reluctance; she has always been an intensely private person. But tonight it was all about me.

"And how are you?" Matt asks, his voice gentling as he gives me a look of sympathy.

"I'm doing okay, Matt." I sit on the edge of the sofa, tense and expectant. After nine years of marriage, I'm used to this dynamic: I race ahead with the plans, and sometimes I forget to bring Matt along with me, emotionally as well as physically. I've had to learn how to ease him in gently to my ideas—buying this house, putting himself forward for a promotion at work, trying for a baby. It takes him a little while, but Matt usually goes along with me in the end. And when he doesn't, I try to slow down and rethink my plans, because I know I can be a bit impulsive, a little too recklessly determined. Matt tones me down and I liven him up; we complement each other. What we have works. And, in any case, this was Anna's idea, not mine. I can at least float it by him.

"Good. I'm glad you're okay." He reaches for my hand, but they are pressed between my knees and so he ends up just resting his hand on my thigh. I smile, and he raises his eyebrows. "What, Milly?" he asks, because he knows me so well.

"So, I told Anna everything about, you know, today, and she came up with an idea." The words feel clumsy, the possibility too overwhelming to explain it in a simple sentence. I can barely take it in myself. *Anna's egg. My baby.*

"An idea?" Matt prompts, his eyebrows still raised.

"Do you remember what Dr. Finlay—Meghan—said about using an egg donor, and IVF?"

"A bit…" He looks cautious, a little confused.

"Anna's offered to be our donor. It means we can skip the waiting lists, the expense of going privately. I could be pregnant in a couple of months, maybe even less." I am practically gabbling in my excitement.

Matt leans back against the sofa, his hand sliding off my leg. "That's a big decision, Mills. And one I don't think we should jump into."

I fight a sense of deflation, even anger, at Matt's understandable caution. Couldn't he be the littlest bit excited? "I know that,"

I say steadily, "and I said the same thing to Anna. But the offer is there."

"Had she even thought about it, before she offered?"

"Yes…" Although I'm not sure she did. How could she have?

"For a couple of minutes?" He sounds so skeptical, and can I even blame him? Yet the more I think and talk about it, the more right it seems. Fitting, because Anna and I are best friends, almost like sisters.

"Obviously she hasn't thought about it in extensive detail," I say. "And we're not going to make any decisions right now, Matt. But I wanted you to know. It's a possibility. That's all."

"Still, I don't even know the first thing about egg donation or IVF. I can't agree to something I don't even understand."

"Why don't we look it up?"

"Right now?" He looks startled.

"Why not?" Matt seems reluctant, and I feel a flicker of impatience, even hurt. "Look, it's what it sounds like. We get Anna's egg and it's inseminated." Although I'm not sure if that's the right terminology. Inseminated? Fertilised? "They make a baby in a test tube," I clarify, "and then they implant the embryo in me."

*And then I will be pregnant.* The words feel magical now, a shimmering promise I can almost touch with my fingertips. Maybe it won't be my DNA, but it will still be my baby. I will nurture him or her inside me; I will give birth. I will be a mother to my child. It's the shining, silver lining to this otherwise towering cloud.

"Okay," Matt says after a long moment. "I understand that. But how does Anna feel about it? Has she even thought about what it would mean?"

"Not all the repercussions, not yet, and neither have I. We're *starting* to think about it, Matt. That's the point."

Slowly he shakes his head, like the pendulum of a clock, back and forth. "I'm not sure I want to put Anna in that position."

I prickle at that; he makes it sound as if I pushed her into it. "She *offered*, Matt. And what position are you implying, exactly?"

"I'm not implying anything." Wearily, he rakes a hand through his hair. "But Anna would do just about anything for you, Milly. You know that."

It sounds like an accusation, as if it's an aspect of our friendship I've abused, but I know I would do anything for her too. I fold my arms, feeling stubborn. "So why not this?"

"Because this is in a whole other category than housesitting or watering our plants or whatever. Come on, Milly. You *know* that."

"Yes, and I also know that Anna is my best friend, and I love her like a sister, as she loves me. Who else would offer? Who else would we ask? Who would we *trust*?"

"What about me?" Matt bursts out. "Did you even think about that? How I would feel, raising Anna's baby as our own?"

"It's not like that, Matt," I fire back, even though I was thinking along similar lines back at the wine bar. "Honestly, it's practically like giving blood." I echo Anna's words, even though I don't believe them entirely. "It would be *our* baby. I'd give birth. Genetics aren't that important, you know."

"I know that, but do you?" He straightens to look at me levelly. "Why not adopt?" The words hover in the air and then drop into the stillness. I look away.

"I don't want to. I told you that."

"Yes, but why not? Your family is great, Milly—"

"I know they are." I sound irritable, but I can't help it. I've already had this conversation with Anna, and I don't want to have it again, even though that's not fair to Matt. I know how great my family is, and that is not the point here. "Look, I know it might seem like an obvious choice, but it just isn't for me." I take a deep breath and then blow it out. "I'm the one who knows what it's like to be adopted, okay? And I don't want that for my child."

"But why?" He looks bewildered, as well as a little disappointed in me, as if I've said something unkind. Perhaps I have. "You had an idyllic childhood, and your parents adore you..." Unlike his, who are generally indifferent and wrapped up in their own lives. Genetics don't count for much there. I know that, and yet... I still want my own child. I want to rest my hand on my swelling bump. I want to give birth. I want to hold my baby in my arms and know it came from my body, if not my blood.

"I never said they didn't adore me. That's not the point."

"Then help me understand what is."

I fold my arms, tap my foot. I feel edgy now, as if my skin is prickling all over. This is how I always feel when I talk about being adopted. Over the years, I've learned to mask it—cue the breezy smile, the brisk brush-over. *I'm adopted, but my family is great. I'm adopted, but my parents are wonderful. I'm adopted, but...* That's how it goes. That's how it always goes. The never-ending caveat that I've always been aware of.

"Do we have to talk about this now?" I ask, trying to soften my voice. "Because it feels like a different discussion. What matters to me right now is that I might still have a chance to be pregnant. To have my own—*our* own—baby. Can you understand that, Matt? Can you understand how important it is to me?"

My voice rings out, and Matt sighs. Somehow, we've started arguing and I don't even know how we got here. I left the wine bar feeling so optimistic, so *hopeful,* and now this. I wanted Matt to fall in step alongside me, catch my excitement, even if we needed to be cautious, but as usual I've raced ahead and he can't catch up.

"I don't know that I have any objections," he says after a moment. "I just want to think about it very carefully. There are a lot of emotional repercussions, Milly. For us, as well as for Anna. We can't go into this with our eyes closed."

"I know that."

"In some ways I think an anonymous donor would be better."

"But there's no waiting list this way, and Anna has great genes." I try to take a lighter tone, to defuse some of the tension. "She's gorgeous." Anna has never made the most of her beauty, but the truth is, she's stunning—tall and blonde, with sea-green eyes and perfect curves. The opposite of me in fact, as I'm small and dark and skinny, with pale, freckly skin that burns if I step into sunlight for a millisecond.

"That's hardly the point."

"What is, then?"

"How Anna feels about us having her baby—"

"Matt, it really isn't like that." I have to believe that, or this whole plan falls apart before it's even started to be stitched together. "It's an *egg*—"

"And whose sperm?" he asks quietly. "Mine?"

I feel jolted, as if I've missed the last step in a staircase, a sudden *whoomph*. I haven't thought about that aspect, and in a painful flash I realise just how many things I need to consider. I can't rush ahead with this, as much as I want to. "I don't know," I admit.

"Because, frankly, I'd find it a bit weird, if my sperm is combined with Anna's egg." Matt folds his arms. "Sorry if that's not how you want me to feel about it, but I do."

I nod, realising that's how I feel too. I know it weakens my whole it's-only-an-egg argument, but it's still a deep-seated feeling, ingrained and instinctive. I know it doesn't entirely make sense; it's not as if anything physical or even emotional will have happened between Matt and Anna, and yet I can't escape the offensive and uneasy feeling that it will be *their* baby. Not ours. Not *mine*.

"I understand that," I say slowly. "I feel the same."

Matt leans forward. "Then you understand that we need to think through this *carefully*. Not just start tossing test tubes around."

I start to respond, but then my face crumples and I bring my hands up to hide my tears.

"Oh, Milly." Matt reaches over and pulls me into his arms. I rest my head against his shoulder and let the tears come, even though I don't want them to.

"I'm sorry," I say through my snuffles. "I know I'm rushing ahead with this. I hadn't even thought about it until Anna offered, and it felt as if she was throwing me a lifeline. We've been stuck on this hamster wheel of waiting, always waiting, and being told just to relax, and now we find out that it was going to do bugger all, all along." The words burst out of me, along with the anger. It's so *unfair*. "If we'd started earlier...if Meghan had run some tests earlier..." Bitterness corrodes every syllable. *If only. If only.*

"We don't know what would have happened," Matt says, sounding so frustratingly reasonable. I want him to be angry right along with me. I want him to *feel*. This whole process—the ups and downs, the uncertainty, the endless waiting, he's taken in his stride, unruffled, practically unconcerned. Tonight was the first time he has shown a proper emotion about anything fertility-related—and it was frustration with me. "There's no guarantee," he continues in that same calm voice, "that it would have happened that way at all."

"But it might have."

"Yes, it might have." He sighs and strokes my hair. "But there's no point in wondering what might have happened, because it hasn't. We've got to deal with the here and now."

"Exactly." I ease back, wiping the tears from my cheeks. "Which is what I was trying to do." I didn't mean to get back to this point so soon, honestly I didn't, but here we are. "Please, Matt. Can't we at least look into it together? See if it might work for us?"

He stares at me for a long moment, as if he's trying to burrow into my brain. I stare back, knowing my hope and urgency are reflected in my face, and hoping that Matt sees that. That it means something to him, how much I want this.

"All right," he says at last, and he reaches for his laptop on the coffee table. I sit next to him and he puts his arm around my shoulders as he types in the search engine *is egg donation right for you?*

We click on the first link, a fertility website blog that details one woman's process as a donor. Silently we read about the hormones she takes, the side effects, the aspiration of eggs under sedation, and the fact that ten of her eggs were fertilised and the embryos frozen for later use. Ten little babies-in-waiting, which makes me realise if we go down this route, we could have more than one child, so precious and alone, like I was. We could have three, the family I always wanted, big but not too big, lots of faces around the table, jostling for space.

Matt frowns and then clicks on another page, and then another, both of us gaining information about donors and the intended parents, the process, the cost, the legal ramifications. We are mapping this strange new territory, page by page.

Matt doesn't say anything; he just reads with the same quiet intensity with which he does everything. But I am becoming excited, like a balloon of hope is filling up inside of me. I know better than to say anything now, but I file away every fact like a promise: the 50–70 per cent success rate of egg donation and insemination; the case studies of open relationships with donors that read like one happy family after another; and, best of all, a study that shows a pregnant mother's DNA affects the baby she is carrying, even when genetically it is not her own. This *will* be my child.

Finally, gently, Matt shuts the laptop. We sit on the sofa, silent, expectant. I tell myself I am not going to say anything. I am not...

"This could work," I venture cautiously, after a few endless minutes. "Don't you think?"

"I don't know." Matt sounds as guarded as ever, and I wonder which part of what we read gave him pause. "It's a lot to think about."

"Yes, of course it is. But it's...possible, isn't it?"

Matt turns to me with a tired smile. "I know you, Milly. I tell you it's possible and tomorrow you'll have booked Anna into the clinic."

"Not tomorrow," I object, trying to smile, make light of it, even though everything in me is tense and ready. "Maybe next week," I joke, although I'm not actually joking.

Matt manages a small smile, but he still looks worried. He doesn't want a baby the way I do, with the same desperate, frightened urgency. Yes, he's wanted kids, but he's not *panicked* about it. He hasn't dreamed about finally—*finally*—holding a baby in his arms and thinking *I know you. I've always known you.*

"There's no harm in thinking about this for a little while, is there?" he asks. "Taking a few weeks at least…?"

"Of course not," I say, even though I am disappointed. "I know it feels like I'm rushing into this, Matt. I *am* rushing into it." I blow out a breath. "But it feels right to me. I want to be pregnant, with a lovely big bump. I want to hold my squalling newborn in my arms. I crave that physical connection—I can't explain it any better than that." I feel a lump forming in my throat and I will myself not to break down yet again. "It's important to me. Very important."

Matt's face softens as he pulls me close. "I know that," he says, and he kisses the top of my head. "I know that, Milly."

But I wonder if he really does. I wonder if he understands at *all* how much I long for this, how having my own child will anchor me to this world in a way nothing else does.

At least that's what I thought then, but I had no idea how I would really feel when it came to pass, or how devastating it would turn out to be. And if I had known, would I have done things differently? Would I have walked away, told Anna, *no, it's not for us*?

I still can't answer that question. The truth is, I don't want to.

# CHAPTER FOUR

## ANNA

The weekend after my drink with Milly, I lie in bed and let the wintry sunshine from the window stream over me, as I daydream about what my baby will look like.

Of course, I know it won't be *my* baby, that's not how it works at all, but ever since I put the idea to Milly, I've been...curious. Wistful. Considering the lack of romantic relationships in my life, I doubt I'll ever have children of my own, so perhaps this could be the next best thing? I'll get to see what a child of mine would look like. I might even watch him or her grow up, be a godmother, or an honorary auntie.

The thought makes me smile, but it also brings its own, peculiar pain, because it hurts to remember. But I'm not going to think about that today.

It's Saturday, which are very quiet days for me. I don't have a lot of friends besides Milly, just some casual acquaintances from work, along with a woman I met at a spin class with whom I occasionally get together for a coffee, and another old friend from my evening business course I took years ago.

As for boyfriends, there haven't really been any, which is actually fine. Over the years, I had a couple of dating situations that never went anywhere much, and more recently I haven't bothered with it at all. I'm happy alone. I've learned to be.

But today as I potter about my one-bedroom flat on the top floor of a Victorian terrace, I let my thoughts drift. I let myself dream, in a hazy and pleasant sort of way, about this nebulous future where Milly and Matt have my child, and I'm involved in his or her life.

I feel hesitant about thinking this way, because I know he or she wouldn't be *my* child in any real way. I'm giving an egg, not a baby. But still…would she have my hair? My eyes? The scaly patches of eczema on my elbows? I can't help but wonder.

I've never been particularly maternal, mostly because I haven't let myself. After the turbulence of my parents' marriage, as well as my own teenaged years, I've avoided serious relationships. Milly is the only one who has breached the defences I've put up out of instinct, and then only because she was so determined to.

So, with these vague images of a rosy-cheeked baby, a tow-headed toddler drifting through my mind, I settle myself on my overstuffed sofa, with my cat Winnie purring contentedly next to me and a large cup of coffee on the table by my elbow, and open my laptop.

It doesn't take long to be sucked into the vortex of internet surfing, as I click from link to link, following a rabbit trail of research that tells me in detail all the things Milly mentioned so briefly, and more.

I learn that I'll have to take a rigorous cycle of hormones, as well as undergo at least one session of psychological counselling to make sure I'm okay with the whole process. I'll have to be under general anaesthetic to have the eggs "aspirated"; I picture a Hoover. I'll have no parental rights.

I end up closing my laptop, deciding I need to clear my head. Running always does that for me, and so I change into my gym clothes and pull on my trainers. It's a cold, bright day, the air crisp and clear as I head down my road to Victoria Park.

My heart thuds in time with the pounding of my feet as I pick up my speed once in the park, the trees stark and leafless, the sky a bright, hard blue above. I'm not going to think about eggs or embryos or babies, about how Milly will get to be a mother while I chose not to be. I'm not going to wonder what if, what if, *what if*, because I can't. I've learned to live with the choices I've made. I don't question them, not anymore, and this is about Milly, not me. I can't let it be about me.

On the south end of the park, I finally come to a stop, my lungs burning, my hands on my knees. I straighten as my heart rate slows and I see that I am near the play area by St. Luke's Road. It's not very busy on this cold February day, but a girl with golden plaits, six years old or so, is squealing with delight as her father pushes her on the swing. Without thinking about what I'm doing, I walk towards the play area, resting one hand on the fence as I watch the girl soar, the father pushing her higher and higher. Her head is tilted back, her eyes closed and her mouth wide open with joy. The father is laughing too, just from looking at her. It's such a joyful moment, and I stand there transfixed by it, enjoying it simply by association, but also aching in a way I can't articulate.

Then the dad catches sight of me and his expression morphs into a guarded frown.

"I'm sorry, may I help you?" he asks, pitching his voice pleasant but firm. I realise how creepy I must seem, standing there staring at the pair of them.

"No, no, I'm just...just resting," I stammer, and then I turn away and start running back towards home, faster than before.

On Monday, all baby-related thoughts are driven from my mind when a young intern from the IT department pokes her head through my door.

"Anna?"

I don't remember her name, although I probably should. Qi Tech has a hundred and fifty employees, and I've been working here for fourteen years, since I was twenty, on an apprenticeship in HR.

"Yes? Can I help?"

"Could I talk to you for a second?"

I glance at my computer and then the clock. I have a meeting in twenty minutes with my boss Lara, the head of HR, to discuss the latest round of performance reports. I've barely looked at them yet, but something about this young woman's stance—her hunched shoulders, pink dip-dyed hair sliding in front of her face—makes me pause.

"Okay, sure."

She comes into my small office and I rise to close the door behind her. Something tells me this is going to be personal.

"I'm sorry," I say as I sit behind my desk again. "I can't remember your name."

She blinks uncertainly at me. "Sasha."

"Right. Sasha." I commit it to memory as I fold my hands on my desk. "What can I do for you, Sasha?"

"I'm not sure how to say this..."

"Honest and upfront is always my policy." I smile even as my mind is racing, wondering what's troubling her. "It seems as if something is wrong...?"

"Yes, well." She sighs, sitting down, her fingers knotted in her lap. "I don't want to cause a big problem." She chews her lip as she glances at me from under her fringe. "Or get fired. I mean, you hear things..."

"There's no reason at all to think you're going to be fired, Sasha." But what has happened? And who is involved? As the assistant director of Human Resources, my job ranges from recruiting, to resolving disputes, to the more unpleasant damage control. Some days I do nothing more interesting than file pay stubs. On other days, I try to keep something from blowing up big time online, because that's the world we live in. A single tweet can spell disaster. Right now, I'm sensing today is going to be one of those other days, and I start to feel worried. Lara is not going to like this. "What's happened, Sasha?" I ask gently.

She chews her lip, looking miserable. "I think this was a mistake. I shouldn't be here."

"But you're here now."

"Maybe it's not a big deal." She shifts in her seat, as if to leave. "I think I may have overreacted."

"Perhaps, but perhaps not. I won't be able to assess the situation unless you tell me." I try for a smile, even though I'm starting to feel nervous. If this is a case of sexual harassment, which I am sensing it might be, then it needs to be handled very carefully, especially as Lara is offensively scornful of the whole #MeToo movement.

Sasha continues to chew her lip, looking undecided, while I wait with a patient, encouraging smile on my face. Then Lara opens the door to my office, which is also the reception area for the HR department. Topping six feet in black stilettos, dressed in a fitted black power suit with a silk blouse in deep purple—she has the same blouse in a dozen different vivid shades—she is intimidating on the best of days, and downright scary on others. Her piercing, narrowed gaze focuses on Sasha before she turns to me, ruthlessly threaded eyebrows raised.

"Anna? Are you ready for our meeting?"

"Yes, just chatting through some things." I turn back to Sasha, but she's already scrambling up from her seat.

"I think I'll go—"

"Sasha, why don't we schedule another time to talk?" I rise as well. "So you can tell me a little bit more about what's been going on?"

"It's all right." I watch unhappily as she backs out the door. "I'm all right," she says again, and then she's gone.

I turn to Lara, who looks unimpressed. "What was she whinging about, then?"

For a head of Human Resources, Lara is not the most sympathetic person on the planet.

"She was concerned about something," I say as I click my mouse to print off the performance reports. "But she was uncomfortable telling me." *And you scared her off,* I add silently. I'd never dare say it, and Lara knows it anyway.

"Someone told her she looked pretty, I suppose?" Lara says, rolling her eyes. "Girls these days." She turns quickly, her heels like sharpened points, naturally expecting me to follow. With a sigh, I gather up the reports. I know this meeting will just be Lara's attempt to justify not giving anyone a pay rise, and I am not looking forward to sitting through it. I love my job, but dealing with Lara requires a level of skill and caution I find exhausting, even though I certainly should be used to it after so many years. At least it provides a distraction from the thoughts about eggs and babies that have been circling in my mind all weekend.


As the days pass, I fight a restless, edgy feeling; I realise I am waiting for Milly to ring. I text her once, just to check in, and she gives a brief reply. It's not that unusual, but for the first time it feels as if there is something unspoken that has settled between us, and I start to think about how, if Milly does take up my offer, this might affect our friendship.

I don't want to believe it would, or even could, at least not negatively. Milly and I are solid. We always have been. This, if anything, should bring us even closer together, giving and sharing so much, a child that would bind us together forever. At least, that's how I want it to be. Yet something about Milly's silence niggles at me, like a stone in my shoe.

When another weekend rolls around without more than a few texts from Milly, though, I start to wonder. I can't remember the last time we've gone this long without seeing each other. I consider ringing her, but I wouldn't know what to say—*So do you want my egg?* It feels ridiculous, as well as overwhelming.

And then, on Sunday night, she calls.

"I'm sorry I haven't been in touch," she says a bit breathlessly. "I've just been trying to sort out everything in my mind..."

"It's okay." I sink onto the sofa, Winnie on my lap. I am relieved she has called, but I am also anxious too, waiting for her verdict. Waiting for Milly to call the shots, as she always does.

"I've been thinking about your...your offer a lot," she says after a moment. "It's so kind and so generous, Anna, but..." She pauses, and I tense, unsure if I want her to accept or refuse. My ambivalence alarms me, because I don't entirely understand it. "Could I come over?" Milly asks abruptly.

"Of course. Do you mean...now?"

"Yes, now, if that's okay. It's just...this whole thing...Matt and I have been doing some research. There's so much to think about, and I wanted to talk to you about it. Because I don't want you—or us for that matter—going into this lightly..."

"I wouldn't." My offer might have been made on the spur of the moment, but it was still sincere. "But yes, of course. Come over."

When Milly arrives just fifteen minutes later, she hugs me quickly and then paces the length of my small sitting room, a dark-haired bundle of nervous energy as always. You could power a city with Milly's energy; it practically crackles from her wild hair, the quick strides, the way she rubs her hands together. Today it feels even more intense than usual.

"Do you want a drink?" I ask. "Coffee, tea...wine?" I think I have a dusty bottle in the back of the cupboard. I'm not much of a drinker when I'm home on my own. It reminds me too much of my childhood.

"Just water, please," she says with a distracted smile.

I go to the kitchen and pour her a glass from the tap. When I return to the sitting room, Milly is still pacing. I hand her the glass and then draw the curtains against the dark night. It's raining, the patter of icy drops on the pane sounding like bullets, but it's cosy and warm inside my flat.

"So, what's up?" I ask lightly as I sit on the sofa. Winnie, having sniffed Milly and then decided not to approach, jumps into my lap.

"Everything, it feels like." Milly turns to face me and then sinks into the armchair opposite the sofa, a huge, squashy one in nubby purple velvet that I bought from a charity shop. With sympathy, I notice how tense and tired she looks, Milly amped up, on hyper-speed.

"How are you doing, Milly? This has all got to be so tough."

"Yes, well." She rakes a hand through her hair, which springs wildly up around her face in a dark halo. "There is a lot to deal with. I'll need to start HRT soon, and of course there's this…" She gestures to the empty space between us, and I nod, waiting. Milly leans forward, her eyes bright with both urgency and determination. "Did you mean it, Anna? Do you really mean it, that you'd be willing to do that for me? Because I can't stop thinking about it. It feels like a lifeline, but it also feels…strange, I suppose. It's such a big thing. And I suppose I'm worried you might regret it, you know, down the line."

"Why would I regret it?" I ask as I stroke Winnie, letting my hands slide over her soft grey fur as she purrs like a car motor.

"I know in the past you've said you didn't," Milly says hesitantly, "but considering things now, I have to ask. Do you think you might want children yourself one day?"

I hesitate, turning her question over in my mind. "I don't think I'll change my mind," I say at last. "It's getting a bit late, anyway."

"Yes, but if things were different, if you had someone in the picture... would you want them, then?"

I frown, wondering what Milly is really trying to say. "I don't know. I don't think so. I suppose I've never felt maternal in the way you have."

"It's just... I wouldn't want you to feel cheated, somehow."

"I wouldn't feel cheated, Milly. I want to do this." I think I know what she's afraid of, but she doesn't want to say it out loud. Perhaps she's afraid it would offend me. "Look," I say gently, "I understand that this would be your baby. It would just have my genes, that's all, and we both know genetics don't count for much. Look at my parents. Look at yours."

"Right." Milly smiles, and I can tell she is relieved by my words. I can't blame her, not really. No matter what I've just said, I've thought about what my child would look like. Wondered whether he or she will have my eyes, my hair, my height, never mind all the other traits—would he or she be quiet like I am? Would they find the same things funny?

But I would never admit those thoughts to Milly, at least not like that. And I know, in my head, and yes, even in my heart, that no matter who provides the DNA, this baby would be Milly's. Milly's and Matt's. But I still wonder.

"Matt and I feel we need to consider all the emotional ramifications," Milly explains, "because there would be so many people involved."

I keep stroking Winnie, from her ears to her tail. "You mean me?"

"Yes, and..." Milly hesitates. "The sperm donor, too, because Matt's not comfortable using his own. I know that sounds weird," she continues in a rush, "because we're talking about *test tubes,* not anything... well, you know. But he said he would feel strange, knowing it was his baby—genetically, I mean—and not mine. And I agree."

"Right." I hadn't thought about it being Matt's baby. I realise I am relieved that it won't be an issue, although I'm not sure I should say that, so I remain silent.

Milly leans forward. "Anna, if this is too much for you, I really will understand. You made the offer in an emotional moment—"

"It's not." I speak quietly, firmly. I am sure.

"It's just that I don't want you to feel pressured," Milly persists. "Because you feel as if, I don't know, you owe me something."

I still at that, because *do* I owe Milly something? Does she feel that I do? When I was at my lowest point, eighteen years old and spiralling downwards, kicked out of my house, jobless, rootless, directionless, she as good as saved me. But that was sixteen years ago, and she did it because she was my best friend. She's never acted as if there was a debt to be repaid, but now I wonder if she's felt that. If I do.

"I'm not doing this because I feel like I owe you something, Milly," I say quietly. "I'm doing it because you're my best friend, and I want to help you and see you happy."

"Thank you." Milly sniffs and smiles. "I know you wouldn't... I didn't mean..." She shakes her head, frustrated, tearful.

"I know you didn't."

"Because I have this vision of what it could be like. What I want it to be like. We know each other, we love each other, and raising kids is hard work. Why shouldn't we all be involved? And, of course, you *will* be involved. Honorary auntie, godmother, whatever. I'm going to need you in all of this, Anna, and I'm not just talking about your egg." She laughs a little, wiping her eyes, and my throat goes tight.

"I'll be there," I promise, my voice a bit hoarse. "Of course I will. Always." I think of the father pushing his golden-haired daughter on the swing, the way her head tilted back with joy, and then I put myself in the picture, pushing the swing, smiling, savouring the moment.

"Good. Then…" She hesitates. "We can go forward…with this?"

It feels like one of those defining moments, both of us teetering on a precipice, having no idea what yawns below. Then I tell myself not to be melodramatic, that this can be simple. Easy, even. Because this is Milly…and me.

"Yes," I say. "Of course we can."

# CHAPTER FIVE

## MILLY

I don't remember the first time I was told I was adopted. One of my earliest memories, though, is telling someone else quite matter-of-factly. It came in different versions and guises as I grew up, from *I didn't come out of my mummy's tummy* to *my parents chose me* to the flatly stated *I'm adopted.*

My parents were always up-front about the adoption, always made it a talking point of my childhood. The photo album of my life starts on the day they brought me home from the hospital at six months old.

This framing of my identity around my adoption didn't bother me for a long time. In fact, I wouldn't say it ever *bothered* me, because it was simply part of who I was, the history they imbued me with, the story they told, proudly and lovingly.

But in my teen years I became curious, as is apparently natural with adopted children. When I was about thirteen, I wanted to know more about my roots, and that's where my parents' friendly, open attitude about it all started to falter. They didn't mean for it to, and of course it was hard for them—this longed-for daughter they loved questioning everything, sometimes angrily, in my teenaged angst.

Looking back, I realise how heart-rending it must have been, the words I tossed around with careless defiance—mother, father, *real.* Each one would have been a stab wound, especially for my mother, who took them all painfully to heart.

They tried to placate me with sentiments they'd read in books about adoption: it was understandable that I would want to know more about who I was, and if I wanted to look into my birth mother's identity, the record would be made available when I was eighteen, and so on. They said it with resolute expressions and kindly tones, but I knew. I always knew it would devastate them both for me to look.

My eighteenth birthday came and went and I never did anything, because I knew my parents would be hurt, but also because I'd moved past angry, adolescent curiosity to a worldlier, hardened indifference. I'd thought about it, and I couldn't help but wonder what sort of woman gives up her baby when she is six *months* old. A drug addict? A prostitute? A woman who doesn't care about her child? A woman, I decided, I had no interest in getting to know.

I told my parents as much, and it felt like we'd passed a milestone; we were all relieved, because now we could go on as we were, without any questions or comments or what-ifs.

I was happy with my decision, because I loved my parents and I didn't want to upset them. As Matt said—like everybody says—they're wonderful. They've cheered me on my entire life, have shown up for every sports day or school ceremony, no matter how silly or small. They didn't bat an eye when I went through a brief and unfortunate Goth phase in school; they took Anna into their house and treated her like their own, and they've loved Matt from the first moment they met him. When it comes to my parents, I am so very thankful.

And yet. When it comes to my parents, there is always an infinitesimal, unfortunate *and yet*, because I'm adopted. Because it's always been a point of interest, of conversation, a fact that somehow must be mentioned, even when I'd rather it wasn't. It's a huge part of who I am, and while that's not a bad thing, it's still a *thing*. A thorn. And I don't know if I can explain that to Matt or Anna or anyone.

I also don't know how it makes me feel about this baby-who-isn't-yet, who will be part Anna, part me, part who knows who else. Do I want the fact that my child was conceived in a test tube from someone else's egg and sperm to be his or her *thing*? The fact we trot out, the point of pride because it has to be? I picture my mythical daughter, six years old, standing up in class. *I came out of my mummy's tummy but she's not my biological mother.* Do I want that?

Do I have a choice?

When I told Anna I had a vision, I meant it. At least, I *wanted* to mean it, because it sounded beautiful. Why shouldn't we all get along, work together to raise this child? It takes a village, right? It can be that way for us. The more I think about it, the more it feels like the only way forward, the only way this will work. If it's not a last resort, but a conscious decision, something we embrace rather than merely accept. And so, that's why I suggest, instead of using Matt's sperm, we use his brother's.

"Jack?" He stares at me, dumbfounded, speechless.

"You only have the one brother," I remind him lightly. "Why not?"

"Why *not*?"

"All I mean is, I hear where you're coming from, when you say you're not comfortable using Anna's egg with your sperm. I'm not comfortable with it, either, even if it doesn't completely make sense. But I still don't like the idea of using some anonymous donor—it seems so cold. So mercenary. Just some random person we're choosing." I pause and Matt folds his arms, looking nonplussed.

He's come around to the idea of IVF with donor egg and sperm *mostly*, but at moments like this we both stumble, and something instinctive in us resists. And yet now I turn resolute, because I have to. Because, for me, this is the only way forward for our family, and I like the idea of our child being related to at least one of us. I'll carry this baby, and Matt will share its genes. A win-win in what is, admittedly, a less than ideal situation.

"If we use Jack's," I continue, "then at least it's still close. Still family. Siblings share 50 per cent of their DNA—"

He offers me a small smile, although his eyes are troubled. "So do humans with a banana, apparently."

"That's a bit of an urban legend," I counter. I did my research. "It's a completely different level of complexity."

Matt rolls his eyes. "Whatever."

"Do you have a problem with it being Jack?" Jack is two years older than Matt, and has been living in France for the last ten years, restoring villas. A few months ago, he relocated to the Cotswolds, to turn a barn into a pricey conversion. He and Matt aren't particularly close, but they've always had an amicable relationship. I think.

"Do I have a *problem?*" Matt repeats. "I don't know. I haven't had time to think about how I would feel, raising my brother's baby—"

"I've told you so many times, Matt, it really is not like that—"

"Except it is, a little bit, because you've been telling me how we can all be involved, how Anna will be some sort of second mother—"

"I did not use those words." I'm sure of it. I never would have even *thought* of it like that. "All I meant is, we can all be involved, to some degree—"

"Which sounds great, but it still feels very complicated, and emotionally quite dangerous. What if, for example, Jack or Anna decide they want parental rights?"

"They wouldn't, and anyway, sperm and egg donors are never considered legal parents. They have no legal or financial responsibilities or rights, *ever.* It will be *our* names on the birth certificate, Matt." I have definitely done my research about this.

"Still, it feels different because we know them," he insists. "If it was someone anonymous, someone we could just forget about..."

"But we can see this as a plus," I argue. "Have all the information upfront. And when our child is curious about his or her origins, they won't have some official-looking file, they'll have us, and Jack, and Anna. That makes a difference." I pause, to let him absorb that, and my own experience of having never opened that file. "If you agree to it, of course."

He sighs. "I just don't know. I still need to think about it."

"How about this?" I suggest. "We have Jack and Anna over for dinner, to discuss things. Talk it through. And if, after that, someone decides it's not going to work, we call it off." A prospect that makes my stomach swirl with dread. I already feel as if I've invested so much in this. But I hope having the four of us sit down together might make Matt see how it could work. How it could be something good. Assuming, of course, that Jack agrees. That Anna doesn't change her mind.

"Dinner," Matt says cautiously.

"Yes, dinner. Just dinner."

He sighs again and then nods. "All right, fine."


Two weeks later, I am bustling around the house, plumping throw pillows and lighting scented candles. A Moroccan chicken stew bubbles in a casserole dish in the oven, sending out tantalising smells of cumin and ginger. The lighting is low, and Matt has started a cosy blaze in the wood burner in the sitting room. Everything feels happy and warm. Promising.

Two days ago, on my initiative, Matt met with Jack and asked him to be a donor. Even Matt saw that he had to have a conversation with him, before this dinner. It was a big step, and it was both a huge relief and a little frightening when Jack agreed quite readily. Matt came home a little shell-shocked, a bit incredulous. This really could be happening. Now Anna and Jack are coming over so we can discuss the future, our future. *Our family.*

The doorbell rings, and I hurry to get it. Jack stands there, smiling and looking relaxed. When I first met Jack, back when

Matt and I were dating in uni, I thought this was someone I could be good friends with. He's easy-going, kind, a good listener, with a dry sense of humour. In short, a great guy, but fifteen years on, I haven't gone much deeper with Jack than at that first meeting. He keeps things at a chitchat level, affable and easy but no more than that, and that seems intentional. In all the time I've known him, he's never had a serious relationship, although I know there have been women. Just none he's brought home for Christmas or a family get-together.

"Jack." I stand on my tiptoes to kiss his cheek. He's a few inches taller than Matt. "It's so good to see you."

"And you, Milly. Wow, this place is amazing." He glances around in appreciation. "I haven't been to Bristol since you moved from your flat." He nods towards the open-plan kitchen. "They must have knocked that wall through at some point...do you know when?" Jack always views houses this way.

"A long time ago, I think, way before we looked at it. Come through."

He comes into the kitchen, and he and Matt do that manly half-hug thing, more of a clap on the shoulder than anything else.

I open the fridge. "Beer?"

"Sure."

We stand around, smiling a bit inanely. Jack is Matt's brother, but we hardly ever see him, and we've just asked him to do this major thing for us. It makes me feel awkward, which I suppose I should have expected.

Then the doorbell rings again, and I hurry to answer it.

"Anna!" I hug her tightly. "Come meet Jack." Despite our years of friendship, they've never met; Jack has always been in France, or we've seen him at Matt's parents' in Reading.

She comes into the kitchen, and I notice how Jack's eyes widen as he catches sight of her. So often Anna hides her beauty in shapeless trouser suits or baggy jumpers and jeans, but tonight she's made more of an effort, perhaps for the occasion. She's wearing a corduroy miniskirt in vivid green that makes the most of her long legs, with woolly purple tights and a fitted button-down shirt in mustard yellow. You'd think it would all clash, but somehow it doesn't. She looks vibrant, the skirt bringing out the sea-green of her eyes, and her hair, instead of pulled back into a standard clip, falling in loose, honey-coloured waves around her face.

Jack springs forward, one hand outstretched. "Hi, I'm Jack."

"Anna." She ducks her head, smiling shyly, as she takes his hand and he holds it a second longer than necessary. I watch, uncertain how to feel about this interchange. Of course, I want them to get along, but Jack is a bit of an affable ladies' man, and Anna has had so few relationships. My inner alarm pings quietly. The last thing I want is for Anna to be hurt by all of this.

"I guess we know why we're all here," Jack jokes, and Anna gives a little laugh. Matt and I both smile self-consciously. Then I busy myself taking the stew out of the oven while Matt gets Anna a drink.

In the end, the evening goes well, despite my nerves. I feel as if I've climbed a mountain to get to this moment—the four of us around a table, the possibility of a family, *my* family, in the air.

We don't talk about anything serious as we eat and Matt pours more wine. Jack tells us about his latest house project, and Anna regales us, rather cautiously, with the latest horror story of her boss Lara, whom I've never met but I've heard about. I tell a few stories about some of the six-year-olds in my Year One class; how Toby, a gap-toothed ginger boy, asked if he could marry me.

"I hope you told him you were already taken," Matt teases, and I smile.

"I let him down gently."

I love my class, but lately it has been hard to go in every day and see all their smiling faces, fearing that I'll never have a child of my own. I watch the mums at the school gate; one has a lovely, huge bump that she rubs with unthinking possessiveness, and another had a baby a few weeks ago. She brought her for the first time on Friday, all bundled in pink, with a tiny face peeking out so all I could see were her navy eyes and little rosebud mouth. I made all the right noises, exclaiming and cooing, but inside I felt as if I could break into pieces. I want that so much for myself that it is a physical pain.

"So, do you have a prospective timeline for this?" Jack asks, gesturing to the four of us, as we finish the white chocolate mousse for dessert. I glance at Matt, uncertain. We haven't discussed it, not officially.

He glances back at me, his eyes crinkling at the corners. "I suppose as soon as possible," he says, and my mouth drops open. "In fact..." He goes to the fridge and produces a bottle of champagne he must have bought on the sly. "I thought we could celebrate. Toast the future, because Milly and I really appreciate you guys doing this, and you know, you're both family." He glances at Anna. "Really."

I have to blink back tears as Matt pops the cork on the champagne and then pours four glasses of bubbly. I'd expected a more difficult, awkward conversation, not a simple celebration. And yet it is simple, in this moment. It is wonderfully, miraculously simple.

"To all of us," Matt says grandly, raising his glass. "And to our baby."

And as we all clink glasses in the cosy warmth of the kitchen, everyone smiling and happy, I feel more hopeful than I have in a long time. I feel buoyant, the bubbles fizzing through me. I am finally beginning to believe that this is going to happen. As we drink, I catch Anna's eye and, over the rim of her glass, she smiles at me. It's all going to work out. Everyone is going to get the happy ending we've all been trying for.

Later, after Anna and Jack have gone and Matt is loading the dishwasher, I walk up behind him and wrap my arms around his waist, pressing my cheek against his shoulder.

"Thank you," I say quietly. "I know you've had concerns."

"I still do, but not enough to keep us from trying this. From making you happy." He turns around so he can give me a proper hug, resting his chin on top of my head. "When I talked to Jack, he seemed so okay with it, it made me think it doesn't have to be as complicated as I first thought it was."

I remember Anna's smile. "I don't think it does."

Matt tips my chin up with his finger and gives me a kiss. "Just think, Mrs. Foster, this time next year we could have a newborn baby upstairs, wailing away."

"Or peacefully sleeping." The possibility causes a thrill to run through me, so visceral I nearly shiver with the delight of it.

*This time next year.* The words feel like a promise.

I had no idea they would one day be a threat.

# CHAPTER SIX

## ANNA

"Are you comfortable?"

The nurse smiles at me as I adjust my position on the examining table. "Yes, I think so."

It is six weeks since we all had dinner at Milly and Matt's, and it has been a roller coaster of emotions, thanks to the injections of hormones I've had to take every week. Milly has had to take them as well, and several times we've been at the clinic together, laughing at how ridiculously teary we were because of it all. It has felt unnervingly intimate, doing this together, bringing us even closer.

Besides the excess emotion, I've also had headaches, mood swings, and despite my daily running, I've gained half a stone, all of which are apparently normal side effects of the cocktail of hormones I've been taking.

It's all worth it, though, as I keep telling Milly, because she is still so anxious that this is proving too high a cost for me, that somehow she will owe me more than she can repay, even though I tell her, I promise, it isn't like that. It's never been like that.

The reality, though, is that it's all a bit more invasive than I expected. Besides the hormones and the scans and the medical screening, I also had to have counselling, to make sure I was all right emotionally. It felt like a test I had to pass, navigating questions about personal beliefs and feelings, unsure what the right answers were, although the psychologist assured me there weren't any.

It also felt revealing. She asked about family, romantic relationships, and earlier pregnancies, and that's when I lied. It was instinctive, a basic need to protect myself. I wasn't about to spill my secrets to some stranger, not even for Milly's sake. And it wasn't relevant, anyway. Or so I believed.

So now I'm here, lying on a table, about to be sedated. My lower belly has felt tender and swollen for the last few days; the only way to describe it is ripe.

In three days, Milly will have the embryo transferred to her waiting womb, and in another twelve she will be able to take a pregnancy test. But whether she is pregnant or not, my part will be over; the eggs retrieved today will be used in any further IVF attempts. After today, my job is done, and yet this feels like the beginning.

"You have someone to drive you home?" the nurse asks, and I nod. Milly has promised to come for me after school finishes. I've taken the afternoon off work; Lara wasn't pleased, but I hardly take any holiday so she couldn't do much about it. As I left during my lunch hour, I saw Sasha again, smoking furiously outside and looking rather miserable. She has not been in touch since our meeting six weeks ago, although I sent her a couple of emails encouraging her to reach out.

As I walked past her I gave her a fleeting smile, but I didn't have time to talk before my appointment at the clinic. As I headed towards the car park, she called out to me.

"Hey, can I talk to you sometime, after all?"

I half-turned, keeping my smile. "Of course. I'm out this afternoon, but why don't you come by next week?"

Sasha nodded rather grimly and again I wondered what she had to tell me.

Now I push thoughts of Sasha away as I lie back and the anaesthetist begins his work, fitting a tube into the canula in the back of my hand. The nurse pats my leg.

"Could you please put your feet into the stirrups?"

It's an obvious request, and yet an unexpected, visceral response rushes through me. *Panic.* It feels shocking, the suddenness of it, the way my breath hitches and my mind blanks. The stirrups...the needle poking into my hand...the way the doctor adjusts the bright light so it's aimed right between my legs...suddenly I am eighteen again. Eighteen and so very alone.

The nurse touches my shoulder, her eyes full of concern. "Are you okay, Anna?"

"Y-y-y...yes." I realise I am shaking. There is a metallic taste in my mouth, and the vinyl table beneath me feels slippery and cold. The nurse advised me to keep my socks on because the stirrups were cold, and inside the thin cotton my cold toes clench and curl around the metal. I try to breathe in and out, evenly, but I still feel faint. My body trembles. If I turn my head, I feel as if I could be back in that other office. I would see the technician at the ultrasound machine, the screen angled away from me so I wouldn't see the tiny image curled up on it. The not seeing has tormented me as much as the seeing would have, if not more. *What if...?*

But I can't think that way now. Thankfully, the anaesthetist has finished his work. "Count back to ten for me, Anna," he says and I swallow and nod, trying to keep back the icy tide of panic that doesn't make sense. It's just a *memory.* That's all it is.

"Ten, nine..." I begin in a trembling voice, and that's all I remember.


I wake up in a dimly lit recovery room, feeling achey and disoriented. I put my hand on my belly, expecting some difference, but it feels just the same, a little bloated from the hormones. My mouth is dry and when I sit up the world rushes around me, a fuzzy kaleidoscope of muted colour. I sink back on the pillows and wait for my mind to clear. It's just the residual anaesthetic making me feel woozy. I remember it from before, and so does my body.

And it's because of the *before,* or maybe just all the excess hormones zooming around in my body, that a tidal wave of grief suddenly rises up in me and I have to stifle a sob.

"Anna?" A nurse appears at the door, her head haloed by light from the hallway. "Are you awake?"

I press my fist to my mouth to keep back the guttural sound I can't believe I feel like making. "Yes," I finally manage to croak. "I'm fine. A bit groggy."

"Let me bring you a cup of tea."

By the time she returns, I have regained my composure. I am sitting up on the chaise, the thin blanket that was covering me folded by my feet. I take the tea with murmured thanks, and sip the hot, over-sugared liquid, grateful to ease the dryness in my mouth.

"Was it...successful?"

"Yes, everything went perfectly." She doesn't offer any more information, and I realise that's intentional. My part is over. I am not privy to anything more unless Milly and Matt choose to tell me. I signed the documents; I knew that. Yet in this moment it stings a little. "You can leave in half an hour or so," she continues. "Assuming you feel well enough."

"I will." I want to leave now. Now that it's over, I want nothing more than to be in the cosy familiarity of my own flat, curled up on my own bed, with Winnie purring as she snuggles against my stomach. In a strange and unsettling way, I want to forget this ever happened. I feel raw and wounded when I thought I would be feeling excited for Milly. I don't understand myself at all.

"And when the person who is driving you has arrived," the nurse finishes, and I look at her, surprised.

"Is Milly not here? What time is it?"

"Quarter to four."

She should be here by now, and I feel a prickling of unease. Where is she? This isn't something she would forget, or even be late to.

I sip my tea, trying to remain calm and positive as my stomach cramps, apparently a normal occurrence after the procedure. When I go to the loo, I see a bit of blood, which is also normal, but it freaks me out all the same. It all feels a bit too familiar. And Milly still isn't here.

Then, about half an hour later, the nurse appears in my room again. "Your lift is here," she says, smiling, and relief pulses through me.

"Milly...?"

Her smile falters. "No, not Milly. He says his name is...Jack? Jack Foster?"

*Jack?* Jack, Matt's brother, Milly and Matt's sperm donor, whom I've only met once? I feel completely gobsmacked, and oddly vulnerable.

"Is that okay?" the nurse asks, and I'm not sure what to say.

"Yes, yes," I finally answer. "Please tell him I'll come out to the waiting room in a bit."

After she leaves, I take a few minutes to check my appearance, brush my hair and wash my face. I still feel a bit groggy, my belly tender. And I have no idea what to say to Jack.

"How are you doing?" he asks, standing up with alacrity when I venture out to the waiting room. The brochure I'd been given advised comfy clothes for the procedure and aftercare, so I am dressed in a hoodie and yoga pants, which in this moment feel like pyjamas.

"I'm okay." I shake my head, feeling entirely discomfited. "I'm sorry, but I thought Milly was coming...?"

"I know, I'm sorry about that, and she is too, of course. Her school had an Ofsted inspection called at three this afternoon.

They're coming to inspect it tomorrow." He gives a grimacing shrug and I put on my coat.

"Right." I know a little bit about the inspections from Milly—how important they are, how everyone has to hustle to get their classrooms in shape, all the paperwork ready. I understand, but I still feel disappointed, a little bit hurt. "Bad timing, I suppose."

"Good thing I'm here." He tilts his head, giving me a rather charming smile. It affects me, because he is undeniably attractive, but I also feel uneasy. I don't know this man, and yet...we are, in a very roundabout way, going to be having a baby together. I tell myself not to think that way. It's just too weird.

"I thought you lived in the Cotswolds?"

Jack reaches for the folder of paperwork I've been given. "Let me take that for you." We walk outside; the day is grey and dismal even though it's now late March. The trees are still leafless, and the crocuses poking up through the earth look chilled and miserable. "I live in Stroud for the moment," he says, answering my question, "but I was in Bristol picking up some aged lumber from a salvage yard." He smiles. "So *that* was good timing."

I nod and look away. I want to be in my flat, alone with my cat and a cup of tea.

Jack leads me to a beat-up, mud-splattered Land Rover, the kind of vehicle I'd expect him to have. It's high up, and he puts his hand under my elbow as he helps me into the passenger seat.

"How are you feeling?" he asks as we drive away from the clinic.

"Okayish. A bit...I don't know. Off." I look out the window, inexplicably feeling that threat of tears again, as if I could sob, which is absolutely the last thing I want to do right now. "This is all a bit weird."

"Yes, I know what you mean," Jack murmurs.

"What about your...part? I suppose it's already done?"

"Yeah, a few weeks ago. Not a big deal for me." He shoots me a quick, slightly rakish smile. "Hardly a painful procedure, you know?"

"Right." I look away, blushing. I shouldn't have brought it up.

"Milly gave me your address...Totterdown, right?"

"Yes, Knowle Road, near the park."

We drive in silence for a few minutes while Jack follows the satnav on his phone and then pulls up in front of my home.

"Thanks for the lift—"

"You're on the top floor, right? Let me make sure you get up all right."

I feel the need to protest, but I don't, because the company does feel rather nice. I'm not sure I want to be alone yet, after all.

"Do you want a cup of tea or something?" I half-mumble once I've unlocked my front door and stepped inside.

"I should make you one. Why don't you put your feet up?" He nods towards the sofa in the sitting room. "I think I can find my way to the kettle."

"Okay. Thanks." Even though Jack is a stranger, it feels nice to have someone taking care of me. I sit gingerly on the edge of the sofa, but then the plump cushions give way beneath me, enveloping me in their plush warmth, and Winnie jumps onto my lap. By the time Jack returns with a mug of tea, I am lying down, my head propped against the armrest, Winnie stretched out on top of me like a living electric blanket.

"You look comfy." He puts the tea down on the coffee table and then, to my surprise, sits in the armchair opposite. I was expecting him to make his excuses and leave.

"This is all a bit odd, isn't it?" he says after a moment, his smile sheepish.

I reach for my tea, mainly to stall for time. Yes, it is odd, but I'm not sure I want to discuss it.

"I mean, you, me...it's our genes, together. Our—"

"Yes." I cut him off before he can say it.

"Sorry, am I sounding creepy?" He rubs a hand over his face. "I don't mean to. It's just that I didn't think too much about it, when Matt asked. I thought about it like donating blood, or giving a kidney." I recall Milly's comparison to just that and smile faintly. "But now that I'm thinking about it properly, it feels a bit different, you know? A bit more..."

"Yes, I know what you mean."

"Did you ever want kids yourself?" He gives me another one of those smiles. "Sorry, is that too personal? I just wondered."

"No, it's all right. I don't think I'll ever have my own children." I pause, choosing my words with care. "I'm happy as I am, really."

"No one special in your life?"

The weird, unexpected intimacy of the situation makes the question feel natural rather than nosy. "No, I'm not... I haven't been much interested in all that. Marriage, children." He looks skeptical, so I explain. "My parents fought all the time and then ended up divorcing acrimoniously when I was fifteen. It put me off matrimony for life, I think."

"That must have been difficult."

"It wasn't easy." And then, inexplicably, I feel that well of emotion rise within me again, and before I can stop it, my eyes are full of tears.

"Hey. *Hey.*" Jack leans forward, putting one hand on my arm. My hands shake and hot tea slops onto my fingers. He takes the mug from me and puts it on the table. "I'm sorry. I didn't realise it was such a difficult subject for you."

"It's not that," I say, sniffing. I am trying to hold back the tide of tears, but I can't. "I've been jacked up on hormones for six weeks," I manage thickly. "It's no wonder I'm a blubbering wreck." I wipe my eyes, because they have started to stream. "Sorry. I don't mean to cry."

"Are you sure it's just the hormones?" Jack asks gently as I keep wiping my eyes and taking gulping breaths.

I open my mouth to say, yes, of *course* it is, and then something else comes out. "Today was hard because it reminded me of when I was eighteen." I pause, wondering if I really want to say this to Jack of all people, and then I find myself blurting, "I had an abortion."

Something flashes across Jack's face, and in a cringing rush, I realise that he was just being kind, that he didn't actually want me to spill my guts.

"Sorry," I mumble, reaching for my tea and trying to hide my face behind the mug. "I shouldn't have told you that. I don't know why I did. It's just... today..."

"Have you told anyone before?"

I shake my head, my nose buried in my mug.

We sit in silence for a moment; the wind rattles the window-panes and I can hear both our breathing.

"Perhaps you needed to tell someone," he says at last. "Since this brought it back up for you. Do you... do you want to talk about it?"

*Do I?* I've bottled it up inside for so long, pushed it down, pretended it never happened. Milly has never known, never even guessed, and thankfully, kindly, she's never asked. I suppose she always knew there was *something*—why else would I go off the rails so spectacularly at the end of sixth form? But she could tell I didn't want to talk about it, and so she never pushed, which was a huge relief.

Even so, it was always there—an invisible, oppressive weight, a pain behind my eyes, a burning in my chest. It has always been an active thing, not to think about it. It requires effort.

"Perhaps I do," I say, and then we sit in silence some more. I pick at a loose thread on the sofa, pulling it taut before I let it go. "It was a hard time in my life," I say finally.

"Because of your parents?"

"Yes, and because I..." I blow out a breath. Do I really want to go into this? Dredge it up, like the sludge from the bottom of my soul? "I was in a relationship that I shouldn't have been," I say, which is one way of putting it. "And when...when I fell pregnant, he wasn't...well, he didn't want to know."

Jack grimaces. "I'm sorry."

"The truth is, *I* didn't want to know. I put it off and off, thinking somehow it would just go away, and then when I finally decided I had to do something..." My throat thickens once more and my eyes sting. "I was farther along than I realised. And that made it..." But now I can't go on. Because remembering hurts. Because no one wants to hear about the messiness of it, the guilt and regret, and certainly not the pain and the blood.

"Anna, I'm so sorry. I shouldn't have brought this up." He reaches over to place his hand on mine, the dry, warm weight of it reassuring.

"You didn't," I manage. "I did."

"Still, I feel as if I was prying." He smiles apologetically, and with a jolt I realise he is backing off, because, like everyone else, he doesn't want to know. And so I slip my hand from his and sit back against the sofa, giving him a repressive little smile as the tears thankfully dry up.

"It's okay, Jack. Today brought up some bad memories, that's all, and the hormones I've been on made it worse. I'm fine, really. Sorry to have offloaded on you there for a moment." I take a sip of my now lukewarm tea.

Jack looks at me for a moment. "Is that why you agreed?"

"Agreed...?"

"To donate."

I stare at him, shocked by the question, and because, no matter how I've tried to keep things separate in my mind, I acknowledge in this moment that they are related. All along there has been some part of me that felt as if the scales needed to be balanced. That one procedure makes up for another, in my own mind, if not in the cosmos.

"Perhaps it had something to do with it," I say slowly, and it is a confession. "On a subconscious level." I wonder how Milly would feel about it, if she knew. Would she mind? Does it matter?

"I'm glad you told me," Jack says, and I give him a small smile. I'm surprisingly glad too, even if I might cringe about it later. It felt a little bit how I imagine a bloodletting would feel, a release of pressure, or a held breath. "I should probably go..." he begins, half-rising, and I nod.

"Of course. Thank you for everything—"

"You're sure you're all right?"

"Yes. Fine." I smile brightly, too brightly. "Sorry about before. I don't know what came over me."

"You don't need to be sorry, Anna."

"It came out of nowhere. Honestly, I'm okay." My smile turns fixed and Jack stares at me. His eyes are brown like Matt's, his hair just a little bit darker. He hasn't shaved today.

"Maybe...would you like to get a coffee sometime? Or a drink?"

I stare back, unsure if he's asking me out on a proper date, or just as some sort of friend. Perhaps not even that, but simply because we have this weird link.

"Sure," I say after a moment, and Jack smiles and nods before leaving, the door clicking shut behind him.

I stroke Winnie as I drink the rest of my tea; my abdomen still aches and even as I feel a strange sort of emptiness inside, a peace settles on me like a violet twilight, soft and dark and comforting.

# CHAPTER SEVEN

## MILLY

When I was about six, a woman at a party—I can't remember where or what for—asked me why I didn't look like my parents. She didn't phrase it as bluntly as that, of course; she said something about genes and dark hair and changelings, laughing a little, and without a blink or a blush, I informed her that I was adopted.

I remember the look that flashed across her face; in hindsight I realise she must have been horrified by her unwitting faux pas, but at the time all I knew was that the expression on her face wasn't a good one, and I felt as if I'd done something wrong.

Then the woman backpedalled quickly, her voice rising loudly as she exclaimed how wonderful it was that I was adopted, and how my mummy and daddy were so lucky, and they must love me very much. But children are smarter than adults ever think; I knew she was overegging the conversational pudding, that her smile was too wide, her voice too cheery. I knew she wasn't telling the truth.

When I asked my mother about it later, she looked stricken for a second before gathering me into her arms and telling me that it *was* wonderful, and she and my father *were* lucky. It was all so perfectly perfect, our very own fairy tale, happy ending guaranteed. And even though her voice brimmed with sincerity, and her smile wasn't too wide, I had the same impression from her as from that strange woman—she wasn't quite telling the truth. I never pressed her on it, and I never doubted her love for me, but the impression remained.

I have a lot of memories like that. They aren't terrible, and I don't regret anything, but they're there, like stones in my mental shoe. And, for some reason, I think of that woman as Matt holds my hand and the doctor transfers a precious embryo into my uterus. We decided on only one because of the potential risks involved in carrying multiples, and we figured if it doesn't happen this time, we'd just try again. But I am hoping—I am *praying*—it happens.

As I lie still, my feet in stirrups, my eyes on the ceiling, I think of that woman and I promise myself that my child will not have moments like that. She will feel loved, accepted, *part of me* from the beginning. All the time. Always.

It's finished in twenty minutes, and as I stand up, I have the urge to tiptoe, as if this newly planted embryo is in danger of sliding out. When I say as much, the doctor assures me this is a normal feeling, but not one based in reality. He advises me to take the rest of the day off, and keep activity to a minimum for the next two weeks, which begs the question—why? Perhaps it can fall out, after all.

It's not easy to take a day off work, especially on the heels of a fairly brutal Ofsted inspection. Monkton Primary is a small, cosy village school thirty minutes from Bristol, with only one class per year group, and a very stretched staff. I've been working there for twelve years, since I finished uni, and while I've been tempted to look for jobs closer to home, it's hard to leave a place where you're known.

When the call from Ofsted came just as I was about to leave to pick up Anna, my heart sank right down to my toes. The last time Ofsted had come they'd given us the dreaded "Requires

Improvement" rating, so there was no question about staying late and pitching in to make sure it went well.

But *Anna*...I hated the thought of letting her down at that crucial moment, even though I knew I didn't have a choice. I texted her and left two voicemails, but I still felt wretchedly guilty for sending Jack in my place. As soon as I got home, I rang her land-line, but she didn't answer, which somehow made me feel worse.

On Saturday I rang again, wondering as the phone rang and rang if I was badgering her. Perhaps she was tired from the procedure and wanted to lay low. Maybe she needed some space. Finally, on Sunday afternoon, she rang me back.

"Hi, Milly. Sorry I didn't return your call earlier." She sounded tired.

"Anna, I'm so sorry I didn't pick you up from the clinic. Jack told you about the Ofsted—"

"Yes. Bad timing."

"Yes." Things felt stilted in a way I didn't expect. "Can I come by? I'll bring croissants." Almond, Anna's favourite.

"Okay," she said after a pause. "Sure."

I brought a bag of fresh croissants, and Anna's favourite chai tea, but when I hugged her hello, something felt just the tiniest bit off. I told myself I was being paranoid, that Anna was just tired. That nothing was wrong, nothing had changed from the way we'd envisioned it all. Anna wasn't having second thoughts or regrets; she *couldn't* be.

"How was it?" I asked as Anna sat cross-legged on the sofa and sipped her tea. "Did it...did it hurt?"

"Not really." Her gaze was lowered and she seemed slightly brittle, in the way she held herself, the set angle of her jaw. I was at a loss, my voice too cheerful, my manner forced. It was as if neither of us knew how to *be* anymore.

"I'm so grateful—"

"I know."

I sat back, feeling a bit scolded. "Anna, is everything okay?" I finally ventured even though I hardly wanted to form the words. "Are you...are you having second thoughts about it all?"

"It would be a little late for that."

I jerked back, but then Anna smiled a bit wearily.

"That was meant to be a joke, Milly. I'm sorry. The whole thing just left me feeling a bit...raw, I suppose. I didn't expect it. I'll be fine in a few days."

I searched her guarded expression, trying to figure out how I should respond, but my mind felt blank. What on earth did *raw* mean? Should I be worried?

"I'm sorry I wasn't there," I finally said. "I really wanted to be."

"I know."

"Was Jack..." I didn't know how to finish that question.

"It was fine. Honestly, it's all fine." She roused herself a little bit, eyebrows raised. "And tomorrow is your big day."

"Yes..."

"Let's focus on that." It felt like a reminder to herself as much as to me.

Now, as Matt takes my arm and leads me like an invalid from the clinic, I try to blank all the worries from my mind—Anna's unexpected aloofness, the wretched Ofsted inspection, which resulted in another "Requires Improvement," or how long the next two weeks of unknowing are going to feel.

"You okay?" Matt asks as we drive back home.

"Yes. Scared to death, and feeling as if the next twelve days are going to be the longest of my life...but yes, I'm okay."

Back home, Matt insists I go right to bed, as if I've had major surgery rather than a procedure akin to a cervical smear. And I obey, because I'm so frightened that I will do something that will knock my precious cargo right out of me. If I did, I know I would never be able to forgive myself. I would have failed at motherhood before I'd even started.

I say as much to Matt when he brings me a cup of tea, and his eyes crinkle in concern as he sits on the edge of the bed.

"Milly, you're too hard on yourself. You always have been."

"Maybe, but how could I not feel that way?"

"If it doesn't happen, perhaps it's not meant to."

I feel a bit stung by that pronouncement. "You don't really believe that, do you?"

He sighs. "I don't know. Sometimes it just feels as if we're forcing it, you know? All this intervention..."

He's having second thoughts *now*? "It's not that much intervention, Matt," I say, trying to keep my tone reasonable. "And if I am pregnant, it will be worth it, don't you think?"

He smiles tiredly. "Yes, of course it will be."

But I am not entirely convinced by his tone, and that feels like something else to worry about.

Anna stops by that evening, and to my relief she seems more like herself, plumping my pillows and bringing gossip magazines and celebrity tabloids, my secret vice.

"Don't feel guilty for taking it easy," she admonishes me. "You have every right."

"I still have to work."

She sits on the side of my bed and holds my hand, her expression turning serious. "Be kind to yourself, Milly."

"Look at me," I try to joke. "I'm *relaxing*—"

"I just mean, this isn't something you can will to happen. Don't blame yourself if it doesn't. It isn't all up to you."

Her perception both rattles and touches me. "I know that," I say, but I wonder if I do. I feel such *pressure*, because this *is* up to me. It's up to my body. And my body has betrayed me before.

The next twelve days do feel like the longest of my life. I can't keep from tiptoeing through them, as if I am holding an ancient and precious Ming vase that no one else can see. When Seth, one of my Year Ones, pokes me in the stomach to get my attention, I am seized with both terror and fury that he might have injured the tiny life inside me.

Anna and I check in with each other almost every day, and I know she is nearly as hopeful and excited and scared as I am. She is nothing but supportive, stopping by with coffee and doughnuts on Saturday, asking how I feel. That weird aloofness I first felt from her has disappeared, and I am grateful.

The day I am to go in for a pregnancy test, Anna texts me a raft of emojis—champagne, a baby, fingers crossed, and a pregnant woman with a lovely big bump. They make me smile, but they also terrify me. I want this so badly, I feel as if there's no way I will get it. Hard work and determination are no longer enough. Just as Anna said, I can't will this to happen, and I hate that. I want to be in control. I need to be.

My heart feels as if it is climbing into my throat as I am called into the examining room; Alicia, my specialist, takes a blood test, then suggests I take a urine test as well, because although the blood test is more accurate, the results won't be available for a few hours, and there's a chance I could know right now.

*Now.* The moment I've been waiting for, the moment I've been dreading. I don't think I'll be able to handle the disappointment if it's negative. I'm afraid of the intensity of my own reaction, the crushing sense of failure that will overwhelm me.

I go into the bathroom, dizzy with nerves, my hands shaking as I unwrap the stick, and then sit, wee, wait.

It's a universal motherhood moment—the test, the sight of the double line or cross or whatever it is. I've heard mums at the school gate sharing their stories. *I couldn't believe it ... I took five tests ...*

And now here I am, stick in hand, needing only to turn it over to know whether I am going to have a baby ... or not.

*Just do it, Milly,* I tell myself, but I feel as if I physically can't; my limbs are concrete, my body paralysed. At least in the not knowing, I can hope. In ignorance, there is still possibility. But if it's negative...

Then my phone pings with a text from Anna. *News?*

On impulse, I swipe the screen to call her. She picks up on the first ring, her voice hushed because she's at work.

"Milly? Have you found out?"

"I'm sitting in the bathroom at the doctor's," I whisper with a shaky laugh. "Holding the pregnancy test."

"Is it—"

"I don't know. I'm scared to turn it over, Anna." I laugh again, because this is *crazy.* "I can't do it."

"You *can.* And, if it's negative, you can keep trying. Another couple of weeks and you could be sitting right here all over again."

"I know, but still. It would be starting over. And maybe it will never happen. Maybe I'm too far gone with this whole premature menopause." It's my worst fear, and Anna counters it immediately.

"And maybe you're not. Maybe you're sitting there, holding the best news of your life."

A little, incredulous giggle escapes me; I so want that to be true. "Keep talking," I say, because Anna might be able to talk me into being brave enough to look. To know.

"You can do this, Milly. It's the only way forward. What else are you going to do? You're in the bathroom, right? You can't live in there forever."

"I could," I joke. "There's water and a toilet."

"But no TV."

"I've got my phone, and the doctor's office has internet."

"What about food?"

"Matt would bring it to me." This conversation is utterly inane, and yet it grounds me.

"What about sleeping?" Anna asks, as if this is a real issue. "Is there a bathtub? Because that could work." I laugh out loud, and I hear the smile in her voice as she continues, "Just turn it over, Milly. You want to know. You need to, no matter how many little lines are on that stick."

"I know I do." I take a deep breath, and I think Anna does too. And then I turn it over.

My breath whooshes out of my lungs as I stare at two blazing-bright pink lines. *Two.* There's no doubt, no faintness, they're both bright and *there.* I let out a wavering laugh, but it sounds more like a sob.

"Milly..." Anna sounds worried, and then I laugh again, the sound definitely one of joy.

"Anna, I'm pregnant." I whisper the words, as if they're sacred, and they *are.* "I'm *pregnant.*"

"Oh Milly." Anna lets out a laugh-sob of her own. "I'm so happy for you. So, so happy."

Matt taps on the door, most likely wondering what on earth I've been doing in here. "Milly?" he calls, sounding anxious.

"Just a sec. I should go," I tell Anna. "I'll ring you later."

"Congratulations, Milly. This is the best news." Her voice is full of warmth.

"Thanks, Anna. You know this couldn't have happened—"

"Without me. Yeah, yeah." She is laughing. "I know. You've only told me about three hundred times already."

I laugh too, and then, as I ring off, I shake my head, still incredulous that this is happening. I press my hand to my flattish stomach. *Hello, little bean. Nice to know you're there.* Then I wash my hands and flush the toilet, trying to collect myself, because I feel as if I could burst into tears or song, I'm not sure which.

Finally, I open the door and grin at Matt even as tears start in my eyes. "Congratulations," I tell him, my voice wobbling all over the place. "We're going to have a baby."

# CHAPTER EIGHT

## ANNA

The week after my procedure, I find Sasha waiting for me by the door to my office. I've had trouble shaking off the melancholy the whole thing created in me, and twelve hours after telling Jack about my abortion, I am in the mentally cringing stage of remembering, and wondering why on *earth* I thought it appropriate or wise to divulge that information to a complete stranger.

Thank God I kept the details to a bare and unpleasant minimum, and there's no real reason to think I'll see him again, despite his offer to go out sometime. After everything I unloaded onto him, I doubt that invitation will be forthcoming, and I tell myself I am relieved.

"Sasha." I do my best to inject some warmth into my voice, even though I'm not at my best. I didn't sleep well, and I felt achey enough this morning to skip my morning run. "I'm glad you came. Would you like a cup of coffee? Tea?"

She shakes her head as I open the door to my office and usher her inside. Office is a rather grand way of putting it; my desk is in the reception area of Lara's office, along with some filing cabinets and a sofa, and sometimes I do feel like her glorified receptionist rather than the Assistant Director of HR, which is what I am since my promotion four years ago.

I close the door behind me, while Sasha perches nervously on a chair in front of my desk.

"I'm glad you've come," I tell her as I sit down behind my desk and fold my hands on the surface in front of me. "I was hoping you would."

"I'm still not sure I should be here..."

"But you are, so why don't you tell me what's been bothering you?"

"I think I've been sexually harassed," Sasha blurts, and my heart sinks, because this is going to be difficult—for Sasha, and for me. Sexual harassment is a huge issue in the workplace, and it's so challenging to deal with appropriately in today's heightened climate.

And then there's Lara, who, despite being a woman herself, is remarkably unsympathetic to the sort of cases that come to our attention—inappropriate comments or unwanted touching, words or actions that a male colleague blusters were only a bit of harmless flirting, if that. Misconstrued invitations and pressured acceptances, both of which unfortunately make Lara roll her eyes. She usually tries to shut the complaints down before they even start, and generally, sadly, even in this day and age, she's successful. But this time Sasha has come to me.

"Why don't you start from the beginning," I tell her.

"I started at Qi in September," she begins haltingly. "I'm in the graduate scheme, in the IT department. And it's a fab environment... I've really loved it, right from the start. Everyone joking and having fun, going out to the pub together after work... it's the kind of thing you dream of, you know, when you're in uni?"

"Yes, I'm sure," I murmur. It's not my experience of work, but I was the only graduate apprentice in a small department, and Lara was not exactly the chummiest of bosses. In any case, I've never been particularly good at socialising anyway.

The IT department, however, is different; it is both nerdy and cool, with a lot of young guys in ironic T-shirts and statement glasses, and a few sharp-looking older ones in button-down shirts, skinny ties, and jeans. They joke they're the IT of the IT, the cream of the crop, as Qi Tech specialises in troubleshooting companies' IT issues, from dealing with databases to managing telephone systems, and our IT department deals with our own IT problems.

Sasha has fallen silent, and after waiting for her to speak and realising she isn't going to, I try a gentle prompt. "So what happened, Sasha? What went wrong?"

"I don't know..."

"You can tell me."

"And it won't go any further?" She asks this almost eagerly, and I hesitate. Surely she wouldn't have come to me if she was unwilling for it to go any further? And yet she's so young, only twenty-two or so, probably one of only a few women in the department, her whole career—her whole life—in front of her. I understand her not wanting this to derail her life, not to mention her job.

"I can't promise that, Sasha, because I don't know what you're about to tell me. But I can promise that I will not tell anyone else unless I judge it is legally and ethically necessary." I smile encouragingly at her and wait.

Sasha takes a deep, shuddery breath. "I don't know, maybe it's my fault," she says slowly. "I might have given out the wrong signals..." She bites her lip, and I wish I could give her a hug.

"The first thing we need to do is establish the facts of what happened. Can you tell me those, Sasha? Was there a particular incident—a conversation, or...?" I trail off, waiting for her to fill in the unfortunate blanks.

"I suppose there have been a few things...over time..."

I release a long, low breath. I still don't know whom we're talking about. "Okay..."

"I don't know, though." She looks at me miserably. "I don't want to get him in trouble."

I feel as if we're circling around the vortex of the problem—the black hole of accusation and insinuation. "I understand you not wanting to cause trouble, Sasha, but that's not what this meeting is about. If some kind of sexual harassment has occurred, then Qi Tech needs to know about it so we can deal with it appropriately. In a sense, the concern isn't about you getting someone into trouble—it's about the company's responsibility towards all of its employees." It's written in the employee handbook, although I don't know if Lara would agree with me.

In my fourteen years at Qi Tech, all under Lara, we have had six official cases of sexual harassment. Four were dismissed, one was dropped by the accuser, and one was settled quietly, behind closed doors. All were essentially hushed up.

But the climate is different now; I think it's better, even if Lara doesn't, and we both know we have to be so very careful.

I pull a notepad towards me. "I need to make a record of this meeting, okay? Is that all right with you?"

"Yes..."

"So why don't we start back at the beginning. You mentioned the atmosphere of the IT department, which you enjoyed. Jokey and friendly?"

"Yes..."

"But then something changed?"

"Yes, with the Dobson account."

I nod, although I'm not aware of the Dobson account. I'm aware of very little that Qi Tech does, and much more about how employees are paid and treated. I know about their illnesses, their time off for personal or sick leave, their pay rises and their bonuses, the staff that don't get along and the ones who do—perhaps too much. But as for actual *work*?

"We were staying late," Sasha continues haltingly. "Because we had to implement their new IT system by the end of the year."

"Right..."

"And then, a few evenings, it was just me and...and Mike."

*Mike.* My heart sinks a little. "Would this be Michael Jacobs you're referring to?"

Sasha bites her lip and nods. Michael Jacobs is the head of IT, an affable guy in his forties, with a booming laugh and a backslapping manner. He's friendly to everyone, knows most people's names, and has been with the company for fifteen years. He has a wife who bakes brownies and sends them in with him regularly, and two young kids who have accompanied him on the Bring-Your-Kid-to-Work days Qi Tech sponsors every year. He's a staple, practically an icon, here. This is not going to be easy.

I take a deep breath and place my hands flat on my desk. "So you and Michael Jacobs were working in the evenings—alone? There was no one else with you?"

"Sometimes there was, but a couple of times there wasn't."

I pick up my pen once more. "And when you were alone...?"

"It wasn't anything much at first..."

The door bangs open and Lara stands there, dressed in her usual work uniform of a black power suit and a silk blouse in a vivid shade, this time chartreuse. Her shiny black bob swings in a hard angle against her chin as her eyes narrow.

"Sasha, isn't it?"

Sasha has already jumped out of her chair, nearly knocking it over, before nodding quickly and then scuttling to the door.

"I'd better get to work..." she mumbles, and I fling out a hand, willing her to stay even though I know she won't.

"Let's continue this conversation, Sasha," I call a bit desperately. "How about next week?" But she's already gone.

"Let me guess," Lara says flatly as she sheds her coat and blazer and marches on stiletto heels into her office. "She came whimpering to you about some kind of sexual harassment."

I flinch, wondering if Lara realises how insulting she sounds, how much trouble she could get into for speaking like that. I suspect she does, just as I suspect the CEO and VPs of the company do—and none of them care all that much. Tech companies tend to be a man's world.

"She was speaking to me about a sexual harassment complaint, yes," I reply as I follow her into her office and close the door. "I've started making notes, but it's still very early stages..."

"That's good," Lara affirms. "These things never need to go too far, do they?"

"I'm not sure about that, Lara—"

"Sasha didn't seem very sure, either," she remarks as she sits behind her desk and pulls her laptop towards her. "Hemming and hawing all over the place. Is it a case of morning-after regret, do you think?" She smiles at me expectantly, as if we're having a chat about HR strategies, and not a possible case of harassment, assault, or worse.

"I don't think so, no," I say after a moment.

"Who's the bloke, then?"

I hesitate, because I know Lara won't react well to this.

She taps her acrylic nails on her desk. "Anna?"

"Mike Jacobs," I admit, and Lara blows out a noisy breath.

"That is not good. No. That cannot happen."

"Lara, it's not a question of what can or can't happen, but what *did*," I protest, and predictably she rolls her eyes.

"Mike Jacobs? Come on, Anna. He's Head of IT. He's been here donkey's years. He has a *wife*."

"None of those facts have any bearing on whether sexual harassment took place," I say quietly. My heart is starting to beat hard because Lara does *not* like it when I push back, even gently, and too often I don't. But I think of Sasha's stricken face, her bitten nails, and something in me aches to be her advocate, not her betrayer.

Lara cocks her head. "If you don't feel you can handle this case, Anna, then I can certainly do so."

And Lara will bulldoze straight over Sasha.

"I'm just saying," I reply as carefully as I can, "that the climate has changed significantly since the last sexual harassment complaint we had in—what? 2016?" She nods tersely. She most likely keeps them all in a mental rolodex. "With the advent of the whole #MeToo movement—"

"Oh, please," Lara interjects with a scoffing laugh, and I try to keep my voice and face both neutral.

"Lara, it's an issue. We both know that. And Qi Tech needs a viral smear campaign a lot less than it needs one sexual harassment complaint."

Lara stares at me levelly. "So what are you suggesting? Throw Mike under the bus?"

"No, I'm suggesting we follow the proper protocols and procedures. Encourage Sasha to relate her experience with a colleague, friend, or union representative present. Make detailed notes and record the conversation if necessary. Ask Mike for his perspective on whatever happened, with an appropriate representative. And consult the company solicitor to make sure we're covered legally."

"Fine." Lara exhales again, shrugging impatiently. "We'll follow the protocols. Let me know when the meeting is arranged."

I'm not sure it's a victory as I leave her office on shaky legs, but I decide to count it as one. This will be the first sexual harassment case I've handled since I became Assistant Head of HR. My experience of the other cases has been typing up notes and watching teary-eyed employees leave Lara's office clutching a bunch of tissues. I want to make sure I do this right.

Of course, I know I can't assume Mike's guilt, and I don't. I even feel a flash of pity for him, because whatever happened, I doubt he thought it would end like this.

For a second, my mind drifts back down the years, to when I was younger than Sasha, and just as uncertain and afraid. When I wasn't sure what was right or wrong, or who, if anyone, was to blame. But then I shut down that line of thinking because I try to think about it as little as possible.

Sasha doesn't come back the next day or the day after that, and when I send her an email reminding her to return, she doesn't reply. I decide to leave it for a bit; I don't want to be accused of harassment, either, and maybe she just needs a little time to gather her courage, or perhaps she has rethought the whole situation, and it's not as clear-cut as it seemed. When Lara asks me about it, I tell her Sasha has gone silent, and she smiles, satisfied.

On Monday night, I call Milly to ask her about the embryo transfer, and she says she'll know whether she's pregnant in twelve days. It seems like a long time, but in less than two weeks everything could change. Milly might be pregnant. And in the smallest, strangest way, it will feel like my pregnancy too. But that's not something I tell her. It's not something I let myself think about too much, because it makes me feel guilty, as if I'm doing something wrong.

So I overcompensate a little over the next few days, by being the most supportive friend I can. I text Milly, I listen to her monologues about phantom pregnancy symptoms and whether it's too early to feel nauseous/tired/dizzy, and on Saturday I bring over some doughnuts and coffee, and we eat them at her kitchen table, Matt having gone for a run.

"I bought a pregnancy magazine," she whispers, as if confessing to looking at porn. "Isn't that terrible? I'm going to jinx it—"

"Milly, you aren't even superstitious."

"Still, it feels... presumptuous. There is such a thing as tempting fate or God or whatever, don't you think?"

I consider that for a moment. "No, I don't, not unless fate is some mad bitch with PMT out to get you."

Milly smiles a little at that. "Maybe not. But I don't think I should have bought it, anyway."

"Why not?"

"Because there's this whole pull-out section in the middle…
like a centrefold, except it's pictures of a woman giving birth. I'm
serious, Anna," she says sternly, because I've started to laugh, "it
shows right up her you-know-what. And I mean *right* up, with
the baby's head *right* there."

"Who on earth wants to see that?"

"Exactly! But there are multiple photos and—good *grief.*" She
shudders. "I do not want to think about that part of it at all."

"You could always have a C-section."

"No, I wouldn't want that, either." She rests her chin in her
hand, sounding wistful now. "The truth is, I do want it—the
contractions, the pushing, all of it. I don't care if it hurts or my
lady parts are never the same—"

I shudder theatrically. "Eugh, Milly—"

"I mean it, Anna. I want it all. I want to push her out, hold
her in my arms." She smiles with self-conscious zeal. "I'm already
thinking of her as a girl, and I might not even be pregnant."

"But maybe you are." I reach over to squeeze her hand, ignoring
the pang that goes through me—the pang I don't want to analyse
or name. A pang I suppress so quickly I'm able to convince myself
I didn't feel it at all.

The evening before Milly's appointment, a text pings on my phone.

> *I got your number from Matt. So how about that drink?*
> *Jack*

For a second I feel nothing but surprise, and then a flicker of
wary pleasure. So Jack wasn't scared off by my tearful confession?
I didn't think he'd call again. I'd told myself not to expect it, and
now, looking down at his words, I realise I'm pleased he's been
in touch. I want to see him again. At least, I think I do.

I wait another few minutes, deliberating, and then, my heart fluttering just a little, I text a reply.

*Sure. When and where?*

# CHAPTER NINE

## MILLY

I'm pregnant. I'm actually pregnant. I hug the secret to myself, even though part of me wants to go up to every stranger in the street and shout the truth. *I'm pregnant! I'm pregnant! I'm going to have a baby! Me!*

Instead, I float around in this translucent baby bubble, hardly hoping, barely daring to dream. It's still such early days, and so much could go wrong. I will be seen by my specialist Alicia until I'm twelve weeks and out of the typical danger zone, and then I can transfer to a regular midwife.

Matt and I agree not to tell anyone until then—except for Anna and Jack, who were both thrilled—because it would hurt too much to have to explain to everyone if it all goes wrong, which, unfortunately, is still a distinct possibility.

We don't tell our parents, which isn't such a big deal for Matt's, who are in the middle of a four-month cruise, but I know mine will be hurt. My mum has rung after every appointment, asked me about every development. Until the last few months, I've always been happy to share my news, but I made the choice not to tell her about the premature menopause diagnosis or the IVF. I knew I couldn't cope with her anxious interest and constant analysis; it was hard enough as it was. But now it feels as if I've been keeping too many secrets, and my pregnancy is one more.

In any case, my parents haven't been in touch these last few weeks, something I realise in hindsight is unlike them. I've been so busy that I haven't noticed their absence, and it makes me feel guilty as well as concerned.

I leave a message on their answerphone, asking if we can see them on the weekend, and then, on Saturday afternoon, we drive across the Severn Bridge from Bristol to Chepstow, where I grew up. It's early April, and everything feels fragile and new, from the daffodils waving in the still-chilly breeze to the sunlight making the surface of the Severn shimmer, and the very slight swelling of my stomach.

I am only eight weeks pregnant, just starting to feel sick, the waistband of my clothes the tiniest bit tight. I relish the symptoms, and I've shared each one with Anna, because they feel like milestones, triumphs. She has marvelled in them too, reminding me how wonderful it is that we are in this together. I feel like we're a team, and it feels good. Maybe this pregnancy, this baby, will bring us together closer than ever before.

My parents have set up lunch in the conservatory at the back of the house, overlooking the garden, my father's pride and joy. It is not quite as well kept as I would have expected at this time of year, when the flower beds have normally been dug out, the raised vegetable beds freshly tilled. It reminds me, with a pang, that they are both getting old; my mother will be seventy-five this year, my father seventy-seven.

*"Milly."* When my mother hugs me, she feels fragile too. My parents are both tall and blond like Anna, Nordic giants, while I am small and dark and fey. It's no wonder people have commented on our differing appearances over the years.

"I'm sorry I haven't been in touch recently. Things have been manic." As I sit down, I can't keep my hand from creeping to my belly. Now that I am here, facing both my parents with their benevolent smiles and kind eyes, I feel as if I shouldn't keep this news from them any longer. I *want* to share it, but I am also scared, because it is still so early and it could all go wrong. I can only cope with so much disappointment, so much sympathy.

"That's all right," my mum says quietly. "We haven't been very good at keeping in touch, either, lately." My father goes to the kitchen to bring out the lunch, and I have a jarring sense of having missed something important, yet with no idea of what it is.

My father brings in a wooden board laid out with various cheeses and meats, along with a sliced baguette and a salad. Matt chats to them about the latest NHS funding crisis, and I only half-listen as I observe how my parents aren't quite meeting our eyes, and my mother picks at her food.

At first I wonder if I've hurt them, by not being in touch. Perhaps they've realised something has been going on, and that I wasn't sharing it with them. My parents have always wanted to be involved in absolutely every aspect of my life, and occasionally it has felt suffocating—the endless questions, the picking over of details, the over-the-top concern and sympathy.

Not keeping them involved in this, the most intimate part of my life, is a big deal, and I know I should have told them, but I wasn't ready for my mother's gushing concern, all the probing questions she would ask that I wouldn't want to answer.

While Matt and I weren't planning on telling them about my pregnancy for another four weeks, I'm not sure I can last the meal without admitting the truth. And part of me—a large part—wants them to know, to rejoice and be glad with me.

But, over the course of the meal, it becomes clear that this isn't about me. The more I sit there, watching my mother toy with her food, the more I realise this is about *them*. And then, when I've cleared away the dishes and my father puts on the kettle, my mother breaks it to us both.

"Milly," she says. "Matt." She pauses, and I tense. I feel frozen inside, like I can't move, can barely breathe. "We haven't been in touch these last few weeks because...well, your father and I received some news and we wanted to process it ourselves first." She smiles with sorrowful wryness, a smile that tugs at me. It *hurts*. "Anyway, it's not good news, as I'm sure you can imagine by now."

Dad comes in with a tray of teas and coffees which he puts on the table before going to stand behind my mum, one hand on her shoulder. She reaches up and clasps his hand with her own. I swallow hard.

"I have cancer," she says, with that same sad smile. "Perhaps you knew I was going to say something like this."

And I did, even though I didn't want to admit it to myself. All through lunch, I did. "Oh, Mum..." I can't get any other words out. I feel guilty for not calling, for being too wrapped up in my own little life.

"It's stomach cancer," she continues. "And I'm in stage three."

"What..." I don't want to form the words. "What does that mean, in terms of treatment and a...a prognosis? Have they said...?"

"It could be better," Mum answers with a small, wobbly laugh. "They could have caught it earlier—"

"But it's not too late," my father interjects, sounding determinedly upbeat. "She's eligible for surgery, and it's going to be scheduled in the next few weeks, and then a course of chemotherapy afterwards."

"That's good." My voice is shaky and Matt reaches for my hand.

"But I am nearly seventy-five," Mum reminds us. "I've lived a good life—"

"Oh don't, Mum." The words are out before I can stop them, and a hurt look flashes across her face. "Don't write your epitaph just yet, is all I mean. This is the beginning of treatment, surgery..."

Mum is silent for a moment. "I don't think I like these kinds of beginnings," she says at last. "And I'm honestly not sure how much of a beginning it is. At my age, Milly, they can't do the really strong chemotherapy or radiation that they might try on someone younger. I wouldn't be able to withstand it." She speaks gently, but it tips me over the edge anyway. I blink back tears, not wanting to cry, not wanting to make this about me. More than ever, I want to tell them about my pregnancy, about something good that truly is a beginning. But it doesn't feel right in this moment; this is about their news, not ours.

"I'm so sorry, Mum." I reach over to hug her, and again I feel how fragile she is. Normally so comfortably solid, she is now diminished in my arms. I fight the urge to hold on, to squeeze, as if I can somehow anchor us both to this moment.

Matt and I leave a short while later, and we're both silent in the car until we cross the bridge. "Should we have told them, do you think?" Matt finally asks.

"I thought about it, but I didn't want to take away from what they were telling us." I press my hand against my belly. Will this baby ever know my mother? "Perhaps we should have. I know my mother especially would want to know…" What if her time is limited? My father insisted the odds were good, that at her stage of cancer the five-year survival rate was over fifty per cent, but it still feels tenuous and uncertain, and that makes me want her to know even more. To have more time knowing. "We'll tell them the next time we see them," I decide.

Matt reaches over to hold my hand. "I'm sorry, Milly."

I shake my head, still reeling. I've known my parents are getting older; they were forty and forty-two when they adopted me. But they've been so hale and hearty, hiking in the Chilterns and spending hours in the garden. Yes, they've had creaky knees and the odd senior moment, but this still feels like a shot out of the dark, shocking in its force.

And it makes me realise how much I love my parents. How much I depend on them—and how much I take them for granted.

I've found my mother's concern exasperating, even annoying; I've rolled my eyes at my father's jolly bonhomie. Now I feel like such a selfish cow, for having so much while acting as if I don't have enough. For feeling as if something was missing in my family, when perhaps nothing really was. Do families ever get it right? Do they ever truly *work*?

Again, I press my hand against my non-existent bump. Our family will be different, I promise myself. We won't take each other for granted. We won't get annoyed at the little things. We'll treasure every moment, mark it as precious, even if it is hard. I know these are promises no one can keep, at least not perfectly, but I mean them all the same. I mean them utterly.

The next few weeks seem to pass in a haze. My mum gets an appointment for her surgery at the end of June, when I will be fifteen weeks pregnant. I tell Anna about her cancer, and she drives out to Chepstow to visit my parents herself, taking a huge bouquet of flowers and a stack of paperbacks for my mum to read in hospital, things I feel I should have done, brought, but I've been so stunned by it all that I didn't. She also sends me a card and flowers, and I am touched by how thoughtful she is, because I know this news will hit Anna just as hard as it is hitting me.

At twelve weeks, I have my first scan, and it feels miraculous. Matt and I hold hands as we watch the monochrome squiggles and lines morph into a baby with arms and legs, a beating heart. *Our baby.*

"Everything looks healthy," the technician tells us cheerfully. "All good. Shall I print out a photo?"

That evening, I meet Anna for a celebratory drink—sparkling apple juice for me, champagne for her. I feel extravagant, as well as grateful. So, so grateful—my baby is healthy, my mother is scheduled for surgery. Despite the hard things, life is good.

Anna squints comically at the photo of the scan, her face screwed up with concentration. "I see it," she finally says, her voice ringing with excitement that makes a few heads turn. "I actually see it. An actual *baby*."

"Well, that is what it is." Anna's excitement makes me smile; she looks so happy, her eyes alight, her mouth curved so I can see her dimples.

"Yes, but still... how big is it now? The baby?"

"I don't actually know."

"Let's check." Quickly she swipes and scrolls on her phone. "Twelve weeks, right?"

"Almost thirteen."

"Your baby is as big as a lemon," she reads off her phone. "And weighs almost an ounce. An ounce!" She looks up, marvelling, making me laugh, before returning to read. "Wow, check this out. Your baby is developing reflexes, and if you poke your tummy, he or she will squirm, even if you don't feel it. Isn't that amazing?"

"It really is." I picture my lemon-like baby nestled inside me, sucking his thumb, kicking tiny legs.

"That is so cool. You are actually *growing* a baby. It's like... Chia Pet, but so much better."

"Chia Pet! You mean those ceramic animals you grow grass on?" I pretend to shudder. "Yes, this is *much* better." We laugh, and I feel a rush of love and gratitude, that I can share this with Anna. That she is so excited for me, that she is happy to walk alongside me in this. "What's going on with you, Anna?" I ask as I sip my sparkling juice. "We can't just talk about baby stuff all the time."

"Well, we *could*." She smiles, and again I think how happy she looks. She's wearing a top I don't recognise, in bright pink with a scalloped edge. It looks good on her.

"Anything new going on?"

Anna purses her lips, considering, and with a flicker of surprise I realise there must be something. It's unexpected, because Anna's life is usually so placid, so predictable. Then she laughs and shakes her head. "No, not really, unless you count Lara being more offensive than usual."

"She's going to get fired one day. Or sued."

"As if." She shrugs. "She's protected by the company. I think she always will be."

"So nothing else?" I press lightly, because I still think there is something, and I wonder why she isn't telling me.

"Nope." Anna smiles and looks away, and I am left feeling as if she has a secret—one she doesn't want to share.

But I have secrets too, although not from Anna.

That weekend Matt and I drive to Chepstow to tell my parents about the baby. It isn't until we're driving there that we talk about what exactly we're going to say.

"Will we tell them about the IVF?" Matt asks.

"Well, yes. Why shouldn't we?"

"And the egg and sperm donation?" I hesitate, and he nods, as if I've said something important. "I know. I don't want it to become this big thing. I don't want to have to *tell* people all the time."

Like I had to with my adoption. No, I definitely don't want that, and yet it feels like something rather big *not* to say. It feels like a betrayal of my original desire to make this a conscious choice, a celebration, the vision I sold to Anna. But it's not as if we have to go around shouting it from the rooftops, surely. People don't trot out these kinds of facts at a dinner party. But then, this isn't a dinner party.

"I don't know," I say slowly. "I know Mum and Dad would understand, but it feels private. I don't want loads of people knowing before we've told our own child." Because all the literature I've read about egg and sperm donation advises you to tell the child about their origins from the outset. Honesty all the way.

And, if I'm painfully honest, I don't like that idea much either. Forget that rosy vision I had; it all feels different now. It feels fraught, opening my child—and Matt and me—up to myriad complications and pain. Questions and doubt and that abominable caveat: *These are my parents but...*

"Perhaps we should have thought about this earlier," I say as Matt takes the exit for Chepstow. "It feels a bit late now."

"There's no need to rush anything. We don't have to tell your parents everything right away. And, like you said, it's private. Not telling them now doesn't mean not telling them ever."

It sounds so simple right then, almost obvious, and yet as we turn into my parents' drive, part of me already knows we've made a big decision by keeping this secret, and it wasn't one we said we were going to make. But right now, as Matt helps me out of the car, it feels like the right decision. The only one.

When she hears I am pregnant, my mother is both incredulous and tearful.

"But this is so amazing...why didn't you tell us?"

"I'm sorry, Mum, but I didn't want to get anyone's hopes up, until it was more certain." I hug her, and then apologise again, because that's what I often do with my parents. "I'm sorry. It wasn't that we were trying to keep something from you..."

"No, no," she says, patting my back, seeming a bit distracted. "It's wonderful news. Truly wonderful. To think you're going to have a *baby*, Milly..." But I know, just as I'd predicted, that she's hurt, and I feel terrible.

"Champagne, I think," my father says grandly, and then winks at me. "Except for the mother-to-be! *Milly*, I can hardly believe I'm saying the words."

I smile. "Me, either."

"We're so thrilled for you, darling."

And I know they are, of course they are, but I still feel guilty.

"I should have told them before," I say to Matt when we're driving home. "Mum feels I've kept something from her, hidden it. It's like a betrayal to her."

Matt shakes his head. "They're thrilled, Milly."

He never picks up the minuscule signals the way I do; he's not finely tuned to that life channel. To him, the afternoon was an outstanding success: we toasted the baby, my dad shook his hand, my mum hugged us both, and they asked us questions about due dates and names, inspecting the blurry printout of the scan as if they were studying a painting by a grand master.

But to me, despite all the happiness and excitement, the afternoon was marked with those infinitesimal moments of tension and disappointment. I felt it in the way my mother shot looks at my dad, the slight shrugs he gave her in response, the silences that stretched on before she struggled to ask another question. Matt saw none of that; he never has.

"Anyway," he tells me gently as we turn into our road, "remember, your mum has cancer. If she seemed a bit, I don't know, low energy, I'm sure that's why."

I say nothing, because I can hardly argue with that, and it's not as if I've forgotten that my mum has cancer. Yet I know it was more than her illness today. I suspect I'll receive a call from my dad tomorrow, when he'll gently tell me about my mum's hurt, in a way that isn't meant to make me feel bad, but often does.

And, sure enough, that's what happens. During my lunch break, while the Year Ones are running amok outside enjoying the spring sunshine, my dad's number flashes up on my phone.

"Milly." His voice sounds so warm, I feel guilty for resenting his phone call. "I just wanted to ring to say how absolutely thrilled we are with your news."

"Thanks, Dad."

"We were just a bit surprised, that you kept it to yourself for so long," he adds after the tiniest of pauses. "Considering how important it is, and how supportive we've wanted to be of you and your fertility treatment."

"I'm sorry, Dad, but I told you why we didn't say anything." I speak as gently as I can. "It was just too hard, in case things went wrong." Which they still could. I'm only thirteen weeks; a miscarriage is definitely not out of the question.

"Yes, but this is us, Milly. Your *parents*." He imbues the word with the special emphasis he and my mother always give it, as if they are somehow *more* my parents because I am adopted. They've certainly been more invested, and I am grateful for that. Of course I am.

"I know, Dad. And I am sorry. But this felt like the right decision to us." I almost add that *they* took a few weeks to process my mother's momentous news, but I don't. It wouldn't accomplish anything.

"All right." My father sighs, accepting, yet I can't keep from feeling that this is another tick in some invisible column. It's so vague, I wonder sometimes if it really exists, this tallying of mistakes and disappointments in my parents' minds. Maybe it's just my imagination, the feeling that I am not measuring up as I should, because I was so wanted, so chosen, and so I have to be extra good, extra grateful, extra everything. "Well, like I said, darling, we're absolutely thrilled for you. Thrilled to bits." He sounds so sincere, and I know he is. Tears sting my eyes and I press the back of my hand to stem them.

"I know, Dad. Thank you."

After the call, I sit for a moment, caught between guilt, grief, and the happiness I've held to me like a promise since I discovered I was pregnant. Then I make myself push the whole conversation to the back of my brain, where a thousand conversations just like it jostle for space.

Now that I've had my scan we can start telling everyone—friends at work, at school, neighbours. We'll celebrate with Anna and Jack, capture a little bit of that vision I shared with her all those weeks ago, us together, raising this child, because it can still be real. We'll have them over for a meal, a celebratory dinner with champagne and cake, all of us toasting this miracle life inside of me—this baby that we are all learning to love, because he or she involves all of us. I believe that. Right now, I want to believe that.

# CHAPTER TEN
## ANNA

By the time Milly calls to invite Jack and me over for dinner, we've been seeing each other—although I'm not actually sure I can or should use those words—for two months. We're not dating precisely, or even at all. Nothing's actually *happened*.

Yet since that first evening when we met at a sleek bar in the city for drinks, we've gone out a handful of times more. Drinks again, dinner once, and a pub quiz with a couple of Jack's mates. Hardly anything, and yet for me and my general lack of a dating life, it feels like a lot.

That first night, I was so nervous I changed my outfit three times, finally settling on jeans and a loose Indian print blouse, not wanting to look as if I was trying too hard. I wasn't even sure what Jack wanted. Was this just a friendly drink, since we shared this admittedly odd connection? Or was it—could it be—something more?

I wasn't sure if I wanted it to be; I'd steered clear of serious relationships for a long time, for a reason. Milly kept trying to get me to go on dates, and sometimes I humoured her, but in general it didn't feel like there was anything missing in my life; I wasn't *lonely*.

And yet I still wanted to see Jack.

He was waiting in the bar when I arrived; he'd already bought a bottle of wine, had the wine glasses ready, and he stood up as

I approached, which I liked, although I told myself not to make much of such details. It was only that I wasn't used to them.

"Anna. It's good to see you again."

"You, too." I sat down, busying myself with my coat and bag so I wouldn't have to say anything. But then I embarrassed myself by blurting, "I thought I'd scared you off."

Surprise flickered across Jack's face and then he smiled. "Not at all. Why would you think that?"

I shrugged, not meeting his eye. "Just that I was a bit emotional before, and I'm not normally like that. I also don't normally air my dirty washing with someone I barely know." I toyed with the rim of my empty wine glass. "I'm usually quite a private person."

"It was an emotional situation." He shrugged my words away as he filled my glass. "It was entirely understandable."

"Right." I took a sip of the rich red wine, feeling both relieved and embarrassed that I'd brought it up yet again.

"Anyway," Jack said smoothly. "You mentioned you work in HR?"

We steered clear of serious topics after that; I told him about my work, and he talked about his various housing projects, and it all started to feel remarkably easy.

The only slightly awkward part of the conversation was when he asked about university. "Milly mentioned you lived together during uni…?" Such an innocuous question, but it brought a tidal wave of dark memories rising in me, a wave that had been lapping at my senses for weeks now, ever since that day in the clinic, when I felt its first cold touch.

"We did, but I didn't go to Bristol as she did." Even though I'd had a place. Jack raised his eyebrows, waiting, so I explained diffidently, "I failed my A level exams. Didn't get the marks I needed." Two Es and a U are just about as bad as it gets when it comes to exams, and they guarantee you a university place precisely nowhere.

"Ah." He nodded in understanding. "So what did you do instead?"

"I did some waitressing, and then I got a graduate apprentice-ship at Qi Tech, where I still work." I didn't mention that I spent eight months either drunk or stoned and most certainly desperate, or that my parents, so acrimoniously divorced that they couldn't exchange two civil words, banded together to give me what they called tough love and kicked me out of the house.

Neither did I mention the two weeks I spent sofa-surfing with people I shouldn't have ever had to meet, and then how Milly rang me, and found me, and brought me back to her flat. If she hadn't, I don't know where I might have ended up, or how low I might have fallen. No, I most certainly didn't say any of that.

At the end of the evening, we had a moment of awkward-ness; Jack insisted on walking me to my car, and then I laughed uncertainly as we bobbed back and forth for a few cringeworthy seconds before he finally kissed my cheek. The touch of his cool lips on my skin was a shock, like being submerged in ice water. I couldn't remember the last time I'd been kissed, even on the cheek.

It was another few weeks before I heard from him again; we met up for drinks at a different bar, and just like before we chatted easily. I was starting to relax, and not to second-guess everything Jack or I said.

"How's Milly doing?" he asked as he poured me more wine. "Is she starting to feel nauseous yet? Doesn't that kick in quite early?"

It surprised me that he didn't know—was he not in touch with Matt? I texted Milly nearly every day; I knew her food cravings as well as the things she couldn't stand: she loved kiwis and hated Parmesan cheese. I'd brought her a fruit salad only yesterday, when I met up with her for a coffee.

And while Milly had told me everything, I'd kept this—Jack—from her. There had been ample opportunity to tell her I was seeing him—if I even was. But I hadn't said anything to her; in fact, I'd deliberately avoided the topic, and I wasn't sure why.

"Yes, she is nauseous," I told Jack. "It isn't too bad, though."

"Exciting times, really."

"Yes..."

"Are you curious? About, you know, the baby? What it will look like, a bit of you, a bit of me..." He rubbed his jaw, looking sheepish, and I had the jolting sensation that he was talking about *our* baby. I'd always tried not to think of it like that, but sitting in a bar, cradling a second glass of wine, with Jack gazing at me so warmly...I did. I thought of it *exactly* like that, and it was a shock to my entire system, every nerve and sense suddenly hyperaware of what he was saying, what it meant, the feelings I'd been pushing away rising up and overwhelming me. *Our baby.*

"I suppose, yes," I answered after a moment. "Sometimes."

"I never thought I'd have kids myself, so it's strange," he continued. "Wondering what it will look like. If I'll see myself in him or her...or see you."

"I suppose you will, at least a little bit." My cheeks had started to warm, because this all felt oddly intimate. *Our baby.* Except it wasn't. I'd told myself I didn't need the reminder, but right then I knew I did, and it horrified me.

The next time Jack texted, he asked if I wanted to have dinner, which felt like a big step, but it was basically the same as before, chatting, laughing, and a kiss on the cheek at the end of the night. Somewhat to my surprise, Jack was quite the gentleman. Or perhaps this was all just friendly, and I was too inexperienced, too nervous, to know. I still didn't tell Milly about any of it, and I told myself that was just because I didn't know what to say. We weren't really dating, were we?

Yet I knew by not saying anything, especially when she asked outright, I was keeping something from her, and it didn't feel right. I have one secret from Milly, and I didn't expect to have any more. I knew, if and when she found out, she'd be hurt.

*

The day before dinner with Milly and Matt, Jack rings, asking me if I want to go together, he can pick me up beforehand. I am startled, because this feels like some kind of statement, and yet it also makes sense.

When we arrive together, clearly having come in the same car, I can tell Milly is surprised, although she doesn't say anything. Her gaze darts between Jack and me and then she turns away, fussing with the drinks.

"We wanted to celebrate the end of the first trimester," Matt says as he pours us all champagne, with sparkling apple juice for Milly. "Since that typically means being out of the danger zone. It's a big relief to us."

"Don't jinx it," Milly protests, and I give her a reassuring smile, which she returns fleetingly before glancing away. I feel the burden of not telling her about Jack pressing down on me like a leaden weight.

"Jack, have you seen this?" Matt brings out the printout of the scan that Milly showed me weeks ago, and Jack takes it, clearly not knowing what it is. I watch his face as he gazes at the blurry black-and-white image, seeing how confusion crinkles his forehead and clouds his eyes before realisation comes like a thunderclap, and his jaw drops.

He glances up at me. "Have you seen this?" he asks, sounding a bit emotional, and almost imperceptibly, the mood shifts, tension twanging through the air, as if everyone has collectively drawn a silent breath.

"Yes, but I'll have another look." I move over to look at it with him, studying the curves and lines of the image, trying to see something recognisable in it, something of myself or Jack, but I don't. Yet sitting next to Jack, remembering how his lips felt on my cheek, feeling the intensity of his emotion as well as my own, I can't ignore the treacherous whisper that steals through me, telling me that this baby truly is, at least in some small way, ours.

*No*, my head fires back. *It's just your genes.*

"You must be so thrilled," Jack says after an extended pause. He hands the photo back. "Congratulations again. Amazing news."

Another awkward pause and then the conversation restarts, with Milly asking Jack about the house he's renovating, and Matt pouring more wine, and then I ask Milly about baby names, which she answers in a slightly brittle way; it's as if her happiness has a slight edge now, and I am afraid that it's my fault.

"Alice for a girl, after my grandmother," she tells us. "William for a boy."

"Those are wonderful names."

She nods in acceptance, not quite looking at me.

The tension thickens when Jack and I make to leave, clearly together, and Matt and Milly are standing by the door.

"Did you come in the same car?" Milly asks, even though she must have already realised that we did.

"Yeah, we did," Jack says, and then to my shock he slings an arm around my shoulders. I stand there rigidly, feeling as if he has just branded me, and not entirely sure if I like it.

Matt looks surprised and Milly's eyes widen and something like alarm flashes across her face, and I know right then why I haven't mentioned seeing Jack. Because I knew she wouldn't like it. And while part of me wants to slip out from under Jack's arm, I don't. Instead I move a little closer, so my hip nudges his, and smile. The silence stretches on.

"Oh," Milly says finally, and then can't seem to think of anything to add to that. "Oh."

"Thanks for a fantastic meal," Jack says, and bends to kiss her cheek, and then shake Matt's hand. We exchange a flurry of goodbyes, and then Jack and I are walking outside into the balmy June evening.

I want to say something, but I'm not sure what, and so we are both silent as Jack opens the passenger door and I slip inside. It isn't until we're halfway back to my place that one of us speaks.

"That was amazing, wasn't it?" Jack says, his eyes on the road. "Looking at that photo. That baby..." He trails off, shaking his head. I don't trust myself to respond, so I stay silent. "That baby... it's half you, half me, Anna."

I feel a weird tumble of sensations—guilt and embarrassment, longing, and something I'm not ready to name. I turn to look out the window, trying to defuse the sudden intimacy that has fallen on us like a silken blanket. "That baby is Milly's," I say as firmly as I can. "Milly and Matt's. Milly did loads of research," I add for emphasis, "and she actually imparts some of her DNA to the baby." Or something like that. I wasn't quite sure of the details, but Milly was adamant that studies showed a baby had some genetic material of its birth mother, even if she was a surrogate.

"But Matt doesn't," Jack says, and I turn to look at him sharply. Why is he mentioning that? Why is he making it sound as if there is something questionable here, something we can pry and probe and perhaps even take apart? Because there isn't. There absolutely isn't.

"No, but he shares fifty percent of your DNA," I counter. "Those babies will have something—a lot—of Milly and Matt in them, Jack, and that's without even mentioning the power of nurture versus nature."

"I know that," Jack says, but he doesn't sound convinced, and a weird panic sweeps over me, because I can't let him make me think this way. It feels treacherous, dangerous. Wrong. There's no point to it, no purpose, no *hope*.

"Milly's adopted, you know. She understands what really makes a mum or dad, and she and Matt will make fantastic parents," I say, a determined, almost savage note to my voice. "Really amazing."

"Oh yes, definitely. Absolutely." He lets out a little laugh and shakes his head. "No question about that." I feel as if we've steered away from some unspoken precipice that was looming before us, and only just in time. My heart is still racing, the post-adrenalin hit of having just avoided a danger.

We don't talk again until we've reached my flat; the street is quiet, twilight just settling, the cherry trees in full blowsy blossom, the flower beds bursting with tulips. The whole world in bloom and expectant. Jack turns to me.

"Anna..."

My breath and heart rate both hitch. Some part of me knew this was coming, after the intimacy of this evening, and I am ready. I am so ready. He smiles and then he reaches for me. The feel of his lips on mine is strange, because it's been so long. Have I forgotten how to kiss?

His hands tangle in my hair. He moves closer, or maybe I do. I feel awkward, all angles and elbows, having to think before I control each limb, a hand here, my hip there, because I don't remember how this works. Maybe I never knew.

But Jack knows; Jack knows very well. His lips are sure, his movements too, maybe a little too sure. He's not worried about my response, and I tell myself I don't mind. At least one of us should know what we're doing.

Eventually he pulls away, smiling, and I smile back. At least I think I do. I feel shaken right down to my core, as if I need to reconstruct myself, and it was only a kiss. He tucks a strand of hair behind my ear.

"See you again?" he says, and it doesn't sound like a question. I nod dumbly, and then I slip out of the car. I feel strange, as if I am floating, but also as if I am leaden. I put my fingers to my lips.

I am still thinking about the kiss the next day, when I wait for Jack's call that doesn't come. Milly calls, though, clearly wanting the lowdown on Jack and me.

"So what's going on there?" she asks, and there is a jolly note to her voice that sounds a bit false.

"Nothing much, really." Already I feel guarded, and it's so bizarre. This is *Milly*.

"Are you dating?" she asks bluntly.

"We're seeing each other," I admit. "It's very early stages, Milly."

"Why didn't you tell me?" She sounds hurt, just as I knew she would.

"I'm not sure. I thought maybe you'd…mind."

"Mind?" Her voice comes out sharp. "Why should I mind?"

"I don't know. Because it's a bit strange? Us being, you know…"

"You being what?" Her voice hardens, and I feel as if I have suddenly stepped into deep waters, and I am flailing.

"The donors. I don't know. It all just seems a bit…" I trail off, unable to put it into words, wishing I hadn't said anything.

Milly doesn't reply, and the silence feels frozen. "Why should that be strange?" she finally asks, and although her tone is matter-of-fact, I sense something dark swirling underneath, and instinctively I back away from it.

"I suppose it isn't, not really. Sorry. I guess I wasn't thinking."

"It's just, Jack is a bit of a player, Anna," Milly continues after a strained second of silence. "I wouldn't want you to get hurt by him. He has a lot more experience than you do, and it's likely that he's not taking this—whatever this is—seriously."

"Thanks for the warning." I am stung, and I am also reeling. More hurtful than her words about Jack is the fact that she said them at all. Milly and I never talk like this. We're not arguing precisely, but somehow it feels worse.

After the call, I end up ringing Jack, which feels a bit reckless. I don't even know if we're at that stage yet; we've been in the mode of me waiting for his call, not the other way around.

"I think Milly is a bit weirded out," I blurt as soon as he answers.

"By what?"

"By...us." He is silent, and my hand turns slippery on the phone. Should I not have called? Should I not have said that? But then I suddenly feel exasperated by it all; I am thirty-four, not sixteen, and if Jack is playing games, I want to know. "Is there an us, Jack?" I ask levelly, and he lets out a light laugh.

"Anna..."

"I'm not asking for a commitment or a ring or anything like that, just clarification. Are we seeing each other?"

The silence stretches on for a few awful seconds, and then Jack finally replies. "Yes," he says. "Of course we are."

And I choose to believe him, even though it comes at a cost: Milly doesn't call or text for a week, and I don't reach out, either. It's the longest we've ever gone without being in contact, and it feels awful.

But I make myself not mind, and after a little while it becomes surprisingly easy. I am busy with work, and with Jack, and when he sends me a bouquet of pale pink tulips at work, any concern about Milly goes right out of my head. For once Milly's friendship is not the centrifugal force in my life. For once I have someone else to think and care about, and that feels like a very good thing.

And then, two weeks later, she does call, her voice full of tears. "Anna," she whimpers. "I need you."

# CHAPTER ELEVEN

## MILLY

I knew it was too good to be true. Deep down, I always knew that. And when, at just fifteen weeks pregnant, it all goes wrong, I'm both utterly devastated and completely unsurprised.

It's the day of my mum's surgery, and so I'm already on edge. Over the last few weeks, I've tried to visit her as often as I can, and every time I see her I'm seized with a terror that she's already leaving me. Each time, she seems paler, thinner, *less*. I tell myself things will get better with the surgery, the chemotherapy, but I'm still afraid. A lot rides on today.

Another worry on my mind, albeit low down on the list, is Anna and Jack. After the dinner where we celebrated the end of my first trimester, I turned to Matt as soon as they were out the door.

"What's going on *there*?"

Matt raised his eyebrows. "What do you mean?"

"*Matt*. Surely you're not so clueless that you didn't realise...?" I stared at him in disbelief. "They came here together, in the same car. He put his arm around her..."

"So?"

"So? Do you think they're dating?"

Matt frowned, and then shrugged. "I suppose it's not really any of our business."

But this was *Anna,* my best friend, as well as Matt's brother. Plus, there was the not-so-little fact that they were the genetic donors of our child. Of course it was our business.

I rang Anna the next day and asked her about it straight out, but her calm reply that, yes, they *were* dating threw me, perhaps more than it should have. On an instinctive level, I didn't like it, but I didn't feel I could say that without sounding mean or paranoid. And so I acted as if it wasn't weird, when we both knew it was.

"I'm worried for Anna's sake," I told Matt when he reminded me once again that it was not my business. "She's had so few relationships...she's innocent, Matt."

"Milly, she's thirty-four."

"I know, and has she ever had a serious boyfriend?"

Matt shrugged. "She's dated a few guys, hasn't she? And she's always seemed happy in her own company, to me. Some people are like that. Jack is like that, for heaven's sake."

"Matt, you can't deny that Jack is..." I hesitated, because even after ten years of marriage, I wasn't always entirely sure about Matt's relationship to his brother. They were friendly without being all that close, which is how his whole family works. Distant without acknowledging it or feeling there's anything amiss, so different from my own tightly knit family. "He's a bit of a player when it comes to women," I finished.

"A *player?*"

"Serial dater, then."

"I don't know the ins and outs of my brother's love life," Matt answered, "but, like Anna, he can make his own decisions. If they want to see each other, we can't stop them."

I fell silent, because something about Matt's repressive tone made me realise he might be almost as uncomfortable with the idea as I was. And he was right—we couldn't stop them, not that I would actually try. Would I?

But, in any case, I wasn't thinking about Anna and Jack the day of my mother's surgery. All day long I was as tense as a wire, ready to snap. I was feeling crampy too, which made me even more irritable and anxious, and then, in the middle of the afternoon, my father rang my mobile.

Although I knew I wasn't supposed to, I excused myself from the classroom, impressing upon my twenty-eight children that they needed to finish their number bonds to one hundred sheet without any talking.

"Dad?" I whispered, my voice urgent as I stood outside the classroom door, my gaze trained on my Year Ones. "Is Mum out of surgery?"

"Yes." He sounded so tired. "It went well."

"It did?" The surprise in my voice made me realise I'd been expecting bad news, and it took a moment for the relief to flood in. "She's okay? They were able to remove the tumour?"

"Yes, they said they think they got it all, although it can be tricky to tell. She'll need to recover for a few weeks, and then hopefully she can start the chemo."

"That's great news." I still sounded stunned. "That's wonderful, Dad."

"It is a relief, darling, it really is. But I should go now. She's going to wake up soon, and I need to be there."

"I'll come as soon as I can, after work." I glanced back at my classroom, all of them still working on their sheets, as my dad rung off, and then I felt it—a sudden cramp banding across my belly, followed by a gush of fluid. Shock nearly rooted me to the spot. *No…*

I hurried into the staff loo, unable to keep from crying out at the sight of the blood staining my underwear and tights. No… *no.* Not this. Not after everything it took to get to this moment. Not when it finally seemed as if things were going well.

I stood up, my mind dizzy with panic, my whole body shaking. I needed to call my doctor. I needed to call Matt.

Matt didn't answer when I rang, his phone switching immediately to voicemail, and I remembered he had a staff meeting all afternoon. My stomach cramped again. I looked at my phone and then I called the person I'd always depended on, the person I needed. I called Anna.

"What's happened? Where are you?" Her questions were calm and no-nonsense, and they grounded me.

"I'm at school. I need to get back to the classroom."

"You need to get to A&E, Milly. Tell whoever you need to that you have a medical emergency. I'll meet you at the Royal Infirmary."

"You have work…"

"It doesn't matter. I haven't had my lunch break yet, anyway. Do it, Milly. I'll be there."

The next hour was a blur, ringing Alicia, leaving a message for Matt, arranging cover for my class and then driving to A&E, terrified. So terrified.

Anna was waiting for me by the front doors, and she pulled me into a wordless hug as soon as she saw me. The two weeks of silence, the tension over Jack, were completely and thankfully forgotten in that moment. All I knew was I needed my best friend. I will always need her.

Now I am here, waiting to be seen, to have a scan, *something* to tell the doctors what's going on, even though I am afraid to know. Anna sits next to me, calm and unflappable, acting as my anchor. She's the one who asks the receptionist for updates, who brings me a bottle of water and finds the best magazines in the pile for me to read, even though I can't concentrate enough to read them. I am too fidgety, my knee constantly jiggling, my arms wrapped around myself to keep myself from rocking back and forth.

Then they finally call my name and Anna and I head into the cubicle, where a nurse assesses me; I am barely able to stammer out my story—IVF, the blood, the cramping. Finally we're called in for a scan, and I stretch out and lift up my top, my heart thudding painfully as I wait for the verdict.

The technician prods my stomach with an electric wand and the images jump and blur on the screen. I hold my breath. Then I see it, a beating heart, and I let out an incredulous laugh of both hope and fear, because that has to be good, right? My baby is still alive. Anna smiles and squeezes my hand.

"You've had a small haemorrhage," the technician says. "But baby still looks healthy. The consultant will tell you more."

And so I learn that while the baby is healthy, the bleeding and cramping mean my pregnancy is now higher risk, and I'm advised to be on bed rest for at least a week, with more regular assessments to make sure I am not at risk for preterm labour.

"But there's no reason to be worried?" I press anxiously. "My baby is all right?" I want promises, but of course they can't give me any.

"The goal," the consultant tells me with a sympathetic smile, "is to keep you pregnant for as long as possible." Considering I'm not even halfway to term, that is not the most reassuring sentiment. The next five and a half months feel as if they will stretch on forever—or not.

Anna comes home with me, fussing over me as she makes my favourite herbal tea and insists I stay on the sofa, feet up, a blanket tucked about me.

"A week of bed rest is no bad thing," she says, "although I imagine it's torture for someone who likes to be as busy as you."

I am about to make a quip back when my face crumples. "Anna," I practically gasp, "I'm sorry. This whole thing with Jack... I've been so strange about it and I shouldn't have been. I'm sorry." And then I am crying, from the emotion of it all—my mum's surgery, the scare, Anna and me.

"Oh Milly, I'm sorry, too." She hugs me and I press my cheek against her shoulder. "I never thought we'd fall out over a *man*."

"We haven't fallen out, have we?" I pull back to look at her anxiously. "I don't ever want to fall out with you."

"And we won't," Anna says firmly. "This thing with Jack... it's not serious, anyway."

"But even if it was..." I am feeling my way through the words. "Anna, you have the right to see anyone you want. Love anyone you want. Marry them..." But already my mind is racing ahead. If Anna and Jack marry, if they have *babies*... their children will be full-blooded siblings of my child. That *is* weird.

As if she can read my mind, Anna smiles and says gently, "Just because this is all a bit weird doesn't make it wrong. Our situation is strange, Milly. We all feel that. We knew going in that it would be, at least a little. But it doesn't have to define us or change anything. I don't regret it, and neither should you."

"I don't," I say. "I really don't." I squeeze her hand, and Anna smiles. I am so thankful to be pregnant. I am thankful to Anna that she made it possible, along with Jack. And yet... she's right. It *is* strange, and her relationship with Jack makes it complicated, whether we want it to or not. We all have feelings, instincts, and something about this situation goes against them. That truth is apparent, uncomfortable, but we can deal with it. We can live with it.

Like Anna said, the strangeness doesn't have to change anything. I hold onto that like a promise, a vow I make to myself and to Anna, even if later I will question everything, and regret so much. Even if those promises will be broken, again and again, by both of us.

# CHAPTER TWELVE

## ANNA

A few weeks after Milly's scare, we've got over that hump of awkwardness, and we're back to our usual routine of texting and seeing each other every few days. Milly is still cautious, and Matt rightly wraps her in cotton wool, but we still manage to go out for drinks a couple of times and even a day shopping for maternity clothes. At nearly the halfway mark, she is finally starting to pop.

We spend a sunny Saturday afternoon at Clifton Village, with its independent shops and gorgeous Georgian architecture. It's a warm, sunny day in mid-July, and everyone is out to enjoy the weather.

"I don't want anything too fussy," Milly says as she riffles through a rack of stretchy tops. "No bows and buttons, that kind of thing. They'd overwhelm me."

"How about this?" I pick out a short-sleeved cotton dress in light blue, and Milly eyes it critically.

"Yes, that might work."

We continue to work our way through the racks, until Milly's arms are overladen with outfits to try on.

"How are things with Jack?" she asks, her voice deliberately casual, as we head to the fitting room.

We haven't talked about Jack in weeks, and I know it costs her something to ask about him now. "Good," I answer, because I don't know what else to say, how many details to give. Jack and I have seen each other about once a week, either dinner or drinks, and while it's been fun, it hasn't progressed quite the way I hoped it would. Something about him seems closed off and elusive, as if he's happy to keep things where they are, forever, and maybe he is. Maybe I should be.

"Is it...is it serious?" She tries to smile, and almost succeeds.

"No, not really." I shrug. "I'm not sure Jack is interested in serious."

"And are you?"

Another shrug. The truth is, I'm not sure what I want. When I'm with Jack, I feel happy, but I'm also anxious. Relationships are hard work, always wondering what the other person is thinking or feeling, wanting to get it right, afraid I'm being too clingy, quiet, boring, whatever. Perhaps that's not the way it's supposed to be, but it's that way for me, and I'm not sure I can manage anything else.

"Well, be careful," Milly says, laying a hand on my arm. "I'm saying that for your sake, Anna. I'd hate for you to get hurt."

*Yes, and you'd also hate for me to end up with Jack.* I don't say it, of course, and I feel guilty even for thinking it. But I know Milly would rather Jack and I weren't dating, and part of me can understand that. Not just because of the baby, but because she's always had my undivided attention, my unwavering support. I've never needed much of a life because I can always help Milly with hers.

What would happen if I were the one getting married, having a baby? Both feel impossible, like mountains in the distance I am completely unequipped to climb, but longing shivers through me anyway. For the first time, I am daring to think about those things a little, to imagine wanting them.

A few weeks later, when the weather has turned sticky and overcast, Sasha returns to my office to discuss her sexual harassment complaint officially, nearly five months since she first poked her head into my office. It has been so long, I let myself forget about her; guiltily, I realise that it was a relief to do so. I should have tried harder to get her to tell her story. Now I try to welcome her warmly, offer coffee, pull out a chair.

She has brought her friend Leanne for support, and Lara informs me she is going to sit in on the meeting as well. It all has to be done by the book, everything noted down and recorded.

"So, Sasha," I say with an encouraging smile, "I want you to take me through the incident you've mentioned, as specifically as you can, and I hope you won't mind me asking you some questions to clarify certain points. And, of course, if you need a moment or a break, we can accommodate that."

"Okay." Sasha gulps, looking terrified. "Like I told you, it started before New Year's..." She talks again about the Dobson account, the late nights, and then mentions one night when she and Mike were working alone.

"When was this, as specifically as you can remember?"

"Umm...right before Christmas? Before the Christmas party..."

Qi Tech has a company-wide Christmas party that I generally only attend for an hour or so. It tends to get a bit raucous, and it's really not my scene. "Okay." I make a note. "And what happened on that evening, Sasha?"

"It seemed innocent enough at first," Sasha says, and I hear Lara give a barely audible snort, which makes me grit my teeth. "We were both tired, we'd been working a long time. He came up behind me and started to rub my shoulders."

"And that made you uncomfortable?"

"Well, I mean, it felt nice," Sasha says uncertainly, "but I was a bit creeped out because it seemed, well, inappropriate, you know?"

I make another note. "Did you tell him that it made you uncomfortable?"

"No...I thought it would have been awkward. I just moved away, after a bit."

"All right." I can picture it all so perfectly—the dim lighting, the discarded containers of takeaway, the clock ticking towards midnight. He comes up behind her, rests his hands on her shoulders. His breath fans her ear.

*You've been working so hard...*

With a jolt, I realise I am not picturing the IT department with Sasha and Mike, but something else entirely. I'm picturing my own story, the one I have tried to bury, the memories I do my utmost to forget because they fill me with so much corroding shame. For a second I can't think, can't breathe; it's as if my own life has been thrown up on a big screen in front of me, and I am living out its worst moments.

"Should I go on?" Sasha asks after a few seconds, and I make myself nod.

"Yes, please." My voice is a bit croaky, and I clear my throat. "What happened then?"

"I started noticing how he'd accidentally touch me. Just brushes, a hand on my shoulder or our hips nudging as we stood next to each other. I felt as if I was making a big deal of it, that I was imagining things."

*That you'd feel ridiculous if you said anything. People would roll their eyes, laugh, sneer: Seriously, Anna?*

I swallow hard. "Did you say anything to him about how you felt?"

"No." She bites her lip. "I didn't feel I could. He might not have even meant it, you know? And then I would have created this whole awkwardness..."

*Yes, exactly. That is exactly why you stay silent, except there is a part of you that is thrilled with the attention, even as it makes you feel sick. There is a part of you that will always feel guilty and ashamed, like there is a stain in your soul that will never go away.*

"Yes, I can understand why you might have felt that way." I try to smile encouragingly, but my stomach is churning as the memories come back to me in flashes—the dark room, the grimy bathroom, the car. His breath. *I always knew you wanted it.*

*But I didn't,* I wanted to cry. *I didn't even think it until you touched me.*

I clear my throat again, and then run my palms down the sides of my skirt. My breathing sounds uneven. "So what happened then?"

"Nothing, that night. But then a few days later I was in the breakroom and he... he came in and stood behind me. Close." She blushes and gulps. "And I could feel his, well, you know, his erection." She looks away, and I struggle to keep my expression neutral.

"All right," I say after a pause. "That must have been very distressing for you." Lara makes a tsking noise, which I ignore.

"It was."

"Did he say anything to you then?"

"No. He... he breathed in my ear. A bit heavily, you know? And I just... stood there, really. I didn't know what to do. He sort of... ground into me, a little." She looks down at her clenched hands in her lap, trying to compose herself. "And then someone else came in and he moved away."

"Okay." I make some more notes, my hand trembling a little. "Thank you for sharing all this, Sasha. I know it can't be easy." She nods, wiping her eyes. "Did anything further happen?" I ask, when I feel she has composed herself enough. I am holding onto my own composure by a thread; this feels so raw, so *real.* I am fighting the urge to get up and walk out of the room, to get out of my head, if only I could.

Sasha gulps and shakes her head. "No, after that he backed off. But a few weeks later I wasn't picked for a project, and it made me wonder. And then the same thing happened again... I've been given the most basic work since that time in the breakroom." Her chin lifts. "And that's discrimination, as well as harassment."

For a second I struggle to find the right words to say. I am conscious that I have to get the truth of the story from both Sasha and Mike. I am also painfully aware of my own memories, the way they are crowding in, pushing everything else out. "I really appreciate you telling me all this," I finally say. "I'll make an official report, and we'll need to talk to Mike, of course, to hear his…" I trail off, because for some reason I can't say *version of events*. It makes it sound as if I don't believe her, and I do. I most definitely do. "And then we'll need to have a mediated discussion."

"I want a tribunal," Sasha says, thrusting her chin out, surprising me with her sudden boldness. "I looked it up online and I can take the case to an outside committee if I don't feel it's being handled fairly."

I am startled, and a little hurt, by this. "Sasha, I assure you I will do everything in my power to make sure this is handled fairly for both you and Mike."

*"Mike?"* she returns scornfully, and I flush. Did I make it sound as if I were friendly with him? As if I'm biased? Because, if anything, I'm biased in Sasha's favour. I feel her pain and confusion. And yet there's Lara.

"Not a chance," she says after Sasha and Leanne have left, and I look at her warily, drained from the conversation, from fighting with myself. All I want is to lie down in a dark room and sleep. Forget about everything this has brought up in me.

"What does that mean?"

"Are you honestly taking that seriously?" Lara demands, now as scornful as Sasha. "Look, she's a young, pretty girl. Did you see what she was wearing?"

"Lara, that has absolutely nothing to do—"

"Her skirt barely covered her arse, and that wasn't even for a night out. Look, Mike might have got carried away, I accept that. But did she ever actually *say* no? Did she ever tell anyone? Or did she respond and then regret it?"

I taste bile. Lara's reaction is exactly why I stayed silent so long ago. Still, I try to sound reasonable, even though part of me feels like flying into a rage, like screaming. "There's no reason to think—"

"Let's talk to Mike," Lara cuts me off flatly. "Not that I want it even to go that far, because Mike is a good employee and his wife is pregnant. This is the last thing either of them needs. But we will tick all the boxes. As for a tribunal…" She shakes her head. "That's never going to happen."

No, it won't, I realise with a sickening rush, because more than three months had passed from the incident when Sasha first reported it. With all her hemming and hawing, and my wilful forgetfulness, it's been over the requisite three months since it happened. She can't take it to a tribunal, and that is my fault, for not following her up. For not encouraging her to come back after that first meeting in February, because it was easier to let it go.

"Clearly she didn't look up that much online," Lara says, and for a second I think I might be sick. My stomach churns and my vision blurs as everything presses down on me—Sasha's story, and my own. It's too much. "Don't take it so much to heart, Anna," Lara scolds. "Or you'll never last in the job."

"Clearly I don't need to give you the same advice," I manage before I walk out of the office, to the bathroom, where I rest my forearms on a sink and take several deep breaths, waiting for my mind and vision to both clear.

But it's no good, because standing there at the sink, staring into the mirror, I see something else entirely. I see myself at seventeen years old, in a darkened room. I hear a low, persistent voice, smell cheap aftershave and stale smoke. *You want this, Anna…*

*But I didn't*, I cry out silently. *I only pretended I did, because I was so lonely and so scared.*

And sixteen years later, I still feel like that young, frightened girl, the girl I try to hide. The girl who lives alone, who can't handle relationships, who donates an egg because she's scared to have a child—a *life*—of her own.

I push away from the sink, stumbling a bit, before I right myself and walk out of the bathroom. These thoughts are too much to take, to process, so I do my best to blank them out, but for once I can't. They're finally screaming to be heard, to be acknowledged, but I know if I let myself do that, I might fall apart and never put myself back together again.

Later that evening, I am sitting in my car, staring straight ahead, feeling too tired even to turn the key in the ignition. I told Milly I'd stop by that evening with a casserole, because I've been helping out by making a meal or two a week since her bleeding scare, but even with the shepherd's pie on the front seat of my car, I don't want to go. I feel too raw, all my old wounds open and bleeding. Still, I force myself to drive to Redland, because maybe if I act normal, I'll feel normal, and I'll be able to forget everything that's raging in my head.

Milly is anxious herself when I arrive at their house; she's had some slight contractions so she's been on bed rest for another week.

"They say there's nothing they can do, but I don't believe that," she says as I put the pie in the oven and start loading the dishwasher. She's sitting on the sofa, her feet up on the coffee table, her arms wrapped around her middle.

"Surely they would do something if they could."

"There are drugs you can take, I'm sure of it. Terb-something." She reaches for her phone and starts to scroll. "Terbutaline. It stops labour for hours or even days."

"But you're not in labour, Milly," I remind her with a slight edge to my voice. "You're just having mild cramps. If they say there's nothing they can do, why don't you believe them?" Too late, I hear the aggressive note in my voice.

Milly blinks at me. "What's got you in such a huff?"

A *huff*? "Nothing. I'm tired, that's all."

"Tired? You shouldn't have come, then."

She means it generously, but it rankles anyway. I have no more patience, no strength, to make it all about Milly today. "I probably shouldn't have," I agree, "but I did."

Milly frowns. "Anna...what's going on?"

I stare at her and wonder if I could even begin to tell her. *Remember sixteen years ago?*

But then I think of how she never asked me anything back then, not about my A levels or what went so badly wrong, nor about what had happened months later, when she found me in some stranger's grotty flat. My life had derailed and we went months without talking, Milly busy with her new uni life. I always told myself I was grateful that she didn't ask, but now I wonder why she never even tried.

"Just some stuff at work," I say after a long moment. "I'm sorry it's put me in a bad mood."

Clearly it's the right thing to say, because Milly smiles in understanding, already reaching for her phone. "It's okay, Anna. You've been so fantastic. You need to think about yourself sometimes." She starts to scroll through Facebook, and I almost laugh.

I almost say, *Really? You want me to think about myself? Because I think you want me to always think about you.*

But that's not fair, is it? Milly has always been so kind to me. It's been the narrative of our friendship, and yet right now I am questioning it. For the first time, I am wondering what the truth is, but I still don't say anything. I finish tidying the kitchen and make a salad to put in the fridge, and promise Milly I'll see her next week, after she's had her scan.

If there was a moment for me to tell her the truth, to make it about me, it passed. I think it passed sixteen years ago.

As I leave her house, a wave of sadness crashes over me, because I think something has changed between us, perhaps forever, and Milly doesn't even realise it.

# CHAPTER THIRTEEN

## MILLY

When I first met Anna in year seven, she looked like the kind of girl who could be the most popular one in the year—tall, blonde, a little remote—but somehow you just knew she wouldn't be. In fact, if it hadn't been for me, I don't think Anna would have made any friends at all in secondary school. She's always been a bit of a drifter, isolating herself from other people, cloaking herself in quietness.

I don't blame her for that, not with the way her parents were. Her mother was an emotional drunk, her father a philanderer, and they played out their problems on the neighbourhood stage. In our small town, it was unfortunate, to say the least.

Thankfully, she had my parents to step in and act like a proper mum and dad. For a little while, they even signed her permission slips and came to her parent–teacher conferences, when her dad had moved to London and her mother decided she needed to find herself in Bali for a few months. Anna hardly ever sees either of them now, even though her mother at least still lives less than an hour away.

At the end of school, it seemed like everything was about to fall into place; we both had places at Bristol, and we planned to live together all three years. But towards the end of upper sixth, Anna got very strange and quiet, and then when our results came, and she found out she'd failed everything, she didn't even seem shocked. She acted as if she didn't care.

I think back to that time now, wondering if I should have done or said more. Pressed her about what was going on, because something must have been. Looking back, I realise I was a bit impatient with her; why was she stuffing up her future so dramatically and wrecking our plans? And part of me felt aggrieved, as if it was a personal affront. *After all I've done for you...*

As I mentally sift through the years, I realise I might not have been that good a friend then, after all. I think about all that after Anna has left, clearly not having told me whatever was bothering her. But then I think how reluctant Anna has been to ever tell me anything; I stopped pressing her for details years ago, because she so clearly didn't like giving them, and generally that's been fine. That's been how our friendship has always been; I am the one who pushes forward, Anna is the one who hangs back. It's always worked, and it can work now.

And so I decide to let it go. There are too many other things to worry about—my mother, my baby—and if Anna really wanted to tell me, she would. It's what I've always thought, but for the first time I feel a bit selfish and even mean for thinking it.

Anyway, whatever was bothering her seems to resolve itself; she comes by a week later, and we have coffee and chat in the normal way. I even ask her about Jack, although she doesn't say much, and I am a bit relieved. I don't actually want to know details.

In late July, I have my mid-pregnancy scan. Out of instinct, I brace myself for bad news, but for once there isn't any. The baby is healthy, perfect, a little girl. I'm going to have a daughter. I picture pink ribbons, frilly dresses, lace curtains. But, of course, she'll be tough too; Matt will teach her football, she'll dirty her knees and clamber up again. Nothing will stop her. We won't let it. *Alice.* I feel as if I know her already. She is just waiting for me to say hello.

I call Anna to tell her the news, and she brings over a cake to celebrate. Jack comes as well, and we all toast Alice, champagne glasses lifted high, everyone smiling and happy. This is how I pictured it; this is how it is meant to be. How it *is*. Whatever nameless doubts and fears I've felt in my own insecurity, I push them away now, to embrace this reality. *My daughter.*

The weeks start slipping by; Matt and I buy a cot, a high chair, baby clothes, and with every purchase this dream becomes more real. Anna comes over to help paint the nursery; my colleagues at work throw me a baby shower. The intermittent cramps and contractions have stopped for the most part, and I am starting to feel not just optimistic, but assured. *I am going to be a mother.*

In late August, Matt and I go on holiday, our last as a couple, two weeks on the beach in Cornwall. Long, lazy days, reading and relaxing and dreaming about coming back next year, with an eight-month-old baby gurgling on a blanket beside us.

In September, at the start of term, my mother visits; it has been six months since her diagnosis and she has been responding surprisingly well to the chemotherapy, although it will never cure her, just buy her more time. How much, no one knows, but I am trying to enjoy the moments we do have, although between her symptoms and mine, there haven't been as many as I'd like.

"You're looking so well, Milly." She smiles, looking near tears at the sight of me and my bump. "You're radiant. Blooming."

"I feel it." I let out a little laugh. "Finally, after so many weeks of feeling like a lump." I take hold of her hand, which feels fragile, her bones hollow like a bird's. "How are you doing, Mum?"

"I'm all right. Trying to enjoy every moment." She sighs and squeezes my hand lightly, her fingers fragile around my own. "I want to see this granddaughter of mine. Watch her grow up."

Tears prick my eyes and I blink them back. "You will," I promise, but I ache to think of what she might not see—my daughter's first steps, maybe even her first smile. It is something that hurts too much to think about.

"I'm so happy for you," Mum says, her voice hesitant, her hand still in mine. "I hope you realise that."

"Of course I do." There is an odd look of regret on my mother's face that I don't understand.

"The truth is, I don't feel I've been as supportive as I could or should have been," she says quietly.

"Mum, you've had your own things to deal with. I know that—"

"Yes, but it's not just that. The cancer." She falls silent for a moment, and I wait. I've never seen my mother look like this, heard her sound like this. She gazes down at our joined hands for a few moments as she collects her thoughts. "I know I haven't spoken very much about when your father and I were trying ourselves, for a baby."

No, she hasn't, not ever, except to say "it didn't happen for us" in a tone that suggested I shouldn't ask any more questions, and so I didn't.

"It was really difficult," Mum says quietly. "Years of the cycle of hope and disappointment—well, you know how it is."

"Yes..." All too well.

"And forty years ago, there was no IVF." She smiles wryly. "It was still all in the pioneering research stage."

"Yes, I suppose it was."

"And the worst part, well, one of the worst parts, was that there was never any real reason for it. Unexplained infertility, they called it. They kept telling us, as they patted our hands, that there was absolutely no reason why we couldn't have a healthy pregnancy, a normal baby, and yet it never happened. Anyway." She lapses into silence, and I wait, sensing more, but what?

"Adoption wasn't my first choice," she says finally. "Obviously. But I always felt guilty about it, once we decided to go down that route. I never wanted you to feel as if you were second best to a biological child."

"I didn't," I say, but inwardly I am thinking about the running theme of my life story: *I'm adopted, but*... How much of that was in my own head, and how much was in my mother's?

"Because you were wanted so, so much, Milly. You really were."

"I know." She has told me at every opportunity, and yet perhaps that was part of the problem. When someone keeps insisting on something, you start to doubt it.

"And then when you had trouble trying to conceive yourself..." Mum continues slowly, "it was strange. I was so sad you were experiencing the same heartache I was, of course I was, and yet when you did get pregnant, I felt... envious. A little. Which is ridiculous." She bites her lip, looking ashamed.

"It's not ridiculous, Mum."

"And not just envious," she continues with a note of steely determination in her voice that reminds me of me. She is going to say this, no matter what. No matter how much it hurts. "I felt... threatened. Because this baby will be closer to you, in a way, than I am. Your own flesh and blood, in a way I can never be, and that's... that's hard, for me."

I still, implications tumbling through me. We still haven't told my parents about the egg and sperm donation. We keep putting it off, saying there will be time later, if it ever needs to be told. These things are private, after all, even if they're acknowledged and appreciated.

And yet with my silent betrayal comes my mother's. What is she saying? That I'm *not* her flesh and blood? That despite all the assurances that I was special, chosen, wanted, *whatever*, there was always a distance between us that could never be closed?

"I know I shouldn't feel that way," she says, resting her hand on mine. "I know it doesn't really matter."

I stare at her helplessly, at a loss. Now is the time to tell her the truth, surely. To admit that actually, yes, I am just like her, and of course it doesn't matter. Genetics are nothing but that—

mere science, abstract, almost theoretical. Relationships are what matter. I know that, and yet...

If that is true, why do we have to have this conversation at all? Why did I resent the fact of my adoption? Why do I resent Anna's part in the conception of my daughter? Because I do. No matter how hard I try not to, I know in this moment I do. And so I stay silent. I watch my mother smile sadly, feel her squeeze my hand, and I say absolutely nothing.

"I'm sorry," Mum says, giving a little shake of her head. "I don't know why I'm telling you all this now. I just wanted to be honest. My... diagnosis... it makes me want to make the most of opportunities."

"I understand." But I still don't make the most of this one.

"But most of all," Mum continues, "I want to tell you how much I love you. How much I've always loved you."

My chest is tight with emotion. "I know you do, Mum. And I love you, too." I've never doubted that, despite all the other things I've wondered about. Love might not be easy or simple, but it still *is*. I'm sure of that. I've always been sure of that.

Mum lets go of my hand, letting out a little sigh as she gives a smile. "So how's Anna?" she asks after a moment. "She stopped by a few weeks ago, with some lovely flowers, but I haven't seen her since then."

"I think she's okay." I speak cautiously, because I haven't seen Anna much lately. We communicate more by text, and even that has become a bit intermittent. Somehow it's been easier, to have a little space.

"She mentioned something about her job?" Mum's forehead wrinkles. "About taking some time off?"

"Time off?" That doesn't sound like Anna. "She hasn't said anything to me." And I wonder why not. Surely if something big had happened, she would have told me? But then I realise that she might not have, and I wouldn't have asked. More strained silences in our friendship that were never there before.

"Perhaps I shouldn't have said. She never likes to talk about herself."

"I know. I'll give her a ring."

But when I call, there's no answer, so I leave an awkward voicemail. "Hey, Anna. It's Milly. I know it's been a little while. I'm sorry about that." I pause, blowing out a breath, trying to find the words. "I hope you're okay." Which makes it sound as if I think she isn't, but it's too late to clarify what I meant; I've already disconnected the call.

I wait for Anna to call back, but she doesn't. A few days later, she finally sends a text, just a quick message to say she's fine, and that she's been busy. It feels a bit like a brush-off, and I wonder what's going on, if anything. I wonder if I want to know.

"Why don't you just invite her over?" Matt asks when I mention my low-level fears that there might be something wrong. "Have her and Jack over for dinner?"

"I don't know if they're still seeing each other."

"You don't?" Matt looks surprised. "They certainly are, Milly. Jack mentioned it to me a few days ago—he took her up to see the house in Stroud. It's almost finished."

"Oh, really?" I try to sound offhand, but I am shaken. Why wouldn't Anna tell me about *that?* Is it because she knows I feel strange about her relationship with Jack? Or is it because I am realising, more and more, that Anna doesn't tell me anything? "Right, I'll invite them both."

A week later, they are in my kitchen, sitting at my table, and I feel uneasy. Anna looks as if she is in love, and I notice they hold hands under the table. Why am I not okay with this? Am I that insecure, that *selfish,* that I don't want my best friend to be happy?

"So things are going well with Jack?" I ask brightly when Anna and I are clearing up, Matt and Jack outside on the patio.

"Yes, I think so." She smiles quietly to herself, as if she's keeping a secret. I feel excluded, even though she's right here next to me, rinsing plates.

"That's good." For once I am at a loss for words. Anna feels a bit like a stranger to me now, and I realise it's been happening gradually, bit by bit, a chipping away of the security and strength I took for granted, until we're both free floating and anchorless. "Mum mentioned something about work? Is everything okay there?"

She hesitates, and then shrugs. "Lara's giving me some trouble. Just the usual, really."

"Right." And then, for perhaps the first time in our lives, we have nothing more to say to one another.

"That went fine, didn't it?" Matt asks when they've gone and we're sitting on the sofa, my feet in his lap.

"I suppose." I know he'll only roll his eyes at the nebulous feeling I have that something is off between us, the growing fear that perhaps something always has been, and it's taken this—this baby, this situation—to show me.

"Don't worry so much, Mills. You're almost in the home stretch." He pats my bump lovingly. "Thirty weeks now."

"I know."

"Once the baby comes, you'll be able to put all these little ups and downs into perspective," he continues. I know he means to be encouraging, but I feel patronised.

"These little ups and downs aren't so little, Matt. Anna is important to me. We've been friends for over twenty years."

"And nothing's actually wrong between you, right?"

"Right." I know I can't explain it to him, not so he'd understand. What would I even say? That things feel a bit awkward?

Anna herself said things were bound to be a bit strange, and perhaps Matt is right. Once I have Alice, things will be different. Everything will make sense. It will all be worth it.

I repeat those promises as if I can make myself believe them, and I almost do.

# CHAPTER FOURTEEN

## ANNA

After keeping so many secrets for so long, I've finally told my biggest one to Jack, and it felt like the scariest and most wonderful thing I've ever done.

When he called, months ago now, and I asked him to come over, he came straight away. He held me in his arms and let me speak, the words spilling out, freeing me.

"I'm dealing with a sexual harassment case at work," I began, feeling as if I were taking my finger out of the hole in the dam. "And it brought up some memories..."

"You mean the relationship you were in, back when you were eighteen?" Jack asked gently.

"Yes." I continued to wipe my eyes, which seemed determined to stream. "Yes. That. At work, one of the graduate apprentices was...propositioned, I suppose, by her boss." I shouldn't have been telling him that much, and yet I had to, for context. Because I had to tell him about me. "And it reminded me...about when I was eighteen. Well, seventeen to start..." I stopped, and Jack put his arms around me.

"You can tell me, Anna."

I take a deep breath, preparing myself for admitting something I've never told anyone. Ever. "The man I was in a relationship with...not that I should even call it that...he was my teacher. He taught history." As if that mattered. The strange thing, or at least one of them, was that Mr. Rees wasn't young or fun or particularly good-looking, all the usual suspects when it comes to student-teacher affairs. He was forty-five, balding, okay-looking for his age, but certainly nothing special. Looking back, I can't explain it even to myself, except perhaps that after my parents' divorce I was lonely, and having someone pay attention to me—a man like my father, even—felt good, sick and sad as it was, as horrible as it felt.

"What happened?" Jack finally asked.

"What you'd expect. I stayed after one day for help on an essay..." And just like Mike Jacobs, he came up behind me so I could feel his breath on my ear, his body so close to mine. I remembered feeling frozen, and then foolishly, pathetically flattered.

"Did you report him?" Jack asked with a note of vehemence. "You should have reported him."

I shook my head. "No, I never did." It all ended predictably; a few sordid trysts at school, one late-night meeting behind a pub that left me feeling dirtier than ever. And then I fell pregnant, and Mr. Rees gave me three hundred pounds to take care of it, and we never spoke again. He was probably terrified I was going to point the finger at him, but it never even crossed my mind, whether out of shame or disgust or just relief that it was over. I didn't think of it once.

"I'm sorry," he said after a pause. "I can't even imagine..."

"It's okay." I sniffed, trying to regroup. "I've never told anyone before. And today... after everything... I needed to tell someone."

"I'm glad it was me." He kissed me gently, and something in me loosened and let go. He wasn't repulsed; he wasn't backing off as I'd feared. "What happened to you, Anna, it was wrong. I hope you know that."

"I think I'm starting to. Hearing Sasha tell her story... it made me realise how much I've doubted myself. How I've felt it was my fault..."

"It wasn't."

"Thank you." I tried to smile. "That means a lot."

Telling Jack freed me, but not enough to tell Milly any of it. I thought about it sometimes, when we were out together, although that was happening less frequently. I thought about sitting her down, letting it all spill out. But it felt like such a big thing, the biggest thing in my life, that I didn't know how to begin, and I was afraid to navigate the why-didn't-you-tell-me conversations, opening up a whole new arena of hurt.

Part of me wondered if Milly even wanted to know. Was that why she'd never asked, back then or now? Why she's never said a word?

And in my meaner moments, I wonder if that has always been the nature of our friendship. From the beginning, I have been relegated to the supporting role, the sidekick, and I've never minded. I've been so grateful to have Milly at all, to have her fierce and unwavering loyalty—and yet I am now realising it has come at a price, albeit one I've always been willing to pay.

I am willing to pay it now, not least because Milly is an important part of my life, she is pregnant, she needs me, and most of all, because of *Alice*. I want to be in Alice's life. I want at least a little bit of that vision Milly painted for me, way back when.

And so I keep texting and meeting for coffee every so often, listen to her moan about swollen ankles and stretchmarks, enthuse about the lavender-themed nursery, with its walls of pale violet, the framed botany prints, the glider with its cushion of cream velveteen. But there is a growing part of me that is starting, with a quiet ferocity, to resent it all, resent *her*, and I feel both vindicated and horrified by that. How can I be this way? How can I not?

Then I find out I've been fired.

First Lara met with Mike Jacobs on her own, and managed to get Sasha's case dropped, most likely through intimidation. I wasn't even surprised, but for the first time I didn't feel like rolling over.

"I should have been at that meeting," I told her, trying not to let my voice tremble. "I was in charge of this case..."

"Honestly, Anna, you seemed a bit too personally involved." Lara eyed me coolly from behind her desk. "So I decided it was better if I handled it myself."

My nails dug into my palms. "And now it's been dropped?"

"Better for everyone, and certainly better for Qi Tech. Sasha sees that. She was a bit of a silly girl." Lara smiled at me almost pityingly, as if she suspected that once upon a time I had been a silly girl, as well.

For a second, I just stared at her and then I heard myself saying, "She was not a *silly girl*, Lara. And it was wrong of you to strong-arm her into dropping her complaint."

Lara's eyes narrowed. "Then it's a good thing I'm in charge and you're not."

It felt as if the very air between us was shimmering with tension. I'd put up with Lara's crap for nearly fifteen *years*. I'd turned a blind eye, shut up when I'd needed to, ignored all the rude, racist, and derogatory remarks she'd made, because she was my boss and, despite everything, despite *her*, I still loved my job.

But now a line had been crossed. Because Sasha was just like me, and I couldn't let her feel the way I had for so long. I couldn't live with myself if I did, not when I knew how the pain and shame felt. How they corroded you from the inside out, even a decade and a half later, until you felt like nothing but rust.

"Do you know how much I know about you?" I said, and Lara looked startled. My voice was quiet and steady, surprising me because I was terrified. "How many things you've said to me that could get you fired?"

She let out a huff of scornful laughter. "Seriously, Anna?"

"Seriously." I stared her down, my heart thumping. "I get that you're a bit of a personality at Qi Tech, Lara. You're your own thing, and so people put up with you. But in today's climate?

Today's *viral* climate? I could get you fired." The words came out of me low, deadly, and completely serious.

She stared at me for a long moment, her eyes narrowed to dark slits, her crimson lips pursed. "If anyone's going to be fired," she said in a deceptively pleasant voice, "I assure you, it's you."

I shook my head. "I don't think so, Lara. In fact, I'd think very carefully about Sasha's complaint. Because it won't be her head on the chopping block if this all comes out, if the media gets hold of it. It will be yours." And then I turned and walked away from my boss, and went to the toilets, where I promptly threw up from nerves.

I knew it was all talk on my part. I couldn't get Lara fired. In fact, I'd just about fired myself, and the blow came two weeks later, when Lara called me into a meeting with Qi Tech's CEO. The company was being reorganised, and my position was no longer needed. I was offered a standard severance package, enough to manage for a few months, at least. Lara requested I clear out my desk immediately, "to make things easier."

"So is the whole company being reorganised?" I asked her as I took down my photo of me and Milly, and another one of her parents. "Or just HR?"

Lara didn't even look at me as she answered. "You knew this was coming, Anna. You can't threaten me and expect to keep your job."

"No, you're the only one who can make threats." I spoke wearily, too worn out to pursue it.

I see Milly a few days later, and it occurs to me, as we sit in her living room sipping herbal tea, that I hadn't texted her right away about being fired, as I once would have. At least, I *think* I would have, but I'm not sure of anything anymore. Did I ever tell Milly what was really going on in my life? Did she ever want to know?

"You *left*?" Her eyes widened as she looked at me, hands laced over her lovely big bump. "Why?"

"Well, technically, I was fired."

"Fired? Oh, Anna…"

"It was over a sexual harassment case. I wasn't willing to let it lie." I pause, waiting for her to ask more. *Why not, Anna? What happened? Do you want to tell me more? What can I do to help?*

But she just shakes her head slowly and says, "What will you do now?"

"Update my CV, I suppose. Possibly retrain. I got a fairly good severance package, at least. Who knows?"

"Well, at least you have some time, with your severance pay." Milly sighs and stretches her arms over her head. "Can you believe how big I am? I feel like a house."

I stare at her for a moment, amazed that my news is being brushed over so quickly. I've been *fired*, and it warrants only two minutes of conversation. But perhaps it has always been this way, and it's just that I've never minded. Perhaps it's not fair of me to start minding now. And so I tell her she looks beautiful, and ask about her birthing classes, and nod and smile and sip my tea. But in my head I'm miles away. I'm barely listening at all.

With more time on my hands, I spend it with Jack. I help paint the upstairs of the house in Stroud, and I sit with him in the empty sitting room, drinking wine and eating takeaway, unable to keep from the temptation of imagining how life would be if this was our house, our life. Trying not to want it too much, because as lovely as Jack is, I'm still not sure how serious about me he is. He's never said and, true to form, I've never asked.

October becomes November, the days dark and cold and empty. Jack goes back to France for a few weeks, and as he doesn't ask me to go with him—I was hoping, just a little—I stay behind and brush up my CV.

I stop by Milly's, and listen to her talk about Braxton Hicks and the Bradley method of breathing during labour. I know so much about pregnancy and birth, I could write a manual about it. The Best Friend's Guide to Pregnancy. Surely it would be a bestseller.

I send out my CV and don't get any responses, and Jack texts to say he has to be in France for another week. I feel as if I am waiting for my life to begin, my real life, the one I've missed out all along, but I don't know what it is. What am I waiting for? A job? A husband? *A baby?*

Then one morning, when the rain had finally stopped and the wintry sunlight made the frosted grass shimmer, Milly rings me.

"Anna?" Her voice wavers. "I'm in labour. My waters just broke, and Matt's gone to Gloucester for a training day." Her voice wobbles, then breaks. "Please, can you come?"

# CHAPTER FIFTEEN

## MILLY

It's funny and wonderful how, in the moments that matter, your friends will be there for you. Even if things have felt awkward and stilted. Even if you think you might need to say sorry, although you're not sure for what. *Even though.*

And when I feel those first contractions tighten around my belly with an alarming amount of pain, and then a gush of fluid, I know only two things: I want Anna, and she will come.

"Have you rung Matt?" she asks as we drive to the Royal Infirmary.

"I've left three voicemails, but I think his phone is switched off." My voice is high and thin with panic. "I thought the risk of preterm labour was over. I never thought this would happen so early..." *Too early.* Six weeks is premature, maybe even dangerously so, but I can't let myself think that way.

"Do you think they'll give you that drug to stop the labour?"

"I hope so." But the contractions are coming with fierce regularity, and have been now for over an hour. What if they can't stop it? "If only Matt left his phone on..."

"He'll check it soon," Anna says firmly.


"You're already three centimetres dilated," the consultant informs me after she's done a check. Matt still hasn't rung. "Although we'd often try to hold off labour at this gestation, I don't think that's going to be possible this time."

"But won't she be too small?" My voice wavers. "Six weeks early…"

"Thirty-four weeks is still a good length of time," the consultant reassures me as she pats my arm. "And your body, along with your baby, is telling you she needs to come out, so that's what's going to happen."

But I'm not ready. *She's* not ready. What if she's too small? What if she can't make it, or she has chronic health problems? *And why isn't Matt here?*

"Milly." Anna speaks gently, looking right into my eyes as the unspoken tension between us evaporates as if it has never been. "It's going to be okay."

"How can you be sure?" My voice wobbles.

"Because of what the consultant said. Because this baby is so wanted, so cared for already. I believe it, and you need to believe it as well. That's what Alice needs right now."

"Okay." I manage a small, trembling smile. "Okay, I will."

They settle me in a room to labour in, with a midwife coming in regularly to check my blood pressure, the baby's heartbeat.

"This is all happening so much faster than I thought," I say as Anna adjusts the blinds of the window overlooking the car park. Wintry sunshine streams in, bathing the room in crystalline light. I am lying in bed, already in a hospital gown, feeling as if I am playing at a role even though I can feel my tummy tighten and release. It's painful, but not in an unpleasant way. Not yet, at least.

"But that's a good thing, in a way," she says. "You were getting tired of waiting, weren't you? Now you don't have to."

"Yes, but I wouldn't mind waiting a bit more now."

Anna smiles and comes to sit by my bed. "We always want what we don't have, I suppose." For a second I think about asking her about these last few months, the unspoken tension that has existed between us, but the words fall silently to the ground before I can even think what they would be—*Why? I'm sorry? Are we okay now?*

She pats my arm. "Focus on your baby now," she says, almost as if she could hear those silent words and knew what they would be. "Focus on Alice."

*Alice.* In a few hours, I might be holding her. The prospect fills me with fear and joy in equal measure. My mobile rings, and I snatch it up and see with relief that it's Matt.

"Matt—"

"Milly?" His voice is a ragged cry. "Are you okay? The baby—our little girl—"

"I'm at the hospital. I'm in labour. Matt, she's *coming*."

He swears, which is so unlike him. "I'm stuck in traffic on the M5. I don't know how long I'll be. Maybe an hour—"

"Just get here as quickly as you can. Anna's with me."

"Anna? Oh, that's good. That's good."

I smile at her, and she smiles back. No matter what still might be unresolved between us, I'm glad she's here. I need her more than ever.

The midwife comes in, and so I end the call with Matt, and when she checks me, she frowns, which sends me into panic mode.

"Is everything okay?"

"Ye-es, but baby's heart rate is a little higher than I'd like. I think we should have it monitored."

A few minutes later I watch the screen of a machine that flashes a graph, jagged lines jerking up and down. I am starting to get scared.

"Try not to worry," the midwife says. "I'll have the consultant come in to check you, in any case."

After she leaves, Anna rests a hand on my shoulder. "This isn't something to get panicked about, Milly. Trust me. They'd tell you if it was serious." I nod, wanting so much to believe her, but I am starting to doubt. "How about we put on some music? I brought my Bluetooth speakers. Some mellow jazz to get everybody's heart rate down, Alice included."

She sets up the speakers and then the soulful saxophone notes of a jazz piece drift out. The music relaxes me, but not enough. I turn to stare at the jagged lines on the screen, wishing I knew what they meant and yet half-relieved that I don't.

"See, this isn't so bad," Anna says as she sits next to me. "And Matt will be here soon."

I nod, but after only a few minutes it all goes to pieces. The consultant comes in to check how I'm doing, and whatever she sees on the screen, she doesn't like, because she barks out something to a nurse, and then the next thing I know she is telling me that my baby is in foetal distress and they need to get her out quickly.

"Her heart rate is too high," she explains, her voice steady but clipped. "The best thing for you now is an emergency caesarean section."

I stare at her, feeling my own rapid heartbeat, in time with my daughter's. "But…"

Anna squeezes my hand. "This is for the best, Milly."

I *know* that, but I still don't want it, and I'm filled with an icy terror that at the very last moment things might still go terribly wrong. I'm wheeled to the operating theatre and prepped for surgery, while Anna waits outside, by the doors. I am alone, surrounded by faceless surgeons in green scrubs, all of them moving so quickly I know it's urgent. It's dangerous.

"You'll be holding your baby very soon, Milly," the consultant says kindly, and I hold onto that promise as they inject the anaesthetic and ask me to count backwards from ten. Before I get to eight, the world goes dark.

# CHAPTER SIXTEEN

## ANNA

I stand outside the theatre doors, listening to the different sounds of the hospital around me—a beeping monitor, a woman in labour, the squeak of a trolley wheel. The last few minutes passed in a blur of motion as they rushed Milly out of the room and into surgery. As calm as I tried to be for her, inside I am filled with fear.

She can't lose that baby. *Her daughter.*

"Why don't you wait in the visitors' room?" a nurse asks me kindly, more command than suggestion. "You'd be far more comfortable, and we'll make sure to tell you when there's any news."

"Milly's husband is on his way..."

"I'll direct him to the visitors' room when he comes."

I find myself in a bland little room with a sofa and chairs, a coffee table and a couple of magazines a year out of date. I pace the small confines, too restless to sit. How long does a caesarean section take? When will I find out how Milly and her baby are doing? *What if...?*

But I don't let myself think that way. I can't, for Milly's sake—and also for mine. I can't imagine life without Alice in it, and she's not even here yet.

Half an hour passes with agonising slowness, and no one comes. I flip through a *Woman's Weekly*, my mind pinging all over the place like a butterfly, unable to land anywhere for long.

Out in the corridor, I see a man holding a couple of glittery blue balloons walk by. A few minutes later, a pregnant woman, clearly in early labour, hands resting on the small of her back, lumbers past, her husband at her elbow. Then a couple of grandparents come, holding the hand of a little girl, maybe three or four, who is clutching a brand new baby doll. This is the place of new beginnings as well as happy endings. It has to be that way for Milly.

Then I start to think about my own pregnancy. I was seventeen weeks when it ended. I'd started to feel flutters. Even now, it hurts to remember those butterfly kicks. It's the worst form of self-torture, but I begin to imagine a rosy what-if scenario, one I haven't let myself consider before because it's been far too painful. But now I imagine that I kept my baby, that I told my parents, that they supported me rather than threw me out.

But even as I envision this warm, fuzzy scenario, it starts to fall apart. I was eighteen years old, and I'd stumbled through the last six months of sixth form, sitting my exams without writing much more than my name. My pregnancy had ended just two weeks before I sat them. If I'd kept the baby, would I have passed my exams? Would I have taken them? And what about afterwards?

I wouldn't have been able to go to uni; I would have had to live at home, and found some minimum-wage job. I would have had to depend on my bitter and resentful mother for childcare. Hardly a dream scenario, and yet I would have had my baby. A boy. They told me, afterwards—even though they didn't want to—because I'd insisted. I'd needed to know, even though it hurt.

Now I release a ragged breath, my hands clenched so hard in my lap that my nails have made crescent moons in my palms. I can't think about all that now. I have to focus on Milly. The visitors' door opens, and a nurse smiles at me, the same one who suggested I wait in here.

"Anna? Milly's out of surgery, and she and her baby are doing well."

"Oh…" A rush of relief floods through me, so I nearly sway. "That's wonderful."

"Would you like to see her?"

"Milly…?"

"No." The nurse's smile is gentle, apologetic. "Milly isn't awake yet. She had to be given a general anaesthetic, due to the urgency of the procedure, and it will be another hour at least before she's ready for visitors."

"Oh…"

"I meant the baby."

"*Oh.*" Should I be the one to see Milly and Matt's baby first, even before they do? But I can't exactly say no, can I? And I don't want to. "Yes," I tell the nurse. "Thank you."

I follow her down a brightly lit corridor to the nursery. "She's a good weight for thirty-four weeks," she tells me, talking over her shoulder as she walks briskly along. "Five pounds three ounces."

"That's great." I don't know what a good weight is, but five pounds sounds tiny.

"And healthy, too. Screaming her lungs off when she first came out. Here she is." She stands in front of the nursery and taps the window. "She's the one on the left, with the striped hat."

I lean forward so my nose is nearly touching the glass and drink in the sight of the tiny baby swaddled in white, her little pink and blue striped hat nearly covering her eyes, her mitted fists up by her face.

She is *tiny*, her skin a peachy yellow, which the nurse tells me is due to jaundice. "But she'll be fine after a few sessions under the heat lamp." She pats my shoulder. "I'll leave you to it, then."

I stare and stare at those navy eyes, the plump cheeks, the tiny rosebud lips that make perfect cupid's bow. I don't mean to, but I look for recognisable features, something that will tell me she comes from my genes, but there's nothing I can see yet.

And then she smiles, or perhaps grimaces, and I let out a gasp because she has dimples, one in each cheek. Just like me. Neither Matt nor Milly have dimples; Jack doesn't either. They come from me. Just me.

"Anna!"

I turn, startled, feeling a bit guilty as I see Matt hurrying down the hall.

"Thank God I found you. They're telling me I can't see Milly, she's still in recovery..."

"She's okay, Matt, and so is your daughter."

Matt turns to the nursery, scanning the plastic bassinets and their tiny occupants eagerly. "Which one is she?"

And it strikes me as so odd, so unbearable, that I know who his daughter is and he doesn't. And Milly hasn't even seen her yet. Everything is the wrong way round, and yet something about it feels right, which is also jarring.

"She's on the left," I say softly. "With the striped hat."

"Oh..." His breath comes out in a rush as he stares at his daughter. *His daughter.* I need to remember that, now more than ever, when my own emotions are so raw and exposed, when memories and longings keep resurfacing and grabbing me by the throat.

I watch as Matt places his palm flat on the glass, transfixed by the sight of his child. "Can I see her?" he asks me, as if I am the authority. "Can I hold her?"

"I don't know." The nurse didn't invite me to, and I don't know what I would have done if she had.

"I should wait for Milly," he murmurs. "It's just so amazing... she's right *there.*" He lets out a laugh of pure joy.

"Did the doctors tell you when Milly might wake up?"

"They said soon, and that they'd get me...but I suppose I should go back." Reluctantly he turns away from the nursery window. "She's going to be so excited." He grabs my arm, his face lit up like a firework. "Isn't this amazing, Anna? That's my *daughter!*"

I laugh, because I can't help it, because his joy is so infectious. "It is amazing, Matt."

His expression suddenly turns serious, his eyes bright with emotion. "This couldn't have been possible without you, Anna…"

I can't bear to hear his heartfelt thanks just now. So I merely smile and nod, gently removing my arm from his enthusiastic grip. "You should check on Milly, Matt."

Sure enough, a nurse intercepts us on the way back to the visitors' room to tell Matt that Milly is waking up and has been moved to a private room. He gives me an apologetic look and I wave him away.

"Go. Go."

"I'm sure she'll want to see you soon…"

"You both need some time together. I'll be fine. I could use something to eat, anyway."

"Okay." Matt reaches for my hand. "Thank you, Anna—for everything."

I wait until he has disappeared around the corner before I head for the doors out of the ward, and the café downstairs. I feel lonely in an unsettling way, like something is missing even though I know nothing is. Nothing should be.

I order a coffee and sit at a table in the café by the hospital entrance, watching all the different people come and go—some in wheelchairs, some walking briskly, some holding each other up in their worry or grief, others filled with purpose or delight. So many different reasons to come or to leave a hospital, and I watch it all play out by a pair of automatic sliding doors.

An hour slips by as I sip my cooling coffee, my gaze still on the steady foot traffic, my mind thankfully empty, although it keeps pinging back to that tiny form in the bassinet, those dimples.

Then I see a familiar figure come through the doors, walking with his long-legged, easy stride, and I half-rise from my chair.

"Jack..."

"Anna!" He gives me a quick hug before stepping back. "I got back last night, and Matt texted me this afternoon." He speaks quickly, an apology of sorts for not being in contact, and I decide to let it go.

"Milly and Matt are upstairs. Alice is fine."

"That's great news. Shall we go up to see them?"

"Yes, okay." We head towards the bank of lifts, and Jack pauses by the gift shop with its schmaltzy tat, all glittery balloons and cheap teddy bears.

"I should get something for them..." I wait as he selects a big pink balloon and a matching teddy with a rictus grin, clutching a fabric heart. Milly would usually hate both, but perhaps she'll love them now because of the occasion. I picture her upstairs, cradling her daughter, perhaps even trying to feed her. They encourage mothers to breastfeed right away, I remember Milly telling me.

"I don't actually know where Milly is," I say, heading for the nurses' desk on the maternity ward, but Jack stops me.

"Matt said room six."

We head in that direction, passing several doors that are partially ajar, so we catch glimpses of parents and babies, snapshots of happiness. A mother nursing. A father taking a photo. A toddler trying to climb onto a bed.

Then we reach room six and the door is firmly closed. We both hesitate, and then Jack raps on it softly. A moment passes and we glance at each other uncertainly.

Then Matt opens the door, his expression a bit dazed, his hair mussed as if he's raked his fingers through it more than once.

"Hey, mate." Jack claps a hand on his shoulder. "Congratulations—"

"Thanks." He steps out of the room, closing the door behind him. "Sorry. I just want Milly to have a bit of space."

"Space?" I echo. What's going on? What's wrong?

"She's...she's having a bit of trouble adjusting. It all happened so fast, I suppose...and she's groggy still from the anaesthetic." He sounds as if he is trying to convince himself of something.

"What do you mean, Matt?"

His voice drops to a whisper, a confession. "She doesn't want to hold Alice," he explains, sounding wretched. "She doesn't even want to see her."

# CHAPTER SEVENTEEN

## MILLY

I wake aching, the world a muted blur. One hand creeps to my bump, but it isn't there. I am empty and sagging, with a deflated balloon of a belly. Panic takes over, a metallic taste in my mouth.

"What…where…" I am struggling to a sitting position, despite the fiery pain spreading through my middle. I can barely get my head off the pillow, in any case, no matter how hard I try.

"Milly. *Milly*." Matt puts his hands on my shoulders, anchoring me to this bed. "It's okay. You're in hospital. You had an emergency caesarean. Our daughter is fine. She's beautiful, Milly. Just beautiful."

I stare at him, blinking slowly, trying to take in the words. Everything happened so fast. I try to put the memories together, but they're like broken puzzle pieces that won't fit no matter how hard I try to jam them together. My waters broke, and Anna was here, and my daughter's heart rate was too high. The consultant looked scared. I remember her saying something about not enough time before fitting a mask over my face. And then…nothing.

"Milly?" Matt looks at me hopefully. "Do you want to see her?"

*Her?* I blink. My mind is still fuzzy, and my mouth is horribly dry. My empty belly is blazing with pain.

"I…" I can't manage much more. My eyes flutter closed. The world feels too much. I fall asleep.

When I wake up again, I feel more focused, the memories that felt so disparate and strange starting to come together into an unsettling whole. I missed it all—everything I had looked forward to and longed for—the labour, the delivery, my darling, squalling newborn placed on my chest, that important skin-to-skin contact I've read about, how you need to breastfeed right away... How long has it even *been?* I turn my head and see that it's dark outside.

"Milly, you're awake." I open my mouth to speak, but only a croak comes out. "Here, let me get you some water."

Matt hurries to fill a glass from the pitcher by my bed and then holds it to my lips. I try to swallow, but most of it dribbles down my chin. I feel utterly helpless.

"How are you feeling?" Matt's eyes are shining and he looks so excited. I can't muster a millionth of his emotion, and I barely manage to shake my head. "Do you want to see her, Milly? Alice. Our daughter. She's beautiful."

*Alice.* The name we chose, but for some reason it feels unfamiliar now. Everything does. I feel so disoriented, as if my brain has separated from my body. I don't know who I am anymore. I certainly don't know who Alice is.

"What... time is it?" I finally manage. I don't know why I ask that first. Perhaps I just need something to ground me in this present reality.

Matt looks surprised, and then a little disappointed. He checks his watch. "It's almost seven o'clock."

*Seven o'clock.* Eight hours since I was awake with Anna, cradling my bump, bracing myself for what was ahead. It feels like forever. "Where's Anna?"

Matt looks even more discomfited, as if he can't understand my questions, how I need to remind myself of these facts. "I... I don't know. She went for a coffee a couple of hours ago. She wanted to give us some time alone." I nod slowly. "I texted Jack too, he's back from France, and all our parents, of course. He wants to stop by later tonight and your mum and dad are hoping to visit tomorrow morning…"

I stare at him, numb to everything, even the pain blazing through me. Everything has happened and I haven't been a part of any of it, not even my baby's birth. *My baby.* The words roll around like marbles inside my head. Do I really have a baby?

"Milly…" A touch of impatience to his voice now. "Don't you want to see Alice?"

I'm not sure I can make any other response, and so I nod. Of course I want to see her, and yet I'm terrified. Nothing feels the way I expected to, least of all myself.

"I'll ask the nurse to bring her here," Matt says.

I must have drifted off, because when Matt returns with a nurse and plastic bassinet on wheels, I startle awake.

"It's good to see you awake, Milly," the nurse says, although I don't recognise her. How does she know my name? I feel as if I've entered some alternate dystopian reality, and while I can remember most of the day before they put me under, it still feels distant, separate from myself, from my present.

"Here she is," the nurse says cheerfully, and wheels the bassinet close to me. There is a baby inside of it.

"Isn't she gorgeous, Mills?" Matt whispers, enthralled by the sight of the tiny creature wrapped in white, looking wizened and red and *strange*.

I blink and stare, knowing I should feel something. *Wanting* to feel something. Joy, or at least relief. But I feel numb, and underneath that, like freezing water beneath black ice, something dark is swirling around—fear, or something worse?

"I'll just leave you two alone for a few minutes," the nurse says. "Have some bonding time."

She tiptoes away while we both stare at the baby. What am I supposed to say? What am I supposed to feel? I know, in a distant, abstract way, what emotions I should feel, what words I should say, but they feel so far away. I can't even pretend.

"Milly," Matt asks gently. "Do you want to hold her?"

"I don't know if I can." I gesture to my stitches. "I can't do anything, Matt."

"Let me hold her to you," Matt says, and inexpertly but carefully he picks up the baby from the bassinet. I can tell by the way he cradles her head he's done it before. How many times has he held her? Has Anna held her? And even Jack? I am the last to this party; I feel like a fake. *Look at you. You're not a real mother. No matter how hard you tried.*

Matt inches over to my bed, Alice suspended over me. She is asleep, but she stirs as he moves her. It's an awkward angle, and after a second she lets out a tiny, mewling cry of protest. Matt quickly puts her back in the bassinet.

"Sorry, that wasn't great," he mutters. "But you can hold her soon, I'm sure. The nurse said you could, anyway…"

"It's okay." I turn my head a little bit away. "I don't want to." As soon as the words are out, I know I shouldn't have said them. I shouldn't have *thought* them. "I'm just feeling a bit out of it still," I say, and I close my eyes, because maybe then Matt won't ask me any questions.

I must fall asleep again, because a little while later I wake up, and I am alone in the room. No Matt. No baby. Outside, the sky is black and starless, and the hospital ward seems quiet. Silent, in fact. I can't hear anything, not even murmuring voices in the distance, and I am suddenly filled with a wild panic. Has Matt *left* me here? Has he taken Alice and gone?

I struggle to a sitting position, even though it makes my midsection burn. I don't think I can walk, not without assistance, but I still try, swinging my legs out of the bed, my feet hitting the cold tile floor. I let out a gasp, icy sweat prickling on my brow and between my shoulder blades. I can do this…

Except, of course, I can't. When I try to rise from the bed, I stagger and fall back, letting out a cry as pain rips through me. The door opens, and Matt rushes towards me.

"Milly, *Milly*. What are you doing?"

"Where were you?" I cry, my voice sounding broken.

Matt blinks, his hand on my arm as he guides me back to a lying position. "I was with Alice."

*Alice, Alice.* The way he says her name as if he knows her, and I don't. I don't know her at all. I jerk away from him, and he blinks.

"Milly…"

"I don't want to lie down. I want to sit up."

"Okay, let me help you."

I don't want to be helped either, but I need it. I suffer silently as he moves me around, adjusting my limbs as if I am a marionette. He steps back, his forehead crinkled with concern as he looks at me.

"Milly, I know this is challenging," he begins hesitantly. "It's not the way either of us would have wanted things to happen, but we've made it through and you're healthy and so is our daughter." I'm not sure where he is going with this, so I just stare at him silently. "The nurse said you might find things…difficult…at first, because of the emergency caesarean, not being awake for the delivery, needing to recover, that sort of thing…"

"So now you're talking about me?"

"Not like that," Matt protests. "Milly, for heaven's sake…" He lapses into silence, seeming to realise there is no point in berating me.

"I know." Everything in me crumples. "I'm sorry," I gasp out. "I just feel so…" I can't explain how I feel, as if I am suffocating. As if this reality that I longed for is now unbearable, and I don't even understand why. "Matt, will you bring her to me? I want to hold her."

"Are you sure?"

His doubt hurts, but I force myself past it. "Yes, I'm sure."

He leaves the room, returning a few minutes later with the plastic bassinet on wheels, Alice swaddled inside. Matt lifts her out almost reverently, and I hold out my arms, the effort making them tremble.

"Here she is." Matt places Alice gently in my arms.

She is beautiful, her golden lashes fanning her cheeks, her tiny rosebud mouth puckered, little mittened fists up by her face. She is perfect. And yet I feel as if I could be holding anyone's baby, even a doll. She doesn't feel like my daughter. The groundswell of maternal love that I expected in this moment, that I'd been building all along, is entirely absent, and that terrifies me. I don't want Matt, or anyone else, to know, and yet I'm afraid it must be evident on my face, in the way I hold her, like a bulky parcel.

"Milly..."

"She's lovely." The words sound wooden. "Lovely."

"Do you want to try breastfeeding her?"

The thought of doing *that* right now nearly makes me flinch. "Tomorrow," I say, and gesture for him to take her. "I'm still so tired."

"Okay." Matt looks worried and I know I'm not handling this right. The trouble is, the right words, the right feelings, seem utterly foreign and impossible.

I turn on my side, away from him, afraid of what he can see in my face. I have to hide how I feel, how I *don't* feel, and I'm not sure I can.

What is *wrong* with me? Or is nothing wrong with me, and it's just I'm finally realising what I've known all along—that Alice isn't really my child?

The next morning, I wake up, half-hoping I'll feel different, better, but I don't. I feel exactly the same, only worse, because I was hoping this dark cloud would have dispersed in the night, and it hasn't. It's thick and black and covering every part of me. And I don't want to admit it to Matt, or to anyone.

At least I am feeling a bit better physically; I manage to shuffle along the corridor like an old woman, my hospital gown flapping around me, Matt holding my elbow.

When I've showered and managed to change into my own comfy clothes, Matt asks me, his voice full of hesitation, if I'd like to see Alice again, and perhaps try breastfeeding.

"Yes, all right," I say, offering him a small smile. I am play-acting, but perhaps if I stay in the role, I will start to feel something. The instinct I am missing will finally kick in.

Matt goes to get Alice, and I perch on the edge of the bed, my heart flip-flopping in my chest. I can do this. I need to do this. I want to want to do this, and yet I know I don't.

A few minutes later, Matt comes in, wheeling that plastic bassinet. "Here she is," he says, his voice pitched just a bit too jolly.

I try to smile as he lifts Alice out of the bassinet. *Alice.* I say her name again and again silently, trying to get used to it. We picked it out months ago; we always called her by her name as soon as we knew we were having a girl. Why does the name seem strange now, almost as if I never chose it?

I hold out my arms and Matt places her in them gently, and I hold my breath, waiting again for the rush of maternal love, the feeling that things finally fit. I am so hopeful, so desperate to believe that in this moment it's going to happen.

But again, nothing does. And when Matt suggests breast-feeding, I steel myself for an attempt, which is awkward and unbearable, and ends up with Alice mewling plaintively and me thrusting her away from me, back at Matt.

"Take her," I say, a desperate plea. Matt scoops her up, already an expert, while I am floundering.

"Milly, it will get better."

I nod, because it *has* to get better. I can't bear to think about what will happen if it doesn't.

# CHAPTER EIGHTEEN

## ANNA

"Oh, Anna." Milly's mother Claire envelops me in a hug, her face crumpled in anxiety. It's been four days since Milly gave birth, and as far as I know, she's barely looked at Alice and only held her a few times, all of them difficult. She's coming home from the hospital today, which is why her parents are here, even though Matt is clearly alarmed by the prospect of having Milly here. He's due back at work by the end of the week, and Milly doesn't even want to look at her child.

The midwives and consultants have given him support, at least, mainly in the form of pamphlets on caesarean recovery and maternal bonding, but the words *postpartum depression* have been murmured. A health visitor is going to stop by tomorrow; an appointment can be booked with the GP to discuss antidepressants, if it comes to that, but I know Matt is hoping it won't.

"We're going to get through this," he said last night, his chin tilted at a stubborn angle, reminding me of Milly. I had come to the hospital to see them both, but Milly was sleeping, or perhaps pretending to. I've seen her once, and it was awkward and strange, with Milly not quite looking at me. In any case, the real reason I came to the hospital was to see Alice.

I'd held her now, twice, cuddling her close to my body, breathing in her warm, powdery scent, feeling both guilty and defiant for holding her at all. But Milly didn't want to, and she's needed cuddles. I'd read online about the importance of skin-to-skin contact during the first few days and weeks of a baby's life. So I pressed my cheek to hers and imbued her with my touch, my love, because Milly wouldn't.

Now I step back from Claire, giving her and her husband Simon a sympathetic smile. Matt has told them that Milly is struggling, without going into the painful specifics.

I came to Milly and Matt's house this morning to do a quick clean; I brought over some banana bread, now warming in the oven, as well as a casserole for dinner tonight. I've made up all the beds with fresh sheets, including the Moses basket by Milly's side of the bed, tucking in the soft, fleece-lined blanket, imagining Alice snuggled there.

I've also made up some bottles of formula, at Matt's request, because although her milk has come in, Milly doesn't want to try to breastfeed.

It's so strange to think of her this way, refusing to be the mother she has always dreamed of being. In a million years, I could have never imagined it. I keep waiting for her to snap out of it, for Matt to laugh and shake his head and say, "Oh, that? Yeah, that was just a blip. Everything's fine now." But every time I've seen him in the last four days, he's looked haggard and dazed, as if he can't believe this is happening either.

"How is she, Anna?" Claire asks now, grabbing my arm. "Is she doing any better?"

"I haven't actually seen Milly recently, Claire." I give her a grimace of apology. "I saw Matt last night, and things seemed to be...the same." I feel badly for saying the words. "But perhaps things will be different once she's home, in her own space, away from all the nurses and doctors."

"Yes..." But Claire doesn't look convinced. "Should she see someone? Get some medication? You hear about things like this..."

"I think Matt wants to wait a few days before they go down that route, see if this clears up on its own." I'm no doctor, but if I were Matt, I'd be asking for the meds.

"Right." Claire walks into the sitting room, sinking onto the sofa with a tired sigh. She looks a decade older from the last time I saw her, her skin pale and papery, her hands reminding me of claws. I know from Milly that she's responding to the chemo, but it's certainly taken its toll. "I wish we could do more," she says with an unhappy frown.

Simon, Milly's father, joins her on the sofa and pats her hand. "You can't push yourself, love, and I'm not sure there's much we could do, anyway."

"But the baby...poor little Alice..."

"She's got Matt." Simon smiles at me. "And Anna."

I smile back uncertainly. I'm not sure if they know about the egg donation. I have a feeling they don't, not that I'd ever mention it. The knowledge sits on my chest like a weight, making it hard to say anything.

"Still." Claire sighs, and Simon puts his arm around her.

"You need to think about yourself right now, Claire."

"I'm a mother," she protests. "When do I think about myself?"

The question reverberates through me as I go into the kitchen to put the kettle on for drinks. *I'm a mother.* Do those instincts always kick in naturally? Did they for Claire, even though she hadn't given birth? Will they for Milly?

And what about me?

*I'm a mother.* Can I say that now, when I chose to end the life of my own child? When the baby coming home this morning has my genes but nothing else? *But I've held her. I've breathed her in. She has dimples.*

I feel confused and guilty, aching for Milly and what she's going through, but also aching for myself. This feels far, far more complicated than it was ever supposed to be, than I ever thought it would, even in my darkest and most difficult moments during Milly's pregnancy. It's so real now, with a real baby I've cuddled and kissed, a baby who looks like me—and my boyfriend.

I feel like I need some distance from it all, but I know I won't create it. I will stay as close to Alice as I can, even if it hurts. I feel as if I don't even have a choice.

I've just brought a tray of teas and coffees into the sitting room when the front door opens and Matt stands there, one arm around Milly, the other holding a car seat.

"Let me help." I put the tray down and spring forward, unsure whether I should help Milly or take the car seat. Matt decides for me, by handing me the car seat. I look down at Alice, snuggled in a fleecy pink snowsuit, fast asleep, her golden lashes sweeping her rosy cheeks. She is so tiny, and she is perfect.

"Milly." Claire's voice is full of emotion. They didn't come to the hospital, because of the risk of infection for Claire, and so this is the first time she has seen her daughter or granddaughter since the birth. "I'm so glad to see you, darling."

Claire goes to hug her, and Milly returns the embrace, clinging for a moment before she moves away.

"Milly should get into bed," Matt says firmly. "It's been very tiring, having all the checks and things this morning, and then leaving the hospital."

"Of course, of course." I put the car seat down carefully. "Would you like a cup of tea, Milly? I can make chai—"

"I'm fine." Her voice is barely audible.

Matt throws me an apologetic look before helping Milly up the stairs.

Claire, Simon, and I all look at each other a bit blankly. What now?

"May I hold her?" Claire whispers, once Milly has gone upstairs, and I glance at Alice.

"Of course, I'm sure..." I fumble with the complicated buckle of the car seat, before carefully lifting Alice out. She's like a mini snowman, bundled in her fleece suit, and fast asleep, so she doesn't even stir as I hand her to Claire.

Claire cradles her gently, her face suffused with love. "My granddaughter," she murmurs, and I am struck by how strange the situation is, on so many levels. Will Claire see the similarities to me? Will she guess? I shake my head a little, as if to clear it. I need to stop thinking like this. It's not helpful at all, for anyone, and especially not me.

Matt comes down a short while later, looking exhausted. "She's sleeping," he says, and then he takes Alice from Claire and presses a kiss to the top of her head, his eyes closed. My heart aches for him too.

"Matt, how are you managing?" Claire asks in a whisper. "This is all so unexpected..."

"It's not what we wanted, but we'll get there." He sits down, Alice in his arms. "Milly just needs a little time."

"Are you sure that's all it is? Don't you think she should see a doctor?"

"The health visitor is coming tomorrow. Milly has been through a lot. Give her a chance to recover. If it turns out she needs... something more, then we'll do that. I'm committed to caring for my wife and my daughter." His voice sounds steely. "Trust me on that."

"Of course we trust you." Claire looks near tears. "And what about little Alice? She's so tiny. Is it safe for her to come home this early?"

"Yes, although we need to put her in sunlight as much as possible, and we'll need to take her in for light therapy for jaundice a couple of times a week." He cradles her closer to his chest. "But, considering her weight, she's doing well. We just need to get the feeding sorted."

"Will Milly...?"

"She'll get there." His tone has turned repressive, and we all lapse into silence.

"How can I help, Matt?" I finally ask. "Just tell me what to do."

"I don't even know." He shrugs, looking defeated for a moment before he rallies again. "What you're doing is amazing, Anna. The meals and the cleaning…everything…but if you could talk to Milly, that would be great. Just normal stuff. I don't want everything to be about the baby."

"Okay." Of course I'll do it, but I feel nervous. Milly is like a stranger to me right now.

Claire and Simon leave a short while after that, because she's clearly tired, and then Milly wakes up and after Matt checks in on her, he asks me to go up.

I walk up the stairs, my heart thudding with anxiety. This conversation feels important, and yet I have no idea what to say.

"Hey, Milly." I stand in the doorway uncertainly; she is sitting up in bed, looking a little more like herself. Her face is pale, her hair brushed. She doesn't respond.

I take a step in and then sit on the edge of the bed, although it feels a bit invasive.

"How are you feeling?" She shrugs, biting her lip. "This has got to be hard," I venture cautiously. "The emergency caesarean, everything so rushed and strange…"

"Yes." Her voice hitches, and she takes a trembling breath. "Anna, I'm scared."

"Scared? Why?"

"Because everything is different. *I'm* different."

"It's natural to feel that, Milly—"

"No, it isn't. Not this." She shakes her head. "I feel like…like a fake." She turns her head away, as if she regrets admitting that much.

"But you're not a fake," I remind her, even though, to my own shame, it hurts a little to say that. "Alice is your daughter." It hurts even more to say that.

"Have you held her?"

I hesitate. "Yes, a few times." She doesn't answer, and I try to offer more reassurance. "Why don't I go fetch her? You could have a little cuddle..."

"No, she's sleeping, and I'm tired." She looks away. "I shouldn't have said anything."

"It will get better, Milly..."

"Yes, I know it will." Her voice is little more than a monotone. "I'm going to rest now." It is clearly a dismissal.

"How can I help? Can I get you a cup of tea, or—"

"No, thank you." She sounds scarily polite. After a few uncertain seconds, I leave, feeling as if I've failed.

Downstairs, I reach for Alice, unzipping her snowsuit and wrapping her in a soft blanket, while Matt goes up to Milly. I walk up and down the room with her cradled against me, wondering how serious things are with Milly. Is this normal first-time jitters, or is it something more? And what is my part in it all?

After a little while, Alice starts to grizzle, so I take one of the bottles out of the fridge and warm it up. I manage to feed her half an ounce, although it takes an age, and then she falls asleep in my arms. I remain completely still, memorising her face, savouring the solid warmth of her in my arms. Then, after another hour or so, Matt finally comes downstairs.

"Thanks, Anna."

"How is she?"

"The same, really." He sighs and shakes his head. "I never expected this."

"No one did."

"I'm taking the rest of the week off, but then I have to go back to work." He frowns. "I didn't schedule my paternity leave for another five weeks."

I hesitate, then blurt, "I can help." Matt's frown deepens. "If Milly needs me. I'm not working at the moment...I'm happy to come round and be a support to her, help with Alice." I smile, trying to sound casual but sincere, instead of how I feel, which is desperate. I want this. I want this more than I should.

"That's really kind of you, Anna..."

"I don't mind, Matt, if you think Milly needs some support. I really don't mind."

"I'll ask her," he says, and I wonder what Milly will say—and think. Will she agree? I have no idea, but as I gaze down at Alice's tiny face, I do know how much I want her to. I want it more than I've wanted anything else in my life.

# CHAPTER NINETEEN

## MILLY

I tell myself I am going to try. Even if I feel as if I am living underwater, everything muted and distant, the smallest tasks feeling impossible, I can still *try*. And so, the next morning, I wake up, shower and dress, and go to my daughter.

She is downstairs with Matt; he has her in the crook of his arm as he gives her a bottle. He was the one who got up with her in the night; I heard her thin cry and the rustle of bedcovers but I didn't move. I couldn't. The bed felt as if it were made of wet concrete and I was entombed in it; it could have been my own grave.

But that was in the exhausted blur of a troubled night, and now it is morning, the day bright and wintry. I am determined things are going to be different. *I'm* going to be. Alice is six days old and I am going to start being the mother I want and need to be, the mother I intended to be all along.

"Why don't I give her the bottle?" I suggest. Matt hasn't brought up breastfeeding again, and I don't suggest it now even though my milk has come in and my breasts are heavy and aching.

"Sure." He pats the seat next to him on the sofa, and I sit down. Gently, he hands Alice to me, and I gaze down at her, willing myself to feel that warm rush of love. And for a second I do—a faint flicker at least, like the ghost of an emotion. It is gone before I can catch hold of it.

Matt hands me the bottle, and I fit it to Alice's tiny mouth, her little lips pursing around it expectantly. It should be easy, but it's not.

"Careful," he says, as the milk comes out too quickly and Alice starts to sputter and choke. "She can only manage a little at a time. If you hold the bottle at less of an angle…"

I adjust the bottle, but after only a few seconds she turns her face away, screwing up her features, before letting out a bleating cry of protest. I can't even do this.

"Try again, Mills," Matt urges, and I take a deep breath. I'm not going to give up right away. I'm *not*.

"Come on, Alice," I say, and although I meant to sound encouraging, I hear an edge to my voice. I try to fit the bottle into her mouth, but she's having none of it now. Her fists flail and her face turns red as her cries become rattling screams that make my whole body tense. I thrust her at Matt. "You do it."

"If you just try, Milly—"

"She's upset. It's not going to work." I get up from the sofa, not looking at him or Alice. "I'll make some coffee."

When I look back, Matt has Alice cradled in his arms, and he is giving the bottle to her easily. My eyes sting and smart and I focus on the kettle, the canister of coffee. This, at least, is something I know how to do.

"The health visitor is coming by later today," Matt says when I am sitting at the table, my mug cradled between my hands. He has finished feeding Alice and she is settled in her car seat, drowsy and content, a milk bubble frothing at her lips.

"Okay."

"I was wondering…maybe you should talk to her. About… about this."

I turn slowly to look at him. "This?"

"Just that it's hard, Milly, harder than either of us expected it to be—"

"It's not hard for you." My voice is equal parts anger and self-pity.

"All I'm saying, there's no shame in admitting you're having a rough time. Maybe even getting something for it."

"You mean pills? You think I need to be *medicated*?" Now I feel insulted, although I'm not sure why. Something is wrong with me, clearly. Even I can admit that.

"No shame," Matt repeats feebly.

I make a sound of disgust—but it's aimed at myself. Yes, there is most certainly shame. What sort of mother can't feed her own child? What sort of mother doesn't even want to?

"Anna said she could come over as well, if you like," he continues after a moment. "Help out a bit."

"Oh, did she?" I hear the acid in my voice and I wonder at it. I need Anna now, because I know I can't take care of Alice on my own, and clearly Matt knows it as well. He's going back to work in a few days. "That's nice of her."

"She just wants to help. Whatever you need..."

But I don't know what I need. I feel as if I could claw at my own skin, scream inside my head, but nothing helps. Anna certainly won't. And yet I say what I know I need to, because I don't really have any choice. "That's great. It will be good to see her." I know Matt doesn't believe me; he just pretends to. We're both becoming experts at this masquerade.

The health visitor has clearly been briefed, because she gives me a sympathetic squeeze of my arm as she sits on the sofa with me, Alice asleep in the car seat by our feet. "How are you finding things, Milly? Your partner said it was a bit difficult, during these early days?"

I shrug, unable to put it into words. Knowing if I try, I will fall apart. I will shatter.

"Baby blues are quite normal at this stage," she continues. "Especially when you've had a traumatic delivery as you have. How are you feeling physically?"

"Okay, I guess." My stitches hurt, my breasts ache, but it's nothing compared to this black hole I feel inside, sucking all my emotions into it.

"It's important to take time for yourself," the health visitor says, a bit sternly. "You need to make sure you're eating and sleeping properly, although I know that's hard with a little one." Right. As if any of that will help. "And don't be ashamed to ask for help," she continues. "This is a trying time for anyone. Friends, parents, and also professionals. They're there for you. If you're still feeling out of sorts in another week, we can have another chat, think about what to do next."

"Next?" I repeat flatly. What's the next stage for a mother like me, a mother who's failed?

"Perhaps think about getting some professional help," the health visitor says. "Some treatment."

I don't want *treatment*. I don't want to be a problem that has to be dealt with, a disappointment to everyone, most of all myself. I want to solve this, the way I solve everything. Of course I don't say any of that to this woman, whose kindly smile feels like an affront. She pities me. I know she does.

"Thanks," I say, my tone one of finality, my smile not reaching my eyes. "That's good to know."


When Anna comes by later, I am resting in bed. I hear her moving downstairs, her delighted coo to Alice. Then I hear Matt's low voice, the creak of footsteps. When she peeks through my door, I pretend I am sleeping.

Later, I make myself go downstairs and face them all. Anna, Matt. *Alice.* The scene that greets me as I come into the sitting room is the perfect tableau of happy families, except it's not my family. Anna and Jack are sitting on the sofa together, Alice lying on her back on Anna's lap, Anna holding her tiny feet in her hands, as they both coo at her.

They look up as I come into the room, and I swear they both look guilty. For a second I feel dizzy, and I grab onto the door frame.

"Where's Matt?"

"He just went out for some milk." Yes, definitely guilty. Anna scoops Alice into her arms, and Jack helps her to stand. "Do you want to hold her?"

Do I need her *permission*? "In a minute. I'll get a coffee first."

"I'll get it," Anna says quickly. "Here—hold her." She thrusts Alice towards me, and I stare at her levelly. What is going on here?

Anna tries to smile, but her lips tremble. Silently I take my daughter, and hold her awkwardly to me. I'm not as adept as Anna, or perhaps even Jack. I turn away from them, pressing Alice against me, and then she starts to cry.

Damn it. I can't do this. I can never do this. Still, I am determined to try, for my sake, for Alice's sake, and because Anna and Jack are both watching. I jiggle her, patting her back, whispering soft words. Nothing works. She keeps crying, and before I can keep myself from it, I let out a sob of frustration.

"Maybe she's hungry," Anna offers. "Do you want to give her a bottle?"

I think of my one attempt at feeding my daughter, and shake my head. "I think she needs a nappy change. I'll see to it." Still clutching a crying Alice to me, I head upstairs, grateful to be away from an audience.

The nursery is as beautiful as I remember making it, except now it is clearly used. I haven't been in here since I came home, and now I notice the stack of nappies by the changing table, the hamper of dirty baby gros and sleepsuits, reminders of everything I've already missed.

"Come on then, sweetie." My voice sounds manic, a falsetto of fake cheer. I lie Alice down on the changing mat; she is still crying, her face red and furious, her tiny fists clenched. I fumble to unbutton her sleepsuit, my fingers feeling too clumsy for the tiny snaps.

Alice's cries increase, shriller and shriller, making me feel even clumsier and more anxious.

"Come *on*, Alice." I can do this. I need to do this.

I take off the nappy, which is completely dry. Anna must have just changed her, and for some reason this infuriates me. I start to put on a fresh nappy, but the tapes snag and then one tears off. With a growl of frustration, I toss it aside and reach for another one. Alice wees all over the changing mat.

In a different life, this would be funny and cute. I *know* that. I can almost picture it; how I'd laugh and tickle her tummy, how nothing would faze me. But I am not that person. I am not that *mother*, and right now this feels like the most important thing I need to succeed at, and I am not. I am failing.

With Alice screaming all the while, I manage to take off her wet baby gro and sleepsuit. It takes two more nappies before I manage to put one on correctly without tearing the tapes, and now I have the monumental effort of getting her dressed. Alice has stopped screaming, at least, but she almost seems worse, too traumatised to make a sound, her eyes glassy and blank.

When I fit the baby gro over her head, it snags, and she starts up again. Tears smart my eyes and I know I am too rough as I push her tiny arms through the sleeves of her sleepsuit. I didn't think it was possible, but her screaming gets louder and even more shrill.

I am crying now too, unable to keep the tears from streaming down my face as I force her feet into the sleepsuit. I can't do this. I can't do anything. And it occurs to me, for the first time, that Alice might be better off without me.

"Milly?" Anna appears in the doorway, her voice both hesitant and alarmed. "Can I help?"

"Take her." My voice is clogged and I turn away, wiping at my cheeks. Behind me, I hear Anna murmuring to Alice, and when I turn around, she is cuddling her, her cheek pressed against the top of her head, and Alice has stopped crying.

"It will get better," Anna says, but she doesn't sound convinced, and neither am I.

"I'm going to have a nap," I say, even though I've just got up.

"I've made you some coffee," Anna protests. "Why don't you just spend a little time holding her, Milly? The nappy changes and bottle feeds are the tough bits. Just cuddle her..." Matt must have told her about my disastrous attempts at feeding her. And the nappy changes and bottle feeds clearly aren't difficult for her, for Matt, for anyone. Anyone but me.

"You can do it," I say, and push past her.

Alone in my bedroom, I curl up on my side, my legs tucked up to my chest. I feel empty now, of tears, of resolve, of anything. Downstairs, I hear Anna singing "Hush, Little Baby," and a broken sob escapes me.


Over the next two weeks nothing gets better. I try, at least as much as I can; I manage to change Alice once, without her crying, and I give her half a bottle mostly successfully. These feel like huge milestones, but they're not enough, and Anna watching me all the time makes everything worse.

Matt has gone back to work, and Anna is always here. When I changed Alice, she congratulated me, as if I'd scaled a mountain. I felt like a babysitter—a bad one that she has to chivvy along and bolster with fake praise.

And I can't help but notice, at every turn, that it's all so *easy* for Anna. She holds Alice in one arm as she pours cereal with the other, totally relaxed and confident. She asked if I wanted to bathe Alice one morning, after she'd had a dirty nappy, and

I watched in amazed fascination as she did it herself, holding a slippery, wet Alice with one hand as she scooped water with the other. Alice didn't even cry.

It was utterly beyond me, and we both knew it. Everyone knew it—my parents, Matt, even Jack, who stopped by too often for my liking. Everyone was witness to my complete and utter failure as a mother, even if no one ever said as much. I saw it in their eyes, their faces, the pursed lips and sideways glances and telling silences. I saw it and I felt it.

"How are you feeling, then?" the health visitor asks when she comes for her weekly visit. Anna is in the kitchen, making dinner, Alice in the baby swing next to her. "It's nice your friend is helping out," she adds kindly, and I wonder if she senses the disparity, how Anna is more of a mother than I am. Perhaps she is glad of it, because then at least she knows Alice is being taken care of.

"Okay," I answer, because some stubborn part of me refuses to admit I can't get past this. Or perhaps it's just because I *know* I'm a failure, and admitting it won't help. Instead I try, stupidly, pathetically, to hide it from everyone, including this woman.

"The baby blues are fading a bit?" she says with a smile, and I can't believe I might be convincing her. She can't tell that I am holding on by a fraying thread, if that. She can't see the despair in my eyes, the feeling every morning that I, quite literally, cannot get up from bed, because my limbs are too heavy, as if I've been replaced by concrete. How can she not see? She's a *professional.* But neither do I tell her.

"Yes, they really are," I say. "It was a bit rough at first, but I think I'm getting the hang of it now." I almost want to laugh; what I'm saying is so absurd.

The health visitor nods, all sympathy. "The first few weeks are the hardest," she says, and I nod back, as if I agree with her, as if that's all it is. When she leaves, I fight a sudden, desperate urge to claw her back, to tell her the truth. I'm falling apart and I hate myself. But I can't, I *can't*, and so I just wave instead.

"I'm glad you're feeling better," Anna says after she's gone, making no attempt to pretend she didn't eavesdrop on the entire conversation. "Do you want to take Alice out today, in the pram?"

I am annoyed by her suggestion, the way I've been annoyed by every other one, like I have to be managed, and yet I know I do.

"That's a good idea," I make myself say, because to refuse feels wrong, and at least I'll be away from Anna. "I'll take her out to the park."

I shower and dress, and when I come downstairs, Anna has already bundled Alice into her snowsuit. She puts her in the pram as I get my coat, and I playact at being cheerful and insouciant. *This is going to be fun.*

Of course it isn't. Alice starts crying almost the moment we leave, Anna standing at the door and waving me off. I grit my teeth and try to walk briskly, even though my incision still hurts and a walk is not actually a great idea for someone who has had an emergency C-section a few weeks ago.

"Come on, darling," I say, my voice cheerful and overloud. "It's such a beautiful day today." Alice, of course, pays no mind. She continues to scream, looking too small in the pram; I should have wrapped her in a blanket, or put something under her head. She rolls around in the pram's empty expanse like a marble in a jar. And she cries. Oh, how she cries.

I walk to the park as I once dreamed of doing, what feels like a lifetime ago. Alice cries all the while. Once I am there, I sit down on a bench, because I am tired and my incision hurts and I honestly feel I can't go any further, in any respect.

Halfheartedly I rock the pram back and forth as Alice continues to scream, but then I stop doing even that. I wonder if I will ever move again, if Alice will ever stop screaming.

"Miss, miss...are you all right?" I blink an elderly man into focus; he is staring at me in concern. "Shouldn't you be tending to your baby?" I hear more than a hint of censure in his voice, and I don't blame him. I've been sitting here for nearly half an hour, I realise, simply staring into space, as Alice howls.

Without answering him, I get up and start pushing her back home. I feel dazed and distant from myself; I barely hear her cries now, and I stare straight ahead, not taking anything in, like a mindless automaton.

Anna comes out the front door as soon as I've reached the drive. She looks panicked, and I realise how loud and awful Alice's screaming truly is. When I look down, her face is bright red and she has been sick on herself.

Anna scoops her up as I simply stand there. "Oh, Alice, Alice..." She glances at me, concern warring with judgment. I see it perfectly. "What happened?"

"She wouldn't stop crying."

"Milly..."

"Don't worry," I say. "It's going to be all right."

It's clear to me now, in a way it wasn't before: I'm not good for Alice. I'm not the mother she needs. I go upstairs and stay there until Matt comes home. I hear his lowered voice and Anna's too, their worried murmurs. When Matt comes upstairs, I pretend to be asleep.

But that night, when he is sleeping, I creep into Alice's room. She is lying on her back, one arm flung out by her head, palm up. She looks completely at peace. Her breath comes in little snuffly snores. As I stare down at her, I feel it—that rush of love that I've been longing for, that warm, welcome flood of maternal feeling. I would do anything for her. I know I would.

Which is why, the next morning, I tell Matt I am leaving.

# CHAPTER TWENTY

## ANNA

I can't help but laugh as I blow a raspberry on Alice's tummy, and she gives me one of her gummy grins. She had just started smiling in the last few days; she will be five weeks tomorrow. Milly has been gone for nearly two weeks.

I was shocked when Matt told me, his face gaunt, his expression dazed, the morning after Milly's disastrous walk to the park. "She went to her parents'," he said, his voice hollow. "They picked her up this morning. She said she can't stay, it's been too hard. She needs some space."

I held Alice to me, trying to take it in. Milly had just *gone*? As concerned and worried as I felt, I couldn't keep from feeling something else as well—a treacherous relief, even joy. *I had Alice.*

It was wrong of me to feel that, I know. I tried not to feel it, but it kept pushing through, like a seedling through the soil, determined to seek the light. *I had Alice.*

"Perhaps that's for the best, Matt," I said. "For a little while, at least. She can rest and recover..."

"She needs to be with Alice." He sounded fierce.

"And she will be," I assured him. "When she's ready."

I moved in to their house the next day, bringing Winnie with me, because it seemed easier for both Matt and me if I was on site. It was nothing more than a simple matter of efficiency, or so I told myself.

Alice slept in the Moses basket in my room; it made sense for Matt to get his sleep while he could, since he had to go to work. I didn't mind getting up at night to settle her or give her a feed; I soon came to treasure those moments we shared, the two of us, cocooned by the soft night, where I could pretend this was how it really was, how it always would be.

Soon I fell into an easy routine built around Alice. A feed in the morning, and then while she slept I'd shower and dress, and then tidy up around the house. After she woke up, I'd feed her again, and then if the weather was good I'd take her for a walk, either in the pram or the sling that I took out of its packaging, with her nestled warmly against me. Then I would come home and potter around, feed and change Alice, read while she lay on my lap, or walk with her if she started to fuss. I'd make dinner for the three of us, and we'd eat together.

Sometimes Jack came by, and we'd play with her together, marvel at her lying on a mat on the floor, kicking her tiny legs. Although he never said anything, I don't think I was the only one imagining this was all real.

Although I called Milly's parents every day, and sent her photos of Alice by email, it was easy to let her drift to the back of my mind. There wasn't anything I could do for her besides what I was already doing, and Alice was the one who needed me now. So during those long, languorous days, when it was just me and Alice, I gave myself permission not to think of Milly at all.

At the park one day, I sat on a bench, gently rocking the pram, enjoying the wintry sunshine. It was early December, and the Christmas decorations had come out, with lamp posts spangled with lights and wreaths.

"Oh, how adorable!" A mum with a baby in a sling came to stand near Alice, cooing down at her tiny, flower-like face. "How old?"

"Four weeks, but she was a preemie. Her due date isn't for over another week."

"Oh, wow." The mum looked at me in frank admiration. "You look amazing."

"Oh..." The syllable slipped through my lips softly, like a sigh. And then I didn't say anything else. In my defence, how could I? It was hardly the moment to say I wasn't the mother, that her actual mother had abandoned her, at least for the moment. Of course, later I realised I could have just said I was babysitting. But that didn't occur to me at the time.

"And she's doing well? Feeding well?"

"Yes, she is, actually. She's doing amazingly, considering, well, everything." I smiled and rocked the pram.

"She's your first?" I opened my mouth to say I knew not what, unable to perpetuate the fiction quite that much, but the woman steamrollered over me before I could respond. "Do you know any other mums in the area? Because there's a mums and babies group that meets in the community centre on Thursday mornings, from ten to twelve. We have a coffee and a chat, while the babies feed or scream." She smiled, with a little eye roll. "You know how it is."

"Yes, I do..." That much was true.

"So you should come along. Meet some other mums. It can be lonely, can't it?"

"Yes..." I was starting to feel out of my depth. I never should have gone along with being Alice's mum. Then the woman leaned closer to look at her.

"Wow, she's the spitting image of you, isn't she? Those dimples. Adorable. And the same eyes and chin."

"Thanks," I murmured. "And I'll definitely think about the Thursday group."

As soon as she'd left with a cheery wave, I peered into the pram. Did Alice really have my chin? Then I felt a curdling rush of guilt. What had I been thinking, having that conversation? Acting as if I were Alice's mother, if just by silence?

I got up abruptly, pushing Alice out of the park as if a bunch of real mothers were chasing me, accusing me of being the fake I knew I was. Of course I couldn't go to the group, not without explaining. And yet, as I pushed Alice along, I knew I wanted to.

But I didn't go. I knew it would be a mistake. And what if Milly decided *she* would go one day, once she had come home? Because she would come home, I knew that. I had to keep reminding myself: this was a dreamtime, suspended and separate from reality. At some point it was going to end, and I was going to wake up.

Then, one evening when Milly had been gone for over a week, I came downstairs from settling Alice to sleep, and saw Matt slumped in the sitting room, a nearly-empty bottle of beer on the table next to him. I doubted it was his first.

"Maybe this has all been a mistake." He spoke into the stillness, staring into the distance. I hesitated on the bottom step, unsure if he was talking to me.

Over the last week, Matt and I had developed our own separate routines. In the evening, when Alice was settled, he worked or watched telly, and I read or surfed online or slept. We didn't hang out together too much, by silent agreement. He didn't even spend that much time with Alice, content to give her a feed and a cuddle in the evening at most. So I stood there, unsure how to respond.

Then he turned to me. "Anna? Do you think it was a mistake?"

"What was a mistake?" I came into the sitting room and perched on the edge of a chair. Matt took a final slug of his beer.

"This whole thing. The IVF. The sperm and egg donation. All of it."

Each sentence echoed hollowly within me. "What do you mean, Matt?"

He gazed at me blearily, clearly exhausted by everything, overwhelmed. We hadn't really talked about Milly; I didn't know how she was doing, besides the basics—that she had agreed to take antidepressants, that her parents were supporting her. Both good things. "What do you mean, Matt?"

"I don't know." He rubbed a hand over his face. "Just that... it feels like this is retribution somehow. There we were, playing God, making some kind of designer baby, not caring what the cost was, or who would be involved. *Affected.*"

I remained silent, trying to piece together his disjointed thoughts. "You weren't making a designer baby," I finally said. "You just wanted a child."

"But don't you wonder if technology has got the better of us? Who are we, to manipulate life that way? I mean..." He shook his head. "I just wonder, if we hadn't gone down this route in the first place..." He paused, the silence heavy. "Perhaps Milly wasn't meant to be a mother."

The words felt like a slamming door, the sound echoing all around us.

"Sorry," Matt muttered, clearly appalled by what he had just said. "I didn't mean that."

"I know you didn't. Matt, you're tired, and this is all so overwhelming. Give yourself a break."

He covered his face with his hands as he let out a ragged sigh. "You have no idea, Anna. I feel so completely spent..."

"That's understandable."

"But I *can't* be. I need to be stronger than this." He sounded angry, and I knew it was directed at himself.

"How is Milly, Matt? Do you... do you think she'll come home soon?"

"I hope so. I keep asking her."

"And the medication...?"

"I think it's helping a bit. She sleeps a lot, and she doesn't always want to talk. To tell the truth, I can't imagine her back here yet, taking care of Alice. I don't think she can imagine it, either."

"But one day, certainly..." My mind was racing, already wondering how much time I had left. I knew, I absolutely knew, I shouldn't have been thinking that way, but I was.

"Yes, one day," Matt agreed heavily. "But when?"

It was at that moment that an idea slipped into my mind, coiling around my thoughts, like a serpent. *What if.* Two tempting, treacherous words. *What if...?*

I didn't get further than that, not right then. But then, a few days later, I see the same mum at the park again, and we get to chatting. Her name is Rhiannon and we end up having coffee at a nearby café, and she invites me to the mums and babies group again, and this time I say yes. It would be rude not to, and anyway, it isn't happening until after Christmas, which is ages away. And all the time I am thinking, dreaming, planning. *What if.*

A little while later, with Matt at work, Jack comes over and as he dances around with Alice in the kitchen, wintry sunlight streaming through the windows, he stops and looks at me.

"Do you ever stop to think...this could be us?"

My heart turns right over, but I do my best to keep my expression neutral. "Sometimes."

"This *is* us." He holds Alice out like exhibit A before cuddling her close to his chest. *He would be a good father.* The thought slips through me like quicksilver. "Right now, I mean." He pauses, one hand resting lightly on top of Alice's downy head. "What if Milly doesn't get better?"

The words fall into the stillness and stay there. I glance down at the homemade soup I'm stirring, swirls of carrot and coriander. The moment feels suspended, crystalline in its detail—the soup, the sunshine, Jack's hand resting on Alice's head. I want it all.

"Even if she does..." I say softly. The words are forbidden and thrilling. *Even if she does...*I glance up at Jack and we stare at each other for a long moment.

"Anna," he finally whispers. "What are you saying?"

"Look at us, Jack. Look at Alice." I keep my voice calm and reasonable, even though I am fizzing inside. I wasn't going to suggest this now, but the moment feels right, even providential. "She's our daughter. In absolutely every way, she's our daughter."

Jack doesn't say anything for a moment, and I turn back to the soup, giving him a few moments to absorb what I'm saying.

"It doesn't change anything," he says at last.

"Why not? Why shouldn't it? Alice is *ours*. You've felt it from the beginning, and so have I. And we feel it even more so now, when we're the ones taking care of her, loving her." My voice throbs with intensity. "Jack, why shouldn't we?"

"Why shouldn't we *what*?"

I take a deep breath. "Apply for custody."

"Apply? We're not talking about a passport, Anna."

"I know that." My voice sharpens and I strive to moderate it. "Don't you think I've thought this through, Jack? I've talked to a lawyer—"

*"What?"* He stares at me in open-mouthed shock, and I quickly backtrack.

"Only on the phone. Only to see." I rang her yesterday, my heart thudding so hard it hurt, my voice a papery whisper as I explained the situation, asked the question. *Could I...*

Jack puts Alice back in her little bouncy seat, where she coos contentedly. "What did they say?" he asks, and the fact that he wants to know encourages me as the actual phone call did not.

"She said it would be difficult." In fact, the lawyer specialising in fertility issues said it would be incredibly messy and painful for everyone involved. "But possible. Potentially."

"How? Donors have no parental rights. Matt told me. Reassured me, in case I was worried."

"The situation is different, because we're together, and we're taking care of Alice as it is."

"I'm not taking care of her, Anna. I'm stopping by every couple of days."

"Still."

A moment passes, and then another. Jack stares at me. "Anna..."

I'm losing him. I can feel it, even though he hasn't moved or said anything more, and I can't stand the thought. "Look," I cut across him, "either Milly is very ill, and she cannot take care of Alice for a long time, or she's *not* ill, and she doesn't care enough about Alice to come home. It doesn't surprise me, really," I add abruptly. "Milly was adopted, as you probably know, and her parents are fantastic. They practically subbed in for my parents since I was about twelve. But Milly's always had this *thing*, like because she's adopted, they're not her real parents or something, even though she never got to know her birth mother."

"What are you saying?"

"Just that genetics count. They matter. And Milly knows that most of all."

"Still," Jack says, but it feels as if the fight has gone out of him.

"We don't have to do anything right now," I reassure him. "Think about it for a while."

Jack leaves a short while later, and I clutch Alice, pacing the house, buzzing with nervous energy. Do I feel guilty for what I suggested? Am I betraying Milly? I think about it, as carefully as I can, and I decide that I am not. This is the best solution; it has to be. And so I tell myself that Jack will come around, the lawyer will come around, maybe Matt and Milly will, as well. It might just be a matter of time, because in my own head, it makes so much sense.

That evening, after I've put Alice to bed, I come downstairs, thinking I might talk to Matt, feel him out just a little. Perhaps I'll ask if I can bring Alice back to my flat for a bit. After all,

I should return to my own life, and yet Alice still needs me. It seems like a sensible first step.

But before I can say anything about that, Matt speaks first. "Anna, I've got some good news. I wanted to make sure it was happening before I said anything, but now it definitely is." He smiles at me, his expression weary yet full of joy. "Milly's coming home tomorrow."

For a few seconds, I can't make sense of the words. I simply stare, while Matt's smile fades into a frown.

"Anna...?"

"Sorry," I say, although I can barely think straight enough to say anything sensible. "Sorry..." I sink into a chair, my mind spinning. Beneath the dazed shock, I realise I am angry. "It would have been nice to have some warning, Matt..."

Matt's forehead wrinkles in confusion. "Warning...?"

Staring at him, I realise how clueless he is. He doesn't get it at *all*. He probably thinks this is a relief for me, because now I can finally go back to my flat, my life. He has no inkling about what I've been feeling, thinking. *Planning*.

"I mean, it would have been nice to know, so I could change the sheets, tidy up..."

"Don't worry about that, Anna. You've done so much already. I can manage."

"Yes, but... can Milly cope? I mean, is she ready to...?" I'm not sure how to phrase what I'm trying to say sensitively, when what I really want to do is scream, *how could you do this to me? How could you just expect me to hand over my baby?*

"I'm taking the next week off, to help ease us back into the routine. And her mother is going to come by every afternoon for a couple of hours, so I think it will be all right."

His dismissal feels worse than a slap. I'm not needed anymore; I'm not wanted. He's not even thinking about me, about how I might feel. He never has... *just like Milly.*

I nod slowly, trying not to show my hurt, as determination crystallises inside of me. I don't care what Matt said. There's no way I'm walking away from this—from Alice—without a fight.

# CHAPTER TWENTY-ONE

## MILLY

For the first few days after I arrive at my parents' house, they don't ask me any questions. They let me sleep, or simply sit and stare. They tiptoe around me as if I'm a ticking time bomb, when in fact I feel as if the pin has already been pulled out of the grenade. I've already exploded. I've left my child.

As the days pass, the fleeting feeling that I was doing the right thing trickles away and in its place I feel a deep and abiding guilt. *How* could I have left her? How could I have not?

When I told Matt that I was going to my parents' for a while, he looked shocked but also the tiniest bit relieved, which confirmed to me that I was doing the right thing. No one wanted to be around me, least of all my own child. *If* she even was my own child. More and more I wondered—and doubted.

Sitting in my parents' house, with basically nothing to do, I had plenty of time to think, and none of it was good. I questioned everything—whether I should have ever agreed to Anna donating, whether I deserved to be a mother. Whether there was still hope for me—and Alice.

When Matt came to visit after a few days, he brought pictures of Alice and looked at me with puppy's eyes, begging me to see a doctor.

"You could at least try some medication. Just *try*, Milly, for Alice's sake as well as yours. If you react badly to it, or you don't like it, or whatever, you can stop."

"I'll think about it," I said. It felt selfish, not to try antidepressants when they might have been the magic fix, but the truth was, I was scared. What if they *didn't* work? What then?

And meanwhile Alice was doing fine without me; I could see it from the photos. Already, in just a week, she looked bigger, chubbier. She wasn't missing me; she didn't feel my absence the way I felt hers, like a gaping hole in the middle of my chest, but one I didn't know how to deal with.

After a week at home, my mother finally broaches the subject. I am lying in my old child's bed, feeling as if there is a heavy weight pressing down on my chest when she comes to stand in the doorway. She is on a break from the chemo, and although she still looks wan and frail, there is a bit more energy to her step.

"Milly." Her voice is gentle as she sits on the edge of the bed. "Darling, we want to help you. What can we do to help you get back home and be the mother I know you want to be to your darling Alice?"

I feel too weary even to form the words. "There's nothing, Mum."

Mum is silent for a few moments, while I simply lie there. "I don't think I've ever told you," she finally says, "how difficult it was, when we first brought you home." I move my head a bit to look at her; her lips are pursed, her gaze distant. "You cried nonstop for days. You'd been with a very kind foster mother for the last two months, and I think you missed her."

"I never knew that." The details of my adoption were simply relegated to before and after. Sad and then happy.

"Yes, well." My mum tries to smile. "I think I wanted to put a positive spin on everything, because I didn't regret it for a second. You were so wanted, Milly, just as Alice is wanted. But it was hard for a while. It was bloody hard."

I appreciate my mum's empathy, but this isn't *bloody hard*. It's impossible. I can't explain to her how powerless I feel, as if I'm sinking into quicksand and no one even notices. They just want me to put my chin up and soldier on, and I can't. I *can't*.

"Depression is quite normal at a time like this," my mother continues. "And these days there's no shame in it."

"It's not just that I'm depressed," I say quietly, although I'm not sure what it is. Maybe antidepressants would be the magic fix I need, who knows? I'm still afraid to take that risk.

"What is it then, Milly?" Mum sounds so loving, so concerned. She wants to know.

I take a deep breath. "It's me, Mum, and Alice. She's...she's not mine." Saying it feels terrible but also freeing. *She's not mine.*

"Milly, I know it feels strange right now—"

"No, I mean it. She's not my biological child. I was diagnosed with premature menopause almost a year ago, and was told I would never be able to have my own baby. Alice came from donated egg and sperm—Anna's and Matt's brother, Jack's." This is another relief, to admit the truth. To lay down the burden I've been carrying for so long, without realising that's what it was.

Mum looks stunned, her mouth hanging open, her eyes wide. "Anna?" she finally says faintly.

"Yes. Anna."

"Why didn't you tell me any of this?"

I sigh heavily. "Because I didn't want you knowing. I didn't want it to become this *thing*."

"A thing?" Mum still looks dazed as she shakes her head slowly, not understanding.

And so I say it. I say what I've never let myself say before. "Yes, a *thing*. A thing you always have to mention, always have to make as the addendum to your story. Like my adoption."

My mum doesn't move, but it feels as if she's staggered. Slowly, she presses one hand to her cheek. "Is that how you've felt about being adopted?"

"Yes." I hate hurting her, but I know this needs to be said. "I don't mean it as a criticism or insult, honestly I don't, but it was always mentioned. Always trotted out. 'This is our daughter, Milly. She's adopted.' Why couldn't I just be your daughter, full stop?" As I say the words my voice breaks and the tears come. They slip down my cheeks silently as my mother stares at me in horror.

"Oh, Milly. *Milly.*" She is crying too, the tears falling freely. "I never knew you felt this way. I never thought for a moment..." She dashes the tears from her cheeks. "As a parent, you try so hard to do right by your child, no matter what it takes, but sometimes it feels impossible to know what the right thing *is*." She draws a ragged breath. "If we mentioned your adoption so much, it was because we thought it would help you remember how precious you were to us. How loved. We never meant it to accomplish the opposite."

"I know," I say, but I wonder if I did, really. Is this the root of my insecurity both then and now? Because I wasn't related by blood, I felt somehow less—first as a child and now as a mother.

"We'd read stories," Mum continues, "about children who found out they were adopted when they were older, and how it sent them off the rails. We didn't want that for you. We wanted to be open, but perhaps, in our fear, we were too open." She leans forward to clasp my hands. "Darling, darling Milly, you have always felt like you were mine. I'm so, so sorry if you felt that you weren't, even for a second. So very sorry." Tears leak out of my eyes and I find I can't speak. "And Alice is yours, as well," she continues, squeezing my hands. "Even if you doubt it. Even if right now you feel like the worst, most incompetent mother in the world." She tries to smile through her tears. "That's how I felt, at first. But you're not, Milly. You're Alice's mummy, and she needs you. She needs you to get better, whatever it takes. She needs you with her, loving her."

With my hands held tightly by my mother's, I nod slowly. I start to accept, just barely, that maybe what she says is true.

The next day I make an appointment with my GP, and after describing my symptoms in all their honest, awful detail, I am both offered counselling and prescribed antidepressants. I am warned that it can be several weeks before they have any effect, and that feels endless.

But amazingly, just a few days later, I feel that towering black cloud start to lift, just a little. Perhaps it's the placebo effect, or perhaps I'm just lucky. But for the first time in a month, I feel as if I can glimpse the horizon.

When Matt visits, I tell him my progress and see the hope light his eyes. "Milly, that's fantastic news. I'm so glad." He squeezes my hand. "Do you... do you think you'll be able to come home soon?"

It's been almost two weeks, far too long already to have been away from my child. The guilt is still there, that I've left her so long. Perhaps it always will be. "I'm going to try," I tell him, and three days later, I do.

Matt takes the day off work to pick me up and drive me back home, to Alice. I am nearly shaking with both terror and longing at seeing her again. What if I can't do it? What if I really am a failure, the truth that no magic pill can hide? *What if she loves Anna more than me?*

I don't share those fears with anyone; I try to keep them from myself. I remind myself that Alice is my daughter, that I carried her in my body, that she will know me as her mother. But I am so afraid she won't.

I am tensed and ready to see her, but when we go inside the house, it feels empty. It also smells strange—Anna must use a different cleaning spray or laundry detergent or something. It looks different, as well, and I notice a dozen little things that have changed, each one a pinprick to my soul.

Anna has moved a lamp from one side of the sofa to the other, and there are notices pinned on the fridge with a magnet—a date for Alice's two-month immunisations, an invitation to a mums and babies coffee morning. I take it all in with one painful glance; I feel as if I've walked into someone else's life, and then I realise that, in a way, I have.

"Perhaps they're upstairs…" Matt murmurs, and he jogs up the stairs in search of both Anna and Alice.

I walk slowly into the sitting room, taking in more details. A new throw pillow, in a shade of purple I never would have chosen. A litter box in the kitchen—of course, she must have brought Winnie here, even though I'm slightly allergic to cats. Is that part of the smell? Everything feels so foreign, and I wasn't expecting it.

Winnie peers out from underneath the table and glares at me balefully before stalking off.

"They're not upstairs," Matt says, frowning, as he comes into the kitchen. We see the note on the kitchen table at the same time.

*Dear Matt, I thought I'd take Alice out for a bit, so you and Milly can settle in without any pressure. See you soon. Anna.*

That note rankles me. Perhaps it's the way it's addressed only to Matt. Maybe it's the idea that it will somehow create pressure to have Alice here with me, even though I know Anna is right and it will. Still, it doesn't seem like her decision to make, and yet clearly she thought it was. And once again I am forced to face the uncomfortable, unpalatable truth, that Anna has made a lot of decisions over the last two and a half weeks. She's had to, and we've had to let her.

"I could ring her, ask her to come back," Matt says after a moment. "Unless you want to wait? Have a cuppa?"

"Fine. Let's do that." *She'll be home soon*, I tell myself. *She'll be home soon, and then I'll have Alice.*

Half an hour goes by, and there is no word from Anna. Matt calls her, but she's not answering her phone. Then, as we are sipping lukewarm tea in silence in the sitting room, Jack stops by.

"Milly." He gives me a big hug before kissing my cheek. "I'm so glad you're back home. It's great to see you. You look well. Really well." He nods, and keeps nodding, and I realise I can expect a thousand awkward conversations like this.

"Thank you, Jack."

"Where's Alice? And Anna?" He looks around as if expecting them to pop out from behind the sofa and yell "surprise."

"Anna took Alice for a walk, I think," Matt says, "but it's been nearly an hour now. I think they should be home soon, especially considering how cold it is."

"She took Alice?" Something in Jack's tone makes us both look at him, expectant and wary.

"Just for a walk…" Matt begins, and then stops at Jack's stricken expression. "What is it? What's wrong?"

"Nothing, really. At least I don't think…" He trails off and I put my mug down, my hands curling into fists as I brace myself for whatever Jack is going to say, because clearly it is not nothing.

"Jack." Matt's voice is strident. "If there's something you know, something that's going on, tell us, please."

"I don't know anything," Jack protests. "It's just…" He lets out a ragged sigh. "Anna was talking to me a few days ago, and it was all a bit… much."

"What do you mean, *much*?"

"I don't know how seriously she meant it—"

"Meant what?" Matt explodes. "Can you please tell me what the hell is going on here?"

"Anna was talking to me about…" Still he hesitates. "About applying for custody of Alice."

His words feel as if they are hurled into the room like a grenade. We are now just waiting for the explosion. Matt is silent, stunned, clearly having absolutely no inkling of this, and yet I realise I am not surprised. I've been fearing it, bracing myself for it, since I first found out I was pregnant. Perhaps even since Anna first offered to donate. And while I've tried to hide the truth from myself, I accept now how complicated our arrangement was, how conflicted our feelings. How all of it eventually had to lead to this.

"Why would she do that?" Matt asks, sounding so bewildered I almost want to laugh.

"Because she feels Alice is her baby," I say. It is so obvious to me. "Because Alice is her baby biologically, and she's been taking care of her basically since she was born." I wrap my arms around myself. *Because I failed as a mother.* I don't want to go down that dark road again, but I can't keep myself from it. *Is this what I really deserve?*

"She's been helping us out," Matt protests. He looks winded, as if he's been struck and is reeling from the blow. "That's all. Just helping us out."

"But it wasn't just that to Anna," I say quietly.

Jack looks at both of us. "Honestly, I don't think she was thinking straight. I don't think she really meant it—"

"What exactly did she tell you?" Matt interjects.

"She spoke to a lawyer, to see if she had a case. She wanted us..." He stops.

"A lawyer." Now *that* surprises me. Anna, passive, drifting Anna, actually had a plan. She'd thought it out; this clearly isn't merely some passing fancy, a wistful *what if.* Maybe this is what I deserve, and maybe it is what I am going to get.

"I don't believe this," Matt says in a voice that tells me he does. He paces the room, angry and caged, raking both hands through his hair. "Why didn't you tell me, Jack?"

"I thought it was a passing thing..."

Matt shook his head. "How could she *do* this to us?"

"She hasn't actually done anything," Jack points out, looking as if he regrets telling us everything he has. "She just had an initial conversation, that's all, just to *see*. Really, Matt..."

"To see what? How she can steal our baby?" Matt rages. "And now she's out somewhere with our daughter, and we don't even know where or when she's coming back. Should I call the police?"

"Matt, don't," I say quietly. That's the last thing we need right now.

"Milly, did you hear what Jack said?" For once Matt is too upset to treat me with his post-baby kid gloves. It actually feels good, not to be tiptoed around. For the last few weeks *I've* been the grenade. At least now it's something else.

"Yes, I heard what he said." I take a deep breath. "But Anna hasn't kidnapped Alice, and she probably didn't even want us to know about the consultation."

"Of course she didn't—"

"Like Jack said, it might have been a whim or a passing thought." Except I don't really believe that. Panic is clawing inside me, fighting with a leaden certainty that this is what I deserve. "Let's wait till she comes back, and ask her ourselves."

"Damn right I will," Matt growls.

As it turns out, we don't have long to wait. Just ten minutes later, the front door opens and Anna comes in, Alice bundled in a sling on her chest. She stops, taking us all in; Matt has been pacing the room, but he stops to glare at her, his arms folded.

Carefully, she closes the door behind her, one hand cradling Alice's head, an unthinkingly possessive gesture. "Milly. Welcome home." And somehow that hurts, because this is not her home. It is mine. Still, I take a breath. Smile.

"Thank you, Anna."

She glances at Matt. "Is everything okay?"

"No, it most certainly is not," Matt bursts out, unable to keep himself from it for another second. "What the hell were you thinking, Anna, consulting a lawyer?"

Anna stiffens, then shoots Jack a hurt, accusing look. "Jack told you, I suppose?"

"Yes, he certainly did."

"Take off the sling." The words come out of me suddenly, as I stare Anna down. "Take off that sling. I want to hold my baby."

Anna's hands tense on Alice and she hesitates. In that endless pause, I see all I need to know. She doesn't want to give Alice to me—not now, and not ever. And part of me doesn't even blame her.

"I'm the only mother she's ever known." Her sea-green gaze burrows into mine. "For three weeks, I've given her everything. *Everything*. She came from my body as much as yours. Surely you can see that, Milly. That, in this situation, I have some rights."

"How dare—" Matt begins, but I hold up my hand to stop him. This is between Anna and me.

"We owe you a great debt, Anna," I say steadily, "but I was *ill*. I wasn't able to take care of Alice the way I wanted to."

"And I was. And both of you just expected me to—the same way you expected me to donate, to be there when you miscarried, to help you when you were on bedrest, to see you through labour." Her voice throbs with intensity. "And you never even *considered* what the cost was to me, behind a half-hearted 'if it's too much, Anna.' You never once thought about what I might feel or want. I've done everything I've ever been asked for you, and more. Much more. And you've always expected it, because *once* you were so kind to me." I blink, sensing something far deeper here than I ever realised, the dark foundation of our friendship that I was afraid to examine too closely. "But I don't need to pay that debt back any longer, Milly. I don't need to remember how you once rescued me, because I've rescued you over and over again. I want to stop keeping count, tit for tat, because that's how you've always operated."

"I didn't..." I begin feebly, but Anna cuts across me.

"You can't just dismiss me. I won't let you. Alice is part of me. She knows me. She loves me. And whether you were ill or not, that counts for something. It counts for a lot." No one says anything and she turns to Jack. "Jack, tell me you understand what I'm saying."

Jack looks stricken as he shakes his head. "I can't support you in this, Anna. I'm sorry. I know you've been through a lot with—with what happened before—"

"What happened before?" Matt demands and Jack shakes his head.

"I meant a long time ago, when Anna was eighteen, nothing to do with now..."

*Eighteen?* "What happened back then?" I ask Anna.

She purses her lips and lifts her chin, her eyes flashing. "I had a termination. But that doesn't really have anything to do with this."

Doesn't it? I am shocked by this news, stunned by how it changes nothing—and yet everything.

"So you want to make up for the baby you killed by taking ours?" Matt says with a sneer, the words so cruel they seem to steal the air from the room.

"*Matt*," I protest. "That's *not* fair." But what if it's the truth? I feel ashamed for thinking it, and yet...

"Milly, she's trying to take Alice from us!"

And still I can't blame her, as much as I want to. "There's no need to be so cruel," I say quietly.

Anna turns to Matt, her gaze fierce and glittering. "And what about you, Matt? What about all the things you said, about how maybe you and Milly shouldn't have gone down this route? Playing God?"

"I didn't mean for you—"

"What about what you said, about how maybe Milly shouldn't have been a mother?"

I gape with shock, nearly stagger. "What..." I can barely get the word out. I turn to Matt, who is looking furious as well as guilty. *Guilty.* Because he did think that. He said it to Anna.

"Give me my daughter," Matt says, his voice low and deadly. "Give her to me right now, and then get out of this house."

I can hardly believe it's come to this, that the four of us, four friends in this great adventure together, are now facing off as if we're the worst of enemies. Anna stares at Matt, and then at me, and finally at Jack.

The seconds tick by and then at last she starts to unwind the sling, her fingers trembling as she fumbles with the ties. Her face is a mask, but behind it I sense a wild grief. This isn't fair to Anna. I know that. But neither has she been fair to us.

Gently, so gently, she lifts Alice out. My daughter lets out a breathy sigh; she has slept through everything. Anna holds Alice for a moment, touching one finger to her cheek.

"Anna," Matt says warningly, and I want to tell him to be quiet, that we need to give her this much. At the same time, I want to snatch Alice from Anna's arms.

Then Anna finally hands Alice over, not to Matt, but to me. She looks me straight in the eye as she does it, and I see the storm of grief in her face although her expression is composed.

I take Alice, bringing her to my body as I gaze down at her sleeping face. *My daughter.* The words don't completely make sense to me yet, even though I feel them desperately, for the very first time.

"Now," Matt says in a cold, controlled voice, "you can go upstairs and pack your things, and then you can get out."

Anna doesn't reply as she walks past us with her head held high.

No one speaks as she moves around upstairs, packing her things. Matt is still fuming, and Jack looks lost. I gaze down at Alice, touching her cheek, her finger, her downy blonde curls. She's changed so much from the scrawny newborn I left three weeks ago. I'm terrified to hold her, but I don't feel that awful sense of displacement and revulsion that I felt before. She belongs in my arms now, and despite Anna, despite everything, that is the sweetest relief.

The stairs creak and Anna comes back downstairs with a suitcase in one hand, another bag over her shoulder. "I'll put these in my car and then I'll get Winnie," she says, and nobody answers.

She comes back in for the cat and the litter box, and still we stay silent. Part of me wants to scream, to cry, to say sorry, *anything*. I can't believe that as I gain my daughter, I am losing my best friend. But I don't say anything. No one does.

Anna pauses at the door, one hand on the knob. She looks at all of us, her chin tilted, her eyes glittering with either tears or anger. I wait—for what? For something about this to make sense? For us all to be able to take a step back, mend these broken bridges and to move on, together?

But the moment passes, and I feel it is gone forever. With a little nod of farewell, Anna opens the door and goes outside. As it clicks shut behind her, Matt releases a long, low breath and I look down at my daughter. Alice stirs, perhaps startled by the sound of the door closing, and then my daughter opens her eyes, blinking sleepily, before smiling at me.

# PART TWO

PART TWO

# CHAPTER TWENTY-TWO

## ANNA

*Four years later*

I see a flash of golden hair across the park, and I stop running. I double over to catch my breath, my hands on my knees, my gaze scanning the path. *Could it be...?*

But then the little girl comes into view, and I see that she's too old. Seven or eight, at least. It's not Alice.

Four years on and I can't stop looking for her. I can't stop grieving, even though I've done my best to move on with my life. And I have. In so many ways, I have.

After I walked out of Matt and Milly's house, I paced the streets for hours, oblivious to the freezing cold, my mind buzzing, buzzing, looking for solutions. I rang the lawyer again, who basically told me to stop thinking about a custody case, now that Milly was home. I heard pity in her voice, and it felt like a slap. Was it really that impossible? Why did it all feel so unfair?

Then, that evening, Jack came by. He looked both guilty and accusing, as if he couldn't decide who to blame.

"I just wanted to see if you were okay," he said, standing in my hallway; I hadn't invited him in any farther. "After everything that happened..."

"You think I'd be fine by now?" I retorted with a harsh laugh. "A bit rough there this afternoon, but it's all okay now? How *could* you, Jack? How could you betray me in that way? What I said to you...and what about what you said to me? 'This is us,'" I mimicked savagely. "What about that?"

He hung his head like a little boy. "I'm sorry, Anna..."

"You had no right." My voice vibrated with pain. "No right at all, to barge in and tell Milly and Matt what I was considering—what *we* were considering, but you didn't mention that, either, did you?"

"Anna, I was never considering it."

His words made me reel back. "Yes, you were. A little—"

"No." Firm now, with a shake of his head. "No, I wasn't. It was...it was fun to pretend, for a bit, that we were...a family, of sorts. I admit that."

"Fun to *pretend*?" I couldn't believe he was eviscerating our dream so completely, even as I was unsurprised. All along, Jack had been playacting at a real relationship. It was why we had never got more serious, why I'd had to push him into making some sort of declaration in the first place. I'd always known, deep down, that we weren't going to last, but it still hurt to hear him say it so plainly.

"I don't mean it unkindly, but I would never have...I would never have fought for Alice, Anna. I should have made that more clear when you suggested it to me. I'm sorry."

He never would have fought for Alice, and he never would have fought for me. "Yes, perhaps you should have," I managed to get out. "And perhaps you should not have told Milly and Matt about it all, when there was no *need*."

"You weren't there—you were missing, and I panicked—"

"*Missing?* I left them a note. I'd gone out to give them a bit of time to settle, readjust." I shook my head, incredulous. "What, you thought I'd *kidnapped* Alice?"

Jack looked shamefaced as he met my gaze. "It crossed my mind."

And, I didn't admit to him then, it had crossed my mind as well. I'd stayed out so long because I hadn't wanted to go back and face them. I'd even fantasised about getting in my car with Alice and just driving, never coming back. I wasn't so gripped by my obsession to have actually done it, but yes, I did think about it. "If I'd talked to them in my own way, on my own terms," I told Jack as steadily as I could, "things might have been different."

Now he was the one to look incredulous. "You think they would have given Alice to you, just like that?"

"No, not *just like that*. And perhaps I wouldn't have talked to them at all. Perhaps I would have realised there was no point, but you didn't even give me that chance, you blew it all up into a huge storm when it didn't have to be, and it's cost me *everything*." My voice choked as I swung away from him.

"I thought I was doing the right thing..."

"For whom?" I shook my head. "For Matt and Milly, obviously, because I'm no one to you." And, in the end, I'd been no one to them, as well. That hurt almost as much as losing Alice. All it took for me to disappear from their lives was one firm push. "Go away, Jack," I said. "There's nothing you can say that will make me feel better, and you're only here to make *yourself* feel better, anyway. So go *away*."

Jack hesitated, and I saw so clearly in his eyes the battle between doing what I asked—what *he* wanted—and trying to be the good guy. "Anna, look, I don't like leaving you on your own..."

"Trust me, I'd much rather be on my own than with you."

"What about us?" He wasn't asking because he wanted to stay together, I could tell that much. He was asking because he wanted to be in the clear.

"We're over, Jack," I said tiredly. "You know that as well as I do."

As he closed the door behind him, I knew I'd never see him again, and I haven't. Just as I haven't seen Matt or Milly or Alice. *Alice.*

The girl has walked on with her parents; her hand is clasped by her mother's and they are swinging arms and smiling, just another happy family scene, one of dozens I see every day. They don't hurt me as much as they used to.

For several months after losing Alice, I was a mess. I lay in bed and stared into space as my savings trickled away, my own version of postpartum depression, and it hurt so much. Part of me was waiting for Milly to call, to apologise, but she never did. And I didn't call her; I felt I couldn't, with the way things had ended. I didn't even want to, because I was so angry.

I clung to the feeling that I had been wronged, again and again, but at some point, I forced myself to see what part I'd had to play in it all, and I knew I wasn't entirely innocent. I had taken advantage of the situation, of Milly, almost without realising it. Looking back, I've asked myself many times if I would have gone through it—the lawyer, the custody case—and I don't think I would have. At least, that's what I tell myself now.

Eventually, at the start of spring, I roused myself to action. I still felt as if I were sleepwalking, but I managed to book myself on a PR and development course, and I started sending my CV out again. I decided I would no longer work in HR; I wanted to do something meaningful with my life. Something that mattered, at least to me.

I still looked for Alice everywhere, just as I did now. In the park, the supermarket, the street. Passing cars, even when I'm in other cities, wondering if they've moved or are on holiday. I feel certain that at some point I'll catch a glimpse of her. That's all I want, just one glimpse.

About six months after it all fell apart, I walked by their house. Just once, feeling guilty and stalkerish for doing it, but I couldn't resist. It was summer, early evening, the world full of syrupy sunlight and birdsong. I stood on the pavement opposite their house, half-hidden by a tree, and waited for nearly an hour for that precious glimpse. It never came. The curtains were drawn, everything tucked up for the night. I saw a silhouette against the curtain; it looked like Matt, but that was all.

I finally left, sickened by myself and what I'd become. I told myself I wasn't going to obsess anymore, and I booked myself in for some counselling, which helped. Then, in the autumn, I landed a job in marketing and development with Speak Now, a local charity that advocates for victims of sexual harassment and assault. I finally felt as if I were moving on.

Of course, there have been blips and backslides over the years—evenings spent with a glass of wine, scouring social media for something of Milly and Matt, and of course Alice, but they deleted their accounts, erased their online presence. There have been Saturdays when I don't feel like getting up, when I wonder if I'll always be alone. There have been reckless blind dates that ended up with me regretting more than I wanted to, and one ill-advised relationship with a man I met in the ready-meal aisle of Waitrose that lumbered on for several uninspiring months.

Four years on, I am still looking for Alice, but this time, after a few seconds, I straighten and walk on.

Saturdays used to be quiet days for me, but a few years ago I decided I needed to get out more, and after being on a waiting list for several months, I managed to bag a quarter plot of an allotment near my flat. I'd never gardened before, and it felt like another world, on the other side of the green palisading, everything so neatly divided into strips marked by raised vegetable beds and chicken coops and cosy sheds storing chairs and kettles, as well as seeds and tools.

My plot was tiny, and I treated each precious inch of fertile soil with care, planting several rows of vegetables, as well as flowers for their simple beauty, and a dwarf apple tree which has yet to produce a single piece of fruit. Still, I love it all—somehow it soothes me, fingers in crumbling soil, nails rimed with dirt, knees aching. To plant something and watch it grow... I think I've needed that in my life.

On this damp grey morning in early April, the allotment is empty; the keen gardeners have already tilled their plots and are waiting to plant, while the less keen haven't bothered yet and clearly don't plan to until the weather improves.

I don't mind being alone, though, because it's a peaceful oasis in the midst of the city, and I need to clear away winter's debris from my little bit of land.

About an hour in, I hear the clang of the gate and I see a man come through, wheeling a bike, a rucksack slung over one shoulder. I've seen him before, and I even have a nickname for him, although I've never talked to him. I call him Mr. Green, because he has one of the best plots in the whole allotment, a narrow strip of regimental order, with a pristine shed at the back. Once, I peeked in when he was working, the door left open, and saw the labelled tins of seeds, the neatly arrayed tools, and was amazed at how orderly everything was. How did he have the time? Did he have a *job*?

Now he gives me a brief smile before heading for his shed, and I turn back to the wet dead leaves I'm clearing away. We're the only two there and we work in silent solidarity for another hour before the clouds gather and the first raindrops spatter down like bullets. I straighten, cursing myself for not having brought my car. I don't fancy a walk back in this downpour.

"Hey."

I turn, surprised Mr. Green is calling me. He's never said a word to me before.

"Care for a cuppa while we wait out this downpour?" He nods towards the shed.

I hesitate, taken aback by the offer, and then shrug my assent with a smile. "Sure, thanks." I lope over, and we both step into the shed, which is just as neat, if not neater, than I remember.

It's cosy too, with a folding chair and a wooden packing crate turned on its side to act as a table.

"I'm Will, by the way," he says as he puts a kettle on a little propane stove perched on a workbench. "Will Ford."

"Anna Thompson."

We smile at each other, a bit inanely, and then he reaches for a battered tin of tea. "You haven't been here that long, have you?"

"About a year, but I didn't come over the winter." My smile turns self-conscious. "I'm not that committed."

"Nor am I."

"No?" I nod towards the neat shelves. "You look like someone who has invested quite a bit in this."

"Ah, but looks can be deceiving." The kettle starts to whistle and he pours hot water into two tin mugs. "This allotment belonged to my uncle. I took it over when he fell ill. I'm just keeping it going until he can get back to it."

"That's kind of you."

He shrugs. "He did a lot for me." There seems to be a world of memory in that statement, and I don't feel I can press, so I just nod and accept the mug of tea he gives me.

"Thanks for this."

He gestures for me to take the chair while he leans against the workbench. It's awkward at first, but we get into the flow of chatting, and as the rain drums on the shed's tin roof, I learn that he works in consulting, and I tell him about my job at Speak Now. He's unmarried, childless, in his early forties, and he's been working his uncle's allotment for two years.

"He has lung cancer," he tells me. "I don't think anyone expected him to last this long, but he keeps on confounding the doctors. I hope he'll be strong enough to come back here soon."

I think suddenly of Claire, Milly's mother, whom I was once so close to. We completely lost touch after everything blew up; she never reached out to me, just as I never reached out to her.

Now I wonder if she is still alive. It's been five years since her cancer diagnosis.

"Sorry, was it something I said?" Will asks, half-joking, and I realise I must have a strange look on my face.

"Sorry, I was thinking of something else."

"Something sad?"

"A bit. A family friend I've lost touch with. She had cancer, and now I don't even know if she's alive or not." Saying it out loud makes me feel sadder. I'd thought about getting in touch with Milly's parents over the years, but I'd always stopped myself, mostly out of fear. What if she refused to talk to me? She would have only heard Milly's side of the story, and I don't think I could have borne her rejection along with everything else.

"That's tough. Could you get back in touch?"

I shake my head even as I wonder. Has enough time passed? Or too much? "I don't think so," I tell Will. "Not anymore."

"Sometimes life's like that," he agrees, and again I have the feeling that he is referencing something else, something personal. Perhaps his life isn't straightforward, just as mine isn't. Maybe no one's is.

The rain has lessened, and sunlight is peeking out from behind shreds of grey cloud. "Thanks for the tea," I say as I stand up and hand him the empty mug. "I'd return the favour, but I don't have a shed or even a kettle."

"No worries, you're welcome to pop in here anytime."

"Thanks." I leave the shed feeling encouraged that I have a new friend. Although I've made more of an effort in the last few years to improve my social life, I still have only a small circle of friends and acquaintances, and no one has replaced Milly in terms of intimacy or affection—but I've come to wonder if that is no bad thing.

*Milly.* She drifts through my mind, as she so often does, as I walk home. I know nothing about her life now, nothing at all—

whether she's recovered, well, or even if she is still with Matt. Are they still living in Redland? Has she gone back to work? And what about Alice?

*Alice.* I cannot imagine her, even though I've tried to. I picture a phantom child, a mini-me with blonde ringlets and green eyes. *Dimples.* But what is she like? Is she quiet or rambunctious, clever or dreamy or shy?

As I turn the corner onto my road, I tell myself to stop wondering. It always hurts, even now, to probe those old wounds, the gaping holes they left in my life. Deliberately I remind myself of all the good things I have—a job I love, supportive friends at work, a garden, and now a new friend. Milly and Alice have no place in my life anymore, I tell myself, as I so often do. Not even in my thoughts. The past needs to stay where it is, where it has always belonged—in the past.

This little recitation relieves me; it anchors me to my present, and it reminds me to be grateful.

Of course, I had no idea then that in just a few short months Milly—and Alice—would be catapulted back into the centre of my life—or that I'd wish they never had to be.

# CHAPTER TWENTY-THREE

## MILLY

"Mummy, look at me!"

I smile and wave as Alice, for the first time, proudly pumps her legs and the swing sails upward. Her smile is one of pure joy, her blonde plaits flying out behind her as she revels in the moment, the sky a dazzling blue above her.

"Mummy, *look*!"

"Darling, I *am* looking," I say with a laugh. I'm looking and looking, revelling in this moment as much as she is—her success, her joy, the simple purity of a spring day. After everything, moments like these feel both simple and beautiful, gifts of grace. I treasure them all.

It has been over four years since Anna walked out of our house, leaving Alice in my arms. Those first few weeks and months afterwards felt like a prolonged funeral of sorts, an endless grief as I mourned the death of a friendship, of a whole way of life, because even though we'd lost touch at times, Anna and I had been intimately wrapped up in each other's lives for over two decades. At least she'd been wrapped up in mine, but after the bombshell of her termination, I realised how little I actually knew her. Our friendship hadn't been as strong or as deep as I'd thought it was.

It was also incredibly challenging, to navigate motherhood when I was still feeling so fragile and uncertain, my confidence at absolute zero. Everything felt unfamiliar—all the baby apparatus, how to change a nappy, how to make up a bottle, how to hold a newborn, Alice herself. Nothing came naturally, as much as I wanted it to.

Alice cried—a lot. Sometimes she would cry so long and hard, I thought she'd choke or have a seizure. Her face would get red, her fists would flail, her eyes would screw up into puffy slits, and she would become hoarse. She was furious and grief-stricken, because she had lost the one person she'd come to know like no other, as a mother, and she recognised me for what I sometimes still feared I was—an impostor. But since being on the proper medication, I knew that for the lie it was, and I was determined to try with my daughter.

My mother helped in the early days, although she tired easily. She was my rock when I needed one, and our honesty with one another strengthened our relationship in a way I never could have imagined. She took Alice when I needed a break, and she handed her back when I needed to bond with my daughter. She taught me how to change a newborn, how to bottle-feed, how to get through the endless days without feeling like a failure. I couldn't have done it without her, not when I'd already lost Anna.

My mother, amazingly, is still alive. She stopped chemo three years ago and has remained in remission since then. She's still frail, forgetful, *old*. But she's here. She and my father visit on occasion, and I try to bring Alice to them once a week. Everything feels stronger between us, but with the passing of time it also feels fragile. We are all counting the days, and we are grateful for each one.

"Mummy, I'm going to stop!"

"All right, darling." I watch, trying to hide my apprehension as Alice drags her feet along the ground to stop herself, and then she nearly topples off the swing. She's not quite four and a half, a bit young for a big girl swing, but I am trying not to be one of those mothers who hovers.

I did for a long time, an over-the-top reaction to having missed the first few weeks of her life, and so I fretted over every sneeze, pored over every potentially delayed developmental milestone, read every parenting book I could get my hands on.

It was a way of being in control, of feeling like I was coping, or even being successful at this whole motherhood thing, when inside I still so desperately feared that I wasn't. In the park or the baby groups that I made myself attend, I felt as if everyone could see I was faking it, and I imagined silent, accusing or judgmental looks as they assessed my mothering capabilities and found them lacking.

Eventually, though, one painstaking step at a time, I developed more confidence. I started to believe I really was a mother. I was able to go off the antidepressants, and without them I could still see the horizon.

When Alice was six months old, she weed on herself while I was changing her nappy, and I laughed and tickled her tummy before the memory of that first awful nappy change slammed into me.

And then I felt so unbearably thankful, that I had moved past that. That, by grace alone, I'd been able to. I started to cry, and then I almost called Anna, because in that moment I missed her so much. I wanted to tell her, to have her share in my joy. But I didn't, just as I never have once in all these years, because I know our conversation wouldn't go like that, and I was never sure what I would actually say to Anna if I saw or talked to her again.

"Careful, sweetheart." I take an instinctive step forward as Alice gets off the swing. She stumbles, tripping over her own feet, something that seems to happen a worrying amount. The paediatrician assured me that developmental delays are common with preemies, and I shouldn't be too worried that she isn't hitting the targets with her motor skills, that she seems to be so clumsy.

*She's on track, all things considered. Be grateful.*

And I am.

Now, before I can catch her, she's fallen forward and skinned both her knees. "Alice!" I hurry over, but she's already clambering up, brushing the bits of gravel off her legs.

"I'm all right, Mummy." She grins at me, proud of herself for being brave. "I'm all right."

"So you are." I pull her towards me and kiss the top of her head, just because I can. Because I never want to take her for granted. Then we turn and start walking back towards home.

Alice slips her hand in mine as we walk along, the sun shining on this gentle April day, the cherry trees above us giant puffballs of blossom. I listen to her tuneless humming as I mentally review what is in our fridge that I can make for dinner.

In the four years since Alice's birth, I have not gone back to work. I never even thought about it, because why would I leave Alice with a childminder or in a nursery while I went to be with other children? I don't want to miss a moment. I can't, at least not yet, and there's no real financial need for me to, so Matt and I are both happy with the decision.

I unlock the front door and Alice skips in ahead of me, running to the wicker basket of toys in the kitchen and getting out a few of her favourites. I switch on the kettle and open the fridge, humming softly as I scan its contents for the makings of a meal.

Alice is soon absorbed in some little plastic figurines on the floor—fairies or princess or a combination of both.

I get out a packet of mince and an onion and start frying and chopping. As always when my hands are busy but my mind isn't, my thoughts drift—first from Alice's preschool play next week, to the taster day at the local primary in a month's time, to the second vision test her preschool informed us she needs to have since she didn't do brilliantly on the first one, and then to what I want to talk to Matt about tonight, my heart tumbling in my chest at the thought. And then, as I so often do, I think of Anna.

I have not seen her since she walked out of my house. I don't know if she still lives in her flat in Totterdown, or what she does for work. I searched for her on Facebook once, but she didn't have a profile. I didn't think she'd had when we were friends, either.

I go over and over that last day, the charged words, the accusations hurled, the *finality* of it all. Did it have to be that way? Did it really have to be that way? During those last moments, it felt as if we were hurtling towards a terrifying precipice, and no one knew how to stop or even slow down.

I still hadn't been well, not *truly* well. Anna's words had preyed on all the insecurities that had been my demons since I'd given birth. Even worse, she opened up a chasm between Matt and me; after she'd left, the click of the door seeming to reverberate through the room, I'd turned to him.

"Did you really say that?"

"Milly…"

I knew then that he had. "You told Anna that you didn't think I should be a *mother*?" My voice was a hoarse whisper as I clutched Alice too tightly to me and she began to squirm.

"I didn't say it like that. For the love of…*Milly*. I was at a low point, and so were you. I was thinking out loud—not even thinking, just…I don't know, moaning. Grieving. I wondered if we should have gone down the whole donation and IVF route, that maybe we'd been trying too hard…I was tired and afraid and it was late, Milly. That's all it was, I swear." He looked at me pleadingly, his eyes full of fear.

I shook my head, unable to forgive him so easily. Unable to forgive myself, because perhaps Matt had been right. Perhaps Anna was. Perhaps *I* should have been the one walking out the door, and she should have kept Alice in her arms. I glanced down at my daughter and saw her face grow red as she began to cry, as she always seemed to do with me. I had no idea what to do, how to comfort her. I stared at her helplessly and after a few awful seconds Matt took her from me. Then I went up to bed and slept.

Thankfully we survived those first weeks and months, although it wasn't easy. I had a lot of healing to do, and a lot of forgiving of myself. At one point, encouraged by my therapist, I looked up my birth records and discovered that my birth mother had suffered from serious postpartum depression. It both saddened and relieved me, to know that. To understand why she'd given me up, and also why I'd felt the way I did. Genes mattered, but in a different way than I'd feared.

Matt and I also started therapy together, to work through our feelings surrounding Anna, my diagnosis, all of it. And, day by day, step by step, we made it. But our friendship with Anna didn't.

At one point, the therapist suggested we contact her for some sort of closure.

"I don't need closure," Matt said shortly. "It's already closed."

"Still, considering what a long-standing friendship it was..."

"No."

The therapist didn't bring it up again. And the few times I did, Matt was adamant. We'd trusted Anna. We'd trusted her with our *child*, the most important thing in our lives, and she had betrayed us utterly. For him, affable, easy-going Matt, there was no going back. It was a surprising insight into his character that I had never seen before, and I wasn't sure how I felt about it.

But, I admit, it was easier for me to go along with him. I was afraid to see Anna again, to deal with all that hurt and guilt and *mess*. I already had enough to be dealing with. And so the months, and then the years, slipped by, and soon enough it all felt too late...and that felt okay.

When Alice was six months old, Jack went back to France. I think that was, in its own way, a relief. He'd tried to stay involved at first, playing with Alice, having a beer with Matt, but it had all been tinged with awkwardness and tension, which may or may not have been wrapped up in Anna's absence or Alice's parentage or perhaps was just a result of the relationship he and Matt had had over the years—not estranged, but not close either, just like the rest of his family. Matt's parents didn't visit us until Alice was three months old, and that seemed normal to them.

With Jack and Anna essentially out of our lives, something in me breathed easier, and I think it did in Matt, as well. What that says about us, I don't know and don't like to think about. We hadn't told anyone else, except for my parents, about the donation, and I thought now we never would. That, in its own way, felt like some sort of betrayal, although of whom exactly I couldn't say, but in any case I just pushed it aside. We needed to focus on the future now. On Alice. And we'd tell her the truth of her parentage when she was old enough to understand it. When that would be, I didn't need to think about yet.

Still, I think of Anna often, and I think of her now as I chop an onion and my eyes stream. Did she get another job in Human Resources? Is she with someone? *Does she think of Alice?*

"Mummy, can you fix this?" Alice holds up one of the little figurines whose arm has snapped off.

"I'll try, honey."

I root around in our junk drawer for some craft glue while Alice waits patiently, her sea-green eyes so trusting. She looks like a miniature Anna, from her wavy blonde hair to those beautiful eyes, and of course the dimples. I remember how I joked about Anna's gorgeous genes to Matt, and inwardly I cringe. I could do without the constant reminder, but of course I'd never change anything about Alice at all.

"You'll have to leave it for a bit," I say after I've managed to glue the tiny arm back on. It looks wonky, but hopefully it will stick. "The glue needs to dry."

"All right, Mummy." Alice gives me an easy smile before turning back to her toys. I don't know if I am imagining that she has

Anna's placid, passive nature as well as her looks—is that kind of thing determined by DNA, or developed through nurture? I suppose I'll never know, and I really should stop thinking about it. In the end, it doesn't matter. It wouldn't have mattered, if everything hadn't gone so disastrously wrong, and that's my fault for being ill in the first place. If I hadn't been...if I'd been able to take care of Alice right away...

Of course, it's impossible to say, but I think things would have turned out so differently.

Matt comes home an hour later, dropping his briefcase by the door and then crouching down as Alice runs to him, tripping over the hall runner and half-flying, half-stumbling into his arms.

"Whoa there, gorgeous." He scoops her up in an easy armful as he glances at me. "Good day?"

"Yes, a very good day. We went to the park." A beef and pasta casserole is in the oven, and I reach into the fridge to get a beer for Matt. I've become the classic little housewife, but I don't care about stereotypes, I just want to be happy.

"And how was preschool?" Matt asks Alice as he tugs on one of her plaits.

"Good." She snuggles against him. "But Mummy said I need to get my eyes tested *again*."

Matt frowns over the top of her head. "Really?"

"Yes." I shrug as I put the beer on the counter and then go to check on the broccoli. "They had vision tests at school, and I got a notice today saying she needs a second test."

"Why?"

Like me, Matt is protective of Alice, perhaps a little too much. But it's an understandable response, considering everything we've been through, and it surely can't hurt.

"She doesn't have 20/20 vision, I suppose," I say lightly, conscious that Alice is listening to every word we say, and not wanting her to feel somehow deficient. "It's not a big deal." I choose not to let it be.

But Matt returns to it after Alice is in bed, when we're tucked up on the sofa with the latest offering from Netflix on the screen paused in front of us.

"So do you think she'll need glasses?"

"Maybe. We always knew being premature would affect her in different ways."

"You think this is about being premature?"

"I don't know." I glance at Matt, trying to lighten the mood. "But surely there are worse things than needing glasses?"

"Yes, of course there are. You know how I am." He smiles, and presses the remote, the moment nearly forgotten.

If only I'd known how prescient my words were. If only I'd known how this was all going to end.

But I didn't know, and so I dismiss Alice's eye test and instead talk about what I think is really important.

"Matt... I think it's time we thought about another baby."

Matt's eyes widen, his lips parting silently as he presses pause once more on the remote. "Milly..."

"I know it's scary," I say, my heart starting to thud, because in all this time we have not talked about having another child even once. "And there's a likelihood that I'll experience depression again."

"Milly..." Already he is shaking his head.

"Matt, we'd be prepared this time. And I'm not getting any younger." In fact, my POI has advanced to a point where if I don't have IVF in the next year or so, the window will most likely have closed forever. I'm on HRT, and so far it's all been manageable, but still.

Matt leans his head against the sofa and closes his eyes. I wait, determined to be patient. I want this too much to jeopardise it by pressing hard now. I've learned that much over the years.

"I don't know, Milly," he says finally. "I really don't know. What happened before..."

"But it will be managed this time," I can't keep from interjecting. "If it happens at all. It might not, you know. With the medication and therapy and *knowledge* I have now, it might not." I've done my research; I have a fifty per cent chance of experiencing postpartum depression again.

"Even so."

"Alice is so wonderful." I hear the emotion clogging my voice. "So, so amazing. Don't you want her to have a brother or sister?"

"Yes, of course I would like that." Matt sounds irritated, which makes me fall silent. "Do you honestly think I don't? Sometimes I think you believe you're the only one who ever wanted a family."

"What?" I blink, startled by the turn in the conversation. "Of course I don't think that, Matt..."

"Well, all of this has been hard for me too. The POI, the IVF, the PPD, a dozen different acronyms that basically *suck*. I don't think I can go through it again, Milly. I just want to enjoy having Alice."

I sit back, winded by his diatribe, and more than a little hurt. He's acting as if it's all been my fault, and isn't that what I have been trying *not* to tell myself for so long? What I so desperately need to believe?

"I'm sorry," Matt says after a moment. "I didn't..." He rubs his hand over his face. "I shouldn't have said it like that. I'm sorry. I'm just scared, Milly. I don't know if I'm strong enough to face all that again."

"Together we can be strong enough. I've looked into it, and because I'm a known risk, I can have a care plan in place from the beginning. I can consult a perinatal psychologist, I can start taking medication that's safe for the baby even while I'm pregnant."

"What about the high risk? You'd have to have a C-section again, and while you were pregnant, you were on bed rest for *weeks*, Milly. What about Alice during all that?"

"A C-section is one thing, and I might not have to be on bed rest. Look, there were a lot of factors last time that won't be a consideration this time around—my job, my mum's diagnosis..." I gaze at him despairingly. "Will you just think about it, please?"

It takes an age for Matt to slowly nod. "Fine," he says. "I'll think about it."

After a tense moment of silence, we settle back to watch whatever's on the TV. I feel as if I know what the battle ahead is, as if I'm prepared for it, because I have a plan, when actually I had no idea at all.

# CHAPTER TWENTY-FOUR

## ANNA

I am lying in bed one Saturday morning in September, the sunlight through the window spreading over me like golden syrup, when my phone pings with a text.

At first, I think it's Will. We've been dating for a few months, since June, and it's becoming more serious, slowly and sweetly. It started after that first cup of tea while it rained; in the weeks after, we found ourselves running into each other more often, giving jokey, self-conscious smiles and sharing a bit of banter. It wasn't until later that we confessed we'd both been spending more time on the allotment for just that reason.

Chats standing in soil, cups of tea in his shed when the rain came down and then when it didn't, and finally one late afternoon in June, when it was just melting into a golden evening, he asked me out for a drink.

Since then we've seen each other several times a week, drinks and dinners and movie nights in, and I made it official in my own mind by telling my colleagues and friends at work that I had a boyfriend. In July, Will asked me to accompany him to a friend's wedding; in August we spent a day at the seaside, like little children, eating ice creams and even going on donkey rides.

So I am smiling, thinking of him, wondering if he wants to do something together today, as I reach for my phone and then stiffen in shock when I see who it's from. *Milly*.

The text is shockingly brief: *Just checking this is your number.* I stare at it for a long moment, hardly able to believe that such a pithy sentiment is how she'd choose to connect with me after four years of silence, as well as the complete fallout that precipitated it. *Just checking?*

I put my phone down and get out of bed, my contented, languid mood replaced by something edgy and restless. I pull on my workout clothes and trainers and hit the pavement for a run, something that usually helps me gain some perspective.

But the only perspective I gain is an even greater fury and resentment that she's texted me this way, after so long. After so much. And then I question whether I have the right to feel that way, if in fact I'm being unreasonable, considering my part in it all.

The trouble is, I reflect as I pound down the pavement, I have no one to talk this through with. The only person who knows about Milly, and more importantly, Alice, is my therapist Ellen, whom I stopped seeing two years ago. I could ring her, but it feels like overkill. It's just a text.

*Exactly.*

Back at my flat I shower and dress and then stare at my phone again. She hasn't sent another text, and I haven't replied to the first one. I have no idea what I'd write: *Yes, that's right! Still here!* How on earth am I supposed to respond? She sent a text as if she's confirming my address for their annual Christmas card.

I tell myself to ignore it, to forget about it, but of course that's impossible. It's just a text, but it's sent my fragile, carefully ordered world into a tailspin. One text and I start to remember. Wonder. Regret, and worse, *want.*

What if she wants to get in touch for a good reason? What if she wants me to be in Alice's life again? Instinctively I know that's not the reason. It can't be, and I can't let myself hope. It hurts too much when it falls apart.

That evening, Will comes by to watch the latest drama series on the telly, and after just a few minutes he can tell I'm out of sorts.

"Anna." He puts one warm, heavy hand on my knee. "What's wrong?"

"It's nothing, really." I try to shrug. "Just a text I received this morning from an old...friend." The word doesn't sit right on my tongue.

"An old friend? And that was a bad thing?"

"It was...surprising. We fell out a while ago." I pause, deliberating how much to tell. "Quite spectacularly, actually."

Will smiles, his forehead crinkling. "I'm having trouble imagining that."

"Believe me, it happened."

I must sound rather grim for Will cocks his head and asks gently, "Do you want to talk about it?"

Do I? How would I even begin to explain? And yet I know if I don't, I'll have missed an opportunity and, worse, I'll have hurt Will. He's told me some of the secrets of his past—an abusive father, an absentee mother, the uncle with stomach cancer who stepped in, and his own rebellion in the teenaged years that was even more defiant and dangerous than mine. None of that was easy for him to share, and yet this feels like something else entirely.

"It's complicated," I say. I've already told him a lot about me—my parents' divorce, my disastrous sixth form, and even my abortion. He was understanding about it all, but this...

How could I tell him that I have a biological daughter somewhere, except I really don't? That I held her and loved her and had to let her go? Four years on, my own actions—wanting to keep Alice, talking to that lawyer—are a tangled mix of justifiable and completely crazy. I have no idea how Will would respond to any of it.

And yet if I *don't* tell him...what does that say about us? Three months in and I feel good about our relationship. I feel hopeful.

Will this torpedo it before it gets off the ground? Or will keeping this secret be the thing that sends it off the rails?

"Try me," Will says with a smile. He squeezes my knee.

I take a deep breath, let it out. "I had a best friend," I begin slowly. "Ever since we started secondary. She was like a sister to me…" Just saying that much hurts. Over the last four years, I've chosen to cast Milly as a villainess, the manipulative friend that took me for granted and then used me, but that narrative falls apart as soon as I think about her properly. Remember how kind she was, how we did everything together. How I was the one who offered to donate. If anyone manipulated anyone, it was me.

"And what happened?" Will asks gently, and I tell him, in halting, painstaking sentences, explaining about her infertility, and then my part, and Jack's as well, in creating Alice. Will's forehead crinkles as he listens. "So you and your boyfriend donated the egg and sperm? Wasn't that a bit…"

"We weren't dating at the start. That happened afterward." Sometimes, when I remember my time with Jack, it feels like looking back on a hazy dream. *Did that really happen?* I knew all along, whether I wanted to admit it or not, that it was never going to last. And I don't miss Jack the way I miss Milly. Not a bit.

"So how did you fall out?"

"After Alice was born…" I stop, make myself start again. "Milly had trouble coping. She was diagnosed with postpartum depression, and she ended up leaving for a few weeks, while I took care of Alice." And so I tell him, slowly, painfully, how I fell in love with Alice—and how I tried to take her away.

When I've finished, Will sits back, absorbing all I've said. I stare at him fearfully, afraid he'll judge me: *What on earth were you thinking, Anna? Are you insane?*

Then he turns to me. "That must have been so tough," he says, and it's enough to make tears come to my eyes. He understands. He's not judging.

"Yes, it was," I manage, and then Will takes me into his arms. "It's the hardest thing that's ever happened to me." Which is saying something.

He holds me for a moment as he strokes my hair, and I relax into his embrace, into having him know this about me and be okay with it. It feels like a big step—the biggest we've taken so far—and it also feels good. It's a relief, not to carry this by myself. To have it all be known.

"So what are you going to do about the text?" Will finally asks.

"I'm going to ignore it. If she'd said something different, something more real..."

"Perhaps she's planning to, after she makes sure you're still at the same number. I can understand her not wanting to write some heartfelt message when a stranger might receive it."

I've thought of that, but I don't think it's the case. I'm not willing to take the risk that it is. "She could have said that, then," I counter. "Something like 'just checking this is your number—I wanted to reach out' or something."

"True."

One thing about Will is, he doesn't push. He's content to let me come to my own conclusions, make my own decisions, and yet right now I crave certainties. I want someone to tell me what the right thing to do is, to *know*.

"I feel as if responding to this text will open that Pandora's box up inside of me," I say slowly. "And everything will fly out." All the resentment, all the hurt, all the anger, all the grief. I've just got my life on a pleasant, even keel. I don't want to upend it again, and for what?

"Fair enough," Will says. "If she has something important to say, she'll try again."

I reassure myself that that is the case, but Milly's text still niggles at me as I head to work on Monday. We're planning a splashy fundraiser at a luxury hotel at Christmastime, and it's taking all my energy and focus. I can't afford to waste time thinking about Milly, and what she might want from me this time.

And yet I do think about her. As I am ordering flowers for the event, or filling in a spreadsheet, or answering calls from donors, I am thinking of her and I am remembering. It's as if this one simple text has stirred the waters that have been swirling underneath all along, and random memories come floating up to the surface.

I remember walking home from school in year seven, sharing a packet of crisps, our shoulders nudging each other. I remember going as each other's dates to the sixth-form ball, and having a blast.

But then I remember other things, things I'd forgotten— overhearing Milly talking to her flatmate a few months after I'd started living with them. Her friend had been complaining about me—and in retrospect I remember being a bit of a flake, distant and withdrawn. Milly's response stays with me now—*She's not that bad*, said in a half-hearted voice. I remember Milly barely reacting when I told her I'd been fired, how she had much preferred talking about herself and her bump.

All these memories jostle for space in my mind, and they bring out the worst in me. I'm irritable at work, and restless with Will. Everyone notices, and Cara, the other person who works in my department, asks me if anything is wrong. Will backs off a bit, to give me some space, he said, and I don't blame him. Whether it's my fault or Milly's, she's not good for me. Remembering our friendship is not good for me.

And so, two weeks after she sent that first text, I finally reply. *Sorry, I don't recognise your number. I think you have the wrong person.*

After I send the text, I toss the phone aside and draw my knees up to my chest. I feel a wave of relief even as I fight the urge to burst into tears. At least now it's done.

Or at least I thought it was—until a few days later, when the doorbell of my flat rings.

"Anna?" Through the intercom, Milly's voice sounds anxious and urgent, and shocks me to the core. *She came to my flat?* I say nothing, because I have no words. "Anna? Is that you?" Milly's voice breaks. "Please, if it is, let me up. I have to talk to you. It's important." Her voice hitches. "It's about Alice."

# CHAPTER TWENTY-FIVE

## MILLY

It started with little things, things so small I thought I was crazy even to notice them. I thought I was being the paranoid, over-the-top helicopter mum, but I *wasn't*.

First it was Alice's second eye test, which she failed. Her vision was worse than anyone had realised, least of all me. After a moment of feeling wrong-footed, as if I should have caught something that I didn't, I readjusted my expectations. Alice got glasses. They had pink frames and she loved them, and best of all, she loved seeing properly.

"Everything is so *clear*, Mummy!" she exclaimed, her face full of joy that made me smile even as it tore at my heart. How had she felt before she'd got them? Why had she never said anything?

"I feel guilty for not realising she couldn't actually see very well," I told my mum one Saturday afternoon in July. We were sitting in their garden, a blanket over my mum's knees because she got cold easily, even in the drowsy summer heat.

"But she's only four, and why would you think she couldn't? They have these checks in preschools for a reason, Milly, and you caught it before she started school." She reached over to pat my knee. "You can't beat yourself up over these things, Milly. Motherhood comes with so much guilt as it is. She's fine now. That's the important thing."

And I let myself believe her. Like I told Matt, there were worse things than glasses.

But then I began to notice other things. Alice started waking up again at night, the way she had as a baby. I put it down to nerves about starting school. Then, one morning, she told me she couldn't put on her shoes.

We were running late for preschool, and I fought a sense of impatience as I kept my voice cheerful. "Come on, darling, you can do it. You've done it before, loads of times."

"I *can't*, Mummy." She thrust her lower lip out, the picture of stubbornness, so unlike her usually easygoing nature.

"Alice..." I stared at her in exasperation, and she stared back. A standoff, and meanwhile the clock was ticking. "Fine, I'll do it today," I said, quickly jamming her feet into the pink Velcro trainers. "But you do it tomorrow, all right?"

"It's *hard*." Her lip wobbled.

"Take your time, then. There's no need to rush. I know you can do this, darling." I gave her a quick kiss on top of her head and promptly forgot about the whole thing, chalking it up as just one more of those everyday moments with a four-year-old. Until it happened again.

The next day, about to go out to a local farm park, one of her favourites, and she sat on the bottom stair, resolutely shaking her head.

"I can't."

"Alice..." I was at a loss. Alice had been able to put on her own shoes for months. Why this regression, this insistence? And did it really matter if I put on her shoes for her?

In the world of mothering, it's so easy to feel judged. The telling silence, the raised eyebrow in the preschool cloakroom. *Oh, Alice isn't reading yet? You brought in iced party rings for a snack?* I try not to participate in or even care about that awful race, but it's hard not to justify and explain. *She knows her letter sounds. It was just once for a treat.*

So now, faced with the battle of the shoes, I didn't know whether I should have given in or fought till she put them on. What was the right thing to do? Who could tell me?

I ended up surfing parenting forums online, hoping for some titbit of wisdom, and found on a pages-long thread about how four-year-olds should be able to put on shoes themselves, and if you do it for them, you're teaching them to be lazy. A child psychologist weighed in: *This is a skill most four-year-olds should be able to master. Look at what the underlying issue is.*

So the next time, I was ready. When Alice told me she couldn't do it, I knelt down to her, eye-level, and asked her gently what she was really afraid of.

"Do you not want to go to preschool, darling?" She stared at me blankly. "Are you worried about something?"

She shook her head. "I can't *do* it."

"Let me see you try."

She glared at me in frustration, and then she began to fumble with her shoe. I couldn't help but feel she was doing it deliberately; she was really not this clumsy. She couldn't have been.

I waited, patient smile in place, as Alice continued to ineffectually push her foot into the shoe, her fingers fumbling with the Velcro straps. Then, to my surprise, she let out a groan of frustration and threw the shoe across the room.

"Alice!" In my shock, my voice came out in a scolding tone of censure.

"I can't do it! I *told* you I can't!" she screamed, and then she half-ran, half-stumbled upstairs and slammed her bedroom door as hard as she could. I stood there for a moment, completely appalled and perplexed. Alice had never behaved like that before, not even as a tantrumming toddler. What was going on?

"She's most likely just going through a phase," Matt told me that evening, when I relayed the whole experience after Alice was in bed. "Remember when she was two, and she insisted on doing everything herself? And I mean everything." Matt smiled in memory, but I was not so easily reassured.

"This felt different, Matt."

"How so?"

"Because it was as if she really couldn't."

"She *believed* she couldn't."

"It was more than that."

Matt didn't look convinced, and I couldn't explain it any better.

"Maybe she's having a bit of a regression," he said. "Because of starting school. Isn't that a thing with children?"

"Yes..." And so I told myself that's what it was, that Alice would not be refusing to put on her shoes when she was seven or ten or twelve. How little I knew. How much I wanted to believe.

In August we went on holiday to Cornwall, the same cottage we'd rented for the last few years, starting when I'd been pregnant and we'd dreamed of a future, a family. We spent a lovely week frolicking on the beach, playing in rock pools and building sandcastles. Most of the time Alice didn't need to wear shoes. Then, the night before we left, Alice had a seizure.

It was the most shocking thing, as if I'd been electrified, every sense put on high alert. I'd come into her room to help her change into her pyjamas, and she was lying on the floor, staring straight ahead, spittle dribbling from her mouth, her whole body jerking.

"Alice...*Alice!*" The note of raw terror in my voice sent Matt sprinting upstairs.

"What..."

"I think she's having a seizure." I could hardly believe I was saying the words. "What do we do?" I turned to Matt, craving some kind of reassurance. "What do we *do*?"

"I don't know. I think…in a seizure aren't you just supposed to leave them to it? They'll come out of it when…" He gulped. "When they can."

The next three and a half minutes felt like the longest of our lives. Matt looked up seizures on his phone and read that we should put Alice on her side, to help her breathe, so we did that while murmuring encouragements and endearments to her, even though it was impossible to know if she could hear us.

It was agonising to see her that way, so out of control, so in need, and yet there was nothing we could do. It went against every instinct I'd ever had.

Then, finally, her limbs relaxed and slowly her gaze came into focus. She stared at us in confusion, and then in fear.

"What…what happened?"

"You had a little scare, darling," I said, only just managing to keep my voice from trembling as hers was. "But you're all right now."

The day we got back to Bristol, I took her to the GP.

"Febrile seizures are surprisingly common in children," he told us, smiling in sympathy. Alice looked very little in the chair next to his desk; her feet didn't even touch the floor. "Although they can be quite frightening."

"This wasn't due to a fever." I glanced at Alice, not wanting her to hear this whole conversation. "She wasn't ill."

"I can request an EEG, of course, if she has another one."

I gritted my teeth, because our GP has always been a bit too easygoing. I felt in my gut that something was wrong, and he wanted to take the "let's wait and see" approach.

As it turned out, we didn't have long to wait. Alice had another seizure the following week, and the GP booked her in for the promised EEG, which gave no answers except that she didn't have epilepsy.

As much of a relief as that was, the not knowing was making me anxious. I felt as if I were becoming paranoid, seeing everything as a symptom.

"You need to relax, Milly," Matt told me, which was saying something considering how overprotective he usually was. "So she's stopped liking broccoli. It doesn't mean anything."

I rolled my eyes at him, because it wasn't *that* that was worrying me. It was everything else—the restless nights, the refusal to put on her shoes, the increased clumsiness, the way she'd sometimes forget a word, right in the middle of a sentence, and stare at me blankly, until I gently filled it in and she'd give me a beaming smile. The feeling, as we walked to school in early September for the first day of her first year that she wasn't the same Alice I knew and loved.

It hit me suddenly, as I watched her walk in front of me. It had happened so gradually, all summer long, that I hadn't taken it all in, but watching her walk so slowly and carefully down the pavement, even limping a little, as she dragged one foot slightly behind the other, I realised Alice was different. She'd changed, more than I'd ever seen or suspected and I knew in that moment that something really was wrong.

I made an appointment for the GP the next day, by myself, so I could talk honestly, without scaring Alice.

"She's changed, over the last few months, and I'm worried."

The GP gave me a smile of rather indulgent sympathy. "Changed how?"

"She's slower, less confident. She trips or bumps into things more, and she can't do simple tasks such as putting on her shoes." Or taking off her clothes, or even brushing her teeth. With a ripple of alarm, I realised, as I sat there, just how much I'd started doing things for her, because she said she couldn't, and because it was easier.

That first pitched battle over the shoes felt like a long time ago. I'd given in without even acknowledging that I was doing it—a lot, moment by moment, day by day.

"Children this age often exhibit a lack of self-confidence, a period of regression, especially when they're starting school," the GP reassured me. "It's fairly normal for them to say they are unable to complete tasks they were able to do previously."

"It's not that." My voice came out firm, even hard. Alice wasn't limping down the street because of a problem with her self-confidence. "It's physical," I told him steadily. "Not emotional."

The GP frowned, and then, with a sigh, as if he was making a big concession, he told me he could refer me to a child neurologist for an initial consultation.

"Neurologist?" The word threw me for a loop. It sounded so serious.

"Considering the seizures she's had, as well as the other symptoms you're mentioning, I think that is the appropriate specialist to consult."

I felt as if I had stepped off the edge of a cliff into empty space. I was free-falling in my ignorance, hurtling towards this whole new world I didn't want to get to know. It reminded me of that moment when my doctor had told me I had premature menopause, except so much worse. Everything was about to change, and in that moment I knew I didn't want it to.

"A child neurologist?" Matt said when I told him. "Do you really think that's necessary?"

"Just in case, Matt."

"But she's happy. She's enjoying school. She's doing well."

"She's limping," I told him quietly. "Have you noticed?" I'd been tracking it for the last week, and Alice's gait had been consistently, troublingly uneven. "And sometimes she forgets words...easy words."

"Surely that's normal, when she's only four."

I shook my head, because even though I wanted that to be the case, I knew in my clenched gut that it wasn't. "Why wouldn't you want to get this checked out?" I asked. "Just in case?"

Matt stared at me for a long moment. "Because I'm scared," he said quietly, and it was a confession, not just of his fear, but of where we were—hurtling into space, having no idea where—or how—we would land. How far we, especially Alice, might fall.

# CHAPTER TWENTY-SIX

## ANNA

"Milly." I stare at her in shock, still amazed, even after having buzzed her up, that she is standing in my doorway, that she is *here*. I am conscious of my bedhead, my pyjamas. If I had to see Milly again, this is definitely not how I would have planned it.

"Sorry." She looks older, her dark, wild hair possessing a few grey streaks, deeper crow's feet by her eyes. Yet essentially she looks the same—small and fierce, a bundle of nervous energy and purpose. "Did I wake you up?"

"No...not exactly. What's happened with Alice?" It feels strange to say her name, especially to Milly. "Is she...is she..." I can't make myself say it, whether she is in trouble or sick or worse. So I just stare, waiting for Milly's answer.

"Do you mind if I...if I come in?" she asks, deliberately not answering my question, and I shrug and step aside. She walks in slowly, taking in the changes in my flat in the last four years. "I wasn't even sure you lived here anymore," she says as she comes into the living room. I changed the walls from deep terracotta to a more soothing ivory a few years ago. I also replaced the sofa with a big squashy one in grey suede. Winnie stretches and leaps off the sofa with a swish of her tail, avoiding Milly and disappearing into the kitchen.

"Why wouldn't I?" I ask as I stand in the doorway. I want her to tell me what's going on with Alice, not make chit-chat.

"Only because I thought you might have moved. You changed your phone number…" I don't answer, and Milly narrows her eyes. "Didn't you? Or was that you, telling me I'd got the wrong number?"

"What's happened to Alice?"

"Nothing's *happened.*"

"You made it sound as if it was urgent, as if something was wrong." The adrenalin is still coursing through me, just from hearing Milly say those words. *It's about Alice.* "Why are you here, Milly?"

"I needed to talk to you. Something's…come up."

I arch an eyebrow, tense and waiting.

"Are you still working in HR?" she asks, and the words seem to hang in the air. Seriously? We're going to just pick up where we left off, have a bit of a catch-up? I don't reply and she bows her head. "Sorry," she mutters. "This is hard."

"Take a seat," I say, relenting a bit in my aggressive stance. Milly lowers herself into an armchair, and I notice how tired and anxious she looks. Fear needles me coldly. "What's happened with Alice?" I ask again.

"I wish I could tell you." She sighs wearily and rubs a hand over her face. "But the truth is, we don't know. We're trying to find…Matt and I…We've started noticing things. Little things at first. Things that might not even be connected…I don't know. It's so hard to *know.* But we started to get worried, and then our GP referred her for some tests."

My mind is whirling. "What kinds of things did you notice?"

"Really little things." Milly shrugs, dabbing at the corner of one eye. "She's a bit clumsy…she needed glasses…she was regressing in certain areas, verbal and motor skills…and then, last month, she started having seizures."

"*Seizures*…" I can barely take it all in. Alice, lovely little Alice, whom, on some level, I still picture as a baby, having these issues. "So what tests has she had? What have you found out?"

"That's the problem. Nothing." She spreads her hands despairingly. "They've ruled out a bunch of disorders, thankfully, some serious, some not as serious."

"Such as?"

My bullet-like questions seem to take her aback, as if she hadn't expected me to be so interested, so invested, *still*. But then I have no idea what Milly has thought about me these last four years—if she's thought of me at all.

"Epilepsy, ADD, something on the autism spectrum...but she's never had those kinds of symptoms. At least, not until recently."

My stomach plunges, icy with dread. "What's happened recently?"

"I don't know, exactly." Milly looks as if she could cry. "It's all so nebulous...I mean, she's *four*. Should I be worried that her pencil grip doesn't seem as tight as it did a few months ago? Or that she has reversed some letters she had nailed down last spring? You hear all the time that this kind of thing is normal, but since starting school a few weeks ago, her teacher has flagged up some concerns."

My stomach swirls with anxiety. "So how long has this been going on?"

Milly sighs and sits back. "For about a year, I suppose, although I didn't start noticing things properly until the seizure. We took her to the GP right away after that, and he finally referred her for tests in September...we've had several appointments since then but still no answers."

"And now?" My words hang in the air and then gently fall, like snow.

"And now the consultants want to rule out some of the rarer genetic disorders," Milly says quietly. "Finding a diagnosis can take years sometimes, because there are so many conditions that are so difficult to pinpoint, that are so incredibly rare. If they can run some genetic tests..." She trails off, and realisation seeps in. Milly may be Alice's mother, but for the genetics, she still needs me. I wonder how she feels about that, but I know it doesn't matter. This isn't about me or Milly; it's about Alice.

"What do you need from me?" I ask, knowing I'll give or do anything.

"Just a DNA sample."

"Don't you have one, from before? Didn't they run some tests then?" It would seem tragically remiss if they didn't, and I still remember the reams of forms I had to fill out, the blood samples taken. Surely they covered all the bases? Except somehow it seems they didn't, and that makes me afraid.

"Yes, they ran tests before, but not for every condition that's out there. That would be impossible." She pauses. "I could have had an amniocentesis to check for various conditions when I was pregnant, but with the high-risk nature of my pregnancy, it didn't seem like a good option, and I don't think it really mattered anyway. I was going to have Alice, no matter what."

Because she wanted her so much. I remember. How I remember. "So..." I say unsteadily.

"So now we need a sample, if you're willing." She sounds so hesitant, as if I might shout at her, ask her how she *dare* think I'd do anything for her after...well, after. Yet of course I'll agree to anything to help not Milly but Alice. Always Alice.

"Yes, fine," I say, my voice abrupt. "I'll give a sample."

"That would be great." Milly looks so relieved that it makes me angry. How could she think I'd be so selfish as to refuse? Did she ever know me at all? Or is she feeling guilty for her part in our story? "The specialist's office will give you a ring...it's the Bristol Royal Hospital for Children, the clinical investigations unit."

Which sounds terrifyingly serious.

I nod, and Milly slowly rises from the chair.

"Thank you for doing this, Anna."

"It's no problem."

"I wanted to say…" She pauses and I wait, my expression bland. I have no idea what she plans to say next, and in the end I think she changes her mind. "How have you been? Are you working?"

"Yes, I retrained to work in development. I work for a non-profit now, a charity that supports victims of sexual assault."

"Oh, wow. That's… that's amazing."

"What about you? Do you work?"

"No, not since…" An awkward pause. "I never went back."

We stare at each other for another endless moment. There are too many things to say, and yet there is also nothing. Nothing that could bridge the chasm between us now. Then Milly gives a little uncertain smile. "Thank you again. I—we—really appreciate it," she says.

"Of course, I'd do anything for Alice," I say, my voice throbbing with intensity, and Milly looks away. I've made her uncomfortable. She doesn't want to think about my motivations, or what they mean.

She starts to leave, and part of me can't believe that this is the total of our conversation. We were best friends for nearly twenty-five years. How can that all be gone? But I'm not willing to say something that would attempt to bridge that gap—in part because whatever I say will fall miserably short, and also because I don't want to. Part of me is still angry. Perhaps I always will be.

After Milly leaves, I call Will. "I heard from Milly," I blurt. "It's about Alice." I tell him all of it, and he listens, and reassures me, and tells me these tests are most likely just a precaution, to cross out some of the more unlikely and worrying possibilities. But I think of Alice forgetting words, missing steps, and my heart both aches and trembles in fear. A tiny part of me thinks *this wouldn't have happened if I'd been there. I would have kept her safe.* Except, of course, that's not true at all. *I* might be the reason why Alice is experiencing these symptoms. If she has a genetic disorder, then it is either my fault—or Jack's.

A week later, the hospital rings, and arranges for my sample to be taken. It's a simple process—a cheek swab and a blood test, to see if I am a carrier for any hereditary disorders. I ask what kind of disorders they are thinking about, and the nurse tells me, rather repressively, that there are too many to list.

"But are they serious?" I ask, because I need information.

"Some are, some aren't," the nurse says, and I know she's not going to tell me anything.

As I step outside the hospital, it is a beautiful autumn day, both crisp and warm. I think of ringing Milly, to tell her I've given the sample, but really to try to get more information about Alice, but then I don't. The hospital will tell her, and she made it clear on her brief visit what she wanted from me. Now that she's got it, I doubt she'll be in touch again. She didn't even show me a photo of Alice when we spoke, and I knew better than to ask.

But a shaft of longing still whispers through me. *Alice.* I try to picture her, whether she looks anything like me now, but of course I have no idea. She would have started her first year of school last month. I picture a little girl in a bright new uniform, hair in plaits, her gap-toothed smile bright, but I might as well be picturing a child in an advert or storybook.

I don't know anything about Alice anymore. I wouldn't even recognise her in the street, even though I keep looking. And that's the way Milly and Matt wanted it, and it's clear that that's the way they still want it.

Nothing is going to change now, no matter what is wrong with Alice.

# CHAPTER TWENTY-SEVEN

## MILLY

It is going to take as long as six months, perhaps even more, to complete Alice's genetic testing. The information levels me, because I am desperate for answers.

Matt and I sit in the specialist's office, listening to him deliver this terrible news, our hands clasped. Months of not knowing how to treat Alice, months where she is not getting the therapy or medication or whatever it is she needs, because it is late November, four months since we first took her to the GP, and it is clear that something is very wrong.

Neither Matt nor I can explain away her symptoms any longer, as much as we want and try to. Vision impairment? Plenty of children need glasses, and sight loss can be a consequence of premature birth. Clumsiness? The same. Reversing her letters, forgetting words she once knew? At four, that's still normal. As for the seizures... well, childhood seizures can be something you grow out of. I tell myself I was being paranoid, thinking there was something wrong. I've always been hypervigilant, and in reality you could take any person's various quirks and failings and turn them into a syndrome.

These tests, we reassure each other, are just to be safe, to be sure. It's probably nothing. It's almost certainly nothing. But this litany of desperate optimism isn't working anymore, because Matt and I are not the only ones to notice Alice's symptoms.

First it was her teacher, telling us what we already knew—that Alice was unusually clumsy, that she forgot words, that she could not put on her shoes or even her coat.

"I thought it was just stubbornness," Miss Hamilton, a battleaxe of a teacher nearing retirement, told us at the parent-teacher conference in October, "but now I'm starting to wonder. Have you had her tested?"

Dr. Williams, the child neurologist, has taken our symptoms seriously. He's told us so many disorders of this kind are difficult to diagnose, because the symptoms are so terribly nebulous. He's told us to trust our instincts, and I fight against the urge to say I don't want to, because my instinct is saying this is serious. This is *Alice*.

Alice, who gives a deep belly laugh when Matt tickles her. Alice, who plays make-believe stories with her dinosaur-shaped chicken nuggets until we tell her she really needs to eat them. Alice, who listens to my ridiculous made-up story about the fairies outside her window, which I've been spinning chapter after melodramatic chapter for over a year.

Alice, who we've wanted so very much, who we fought for and love with every fibre of our being. How can something be wrong with her? She's perfect. Just the way she is, she's perfect.

"But surely you might find a diagnosis sooner?" Matt asks Dr. Williams now, as we sit there with our hands clasped, his reasonable tone underlain by anxiety.

"Possibly," Dr. Williams allows. "But at this point it's like looking for a very small needle in an absolutely enormous haystack...I know that sounds a bit trite, but Alice's symptoms are a motley collection that could be pointing to any number of conditions." He pauses. "And you should prepare yourself that we might never find a full explanation. I know that's difficult to hear, but new disorders, hereditary or not, are being discovered and classified all the time. I just don't want to set you up for disappointment, by not knowing the facts."

"Trust me," Matt says with a grim smile. "That is not the case."

"Doctor Williams, it seems as if there has been an acceleration in Alice's symptoms." I hate having to say it, but in the last few weeks, she's forgotten even more words, things that can't be explained away by her age.

Last night she asked for lasagne for dinner but she couldn't actually remember the words: "You know, that flat pasta with the sauce?" She screwed up her face. "It's got red sauce and white sauce and it's really yummy…"

"Lasagne?" I said, trying so desperately to sound lighthearted. "Is that what you mean, silly?"

"Yes!" She beamed at me. "Lasagne."

But as I started frying the minced beef, I fought a tide of panic, an urge to cry right then and there. *Darling girl, how could you forget lasagne? You have it every week. It's your favourite dinner. You've been calling it by name since you were two years old, and we were so proud you could say such a big word by yourself.*

I grieved that little girl then, because I knew, in some way, she was gone. And I told myself that we would find a diagnosis, that she would get better. Whatever it took—surgery, therapy, medication, anything. We'd do it. We'd find a way to make Alice herself again.

And yet, with each passing day, I noticed something else. She now had to walk down the stairs one foot at a time, so slowly, when a few short months ago she'd skipped down them happily. We'd taken her for another vision test and it had deteriorated since she'd got her prescription. She had seizures several times a week, and occasionally she'd give what I'd learned were myoclonic jerks—sudden muscle spasms that she didn't even notice but Matt and I certainly did.

"It could be something innocuous," Matt insists as we drive home from the hospital with no more answers than before. "There are plenty of treatable conditions, things that can be handled with

the right medication or therapy. We just need to know what it is."
He hits the steering wheel, whether for emphasis or in frustration
that we don't know, and won't for a while yet, I can't tell.

I tell myself that at least now we're on the right track, hopefully, with Anna and Jack's samples logged in and being compared
to Alice's. If there is something hereditary, surely they'll find it.
My mind drifts back to Anna, because, in some ways, it's easier to
think about her now than about my daughter and all I don't know.

She looked the same—a bit older, as I am, but essentially
the same. Somehow that surprised me, because she seemed so
different. Colder, more contained, less passive. A harder version
of the woman I once called my best friend, and I wonder how
much of that is up to me.

"You haven't even asked about Anna," I tell Matt, and he shoots
me a wary look.

"Why would I?"

"Because you know I saw her. Because she was your friend as
well as mine, once upon a time."

He shrugs. "That was then."

"Why are you so hard about this, Matt?" When we talk about
Anna, which is very rarely, he reminds me of his rather distant
parents. My warm, easy-going husband suddenly turns into a
cold stranger. It's disconcerting, even though the coldness isn't
directed at me.

"I'm not hard, Milly." He pauses, his gaze on the road, his
fingers flexing on the wheel. "But surely we have enough to be
getting on with, without throwing Anna into the equation? She's
out of our lives. End of story."

But she wasn't out of our lives, not exactly, not at *all*. Not
while her blood ran through Alice's veins, her imprint on every
single one of our daughter's cells. Not when we still didn't know
what was wrong, and whatever it was might be because of Anna.
How could she possibly be out of our lives?

The next week, while Alice is at school, I drive out to Chepstow to see my parents. I'd told them a bit about Alice's health concerns, but not the full, terrifying picture. I hadn't wanted to burden either of them with the worry when we still didn't know what, if anything, was wrong.

Just this morning, as I sliced bananas to sprinkle on top of Alice's Weetabix, Matt said in a low voice, "You know it might not be this big thing. You hear stories of people with a load of mysterious symptoms, thinking they're on death's door, and then it just turns out to be some strange virus that goes away by itself." He took a sip of coffee, looking at me seriously, as if expecting me to agree and offer statistics.

And, of course, I would have loved to. *Please, let this just be a virus.* But in my heart, in my leaden gut, I knew it wasn't. How could it be? Alice's symptoms were becoming severe; we'd already talked to Miss Hamilton about having a teaching assistant help Alice with changing for PE and managing her lunch tray. We'd adjusted to this new reality in such small increments that, somehow, we managed to forget how big it was, how overwhelming. Maybe it was the only way we could cope, but right then her condition felt like a shadow looming over me, a stone weighing me down. This could be something big. This could be life-changing. Already, it was.

"We'll just have to wait and see," I told him and then turned to Alice with a smile, sprinkling the bananas over her cereal. "There you go, sweetheart."

Thankfully, Alice didn't seem too concerned about what was happening to her. She was frustrated by her clumsiness sometimes, but she couldn't remember the seizures she'd had and she liked her glasses. When she forgot words, we filled them in for her, and she went on happily. I wanted her to stay in childish, innocent ignorance for as long as she could. I wanted to hide our fear from her, until there was a certain diagnosis, until we knew what we were dealing with. And maybe I wouldn't even tell her then.

Now, as I head across the Severn Bridge, the wintry sun sparkling on the river, I think about how I am going to tell my parents. They will be devastated to know that something might be wrong, and as anxious as I am, waiting for answers. My mother is so frail, I hate the thought of worrying her about anything, and yet I've had enough secrets from my parents; I don't want there to be any more.

"Milly." My mother smiles but does not rise from her chair as my father hugs me. They are sitting in the lounge, the gas fire turned on high, the doors closed, and it is stifling. Even so, my mother has a blanket over her knees, and I notice how scrawny she has become, even more than the last time I saw her, her wrists poking out from the cuffs of her jumper like twigs.

"How are you feeling today, Mum?" I ask as I bend to kiss her cheek. Her skin is papery and dry.

She smiles and pats my hand. "Tired, as I often am. But peaceful."

Peaceful? I pause at her choice of words, and my father smiles sadly.

"We had a scan last week. The tumour's growing again, and he thinks this time the chemo will be too hard on your mother."

I sink into a chair, shocked and yet not surprised at all. I've been waiting for this news for years. The fact that it's taken so long is the surprising thing, not that it's finally happened.

"I'm sorry," I finally say, looking at my mum. She smiles at me, her eyes bright. "What... what does this mean, exactly?"

She shrugs. "Who can say? No one thought I'd live this long, not by a long shot." She sighs. "But when pushed, the consultant said a few months, if that."

I nod, winded, knowing this time is different. This time it's for real. Of course, I've been subconsciously grieving my mother for years, because that's what a bad cancer diagnosis does to you. It prepares you for the end, at least as much as anything can. Still, I can't believe it's actually here—the endgame, the winding down. No matter how expected it is, it still feels like a shock. And how can I tell them about Alice? Yet how can I not?

"How's our beautiful granddaughter?" Dad asks brightly. "Cheerful as ever?"

"She is the sweetest little girl," my mother murmurs with a smile. "And I am *not* biased."

I look at them both, my heart so heavy it feels like a burden I can't carry anymore. Telling them that Alice might be ill, that she might have some disorder or condition, will break their hearts. But they deserve to know. I know they would want to, and yet I don't want to hurt them.

"Actually, I have some news to share as well," I say, clearing my throat. My mother looks at me expectantly, and my father frowns. "It's about Alice. It might be nothing, or something small, but it might also be something…more serious." I hesitate, and my mum puts a hand to her throat.

"About Alice? What is it, Milly?"

And so I explain about the symptoms, the consultants, the tests. "Six months feels like a long time to wait," I finish. "But we might find out sooner. I just want to know what it is, really, so we can start making a plan." My hands are knotted in my lap, my whole body tense. Since we first started noticing the symptoms, my stomach has been clenched with anxiety, my body maintaining a constant level of tension that exhausts me—and it's only become greater the more we find out, the more we have to wait, the more we don't know.

"Oh dear heaven," my mother whispers. *"Alice…"*

"But it might be nothing," my dad insists. "Like Matt said. A strange virus…" I'd thrown that suggestion out there like a lifeline, and as tempting as it is to grab onto it, I know we shouldn't. It will just make the truth harder to bear, when it comes.

"But it might not, Dad. We just have to wait and see."

My heart is still heavy as I drive back to Bristol, having promised my parents regular updates on Alice and, of course, to tell them any news about test results.

We are still waiting for those results in early January, when I stand in the school yard waiting for Alice, as the other mums and childminders stand in clumps nearby, having a good natter. Everyone is talking about Christmas and what they did, how much they drank. Our Christmas was quiet, with my parents, trying to keep the ever-present fear at bay, and most importantly, from Alice. But I notice things. Every day, I notice things. Now a mum offers me a hesitant smile from across the school yard; I try to smile back but I'm not sure I manage it.

At the start of reception, I was making inroads into these little cliques; I knew a few mums from baby and toddler groups, Mummy and Me classes, so it seemed like a natural friend group. I even went out to a drinks evening at a local pub with a few of them, but as Alice's symptoms worsened and finding her diagnosis became more consuming, I found myself standing alone, avoiding others' gazes. It was just easier.

Now I see, with a sinking heart, that she is not trotting out with the others in her year; Miss Hamilton is standing to the side, holding Alice's hand. She gives me a meaningful look and my stomach clenches even harder.

I see the other parents and carers sneaking me curious looks, and I know they think Alice must have misbehaved, that she is some sort of problem child, when nothing could be further from the truth.

"I'm afraid Alice got a little upset today," she says in a low voice once the other children have been dismissed and we're back in the classroom. Alice is sitting a few feet away, playing with some number blocks.

"Upset? What about?"

"Another child teased her, for not being able to hold her pencil properly." Miss Hamilton grimaces. "I spoke to the child, of course, but Alice took it to heart. She told me she can't hold it the way she wants to."

I nod, swallowing hard, trying to keep my expression neutral, not wanting to break down here, over a pencil grip. And yet it's always something like this—loss upon loss. No matter how small, they still pile up. They batter away at me until I feel completely drained and helpless. "I'm afraid we're not going to have any results from the tests she's undergone for a few more months."

"I'm sorry." Miss Hamilton places a hand on my arm, and I struggle not to cry. I feel so fragile, and what about Alice? Clearly she feels fragile too, and I *hate* that. I hate it so much.

"It's just so hard, not knowing," I manage to gasp out, and Miss Hamilton puts her arm around me. I rest my head against her pillowy warmth, trying not to completely lose it in the middle of the reception classroom. Then I feel a little hand tugging on my coat.

"Mummy... *Mummy*." Alice sounds alarmed. "What's wrong? Why are you so sad?"

I push myself away from Miss Hamilton, ashamed that I came so close to losing it in front of Alice. That's the last thing she needs.

"I'm not sad, darling," I say, my voice veering between horribly clogged and manically upbeat. "Not at all." I force a smile and Alice regards me uncertainly. After a tense few seconds, she goes back to her blocks.

"Are you going to tell her?" Miss Hamilton asks in a low voice. "That something...?"

I shake my head. "Not until we know."

Alice is not so easily satisfied on the walk home. "Why were you sad, Mummy?" she asks as we walk along, her little hand slipped in my mind. "Was it because of me?"

I stop and turn to face her. "No, Alice. No. I'm not sad because of you. I could never be sad because of you."

She regards me seriously, her sea-green eyes—Anna's eyes—wide and unblinking. "But something's wrong with me."

I am shaken to the core, but I do my utmost not to show her how much. "Nothing is wrong with you, Alice. *Nothing*." I kneel right down in front of her, on the cold, wet pavement, and take her by the shoulders, wanting to imbue her with that truth. "Absolutely nothing. Please don't ever think that there is."

Her lips tremble as she gazes at me unhappily. "But I'm so clumsy now. And I can't hold my pencil."

"Yes, and we are trying to find out why that is. You know that's why the doctors have been doing those tests? To try to discover why this is happening." We've said as much before, but I don't know how much Alice understands. How much any of us understands.

"Yes, and then they might give me some yummy medicine to make me better," she finishes on a sigh. "I know." It's what we told her back when we first went to the GP.

"Yes, some yummy medicine." My voice thickens and I rise from the damp pavement, feeling heavy and aching and old. "Yes, that's what will happen." That's what I want to happen, more than anything. *Please, let that be all she needs.*

We walk hand in hand back to the house, neither of us speaking, and after a block Alice starts skipping in her new, uneven way; it makes my heart swell with love and tremble with fear. Already she's forgotten about Miss Hamilton and the pencil, but I haven't. How many more things will Alice struggle with before we figure out what is wrong? How much more will she lose?

My mobile rings just as I come into the house, Alice running ahead to scavenge for a snack.

"Can I have biscuits, Mummy, with icing?"

"Yes, darling." My former militant policing of sugar intake has become positively indulgent. There are far worse things to worry about than a few too many sweets.

I smile as I see her on her tiptoes, reaching for the dented biscuit tin, and then I glance down at my phone, everything in me stilling when I see that it is Anna. I almost don't take the call, but then I do, just in case. Of what, I don't know, but I'm not taking any risks.

"Anna?"

"Milly?" Her voice sounds strange, muted somehow, as if something important has been leached out of it. "May I talk to you, please?"

"Talk?" I close the door behind me as Alice grins at me from the kitchen, a biscuit in each hand. I smile back, and she walks unsteadily over to the sofa and flops down on it.

"Yes, in person, both you and Matt."

"Perhaps it would be better if you just spoke to me, Anna. I don't think Matt wants—"

"It's important, Milly. Really important, for both of you." Anna's voice clogs and my heart freezes as she says the same words I once said to her. "It's about Alice."

# CHAPTER TWENTY-EIGHT

## ANNA

I can't stop thinking about Alice. Lying in bed, sitting at work, going out with Will... I am always thinking about her. Wondering if she really has some sort of genetic disorder. Praying with everything that I have that she does not.

Will understands my worries, and while he's always patient and happy to listen, I can't help but worry that he is getting the tiniest bit impatient with my anxiety, my endless, restless wondering. He doesn't know Alice. He understands what she once meant to me, but he doesn't care about her, not the way I do.

Several times over the next few months I pick up my phone to call or text Milly. Would she even let me know the results, if they find a diagnosis? The thought that she might not, that she wouldn't even think of it, hurts me more than it should. I can't escape the suspicion that she got what she wanted from me, and once again I'm irrelevant to her—and to Alice.

"You need to let it go, Anna," Will tells me gently when I bring it up yet again, on a chilly, grey day in late November when we're both in the allotment, hauling dead leaves away from his uncle's plot. "As hard as that it is. And I know it is hard," he adds before I can protest. "I do."

But he doesn't, not really. He doesn't understand how Alice has, on a very basic and very real level, felt like my child. *My child.* How can he possibly understand that?

"I just want to know," I say. "I need to."

"Do you really? What if it's bad news? I mean, really bad news? Some of these neurological disorders are serious, Anna." He says all of this so calmly that I feel like slapping him. Doesn't he realise how his words devastate me, along with Alice?

"I'd still want to," I insist. "And we don't even know if it's something like that."

"True, but it certainly sounds as if it is—"

"Will, *please*. This is Alice you're talking about, someone I care—"

"Someone you haven't seen in four years," he reminds me gently. "I know you don't want to hear that, and I feel mean for saying it, but that's the reality, Anna."

I stare at him, my lips pressed together. "What exactly are you trying to say?"

"Only that you're taking this so much to heart, and it worries me. It's not good for you. I know she feels like it on some level, Anna, but Alice is not your daughter."

"I know that." I bite my lip hard, hoping the pain will distract me from the far greater one caused by Will's words. I know he's right, of course I do, but it's so painful to hear him say it. "Look, Will, whatever I should or shouldn't be feeling right now…it's not so easy to just *let something go*, especially when it's important to you."

"I know." His tone is gentle, his face full of compassion, but I'm afraid he still doesn't get it, that he just wants me to be done with this—with *her*—and I turn away from him, focusing on a pile of wet leaves. "Why don't we talk about something else?" Will suggests. "Like Christmas."

"What about Christmas?" For the last few years, I've spent a rather uninspired Christmas Day with my mother, since we've both been on our own. We don't particularly enjoy each other's company, but it feels like the right thing to do.

"I thought we might spend it together."

I still, a handful of mulchy leaves in my hands, as I stare at him. "Really?"

"Yes, really." Will gives me a lopsided smile. "What do you think?"

I think it's a big step. A good step, but also a scary one. "I usually go to my mother's."

"Then we can do that."

I imagine my mother's open-mouthed shock at having me show up with a boyfriend in tow. I never have before, and I realise I rather like the image. "All right," I say slowly. "Why don't we have lunch with her and spend the rest of the day on our own?" There is, after all, only so much of my mother I can take, boyfriend or not.

I don't hear from Milly for the entire month of December, and I force myself to at least act as if I've forgotten. I focus on the charity fundraiser, which goes well, and on spending Christmas with Will, the first Christmas I'll have ever spent with someone significant.

It is a bright, cold Christmas Day as we drive out towards Chepstow; the sunlight on the Severn has a pure, crystalline quality and the air feels sharp. I rang a week ago to tell my mother I was bringing Will, and she seemed less interested or enthused than I'd hoped, although why I keep hoping for something more from my mother than I ever get, I don't know. I'm almost forty; perhaps I should stop trying.

The reality is, my relationship with my parents has always been fractured, punctured first by arguments and anger, and then later by bitterness and resentment. I try to remember good times, when I was little, but I can't.

One of my earliest memories, when I was five or six, is sitting huddled on the stairs while my mother screamed at my father. I don't remember what she said, what the fight was about, but with years of later experience to draw on, I can guess—my mother's drinking and my father's affairs. They always seemed to relate, and they were the continuing looping reel of my childhood, although I didn't realise the truth of my mother's drinking or my father's infidelity until I was in my late teens.

Often their arguments flew over and around me; they were so wrapped up in their own misery that they seemed to forget I was there at all, although when they did remember, I would have preferred they didn't. I became a bargaining chip, albeit one that didn't seem to matter very much. When I was about ten or eleven, I remember my mother dragging me out of my bedroom and downstairs, thrusting me in front of my fuming father.

"Don't you care about her?" she'd screamed. "Isn't this a reason to stay?"

My father looked at me for a moment, and he almost seemed sorry. I hung my head, feeling weirdly ashamed, and then he turned away. "I'm sorry, Helen," he said over my head. "But it's not."

*It's.* He meant me.

When I was fifteen, they finally divorced. The fighting stopped but life didn't get much better. My father disappeared from the scene, first working in London, and then, when I was in my twenties, accepting a corporate job in Abu Dhabi. When I was twenty-two, he remarried a woman with two young children; I've seen them on social media, although not in real life. I haven't actually spoken to my father in over ten years, although we exchange texts and voicemails a couple of times a year and call that a relationship.

As for my mother...we keep up the flimsy pretence that we're family, and somehow that matters, even though we go months without talking to each other, and she knows next to nothing about my life. She doesn't know about Alice. She doesn't even know that I donated an egg for Milly. Throughout my school years she was distracted and indifferent, except when she wanted to criticise me, usually when she was drunk, and then, of course, the whole debacle happened with my failed A levels, my wrecked dreams, alienated me even further from her.

After Milly rescued me, and I started to get my life back together, my mother reached out, rather sanctimoniously, her attitude one of noble willingness to have someone as difficult and destructive as me in her life again. And while I had no real desire to be in my mother's life, I recognised that she was the only family I had, and so I have endured the few visits with her every year, letting her complaints and criticism wash over me, trying not to mind.

Now I wonder why I'm bringing Will to see her. Do I still think I can change her opinion of me? Am I finally hoping to impress her?

"Maybe we should give this a miss," I blurt as we cross the bridge. Will looks at me in surprise.

"Are you nervous? I thought I was the one who was meant to be nervous."

"My mother is a difficult woman, Will."

"She can't scare me, Anna. Why do you think I'm not having you meet my parents?" He smiles, and I try to smile back, but I'm seriously starting to regret this whole endeavour.

"She doesn't even make a nice Christmas dinner," I half-joke. "The turkey's always dry."

"At least the pudding will be delicious," he replies, nodding towards the chocolate log I made that is sitting on the backseat.

"She's going to be rude to you." I feel obligated to warn him. "And most certainly to me."

"I can take a bit of rudeness," Will answers with a shrug. "But if she's rude to you, we might have to have words." He reaches for my hand, lacing his fingers through mine, and I am jolted by his touch, by the simple fact of his loyalty. It's been a long time since someone has stood up for me.

"Thank you," I whisper.

My mother's eyes widen when she catches sight of Will, clearly not expecting me to bring home such a catch. A trio of Jack Russell terriers cluster around us, sniffing and wagging their tails. Since the divorce, my mother has become a bit obsessive about "her babies."

"How have you been?" I ask, going in for an air hug, where we pretend to embrace but don't actually touch. It's a skill we've perfected over the years.

"Oh, you know." My mother waves her hand. "My knees are playing up. I was hoping you'd visit sooner." She sniffs, and I bite my tongue to reply that she never asks me. She gives Will a glance that manages to be both simpering and accusatory. "I don't see her enough."

"Nor do I," Will returns smoothly. I feel bolstered by his support, but already exhausted by my mother's attitude. This is how it always is, how it has always been, ever since I can remember—the sniping and the indifference, a particularly painful combination.

We stumble through an hour of small talk and sickly-sweet sherry in the sitting room, before my mother makes a big to-do of checking on the dinner, and I go in to help her.

"Will seems all right," she says, her back to me as she empties several ready-made trays of vegetables into microwaveable bowls. She pauses, her hands resting on the counter. "Is it... is it serious?"

I take a quick, steadying breath. "It might be getting that way." It feels like a lot to admit.

My mother stiffens, almost as if I've given her bad news. Perhaps I have. I've never understood my mum, how she can seem to both resent my presence and its lack at the same time. I don't visit enough, but when I do, she can't wait to get rid of me. I've never understood it, but it always hurts.

"Would that be a bad thing?" I ask lightly, trying to make it a bit of a joke, even though I mean it. Why is she standing there so still, as if I've just struck a death blow? Is my happiness that offensive to her?

"No," she finally says, but she sounds unnervingly hesitant.

"Mum, what is it? You don't like him?" Will has been impeccably polite and unwaveringly friendly since we arrived. He didn't even bat an eyelid when one of her dogs humped his leg repeatedly.

"This has nothing to do with Will."

"Then with me?" I can't keep the hurt from my voice. "Why don't you want me to be happy?"

"Oh, honestly, Anna, is that what you think?" She is impatient now, shoving the bowls in the microwave, slamming the door.

"Sometimes, yes."

"Well, this might amaze you, but not everything in my life is about you." This huffy accusation is so ridiculously unfair—*nothing* in her life is about me—that I open my mouth to refute it, but then I realise there is no point.

"What is this about, then?"

She doesn't reply and I watch her, taking in the tension that turns her body into hard angles, the way she won't look at me. She's not telling me something, but I have no idea what it is.

"Mum, what's going on?"

"Not here, Anna, not now." Her voice wobbles and her hands tremble as she takes the bowls out of the microwave. "It's Christmas."

A ripple of genuine apprehension runs through me, a physical sensation that makes me want to shiver. "Not what?" I ask in a low voice. "What is it you're not saying, that you *can't* say here, at Christmas?" Because clearly it is something, for her to be affected like this.

Will appears in the doorway, the furrow between his brows making me wonder how much he heard. "May I help?"

My mum glares at me, her eyes narrowed to commanding slits. *Drop it.* I read her silent command loud and clear.

And so I do, because the last thing I want is an ugly confrontation with Will there. But throughout the mediocre meal, the requisite walk with the dogs and the stilted conversation and even more awkward pauses, I am wondering about that moment—and what my mother chose not to say.

A few days later, I find out. She calls me, asking me to visit her again, two times in one week, which is unprecedented, and makes me feel even more apprehensive. Whatever she needs to tell me, it sounds important.

The day is damp and grey, the lowering clouds a dull reminder that Christmas is over. My mother greets me wearily, shuffling into her sitting room with little more than a mumbled hello. I smell brandy on her breath, and my apprehension turns to fear.

Although she drank heavily throughout my childhood, my mother sobered up through a combination of self-help books and yoga, and has only had the occasional tipple—as far as I know—for about twenty years. But right now she is drunk.

She slumps into her usual armchair, one hand twitching towards the remote control. Often the television is on while we talk, a constant low-level background noise, my mother's gaze flicking to the moving screen every few seconds, but now she keeps it off.

She gazes at me, her face tired and worn, her hair, once a pristine highlighted blonde, now a dirty, dishwater grey. I feel a flicker of pity for her, but no more.

"What is it, Mum? What is it you didn't want to say at Christmas?"

"I'm not sure it's important now. Yet."

*Yet?* "You called me out here, didn't you? Why can't you just say it?"

My mother leans forward, her dull eyes suddenly sparking with anger. "Maybe because it's *difficult*, Anna. Have you thought of that? Maybe because it's painful, and I don't want to." I'm shocked into silence. "Did you never think that?" she says more quietly. "Did you never think about me?"

"I could ask you the same question," I retort before I think better of it. Briefly, I close my eyes. This conversation has not got off to a good start. "I'm sorry, Mum. I don't want to argue. It's just...concerning. Whatever you haven't told me, it seems important."

"How serious are you about Will?"

I blink, jerking back a little in wary surprise. "What does that have to do with anything?"

"I need to know if you might think of...of having children."

I stare at her for a moment, flummoxed. "Why are you asking me this?"

"You're nearly forty already. Perhaps it's too late."

"You almost sound hopeful." I swallow hard. "Mum, why..." I pause to regroup. A feeling of nameless dread is washing over me. "I've already had a baby," I tell her, and I watch as her eyes flare wide and her lips tremble. "Five years ago."

"You didn't..."

"In a roundabout way, admittedly. Do you remember Milly?"

"Of course I remember Milly."

"She was trying for a baby for a long time, and it turned out she couldn't get pregnant on her own, so I donated my egg. Her daughter, Alice, is five years old now." I watch her carefully, my heart starting to thud as her face turns grey.

"Why didn't you say anything before?" she demands.

"It felt private. And I didn't think you needed to know." I press one hand against my thudding heart. "Did you?"

My mum doesn't answer, just shakes her head as she bites her lips. She looks anguished, and I am starting, terribly, to suspect why.

"She's started having some symptoms," I say as my mother jerks suddenly, her gaze fixed on mine. "Random things, some seemingly little, others not so much... but they're worried about it. They asked me to give a DNA sample, to check for hereditary conditions." I watch her, waiting, afraid and yet hopeful that she'll just shrug dismissively.

Mum lets out a sound that is half-moan, half-sob.

I clench my fists, the dread overwhelming me now. "*Mum.* What is it? What haven't you said? What do you know?"

She shakes her head and then says in a low, barely audible voice, "What kind of symptoms?"

"I don't really know." I try to remember all the things Milly said. "Vision loss... some problem with small motor skills... clumsiness... forgetting things. I think." I shake my head helplessly. "Mum, whatever it is, tell me, please."

The silence stretches on for a minute, and then another. Then my mother rises from her chair. She looks even more haggard than usual, her eyes seeming strangely blank. "I'll be back in a minute," she half-mumbles and I wait, stroking one of her Jack Russells, fighting a crashing sense of panic.

A few minutes later she returns, carrying a photograph album with a cover of faded white sateen. She sits back heavily in her chair, the album on her knees.

"What is that?" I ask after a moment, when she doesn't open the book or even speak. Another endless pause.

"It's a photo album," she finally says, tracing the embossed title on the cover with her fingers. "With pictures of your brother."

For a second the words don't make any sense. They bounce off me, refusing to penetrate. I'm an only child. I used to wish for a sibling, someone to share the misery with, but then later I was glad my parents only inflicted themselves on one child.

"What are you talking about, Mum?" My voice sounds strange and tinny. "What do you mean, a *brother*?"

"He... he died when you were two."

"And you never *told* me?"

Her lips tighten as her gaze flashes downwards. "Your father wanted it that way."

The implication being that she didn't. But then why hadn't she ever told me about him, after the divorce? Why keep my sibling a *secret*? "I don't remember him at all." I sift through my earliest memories, trying to slot a brother in, but I can't. There's no one there at all.

"You wouldn't. We never told you about him, and he was in a care facility by the time you were born."

I swallow hard. "A care facility? Why was he there?" But, of course, I already know—not the details, but the awful gist, and that is enough to make my stomach churn and my vision go blurry. "Why was he there, Mum?" I ask, louder this time, because her fingers keep tracing the letters on the book—which I can now see reads *Baby's First Album*.

"Because he was dying," she whispers. "And we couldn't care for him at home."

*Dying.* The word slams into me, leaving me breathless and reeling. I want to put my head between my knees, catch a few steadying breaths, but I'm afraid it might send my mother over the edge. She is staring at the album as if transfixed, tracing those letters over and over. I manage with one deep breath, exhaling slowly, to ask, "What did he have?" My voice is little more than a thread. "What was his...condition?"

"Batten disease." I have to strain to hear the words. I've never heard of it.

"What were the symptoms?"

Slowly she lifts her head and blinks me into focus. "There are many. With your brother, it was vision loss, seizures, and then forgetfulness...childhood dementia." Two words that should never, ever go together.

My throat is so tight I can barely squeeze my next words out. "What about clumsiness? Motor skills...?"

"Yes, those too." She shrugs, as if it is a matter of indifference, but I can see how deeply she is hurting, her body seeming to fold in on itself, her head bowed as she remembers her grief, the grief that has never left her.

My mind is racing down dark alleys, then turning around and skittering back, because I don't want to go there. I *can't* go there, and yet I have to. For Alice, I have to. "And this is a hereditary condition?"

She nods. "Both parents have to carry the gene."

Both parents—which means Jack has this awful gene as well. *If* Alice has it. And yet already I know that she does, she must, and I can't bear it. How on earth can I give this kind of news to Milly and Matt? How on earth can I live with it myself?

"Is there treatment?" I ask, a bit desperately. "Medicine? Something…?"

My mother shakes her head. "There's nothing."

"But this was a long time ago. Perhaps things have changed…" It feels like the smallest, faintest ray of hope in this otherwise impenetrable darkness. Surely science has moved on loads in the last thirty-five years. There might even be a cure now.

"There isn't, Anna," my mother says, as if I've said all of this out loud.

"How do you know?"

"Don't you think I care?" Her voice throbs with pain. "Don't you think I'd know? That I'd find out?" I stare at her, the wild grief in her eyes, the way her arms are wrapped around her body as if she needs to hold herself together, and I realise I've never known my mother at all.

After a long moment, I nod towards the photo album, my body and heart aching with the weight of my new knowledge. "May I see it, please?"

Wordlessly, my mother hands it to me. Despite everything she's already told me, the first photos are a shock—a tiny, shrivelled newborn, a smiling, chubby baby. He has the same green eyes I do—the eyes of my father—and honey-blond hair that curls about his face, making him look like the proverbial cherub.

Silently I go through the first two years of his life, all the milestones, as well as the little moments. Chocolate cake on his first birthday, tottering steps in a garden. It is strange to see my parents laughing and loving together, a happy family that I have absolutely no memory of.

And then the photos stop, sometime after my brother's second birthday. The rest of the pages in the book are blank.

I glance up at my mother, and she shakes her head. "You wouldn't have wanted to have pictures then." I frown and she continues heavily, "He went into the care facility right before he turned three." She swallows, more of a gulp. "He lived another year after that."

"Did you visit him?" The question slips out unbidden, and my mother suddenly glares at me, her eyes screwed up, her mouth twisted. She is ugly with outrage.

"Did I *visit* him? Did I visit my own *son*, my firstborn child? What kind of question is that?"

I shrink back under the force of her rage—except it isn't rage at all, it's grief. Her face crumples and her shoulders shake and I realise she is sobbing—great, heaving sounds of deepest grief that I've never seen her make before.

"*Mum.* Mum, I'm sorry." I haven't actually hugged or even touched my mother in years, yet now I kneel in front of her and put my arms around her. She submits for a few seconds, but then she pushes me away—which, I realise, has been happening since I was a child, or even a baby. The whole story of my life, encapsulated in this moment.

I sit back on my heels as she continues to sob, choosing to be alone in her grief, to shut me out. *Why?* Why didn't she or my father ever tell me the truth? Why didn't they include me in their grief? I am angry, but more than that, I am deeply, profoundly sad, for so many reasons.

I think of my brother, and then I think of Alice. *Alice.* My heart breaks all over again, cracking right down the middle; soon it will be nothing but a handful of jagged splinters.

"Why didn't Dad want to tell me?" I ask quietly when my mother's sobs have subsided to hiccoughs.

She shrugs and wipes her eyes. "It was too painful. When something like that happens...you don't want to be defined by it, and yet you *are.* Of course you are. Richard couldn't see that. He thought if we moved from London, if we built this new life for ourselves, with you, it would be better. A fresh start for everyone, but there never could be any such thing."

"Weren't you afraid I might have it, too?"

My mother doesn't look at me as she answers. "Of course we were. We hadn't intended..."

"I was an accident," I say flatly.

"Do you think we'd want to risk going through it all again?" she demands raggedly.

I understand that, even if I can't help but feel hurt. "Is that why you fought?" I ask. "Because of him?" *Was it why you drank? "Why you divorced?"

My mother looks at me with bleary tiredness. "What do you think?"

I rise to my feet, knowing there is little more to be said. Even now, in the midst of her grief, my mother is choosing solitude over being with me, as she always had, and it hurts. I want to share this with her; I want to comfort her in her grief, a grief I feel even though I never knew this little boy. *My brother.*

"I'm sorry, Mum," I say, and she just shrugs and looks away from me.

I am at the door when I turn back to face her, feeling strangely empty as I take in her shattered look, her still-streaming eyes. If they'd told me... if they'd tried to make us a family again, instead of choosing grief over love... but perhaps they couldn't. Perhaps they weren't strong enough. I know I can't blame my mother, considering the pain and grief she has had to endure.

"What was his name?" I ask softly.

She gazes at me, everything about her broken. "Robbie," she whispers.

As I turn away from her, I wonder how on earth I am going to give this awful news to Milly—and how I can bear to live with it myself.

# CHAPTER TWENTY-NINE

## MILLY

"Anna wants to talk to us?" Matt sounds incredulous that I could have entertained such a prospect for a moment. "Absolutely not."

"*Matt*. She says she has something important to tell us. About Alice." I remember Anna's broken voice and I feel a sharp stab of fear. Do I want to know whatever she is going to tell us? And yet I have no choice, because if she knows something that can help Alice…

"What could she possibly have to say about Alice?" Matt scoffs. We are standing in the kitchen after supper, talking in hushed voices as Alice watches television just a short distance away.

"I don't know, but she sounded worried. Scared, even." Which terrifies me. "Perhaps something to do with the genetic testing—"

"Which is with Doctor Williams, a highly trained specialist. If there is news about that, he'll be the one to ring, not Anna."

"Still, she has something to say to us, Matt." I close the dishwasher and lean against it, my shoulders slumping. I feel so exhausted all the time, and at the same time completely wired, my whole being powered by this endless anxiety. I just want to *know*, and yet I don't. I very much don't.

"I doubt it's anything. She's probably just fishing, looking for a way back into Alice's life."

"And is that so wrong of her?" I ask quietly.

Matt folds his arms. "She talked to a *lawyer*, Milly. She was going to sue for *custody* of *our* daughter."

"We don't know if she would have actually gone through with it."

"And what makes you think she wouldn't have?"

"She gave her back rather quickly, and, after all, it was five years ago. Besides, this is about Alice." I lower my voice even more. "If she knows anything that could help her...help us with a diagnosis...we *have* to listen to her, Matt. For Alice's sake."

"I can't imagine she does," Matt snaps, but I see the acceptance in his eyes. For Alice, he'll do anything. Just like me. "Fine. We'll see her. But she's not seeing Alice."

"Who isn't seeing me, Daddy?" Alice lopes into the room, a shuffling sort of walk we've become used to, glancing between the two of us. I give Matt a quelling look.

"No one, sweetheart," I say, dismissing Anna as simply as that. "It's time to get ready for bed." I reach for Alice's hand, and her little fingers slip through and twine with mine. Together we head upstairs, each step painfully slow, reminding me how much has changed. On the third step, Alice trips and nearly sprawls flat on her face, but I manage to keep her upright—just.

"Sorry, Mummy." Her lower lip trembles and I pull her into a quick hug.

"You don't ever need to be sorry, Alice. Never, ever. Not for falling. Not for anything."

"Why am I falling so much?" she whispers. She pulls away so she can look at me seriously. "What's *happening*?"

My heart feels like a cloth wrung for its last drops as I meet her confused and unhappy gaze. "I don't know, sweetheart. But the doctors are going to find out."

An hour later, Alice is peacefully asleep and I am pacing the downstairs, mindlessly moving toys from one basket to the other in an attempt to feel busy, even though everything is already tidy. Matt is sitting on the sofa, frowning at his phone. Anna is due to arrive any minute.

When I think of what she might say, even in the most vague and nebulous terms, I feel as if I could be sick. My stomach churns and my skin prickles and I continue to pace our downstairs, needing to move, because otherwise I might leap out of my own skin. Then the doorbell rings.

Matt doesn't move, so I go to open it, blinking in surprise at the sight of Anna. She looks...well, she looks terrible. Her hair is piled up messily and there are deep, violet shadows under her eyes. She looks old, as if she's aged a decade since I've last seen her, and I can't bear to think why.

"Anna..."

"I'm sorry to be so sudden with this."

I step aside and she moves into the room, her arms wrapped around herself, her head bowed.

"I'm so, so sorry." Her voice breaks and I stand there, frozen, because even though I'd been dreading this visit and what it might mean, I am still shocked by the depth of her sorrow.

Matt tosses his phone aside, looking unmoved by Anna's agitation and regret. "Just what," he asks, "are you sorry for?"

"*Matt*." Does he actually think this is about what happened five years ago? Because I know it isn't.

"For a lot of things," Anna says quietly. "But mostly for what I have to tell you now."

I open my mouth, but no sound comes out. My mind is blank and buzzing, my mouth terribly dry as my heart starts to thud. I don't want to hear this. I know I don't want to hear this.

Matt's face is stony and he doesn't say anything.

Anna looks at us both, strangely dignified in her misery. "Shall we sit down?"

Then, when we are all seated, when I want to prolong this moment forever and at the same time feel as if I can't stand a second more, she speaks.

"I visited my mother this afternoon. She told me something I had no idea about… no idea at all… but I am afraid it has some bearing on Alice, although I hope—I hope so much—that it doesn't." Her voice has broken again and she dabs at her eyes.

"Just say it, Anna," Matt says, his voice hard. He's acting as if this is no more than histrionics—doesn't he realise this is serious? That this *matters*?

"I had a brother," she states woodenly. "An older brother. My parents never told me about him. I never even knew he existed until today."

"What…" The word comes out in a breath, as I stare at her uncomprehendingly.

"He had a hereditary condition. A neurological disorder that has symptoms that sound very similar to Alice's." Her face crumples before she smooths her expression out, like a hand smoothing a sheet, and takes a hitching breath.

"So you think Alice has this condition?" Matt says, sounding skeptical. "Is that what you're saying?"

"I think it's possible. Of course, this… this condition requires both parents, that is, genetic donors, to be carriers of the gene. So Jack would have to be tested, as well."

"We've already asked him, and he's been tested. What *is* this, Anna?"

"What?" Anna stares at him uncomprehendingly. "What do you mean…"

Matt leans forward. "Is this some bid for attention? A way to get close to our daughter again? Is that what you're after?"

"*Matt.*" Even I, in all my fearful paranoia, can see this is not some sneaky, manipulative move on Anna's part. How could it be? She looks heartbroken.

Anna turns to look at him. "Do you think I'm making this up?" He shrugs, and she leans forward, intent now, her eyes blazing.

"This is the last thing I'd make up. The *very* last thing. I'm here because of *Alice*, Matt, because even if you don't want me to, even if you can't stand it, I care about her." She turns to me, fiercely. "I do. I'm sorry, but I do. And the truth is, I hope to God she doesn't have this condition. I hope and pray with everything I have."

"Why?" I whisper. I can't absorb the rest of what she's said, not yet. "What is this condition, Anna? What…what might it mean for Alice?"

Anna lowers her gaze. She doesn't speak for a moment, but I already know. I think in some dark corner of my heart I've always known, or at least I've feared. But I need her to say it.

"It's called Batten disease. It's a neurological condition that causes vision loss…loss of motor skills…childhood dementia…" A soft cry escapes me. "Children diagnosed with it end up being completely bedridden and dependent…and they usually die by their early teens," she finishes, her voice so unbearably sad. "At the latest."

For a second I can't take it in. I won't. I simply stare at her, and so does Matt, and then I lurch upright and race to the downstairs toilet, where I am violently sick, my insides wrung out. A few minutes later I walk into the kitchen; the world around me is going in and out of focus, my heart beating with hard, erratic thuds. Anna and Matt are both still seated in the living room, frozen as if they are part of a tableau. I pour myself a glass of water and drink it, my mind both numb and spinning.

"Milly…" Anna begins.

"No." The word comes out of me, flat and forceful. "Alice does not have that. Alice *cannot* have that."

"I'm so sorry, Milly." Anna is crying now, and Matt is looking dumbstruck, and suddenly I am filled with so much rage.

"No!" I hurl my glass at the wall of kitchen cupboards, but its loud shatter doesn't satisfy me. I need so much more to break.

"She might not have it," Anna says softly, even though we all know it for a lie. "It could just be a coincidence…"

"No." I press my palms against my eyes, pressing until I feel pain and see flashing lights behind my lids. "No. No. *No.*" The words fire out of me, and then I am collapsing softly, folding inwards, as I crumple to the floor and sobs tear through me.

A few seconds later I feel arms around me, and I realise they are Anna's. And I cling to her, because I am drowning and I need an anchor.

"I'm so sorry," she murmurs against my hair. "I'm so, so sorry."

And I know she is, for so many things, just as I am, but being sorry isn't enough. It won't matter for Alice. It's already too late for her, even though it's only beginning.

After a few moments, I stand, and then Matt comes over and pulls me into a hug. The three of us stand there, our heads bowed, our shoulders shaking, once united by love, and now brought together by grief. There is no going back.

# CHAPTER THIRTY

## ANNA

For a week, I walk around in a fog. I can't concentrate on anything —not my job, not Will, not even the simple matter of sleeping and eating. I am waiting for Milly to contact me, to tell me what the consultant has said, and whether Alice has Batten disease. I am still hoping, ludicrously, I know, that she does not.

I've imagined the call so perfectly—the incredulous relief in Milly's voice, the laughter, the discovery that Alice has some strange virus or some far less serious condition that responds to treatment and medication—because I've looked online, I've scoured all the websites, and the outlook for Batten disease is as unbearably grim as my mother first said.

After I told Milly and Matt, after we embraced in the midst of our sadness, the push and pull of our relationship over Alice ceased to exist, at least in that moment. Who cared what had happened before, when Alice's life was at risk?

But then Matt stepped away and nodded at me, a farewell. "We'll tell you if we have news," he said, clearly a concession, and I wondered how much had actually changed between us.

Then, ten days after that conversation, Milly finally texts me. *You were right.* Three short, terrible words. I stare at the text and am reminded of when she texted me before, when she found out about the premature menopause. It feels like a lifetime ago, and it *is*. Alice's lifetime. I think of how devastated Milly was then, and how neither of us could have ever imagined where that conversation in a wine bar would end up taking us.

On impulse as well as instinct, I text her back. *Do you want to meet? Have a drink later?*

I stare at my phone, willing her to respond. And then, after a few endless minutes, she does. *Okay. How about 6?*

It feels surreal to be winding my way through the wine bar later that evening, clutching a glass of white; I haven't been here since Milly was pregnant, and we were friends. I don't know what we are now.

I find her in the back, hands wrapped around a large glass of red, her hair wild about her face. She looks up as I approach and she can't quite make herself smile. Neither can I; it's simply too sad for that. Too hard.

"Milly." I sit across from her. "How are you?"

She opens her mouth, and then shakes her head. She takes a sip of wine. "I don't even know," she says finally. "I feel . . . flattened. As if a ton of bricks has fallen on top of me, and it's all I can do to breathe."

"I can't even imagine . . ."

"No, you can't." Her words are blunt without being hostile. "No one can. I couldn't, and I still can't, even though it's now my reality. Alice's . . ." She stops, biting her lip, before she resumes. "You know, for about five seconds every morning, when I wake up, I forget. It's the most wonderful five seconds. I feel light inside. I think about what we're going to do that day. I can *breathe*. And then it all slams into me again, and I remember, and everything is awful. So incredibly awful. It's a grief I have to keep living, over and over again."

I have no words, no comfort to offer, and so I just shake my head helplessly and cover her hand with my own. Her face contorts for a second, and then, with a shaky breath, she composes herself.

"Have you learned anything more?" I ask after a few moments. "Any treatments or medication?" When I steeled myself to look online, I didn't find anything, but surely, with the help of specialists, there must be something…

"No, nothing useful, anyway. Nothing I'd ever want to hear." Her voice is so bleak. "No treatment, no medication, no hope." I flinch. "Although that's not quite true. She's on some anti-seizure medication now, so that helps a bit. Her consultant Doctor Williams says, based on her rate of regression so far, she'll likely lose her sight within a year, and her motor skills soon after that. She'll most likely be completely dependent by the time she's eight or nine." She dabs at her eyes, looking at the ceiling so the tears won't fall. "And you know what? At this point that almost sounds like good news." Her voice chokes. "Because that's three or four years away, and at least that means she'll still be here then."

I press my hand to my mouth, unable to take it all in. It keeps bouncing off, as if my mind is insisting on rejecting this information. *No, no. This can't be true. It just can't be.*

But it is.

"The hardest part," Milly continues, "is knowing what to tell Alice. How do you tell a five-year-old that she is going to deteriorate and die? I mean, *how*?" Her voice rises and a few people turn to look at us. "I've bought some books, and I did an internet search on 'how to tell your child she's dying.' Can you even imagine the search results for that?" She shakes her head, annoyed now, angry tears sparkling in her eyes. "But all the advice is so unbelievably *lame*. Do you know how many times I've read 'this is a difficult topic to discuss'? Oh, *really*? You *think*?" More people are looking, but I don't care, and neither does Milly. She is still looking at the ceiling to stop herself from crying, even though tears are trickling down her cheeks.

"And, of course," she continues, "I don't even know how much Alice understands about death. She's *five*. Even the doctors don't know. So, at the moment we're just taking it day by day, giving her information on a need-to-know basis. At this point we just want to give her as much normality as possible, but that already feels impossible." She lets out a shuddering breath. "Sorry. That was a lot of information."

"You don't ever need to be sorry, Milly."

"That's what I keep telling Alice." She gives me a twisted smile, her face crumpling a bit. "She keeps apologising for being clumsy and things. It breaks my heart." She thumps her breastbone. "I feel it, right here, every time, *breaking*."

"I can't help but feel this is my fault," I blurt. I have to say it, even though I don't want to make this about me. It has been weighing on me ever since my mother told me about my brother. "If I hadn't offered..."

"Oh, no, no, no." Milly shakes her head firmly. "I can't go down that route, Anna. I can't let myself think that way. Because if you hadn't offered, and I hadn't accepted, then I wouldn't have had Alice. And even now, *especially* now, that's unimaginable."

"Do you really feel that way?" I ask quietly. I want her to. So much, I want her to.

"I have to." Milly gazes at me brokenly. "What's the alternative? To wish she'd never been born at all?" She leans forward, suddenly urgent. "Do you wish that?"

"What...?"

"I've thought about that day a thousand times, Anna. A million. How it all unravelled so fast, before any of us could do anything... it felt as if I was watching a train crash in slow motion and I couldn't do anything to stop it, but at the same time I was the one driving the train."

"Yes." It's hard to get any other words out. I never thought I'd be sitting here with Milly, talking about that day. "I never should have..." I begin, then stop, trying to frame my words in a way that is truthful to what happened as well as to my own feelings.

"No, *I* shouldn't have," Milly says. "I know we put you in an impossible situation, Anna. We asked too much of you. We didn't give you any leeway, any permission to feel something, or be something, other than our oh-so-helpful friend."

"And I took advantage," I admit painfully. "I was so besotted with Alice. I didn't expect it...the strength of how I felt. I really didn't."

"And I didn't expect not to feel that." Milly looks down at her drink.

"I wouldn't have gone through with it," I blurt. "I've thought and thought about it, and I really don't think I would have."

Milly nods slowly, and I can't tell whether she believes me or not. "I don't suppose it matters anymore."

"Still..." I feel I have to say something, I *want* to, although I'm not sure what. "I'm sorry, Milly," I finally whisper. "For all of it."

"So am I. For so many things." She shakes her head and lets out a long, low breath. "Why didn't you tell me about, you know, your termination? Was that why you bombed your exams? It must have been..."

"It was two weeks before."

"I can't believe I didn't know." She grimaces. "I can't believe I didn't ask."

"I didn't want you to know. I was ashamed." I look down, at my untouched drink.

"Who was it, Anna? The father? I didn't even know you were seeing anyone. I feel as if I've had to recalibrate our whole friendship, based on all the stuff I didn't know—"

"I wasn't seeing anyone."

Milly frowns. "Not even...I mean, there was *someone*. Wasn't there?"

I shake my head. "Not in the way you think. It was..." I blow out a breath. "Mr. Rees."

"Mr. Rees?" Milly's shocked and horrified expression is almost comical. "Our history teacher?"

"The very one."

"But he was so..."

"Old? Unattractive? Yes." I try to smile, but I can't quite manage it, so I take a gulp of wine instead. Even twenty years on, with all the therapy and healing, this is still hard.

"It wasn't...I mean, he didn't..."

"It wasn't rape, if that's what you mean," I say in a low voice. "At least, *he* wouldn't have ever thought it was."

"Oh, *Anna*." Milly reaches for my hand and squeezes it. "I should have known. You should have been able to tell me. I feel as if I wasn't a good friend to you at all."

"You were, Milly." Over the years, I've tried to cast her as the villain, big bad Milly who took me for granted and used me in the worst way, but it's never had the ring of authenticity. It certainly doesn't now, no matter how guilty and appalled Milly feels.

She shakes her head. "I should have made you tell me. Instead, I just dragged you along with my plans, without even considering what you might have been through."

"If you dragged me along with your plans, it was because I never had any of my own. If you hadn't found me sofa-surfing with strangers, I don't know where I would be now." I shudder at the prospect. "I really don't."

"Still, I should have done more for you."

"You did a lot. And even if you'd pressed and pressed, I might not have told you."

"I'm sorry for what you went through. I really am." She shakes her head and then drains the last of the wine. "What a pair we are."

The words warm me, in their way. We're a pair again. At least, I hope that's what she means, and the possibility that it is emboldens me to ask, "Milly...do you have any photos... of Alice?"

Milly hesitates, the glass half-raised to her mouth.

"May I see them?" I ask, trying not to sound too desperate. Surely she wouldn't deny me a photo, not after everything we've just said and shared?

"Let me see if I have a decent one," she says, and starts scrolling through her phone, the screen angled away so I can't see it, while I hold my breath. After a few seconds, she shrugs and puts the phone down on the table in front of me. "Screw it, you might as well see them all. It's only the last few months, though."

Hardly daring to breathe, I start to scroll through the photos: Alice on a beach, grinning with a drippy ice cream cone; the first day of school in a smart new hunter-green uniform; curled up on the sofa, absorbed in a book. I swipe and swipe again. Alice tucked up in bed with a million teddies. In wellies, splashing in puddles. A perfect childhood encapsulated in these precious seconds. Gazing at her, I'd never know she has a terminal disease. Gazing at her, I can't help think, *she looks just like me.* The same hair and eyes, the same dimples. The same lanky build and slightly sticky-out ears.

"She looks just like you, doesn't she?" Milly says with a wry laugh, echoing my thoughts. "Perhaps that's part of the reason I've thought of you so often."

"Is it hard... having her look like me?" I ask tentatively. This is strange, new territory, the two us talking about Alice.

"Sometimes. Sometimes I've wondered why I mind so much."

Reluctantly, I push the phone back to her. I could look at those photos forever, study each one and memorise every detail. "Thank you." Milly nods, and I make myself ask, because I want to so much, "Could I... could I see her sometime? Meet her?"

Milly's expression freezes and I know that it's a step too far. Never mind the drinks, the apologies, the heartfelt conversation, the photos, she still doesn't want me to see her daughter.

"I'm sorry, Anna. Matt and I talked about this already—"

"It's okay," I interject. I don't want to hear her excuses.

"It's just, Matt is reluctant. He doesn't want to complicate things, especially when Alice's health and treatment, such as it is, has to be paramount."

*Complicate things?* What does he think I'm going to do? But, of course, I have to respect their wishes. Perhaps it was selfish for me even to ask. "I understand," I manage, sounding brittle. "I shouldn't have asked."

"No," Milly protests, but she leaves it there.

I wish I hadn't asked, because now the door has closed forever, and I was the one to have shut it.

# CHAPTER THIRTY-ONE

## MILLY

*I'm sorry.*

That's what Dr. Williams said when he confirmed that Alice had Batten disease, having given us all the awful details: that she has a variant called CLN5, that affected children begin to exhibit symptoms after the first few years of life. He tells us it's likely Alice started exhibiting as long as two years ago. Children with CLN5 develop vision and cognitive issues, along with behavioural problems, and they gradually lose the ability to talk or walk. They usually live into their late childhood or teenage years. I can't imagine a worse prognosis; I'd almost rather Alice was hit by a car than this slow dwindling to death. And all Dr. Williams can say is, *I'm sorry.*

It reminds me of Meghan, all those years ago, offering the same kind of apology. *I'm sorry you have premature menopause. I'm sorry you can't have a baby.* And now this. *I'm sorry your child is going to suffer and die.*

*I'm sorry.* I hate those two words. They don't do anything. They just remind you that you are the one who needs to be felt sorry for.

Matt and I walk around in a haze of grief for a week after the news. We don't tell anyone; we *can't.* Telling someone—my parents, Alice's teacher, Anna—will make it too real, and it is enough, it is too much, to absorb it ourselves, the repercussions going on and on, realisation after realisation. We won't see her get married, or finish school, or even discover who she *is*. We might not even see her finish her first year of school.

Although children with Batten disease can live into their teens, many die far sooner. There are no guarantees except one, and it is the worst of all.

Then, after a week of dazed grieving, I kick into gear. I realise that the best and maybe even the only advocates for Alice are Matt and me, and we need information as well as strength to handle whatever is coming next.

So I spend hours on the internet, learning facts, memorising statistics. I read about possible therapies and treatments and how to arrange for an Individual Educational Plan at school. I join the local support group for parents of children with neurological disorders, as well as the international organisation for families with Batten disease. I devour books and blogs and JustGiving sites.

Then, after gorging on a glut of information, of hearing people's heartbreaking stories and sitting in front of the computer, tears streaming down my face as I read about their bravery, I have to stop. I am overwhelmed by Batten disease, by how it has taken over Matt's and my lives along with Alice's. It has become my new hashtag, the huge *thing* in my life; forever I will be known as the mum whose child has Batten disease. *Whose child died of Batten disease.*

Sometimes I whisper it to myself, just to try the words out. To get used to the idea, because it is coming and I know I need to be prepared, even as I know no parent can *ever* be prepared for that. Even as everything in me rails against it.

And so we have entered into the unwelcome reality of life with a terminally ill child. Alice is on a dozen different prescriptions to help alleviate some of her symptoms, even as they create new ones. She has occupational therapy three times a week, and we've been assigned a social worker to help us navigate this brave new world, but I don't like her cloying manner and Matt won't talk to her at all.

Of course, we have to tell everyone—a dozen conversations of grief and tragedy played over and over again, with neighbours, friends, teachers, family.

My parents are the hardest. My mother looks as if she is shrinking right in front of me, her whole self collapsing inwards. "To think I might outlive my granddaughter," she whispers. "Oh, Milly. Oh, *Alice*."

"Don't say that, Mum," I beg. "Please, not yet. I'm not ready for that yet."

"Oh darling, I'm sorry. I shouldn't have said . . . I didn't mean . . ."

"It's all right." I wave her protests away as she fights tears. No one knows what to say, me least of all.

"Are you going to tell her?" Mum asks in a low voice, even though Alice isn't even there. I've driven over while she is at school, Matt at work.

"Right now we're telling her as little as possible. We want things to be normal for as long as they can."

And the truth is, we still have no idea how to talk to Alice about this. How do you tell your child she is going to decline and die? How do you even *begin* to have that conversation? I've searched the internet but have found only pithy bits of advice, and then I bought a load of books on Amazon, memoirs and how-tos, but after just a couple of pages, I found I couldn't read any of them. It was too much, too hard. And, thankfully, it isn't time yet.

But the reality is, and becomes clearer every day, that we will have to tell her someday, perhaps someday soon. Each morning seems to bring a new challenge—putting on her socks, getting a spoon to her mouth, remembering an obvious word like cat or table. I see the frustration in Alice's eyes, the way she becomes angry with herself, and I want to cry.

We *have* told her she is ill, and that all the things she is experiencing are part of the illness, and also that she has some medicine to help with it. Alice hasn't asked any more questions. She trusts us—to take care of her, to keep her safe, and we are trying, oh how we are trying, but ultimately we *can't*, and that still feels impossible to live with.

"What can we do, darling?" my father asked. "How can we help?" He meant well, but my parents are both elderly now and my mother's health has never recovered properly. Besides, there is nothing anyone can do. That is what hurts most of all.

And yet people still try—casseroles appear on our doorstep, and cards in the post, and a well-meaning mother at school, when she hears about it, informs me quite cheerily that she is organising a "fun run."

"For charity, to go towards research," she explains uncertainly; the look on my face must be terrible. I don't want a fun run. There is nothing *fun* about this.

"Thank you," I manage to say. I know she means well. Everyone does—from the parents at school to our neighbours to the people who matter most—my parents, Matt's family, Anna, Jack. Jack just hugged us when we told him; there were no words.

As for Anna... I think back to the drink we shared, how nice it was, to be together again, and I wonder if I should have let her see Alice, even though I know Matt would never allow it. Then I decided I couldn't think about it anymore. I am second-guessing so much already; I don't have enough energy to worry about Anna.

Although Matt and I are in this together, it feels as if we are floating in our own isolated bubbles of grief, handling each day's challenges in our different ways. Matt never wants to talk; he doesn't want to make a plan, the way we always have before, complete with bullet points and to-do lists.

I understand his reluctance, because God knows I feel it, too. Who wants to discuss how best to handle Alice's toileting needs at school, since she is struggling to manage by herself? Or what foods she is able to eat now that she is having trouble chewing? And yet we have to, because we have to make decisions, more and more every day, in order to help Alice.

"I feel as if I'm alone in this, Matt." We are sitting at the kitchen table one rainy evening in February, and Matt has an obdurate look on his face I've come to know well. "I need your input." We have been discussing the school's Individual Educational Plan for Alice, and how it needs to be amended—again. Miss Hamilton has been amazing, but even she struggles to keep up with Alice's increasing needs.

"Why do you need my input?" He sounds surly, and I tense. "It doesn't change anything."

"What is that supposed to mean?"

He shrugs, not looking at me. "Whether Alice has help cutting up her food, Milly. It doesn't *change* anything. It doesn't change what's going to happen to her." Already he's looking at his phone, one thumb scrolling mindlessly, the conversation over.

"Do you really mean that?" I ask quietly. "You don't think this matters?"

He looks up, his expression set, almost angry. "She's going to die, Milly. She's going to decline and die—it's just a matter of how and when."

My hands curl into fists on the table. "And meanwhile her quality of life doesn't matter? You don't care about that?"

"What quality of life?" he bursts out. "Do you think it seriously matters that she learns her letter sounds when she'll be blind within a year? Or that she has her food cut up for her when, according to Doctor Williams, she'll be on a liquid-only diet by the time she's seven? Do you really think *any* of this matters?"

"It matters to Alice." My voice is shaking. "I thought we agreed we wanted to keep things normal for her as long as possible."

"Nothing about this is normal." He pushes away from the table so hard it moves across the floor, and I have to stop it from hitting me.

"Matt—"

"I can't do this." The words come out low, flat, despairing. "I can't do this, Milly." His back is to me, one hand raked through his hair.

"What do you mean, you can't do this?" I'm afraid to dissect what he's telling me. "We *have* to do this, Matt."

"It's too hard." His voice breaks. "Seeing her this way ... losing something almost every day ... it's too hard."

I stare at him, caught between the wild grief I know he feels and anger that he's making this about him.

"And how do you think Alice feels? She's the one who has to endure it all. For her sake we have to be strong. Please, Matt." I don't think I can do this without him, and yet I realise I already am. Over the last few weeks he's withdrawn, not just from me, but from Alice. "Matt, please. I need you. Alice needs you."

He shakes his head again. "I'm sorry ..."

I can't stand to hear that stupid sentiment yet again. "Don't be sorry," I snap. "Be strong. Do you think this is easy for anyone? I feel as if I'm bleeding out, *every single day*, and I have to hide it, act like I'm coping when I'm *not*. But I do it, Matt, because if I don't, what will happen to Alice? Don't you want whatever time she has left as a normal little girl to be happy for her? Don't you want these memories to count?"

"Count for what? The ending is still the same."

"But the way we get there can be different." I think of Anna's mother, who torpedoed her whole life, and Anna's childhood, in her grief. I *won't* be like that. "These moments matter, Matt. They have to."

But he just shakes his head, and then he scoops his keys off the counter. "I'm going out."

"Going out? Where—"

"Just out. I need some space, Milly. I'll be back later." He leaves without looking back at me.

I stand there, staring around the empty room in disbelief. After a few minutes I start tidying up, because I don't know what else to do. I've read the statistics; I know parents who lose a child are more likely to divorce. But I don't want that to happen to Matt and me. I don't want to add another grief onto an already unbearable one.

But what if I don't have a choice? And, even worse, I think as I mindlessly put cups into the dishwasher, what if Matt is right and none of this really matters?

# CHAPTER THIRTY-TWO

## ANNA

"Hey, Anna."

I stare at Jack in shock, amazed to see him at my front door, even though I've just buzzed him in, after he'd texted me this evening asking if he could come over.

It's been a month since Milly and I had a drink together, and I hoped that our friendship might restart. It hasn't, and Milly hasn't been in touch even once; the carefully worded text messages have gone without reply.

I know I can't blame her. Who has emotional energy for fraught friendships when their child is dying? And yet I think of them, and of Alice, almost constantly. I wish I had stayed part of their lives, so I could be the support to them now that I know they must need. Instead, I've been shunted off to the very periphery of their lives, which I know is my own fault. If I hadn't made that desperate, pointless bid for custody...if Jack hadn't said...

I give him a not-entirely friendly look. "What are you doing here, Jack?"

He looks a bit taken aback by my animosity, but I haven't seen him in five years, and the last time I saw him I asked him to go away. What did he expect?

"I just wanted to see you. You know about Alice?"

I stare at him in disbelief. *Do I know about Alice?* "If I didn't, was that how you were going to tell me?"

"I'm sorry." He runs a hand over his face. "I wasn't thinking. It's just so...crap, you know?"

"Yes. I know." And crap is a massive understatement. I consider mentioning my brother, how they found out about Alice's diagnosis, but then I decide there's no point. It doesn't change anything.

"It's just so hard to believe..." Jack continues. "I mean, what are the chances? Both of us having this crap gene."

"Very slim, apparently." One in fifty thousand, or so the internet says, and Alice's version is even rarer than that.

"If we hadn't..." He swallows hard and looks at me. "If it hadn't been both of us..."

"I know." I torture myself with that thought enough; I don't need Jack to say it. "How was anyone to know?"

"I know. I know. It's just so rough. I keep thinking about her. She's such a cute kid."

I feel a twitch pass across my face and I struggle to keep my voice even. "I wouldn't know."

Jack looks surprised. "You mean you haven't seen her...?"

Does he actually not know that I've been estranged from Milly and Matt since *that* day? Is he so unbelievably clueless? I just shake my head, because I have no words.

"I thought you guys would have made up, after all this time."

"It hasn't happened that way." A pressure is building in my chest. "But you must not have kept in decent touch, if you don't know that."

He hangs his head a bit, shamefaced. "I moved back to France a few years ago...but I've come for visits. Milly and Matt brought Alice out one summer..."

And they must not have ever even mentioned me. I turn away, because I don't want him to see my face. All of this hurts. I've missed so much, so many days out and dinners in and long, lazy holidays, and now it's too late. I can't stand the thought. I can't stand to rewrite history in my mind, a montage of cosy moments where I stayed involved in Milly and Matt's—*and Alice's*—lives. Where I mattered.

"How are you doing, Anna?" Jack asks, his voice gentle. "I keep thinking of Milly and Matt, but then I realise this affects you as well. More than...well, more than anyone else, besides them, maybe. You loved Alice..."

An unruly sob escapes me and I press my fist to my mouth. I've cried enough in front of Jack Foster.

And yet I do cry, and he does see, as another sob breaks over me like a wave, and suddenly Jack's arms are around me. He's the last person I'd expect to turn to for comfort. The last person I'd expect to offer it.

"I'm sorry, Anna," Jack murmurs as he strokes my hair. "I'm sorry for everything. I keep thinking back to that day, you know..." Of course I know what day. "And wishing I could have acted differently. Been...more understanding. Shut my damn mouth."

With what feels like immense effort, I step away from him as I wipe my eyes. "That's in the past, Jack. Long in the past. It doesn't matter anymore."

"I think it does." He gazes at me steadily. "If it hadn't...if I hadn't..."

"Alice would still be ill. She'd still be dying." I make myself say the words, even though each one cuts me inside. "Nothing can change that."

"But you'd have known her," Jack says sadly. "You'd have been involved in her life, all along..."

Which is far too painful to think about, so I turn resolutely towards the future, what little of it there is. "I wish I could be involved now. Not just for my sake, but for theirs. They need support, Jack. This has got to be so hard, and they're making it harder by keeping to themselves. Have you seen them? How are they coping?"

"Coping is the word." He grimaces. "I don't really know. Milly seems...manic, I suppose. And Matt barely talks. It's been really rough on both of them."

"Do they have help? Parents, or people from school?"

"A bit. Milly's parents aren't up for much and Matt's and mine have never been too involved in, well, anything." He laughs, a humourless sound. "They have their own interests."

"Nice." I shake my head. "What about friends from school? Work?"

"I don't really know." He looks a bit shamefaced, and I wonder how much he's helped. Has Jack *ever* been the kind of person to go the distance?

"Never mind," I say. "I'll go over there."

Jack looks both relieved and uncertain. "Are you on good terms with them, Anna? I mean—"

"I know what you mean. And no, I'm not on any terms with them, not really. I had a drink with Milly about a month ago." I think of Matt's refusal to let me see Alice. Yet am I really going to let that stop me? "Still, we surely can put aside our differences for Alice's sake. They need support." And in the past, that has always been given by me. Why should things be any different now?

When I tell Will my plans, however, he seems reluctant. He hasn't liked what he considers my obsession with Alice; too often when we're meant to be watching something on TV, I am on my phone, searching out the latest medical research on Batten disease, hoping for some last-minute breakthrough. When we're out and about, I'm distracted and distant; I try not to be, but whether I wanted it to or not, Alice's condition has taken over my thoughts.

"Do you really think this is a good idea, Anna?" he asks as I stir the huge pot of soup I'm making to take over to their house. "You told me that Matt refused to let you see Alice."

"And I won't see her." Although I am hoping to, even if just a glimpse. "They need help, Matt. Jack said they don't have much support."

"And you want to be the one to give it?" He sounds skeptical, and I can hardly blame him, considering everything that has happened.

"I always have before."

"True, and that didn't turn out so well. I'm thinking of you, Anna—"

"And I'm thinking of them."

He nods slowly. "Yes, but things have changed since you helped them before—"

"Exactly. Things have changed. Now is the time to step up." I look at him levelly, and he looks back, and then, after a long, tense moment, he shrugs.

"I understand why you feel the way you do, I just don't agree with it." He sighs. "But fine. Go."

"I wasn't actually asking your permission," I say a bit sharply.

"And I wasn't giving it. I think this is a bad idea. I think this is only going to hurt you in the long run, and yes, it's you I care about, not people I've never met, although I recognise that you care about them. But I really do honestly believe that you need to let go, Anna. Let go of Alice."

"I will have to soon enough," I remind him quietly. "Will, don't you think this is the right thing to do? They need help."

"And they have people in their lives to help them, no matter what Jack says. What does he know? You told me he said he's been in France for years."

"Yes, but—"

"Anna, what I'm afraid of, what worries me, is that you're not doing this for Milly and Matt. You're doing this for yourself, and it's going to end badly."

I stare down at the soup as I stir it, trying not to feel hurt by his words. "We already know it's going to end badly. I just want to be there when it does."

He shakes his head but doesn't say anything more, and the next evening I drive to Milly and Matt's house. It's mid-February, the same time of year Milly came home and I walked out. Five years ago now, which feels like forever and yet no time at all.

I park the car in front of their house and gaze at it—the hanging basket by the front door, now empty, swinging a little in the breeze; the spill of warm light from the picture window out front, with the drapes drawn across. It's half past six, early enough that Alice won't have gone to bed. But have I really come over here just to see her, or did I mean what I said to both Jack and Will about offering support? Will they even accept it?

Slowly I get out of my car, taking the bag I've brought with a tray bake of brownies and the pot of homemade chicken soup. Paltry offerings, but I don't know what else I have to give.

I feel sick with nerves, my stomach knotted with anxiety, as I press the doorbell and wait. I question whether I should have come, if Will is right and this is essentially a selfish act. I hear muted voices, the sound of someone coming down the stairs. Then the door opens, and Matt stands there, slack-jawed at the sight of me before his expression hardens.

"Anna."

"Hi, Matt." It's been strange, how hostile Matt has been to me, even more so than Milly, and so unlike the easygoing guy I used to joke around with. He stands in the doorway now, his body blocking my entrance, clearly not willing to move. "May I come in? Just for a few minutes…"

"Matt," Milly calls from upstairs. "Who is it?" I hear the sound of splashing and then a giggle, and I realise Alice must be in the bath. I picture her sitting in a froth of bubbles, hair piled on top of her head, a grin for her mummy as she pops the translucent bubbles one by one.

"It's Anna," Matt says flatly.

Silence from upstairs. Then, "I can't leave Alice…"

"I'll take care of it." Which makes me sound like some sort of pest problem. I heft the bag I'm carrying so Matt can see it.

"I brought some food…"

"Come in," he says rather ungraciously, and steps aside so I can squeeze past.

It's strange being in their house again. I was here a few months ago, to tell them about my brother, but I didn't notice any details because I was so distraught. Now I look around, and see evidence of Alice everywhere. Crayoned pictures Sellotaped to the fridge. A basket of toys, with plastic unicorns and princesses featuring heavily. A half-done puzzle of a fairy castle on the coffee table. A plastic sippy cup, the kind for a small toddler, by the sink.

"Shall I put these in the kitchen?" I ask, and Matt shrugs. His animosity feels palpable, like a thick, oily substance coating the air, making it difficult to breathe.

I unload the soup and brownies on the counter and spend an inordinate amount of time folding the bag while Matt just waits. Does he expect me to leave now? Should I?

"How are you both managing?" I finally ask and he makes a huff of sound.

"How do you think?"

"I'd like to help…"

"We don't need your help, Anna." The rebuff is quick and absolute, and despite everything, it still surprises me. It still hurts.

I stare at Matt, noting how he clenches and unclenches his fists, his stance one of complete aggression, as if I'm the enemy. *Still*.

"Matt…" I take a deep breath. I wasn't going to talk about the past tonight. I didn't want to resurrect old ghosts, have them drift around us, but with the sound of Alice splashing in the bath upstairs, I find myself saying words I didn't expect to, even though I've already said them to Milly. "Matt, I'm sorry."

He doesn't reply, doesn't acknowledge my apology with so much as a flicker of an eyelid.

"I'm sorry for before," I clarify. "For thinking, even for a moment, that Alice was…that I was…"

"Anna, don't." The words are savage, bitten off. "Not now."

"I don't know what possessed me," I continue haltingly, determined now to say what I have never had the chance to say to him. "It was such a strange time, and I didn't expect to feel the way I did…"

He takes a menacing step towards me. "Don't you dare make excuses now," he says in a low voice. "Don't you *dare*, when you tried to *steal* our child—"

"I didn't steal anyone." For the last five years, I've tortured myself with guilt even as I've nurtured my anger, but I want to be finished with both now. Surely, considering Alice's condition, we should put this behind us, finally and forever? We should be able to.

"You would have, if you'd had the chance—"

"No, *listen*. I admit, I consulted a lawyer. I was thinking of…of applying for custody. But I look back and I don't think I would have ever gone through with it. Even the solicitor was discouraging me from—"

"At least someone in the situation had some sense of morality—"

"Matt, *please*. I know it was…it was wrong. But can't you see it from my perspective, just for a moment? I was taking care of Alice all the time, for *weeks*—"

"We *trusted* you—"

"And even you had said you weren't sure if Milly—"

"And you threw it back in my face. A moment of weakness, when I was at my lowest—"

"And what about me? What about *my* moment of weakness, *my* lowest? Did you ever consider that?" My voice rings out, despairing, broken. "Did you ever think about how it felt for me—"

"A normal person wouldn't think that taking care of a baby when the parents are vulnerable means you then sue for custody." Matt's voice is hard.

I shake my head, impatient now. "I wouldn't have gone through with—"

"You don't know that."

"*You* don't know that." We stare at each other, a standoff. "Is that it, then?" I ask more quietly. "No forgiveness? No moving on? One strike and I'm out? Is that how you operate, Matt?"

He stares at me for a long moment. Upstairs, I hear Milly call Alice softly, and I wonder—I hope—she is going to come downstairs. That I'll get a chance to see her. But then I hear a bedroom door click softly shut, and I realise I should have known better. They are never going to let me see her.

Then, when I am half-expecting Matt to order me out of the house for a second time, his face crumples. I watch in shock as his lips tremble and his eyes start to stream and he shakes his head, turning away from me to hide his emotion.

"Matt…"

"It's my fault." The words are barely audible; I hear them, just, but I still can't make sense of them. "My fault," he repeats, his voice choking. "I shouldn't have left Alice with you." I reel back, shocked. *What is he saying about me…?* "I shouldn't have failed Alice like that. Failed Milly."

Realisation sharpens into focus. "You didn't fail anyone—"

"I was happy enough to let you take all the night-time wake-ups, all the feeds, everything. I checked out, because it was easier. It's always easier."

I have the uneasy sense that he is not talking about then, but now. "You didn't *check out*, Matt, and in any case you had a lot to deal with. You still do." I shrug helplessly. "It was an impossible situation, just as it is now."

"Still…" He draws a quick, ragged breath. "I should have been a better husband. A better father."

I stare at him, unsure where to go from here. Has he been angry at me for five years because he hasn't wanted to admit how angry he is with himself?

"That's all in the past," I say finally. "It all happened a long time ago, and I'm sure you've been a wonderful father and husband in the years since then. What matters is now, Matt—"

"Yeah, and you know what happens now?" Matt swings around to face me, angry again. His moods are changing so quickly it makes my head spin, and yet I understand it. The grief is too overwhelming to make sense of. "What happens now," he continues in a low growl, "is that my daughter declines and *dies*. That's what happens now." His lips tremble and he presses them together. "And I'm failing her now just as I failed her then."

"Matt, please let me help. I want to help you and Milly." My voice trembles. *"Please."*

He shakes his head, but the gesture seems aimed more at himself than at me.

"How is Alice doing?" I brace myself for his rebuff, but he deflates, that spark of anger already snuffed out.

"She's still in school, but she can't hold a pencil easily or even drink from a cup," he states flatly. I recall her sippy cup by the sink. "She can't bring a spoon to her mouth, at least not without getting food everywhere, and she keeps forgetting simple words. She's also got 20/40 vision, which is only going to get worse, and the consultant thinks she'll need crutches within the next few months. She's had eight seizures since the diagnosis, and that's on medication. *That's* how she's doing."

He turns away, and I blink slowly, taking in each detail with dawning horror. Even after all the research I'd done online, I hadn't expected her to deteriorate quite so quickly. It's been less than three *months*.

"Matt, I'm so sorry..." The words are painfully inadequate. "Please, let me help you. What can I do?"

He shakes his head, his back to me. "I don't know what we need." Which at least isn't no.

"I can bring food, do the washing. Whatever..." I trail off, because I realise Matt isn't in a place to brainstorm with me about ways to help, and coming here at all was, in some way, selfish. I wanted to see Alice. That's what motivated me, at a base level. Will was right. I swallow hard as I let go of that deeply held desire, for the first time. "The soup is in the fridge," I say. "I'll bring another meal round in a few days, if you think it helps. I don't have to come in. I can leave it on the front step."

Matt doesn't reply and after another few seconds I turn around and leave, closing the door quietly behind me. It isn't until I'm in the car that I see the silhouettes behind the drapes, and I realise Milly has come downstairs. She must have been waiting for me to leave.

# CHAPTER THIRTY-THREE

## MILLY

I hear Anna close the front door as I wait at the top of the stairs. It might make me a coward, but I wasn't strong enough for a confrontation with her tonight, not on top of everything else. It's been two weeks since Matt walked out of the house, and although he came back after a couple of hours, things have changed between us. A tension exists between us that wasn't there before, but after overhearing his conversation with Anna, the honesty in it, I feel the tiniest bit hopeful that things might change.

As I come downstairs, I see him sitting at the kitchen table, his head in his hands. He looks up as I approach, his expression so very weary.

"She's gone."

"I know."

"How much of that did you hear?"

"Most of it," I admit.

Matt lets out a heavy sigh and drops his head into his hands once more. "I'm sorry, Milly. I'm doing so badly with all of this and making it even worse for you."

My heart twists painfully. I've been trying not to feel angry with Matt for the way he's disengaged, and I haven't succeeded. It's revealed itself in a snippy tone, a frosty look, which has made things worse between us, but right now I feel only empathy—and sadness. So much sadness.

"I want us to stick together on this, Matt. That's all."

"I know. I do, too." He looks up again, despairing. "You're so much stronger than me."

"I'm not, Matt." I put my hand on his shoulder. "I'm really not."

We stay like that for a few minutes, neither of us speaking. It almost feels peaceful, as if this heavy weight that has been bearing down on me has eased, just a little.

"Do you think I was too harsh with Anna?" Matt asks eventually. "She wants to help."

"Then let her help. God knows we need it."

"And Alice?"

The question hangs in the air, as if I can almost see the words spelt out. *And Alice*. Always Alice between us, but for the first time I wonder if it doesn't have to be that way any longer.

But then Matt shakes his head. "It's too complicated. I can't think about it, not on top of everything else."

Which was my excuse for hiding upstairs. Whether she means to be or not, Anna is a complication in our lives that we don't have the emotional energy to indulge, and I know that she is the one who will pay the price.

Any worry or guilt I feel over that, however, diminishes in light of everything else—dealing with Alice's constantly changing and growing needs, her medication, her moods. Our sunny girl has periods of darkness, just as we do—days when she doesn't want to get out of bed, nights when she can't sleep. Sudden rages when she realises there is something else she can't do; yesterday it was brushing her teeth. She threw the toothbrush at the mirror, and then started hitting it with her fists, causing it to crack. We ended up in A&E, getting three stitches put in her right hand where the shattered glass had cut her.

Every day brings itself a new challenge, and yet also surprising graces.

One afternoon in early March, I am standing by the school gate, avoiding everyone as usual, which seems to be the easiest option for both me and them, when another mum approaches me.

"You're Alice's mum?" she says with a smile, and I nod, because everyone knows that now.

"I'm Jane, and my daughter Violet is in year one. I was wondering if Alice could come over for a play date? Although they're not in the same class, they play together so well."

I stare at her dumbly; it is the very last thing I expect. In fact, lately I've been wondering if it's worth keeping Alice in school at all, with all the challenges, and the way some of her classmates have started to look at her. They're too young to understand, or to filter their words.

*Why is she walking funny? Why can't she talk normally? Why is Alice so weird?*

"A play date..." I say slowly, because I'm not sure that's possible.

"I know there are additional needs," Jane says gently. "And if you want to come along too, that's absolutely fine."

Just then Miss Hamilton opens the door, and after the first rush of children, I see Alice walk unsteadily out, hand in hand with a little girl with brown hair and a gap-toothed smile I don't recognise.

"That's Violet," Jane says proudly, and as the two girls come closer, I realise Violet has Down syndrome. Jane confirms it with her next words. "They got to know each other, because they both have support workers," she explains. "And they ended up doing things together."

I nod, fighting a lump in my throat. So the special need kids get lumped together. It's to be expected, and yet I resist the notion. I don't want that for Alice, and yet that seems wrong.

"I know it's hard," Jane says gently. "It's not what you wanted."

Which makes it sound as if I placed an order for a child the way I would for a meal in a restaurant, and picky customer that

I am, I'm going to send it back. "It's what *is*," I tell Jane, making my voice firm. "And I'm sure Alice would love to have a play date with Violet."

The play date is, of course, a big deal. Alice has had only a few play dates in her entire life, back in preschool, and I always went along. This time, however, she is insistent she wants to go by herself, even though I am terrified that something will happen and it will all go wrong.

"Violet's mummy is going to take us from school," she tells me. "And we'll have chips for tea!"

Her words have become more slurred in the last month, and sometimes it's hard to understand what she says. I wonder if Jane will be able to understand her, and I try to quell that persistent tremor of fear. "It sounds amazing, Alice."

But I am still in a ferment of anxiety for the whole day of the play date; I have to resist walking to the school gate, just to check that the pickup goes off all right, at the end of the school day. I tell myself this is luxury, having time to tidy up, pay some bills, look into the conference for Batten families that is in Florida in July. The hours tick by, terribly slow, and finally, *finally*, it is time to pick her up.

I hear the squeals of laughter before I've even turned into Jane's drive. I hesitate, stunned and more than a little apprehensive, as I see them both jumping up and down on a trampoline in the front garden. Should they really be doing that...? Alice falls on her side, and I hasten forward.

"Alice..."

"Hey, Mummy!" She sounds so happy. It stops me where I am, because I can't remember the last time Alice sounded like that.

"They've had a fabulous time," Jane tells me from the front door. "I've been keeping my eye on them—I hope you don't mind?"

I feel disoriented, because part of me does mind, and yet Alice is so happy. She's doing what a million other girls her age can do, and who am I to stop that? To hover?

"I'm glad she's having fun," I finally say, and Jane smiles in understanding, as if she's witnessed my entire thought process.

"Come in and have a cup of tea."

We watch the girls from the front window as we sit in the lounge and drink tea, and I can't believe how wonderfully normal it is, how much of a break.

Jane doesn't talk about Batten disease or Down syndrome or any of the challenges associated with either, and that is a relief. We're just two normal mums, with two normal children. And as we sit and chat, I realise I need to completely redefine what normal is, because Alice *is* normal, just as Violet is.

Listening to them giggle and squeal outside, you wouldn't be able to tell that anything is wrong with them and, for the first time ever, I wonder if there *isn't*.

Eventually the girls come back in, tired but happy. Jane has them wash their hands at the sink, and I watch as they fumble through it, dropping the soap, splashing themselves, but they do it. Maybe I should let Alice do more, even if it's messy and difficult. Maybe it would help her as well as me.

I feel as if I've opened a door into a whole new room I didn't know even existed, filled with sunlight and possibility. Since Alice's diagnosis, I've been living in the dark, head down, always pushing through, soldiering on, but now I wonder if it has to be that way. If maybe, just maybe, we can enjoy more than endure.

But then I remember that Violet does not have a terminal diagnosis. Violet is not going to lose her sight, speech, and mobility in the next few years. Violet is not destined to die when she's still a child. Alice's diagnosis is different from Violet's; there is no escaping that. But for now, they are little girls and they are friends, and that is enough.

"If you ever need to talk," Jane says as we're leaving. Her smile is kind without being pitying. "About anything."

"Thanks, I'm sure I would. And perhaps we can have Violet over one afternoon." I realise I mean it, that I would like to do that.

"That would be lovely," Jane says, and both girls chime in with their delight at the prospect.

"You had a good time?" I ask Alice as we walk home hand in hand, darkness already falling.

"Yes, Mummy, I really did." Alice turns to me appealingly. "Can we get a trampoline?"

My instinct is that no, we cannot get a trampoline, because it's too dangerous, and in a few weeks or months or maybe, just maybe, years, Alice won't be able to use it anyway. But then I am appalled at myself, at my narrow, negative view, because Alice can use it *now*.

"Yes," I tell her with a smile. "I think that sounds like a fabulous idea." And then because I want to grab life and happiness while I can, I add, "Let's order one tonight online."

When we arrive home, there is a foil-covered casserole dish lying on the front step. There have been a few of these nearly every week, and they're all from Anna. As I pick it up, Alice asks me who it is from.

"Just a friend," I say, and we head inside.

"My friend? My friend Violet?"

"No, a friend named Anna." Saying the words feels momentous, but of course Alice doesn't register their import; she just keeps asking questions.

"Anna? Do I know her? Has she met me?"

I keep my gaze on the casserole as I answer. "Yes, you met her a long time ago, when you were a baby."

"A baby? Not since then?"

"No," I say heavily. "Not since then." I pause and then look up. Alice is standing in the middle of the living room, listing to one side like a ship in a storm, blinking at me from behind her thick glasses, but she's smiling, and I realise that even though this terrible disease has stolen so much from her, it can't steal that. She is still Alice. She will always be Alice.

"Alice," I say. "Do you want to meet her sometime? Our friend Anna?"

Her face lights up as she nods. "Yes, oh yes!" she cries, even though she doesn't know anything about Anna. She's always been up for meeting a new friend. "I want to meet her. Can we meet her today, Mummy?"

"No, not today," I say, the words feeling important and necessary, a promise I am making not just to Alice, but to myself. "But soon."

Amazingly, I am feeling optimistic, for the first time in what feels like forever. The sun is shining, and Alice has a friend. For once the future doesn't feel as if it is yawning in front of me, dark and terrible. A few weeks ago, Matt and I started therapy again, and we are stronger than ever. Finally there is a break in the clouds of our lives, and for a few moments I allow myself to enjoy the sunshine, to breathe, to *be*.

Then, that night, Alice has a grand mal seizure, and everything changes again.

# CHAPTER THIRTY-FOUR

## ANNA

The soil is dark and rich as I plunge my hands into it, turning over the earth to plant the tiny seed. It is late May, and Will and I are working on his uncle's allotment; his cancer returned and it's unlikely he'll be able to work it, at least this year.

It's been good for us, working together, growing things. We've cleared away all the winter's debris and have planned raised beds of onions and lettuce, as well as a new chicken coop and six lovely little chicks, fat and yellow. It's a fresh start, something I think we both needed, especially me, after all the sorrow of the winter.

Five months on from Alice's diagnosis, and I have begun to learn to let go. It's been a slow process, a painful separation of myself, and yet I know it's been necessary. It's been five years since I last saw Alice, and I've finally stopped looking for her.

Will, despite or perhaps because of his initial concern, has been unwaveringly supportive. I make meals for Matt and Milly once a week or so, and every so often I send her a text, just to let her know I am thinking of her, without any pressure or expectation.

After five years, I've finally relinquished the expectation that I am somehow owed something from Milly. And while Alice is never far from my thoughts, she doesn't dominate them.

"Tea break?" Will suggests, and I straighten, easing the crick in my lower back. We've been working for several hours, and the plot is taking shape. All around us people are busy on their own strips of land, raking, hoeing, and planting. The world feels lush and brimming with possibility, with new growth and fresh starts.

"Sounds good."

We troop into the little shed, where we've now spent so many happy hours. Will lights the propane stove while I fill the kettle at the outdoor tap.

"I'll make it," he says, taking the kettle from me when I return. I shrug and sit down, grateful to have a bit of a rest.

It's a lovely, sunny day, and I tilt my head to catch the light from the open door, my eyes drifting closed as I listen to the drone of bumblebees, someone calling in the distance.

"Here you go." Will sounds a bit hesitant, even nervous, as I open my eyes and see a tin mug of tea in front of my face.

"Thanks." I take a sip while Will watches me.

"You looked as if you'd fallen asleep."

"I almost had." He's still watching me, and I let out a little laugh. "What is it?"

"Nothing." Abashed, he looks away. I glance down at my mug, and I start at the sight of something floating in the hot liquid. Something bright and glittering.

"Will..."

"What?" He looks entirely too innocent, and I laugh incredulously, unsure even now. Carefully, wincing a bit because the tea is hot, I fish the ring out of the mug—because it is a ring, a diamond ring.

When I look up, Will is kneeling down in front of me. "Anna, I love you so much. Will you marry me?"

I laugh again, still incredulous, and so joyful. "Yes...yes, of course I will."

He slides the ring onto my finger and then I grab his hands and pull him to his feet, as he kisses me. "Shall we set a date?" he asks.

"Already?" I laugh. I still can barely credit the ring sparkling on my finger.

"The sooner the better, as far as I am concerned." He gives a playful grimace. "Neither of us are getting any younger, I am reluctant to admit."

"True." A sudden, terrible thought jolts through me, and Will sees it in my face.

"Anna, what is it?"

"Do you want children?" I ask bluntly. We've never spoken about it before, even when we've talked about Alice.

"If they happen, they happen," Will answers after a moment. "What I really want is a lifetime with you."

"Yes, but…" I twist the ring on my finger. "You know I have this gene? For Batten disease? And apparently, there is a fifty percent chance I'd pass it on to my child." As I've already done once.

Something flickers across Will's face, and I know he hasn't thought of this before. I hadn't either, amazingly. I'd been so focused on Alice, and in any case, even when Will came into my life, I never really thought I'd have children of my own.

"Well, I most likely don't have the gene," Will says, his tone determinedly reasonable. "And I can be tested for it, at any rate."

"But even so, any child we have might be a carrier…"

Will gives me a sympathetic smile. He knows this is hard for me, stirring up old anxieties and longings. A child still feels like an impossibility, something that's almost forbidden for me. *A child of my own.* Can I even dare to dream…?

"Surely we can cross that bridge when we come to it, Anna?" Will says gently. "I know it's a concern, of course it is, but this is the start of our life together. That's what we can focus on now."

"Yes, I know. And I'm so happy…" But thinking of a child makes me think of Alice. How is she? How are Milly and Matt coping? I don't know. Perhaps I never will.

My lower lip wobbles and he draws me to him. I tuck my head under his chin and close my eyes, savouring the steady warmth of him next to me, amazed that he is going to be my husband.

"I know she'll always be part of your life," he says softly and I let out a little hiccoughy sigh.

"How did you know I was thinking of her?"

"Because I know you." He rests one hand on my back. "Have you heard from Milly lately?"

"No, I never hear from her, besides a text to thank me for a meal." I sigh. "I don't expect anything else. I know she'll tell me if…" I can't say it. I wrap my arms around him and tilt my head up to meet his concerned, crinkled gaze. "Let's get married this summer."

"So soon?" he teases.

"Yes." I sound firm and I feel determined. I must shed these old sorrows like the ghosts they are, for Will's sake as well as mine. They don't need to haunt me any longer, even though I know they will always have a place in my life. "Like you said, we're not getting any younger. Why wait?"

Two weeks later, Milly calls me.

# CHAPTER THIRTY-FIVE

## MILLY

A hospital at night feels like a ward of ghosts. It's early June, and outside the world is in full bloom, the cherry blossoms masses of pink puffballs, the flower beds laden with heavy-headed tulips, but inside everything is darkened and silent, save for an occasional cough, the squeak of a trolley wheel. I feel invisible, drifting down the corridor, stretching my legs before I return to sit by Alice, who is, thankfully, sleeping.

We've had half a dozen overnights in the hospital since that first grand mal seizure back in March, to adjust her medication, usually after she's had another seizure. It takes a few days to work out the right dosage, and then we're back home, trying to restart this strange new life we find ourselves living.

And it *is* strange—a deep sadness punctuated with moments of joy, as we adjust to the ever-changing reality of loss. She is still in school, and her best friend is Violet, and her belly laugh makes me smile the way nothing else can. She's Alice. Amazingly, wonderfully, she still is our Alice.

I slip inside her room and stretch out on the makeshift bed they've set up next to her. Matt and I have been taking turns staying the night, and tonight it is mine. Looking at her now, you wouldn't even know she was ill at all, much less so seriously—her hair is spread out across her pillow in a golden sheet, her lashes fanning her pale cheeks.

Watching her sleep, you couldn't tell that her vision loss is now at seventy percent, or that she can no longer hold a pencil or spoon. If you didn't notice the crutches propped in the corner of the room, you wouldn't realise she couldn't walk unassisted. If you didn't hear her speak, you wouldn't know that she slurs some words and forgets far too many others. Watching her now, you wouldn't know anything was wrong with her at all.

And maybe nothing is. Maybe this is who Alice is, who she has been all along. It's a strange and unsettling thought that I sift through my mind, looking for the gold amidst the dross. Maybe this is who Alice was always meant to be, teaching us, loving us, helping us to be strong and thankful even as we grieve and rail.

I shift on the bed, trying to get comfortable even though I know it's pointless. I hardly ever get to sleep during these hospital visits, tensing at every distant noise, or just straining to hear Alice breathe. I should be used to it now, used to the whole sorry load of this wretched disease, but I'm not. Even now, I feel a ripple of surprise—*Wait, really? Alice is sick? When did that happen?*

Sometimes, in these long, lonely nights, I've let myself play the pointless what-if game, a form of self-torture I try not to indulge in. *What if I hadn't had premature menopause? What if we'd gone with an anonymous donor? What if we'd adopted?* What if... Then Alice wouldn't be here at all. She wouldn't exist.

And when I think like that, I make myself ask the hardest question of all. *Would that be better?* Would I—*could* I—wish that, knowing what I do now, bracing myself for all that is still ahead, all we—and Alice—will have to suffer and endure?

Alice stirs in her sleep and I lean forward to smooth the hair away from her face, my heart aching with love for her, just as she is now, as she's always been. No, I could not wish that.

"Mummy?" Alice's voice is disembodied in the darkness, the voice of a ghost.

"Yes, darling?"

"Mummy, am I going to get better?" The question is soft, slurred, but all too understandable. I prevaricate, because the alternative still feels impossible, even after all this time.

"The new medication should help, darling. That's what the doctor said."

Alice, my lovely Alice, shakes her head. "No. Am I going to get *better*?" And she waits for my answer, the answer my heart cries out not to give, even now. Especially now. And yet I know she deserves the truth. She's been so patient, so brave, so trusting. And even though she's only five years old, I see an understanding in her eyes that humbles me.

"The things you've been feeling, Alice...the symptoms... they'll never go away." I take her hand. "I'm so sorry, sweetheart. So, so sorry."

She is silent for a long moment, lost in thought, but I have no idea what she is thinking. Then she looks at me again, those sea-green eyes startlingly direct. "Am I going to die?"

My eyes fill with tears as my heart lodges itself in my throat. I hold her hand like an anchor. I'm not ready for this moment. I didn't think she'd ask; I didn't think she'd *know*. She's still so very little. And yet, looking at her, I can see that she does. "One day, Alice," I say quietly. "Yes. But Daddy and I will be with you. We'll never leave you alone, I promise. We'll stay with you the whole time, and you won't need to be scared at all."

She nods slowly, her expression so serious. "Will it hurt?"

A small sob threatens to escape me, but I choke it down. "I promise you, Alice, it won't hurt. The doctors will make sure it doesn't. It will be like falling asleep, and it's not going to happen for a long time." *God willing.* God willing, we still have years with her, even if those are years of loss, of a certain kind of grief. She'll still be with us, and there will still be joy.

"And then I'll go to heaven?" The question surprises me, because we're not particularly religious, but then I remember that her primary school is Church of England, and they must talk about these things there. If ever there was a time to believe in heaven, to hope and trust that there is a God who loves her, it is now.

"Yes, darling. You'll go to heaven."

She nods slowly, accepting this along with everything else. Perhaps the realisation, the rage and the tears will come later. At least in this moment there is peace. "That's all right, then."

I nod, not trusting myself to speak. Perhaps she is too young to realise all the losses she faces—all the moments and milestones she'll never know. That I'll never see. Perhaps she will be spared that, and it will only be my grief to bear, mine and Matt's. *And Anna's.* The thought slips in and takes root. *Anna.*

I have not seen Anna since that night in the wine bar, although she continues to leave meals for us every so often, and sends the occasional text. I always send one back, thanking her, but it's clear there is still a distance between us, a distance Matt and I have put there.

After that first seizure, I didn't have the wherewithal to engineer a visit with her as I'd planned, with all its accompanying stresses, but now, as Alice falls asleep, I wonder at myself. Can I really deny Anna so much, simply because I don't feel up to it?

Now, as I watch Alice's face soften into sleep, her chest rise and fall, I realise something I should have understood a long time ago. Anna needs to see Alice. While Alice is still seeing, talking, walking, *being*, Anna needs to know her daughter.

# CHAPTER THIRTY-SIX

## ANNA

"Hello, Anna."

Milly's voice sounds quiet rather than anxious, and for a second my heart seems to stop, my phone becoming slick in my hand, as the potential implication punches me in the chest. No matter how much I've told myself I've let go, in this moment I am one hundred per cent invested.

"It's not Alice...?" Surely it can't be the end already. Please God, no.

Milly lets out a wavery sound, something caught between a laugh and a sob. "No, it's not Alice. At least... not that way. Not yet." She pauses to draw a quick, even breath. "She's been in and out of the hospital lately, having her medication adjusted, but she came home a few days ago."

"Okay..."

"And I thought you might like to see her."

For a moment I can't speak. I'm trying to process what Milly said, and more importantly, why she said it. And then I realise that none of it actually matters. She's asking me if I want to see Alice, and there is only one answer to that.

"Yes, I would love to see her. When is a good time?"

"Saturday afternoon? If the weather's nice, we could have a barbecue."

"I'll be there."

"Great."

"Milly…" I have to ask. I need to know. "What made you change your mind? You and Matt?"

"It's the right thing to do," she says simply.

I feel as if I am floating through a dream as I get through the next two days. I keep expecting Milly to text me, to call it off. Has Matt agreed to this? Why has she changed her mind? But I tell myself those questions aren't important. Only Alice is.

I tell Will about the visit too, half-expecting him to be reluctant, or at least concerned, warning me about how I'm setting myself up to be too involved, to get hurt, but he isn't and he doesn't. Instead he hugs me and tells me he is happy for me, and echoes Milly's sentiment, that it's the right thing to do. That I need to see Alice, and maybe, just maybe, Alice needs to see me.

It is a gorgeous, sun-soaked day in early June when I head over to Milly and Matt's for four o'clock. It's the kind of day that encapsulates everything wonderful about a British summer, when the world is tinted with gold and filled with birdsong and butterflies, every moment like something caught on camera, a snapshot of happiness.

I've baked a batch of chocolate-chip cookies and made a salad for the barbecue, and I heft both as I walk up the path to their house, feeling more nervous than I think I ever have in my life. I have no idea what to expect, how I'll feel, what I should do or say. And what about Milly and Matt? What are they expecting from this visit? What do they want from me?

I ring the doorbell, balancing dishes, trying not to look terrified.

Milly opens the door and smiles when she sees me. "Anna," she says, and for a second I think she might actually hug me, but then she just reaches for my hand and gives it a squeeze. "I'm sorry it's been so long. Come through."

I follow her through the house, glancing around at the changes that have taken place since I was last here—the hand railings in the bathroom and by the kitchen, the walker stood by the door.

We step through the French windows to their strip of back garden, the grass, a verdant, Technicolor green, tumbling down to an old horse chestnut tree with a swing hanging from it, the kind with a deep bucket seat and buckles. Matt is standing by the barbecue on the terrace, and Alice—for this little girl before me is of course Alice—sits on a blanket, watching a butterfly float through the air.

It's such a perfect, pastoral scene that I wish I could take a photograph, but I know it wouldn't do it justice. I stand framed in the French windows for a moment, breathing it all in, emblazoning it on my mind, and then Alice turns and looks at me.

The first thing that blazes through my mind is that I know her. I've *always* known her. She looks just like her photos, like me, but the sense of knowing is deeper than that, soul-deep. Then she smiles at me.

"Hello," she says shyly, and my heart is so full I feel as if it could explode right out of my chest.

"Hello, Alice."

I walk towards her slowly, mindless of Milly, of Matt. I drop to my knees on the blanket by her and just drink her in. She watches me frankly, studying me the way I am studying her.

"Do I know you?" The words are a bit slurred, but I still understand them. Of course I do.

Before I can answer, Milly does. "Yes," she says. "You do, although you may not remember. But you've always known Anna, right from the beginning."

And I think it is the kindest thing she could have said. I glance at Matt, wondering how he is taking all this, but when I meet his gaze he just gives a little nod and looks away, not hostile as he once was, but something more accepting, perhaps a little bit resigned. This is still hard.

I sit down next to her. "What have you been doing today, Alice?"

"Watching butterflies. I want to catch one, but Mummy says they're too fr...frag..." she stumbles on the word, and I fill in for her.

"Fragile?" I fill in, and Alice nods.

"Perhaps Anna could push you on the swing," Milly suggests. "While I get the food ready." She glances at me, and I read everything in her gaze—the worry about Alice's mobility, whether I can keep her safe. But she trusts me. In this small, crucial thing, Milly trusts me.

"I'd love to," I say, and I hold out my hand. She takes it, and as her little fingers fold around mine, my heart feels as if it is exploding in my chest, with both joy and sorrow.

We walk slowly towards the swing, hand in hand, Alice's gait stiff and ungainly; she drags one foot behind her a little, and I go slowly, one step at a time, to match her uneven stride, aching inside for all she's lost, and yet so thankful that she's here. That we're here together.

I help her onto the swing, and when she's settled and safely buckled in, I gently push.

The breeze whispers by us and the sun shines down. Alice lets out a giggle as she swings higher.

"Look at me, Mummy!" she calls, and while part of me can't help but think that she could be calling to me, another part knows that she isn't, and that's okay. That's right.

I think of that father I saw long ago, pushing his daughter, the way she tilted her head back with joy, and I smile. Alice smiles back at me.

Later, after hours that I will commit to my memory forever, Milly pours us both wine while Matt gives Alice a bath upstairs.

"I should have called you sooner," she says. "A lot sooner." She pauses. "Years sooner."

"It doesn't matter now."

"It does. You could have been involved in her life all along..." Her face crumples. "Oh, Anna..."

And then we are both crying, and we are in each other's arms, hugging each other tightly, holding each other up. It's as if the years apart never happened, and yet they are more present now than they have ever been. We have been shaped by their scars, by the silence between us, and by some miracle of grace, we've come out stronger, on the other side.

"Do you know," Milly says when we have sniffed and wiped our cheeks and settled on the sofa, "I looked up my mother a few years ago? I finally looked at my birth records, after all this time."

"And what did you find?"

She sighs and leans her head back against the sofa. "She had postpartum depression, the same as I did, only worse. That's why she gave me up." She shakes her head slowly. "All these years I've thought I didn't want to know her. I didn't care, because I was so sure she didn't. I judged her for giving me up at six months." She lifts her head to look at me directly. "But now I feel differently. About a lot of things. About her...about you...about everything."

"Alice is beautiful, Milly. And you're a wonderful mother."

"Thank you." Milly nods slowly. "She belongs to both of us." I know it is a lot for her to admit. "Remember what I told you, way back when? About us all raising her?"

I nod. Of course I remember.

"I wish that could have happened. I really do, now." She smiles uncertainly. "But perhaps it still can. It's not...it's not too late, is it?"

"No." I shake my head, swallow hard. I've let go, and Milly has grabbed on, and somehow all of it feels right, as if we've come full circle, and we've ended up exactly where we need to be. Even Alice. "It's not too late, Milly. I know it can't be easy…"

"It's not. It's the hardest thing I've ever done, and I have to keep doing it, day after day, for who knows how long. And it's only going to get worse. That's the most frightening bit. Will I be able to cope? How will we manage? How will Alice?" Her fingers tremble as she lifts her wine glass to her lips.

"And yet she's beautiful." I smile at the memory of Alice on the swing, stumbling after a butterfly, just *being*. "Inside and out, she's beautiful."

"Yes, she is." Milly's voice wobbles and she sets her jaw. "And I'm so thankful for her, in spite of everything, *because* of everything. Sometimes that doesn't make sense, but it still is." She lets out a shaky laugh. "Do I sound crazy?"

"No," I tell her. "Wise." I pause, and then I ask hesitantly, "And Matt…?"

Milly sighs. "He was angry for a long time, but something like this… it purifies you. It takes away all the dross of anger, resentment, bitterness, hurt."

"If you let it."

"Yes, if you let it. And that's the decision we have to make every day. Every *second*. To let something good emerge, out of the bad. Out of the unimaginable."

I reach over to clasp her hand. "That's a brave thing to do."

"It's the only thing. The alternative is to let this destroy me, and I won't." Her eyes gleam and she blinks rapidly. "I *won't*. None of us will."

A creak sounds on the stair, and I turn to see Matt looking straight at me. I am still half-expecting him to tell me to leave, even now.

"Alice wants you to say goodnight," he says, and for a moment I can't speak.

"Me…?"

"Yes." He manages a stiff nod, a small, tense smile. "She asked for you especially."

And so, I tiptoe upstairs, my heart in my mouth. I find her bedroom, the same one as when she was a baby, but now it's a little girl's room instead of a nursery, all pink princesses and rainbow stencils.

Alice is sitting up in bed, her hair in damp ringlets, her cheeks rosy. She looks perfect.

"I asked Daddy if you could read me a story." It takes me a second to understand her, but then I nod, my heart so very full.

"I'd like that, Alice. I'd like that very much."

She hands me a book and I settle in next to her, both of us leaning against the pillow, my arm around her shoulders. We read an abridged version of *The Velveteen Rabbit*, that old, beloved classic of the rabbit who is loved into being real. My throat thickens as I read about his conversation with another well-loved but now-forgotten toy: "'Real isn't how you are made,' said the Skin Horse. 'It's a thing that happens to you. When a child loves you for a long, long time, not just to play with, but *really* loves you, then you become Real.'" I take a deep breath, willing the tears that threaten to recede.

"Go on, Anna," Alice says softly. "This is the best bit."

And so I continue, each word a painful labour of love. "'Does it hurt?' asked the Rabbit. 'Sometimes,' said the Skin Horse, for he was always truthful. 'When you are Real you don't mind being hurt.'" Alice nods, clearly familiar with every part of this story, savouring the words. I go on. "'Does it happen all at once, like being wound up,' he asked, 'or bit by bit?' 'It doesn't happen all at once,' said the Skin Horse. 'You become. It takes a long time. That's why it doesn't happen often to people who break easily, or have sharp edges, or who have to be carefully kept. Generally, by the time you are Real, most of your hair has been loved off, and your eyes drop out and you get loose in the joints and very shabby. But these things don't matter at all, because once you are Real you can't be ugly, except to people who don't understand.'"

By this point I can't keep the tears at bay, because it's all so unbearably poignant, so tragically bittersweet, so *real*.

Alice smiles and reaches for my hand. "It's all right," she says softly, and I'm amazed that she has the strength—and the grace —to comfort me, even just over a story. "It's all right, because it's good to be real."

"Yes, it is." I sniff and manage to smile. "You're right, Alice. It's very good."

She smiles at me, and I smile back, and if I could cup this moment between my hands and hold it, I would. Oh, how I would hold on to it forever.

I manage to finish the story without shedding any more tears, and Alice's eyelids are fluttering closed by the time I reach the last page. "Goodnight, Anna," she whispers, and my eyes sting with tears.

"Goodnight, Alice." I close the book and just watch her sleep, the gentle rise and fall of her chest, the soft, little breaths. The whole house, the whole world, is hushed and still. At peace.

Will I have another moment like this? Will Milly, or Matt? More than ever, I am aware of how little any of us can know what the future holds, what sorrows we will have to bear, what hope we will find in the most unexpected of places. And yet, in this moment, I am glad—and I am thankful, for everything, even the heartache, the grief, all of it, because it brought me here. It brought *us* here.

"I love you, Alice," I whisper, and her eyelids flutter once more as I lean over and kiss her cheek, breathing in the scent of strawberry shampoo. She lets out a breathy sigh, and then, slowly, a smile on my lips, I rise and go downstairs.

# EPILOGUE

## MILLY

### *Three years later*

"Look at me, Mummy!"

"I see you, darling." I wave and smile at my son, five years old and so very proud of swinging by himself. We adopted Toby six months ago, after a year of paperwork and planning, assessments and visits. He's had his challenges, as any child in his position would, but he's also been a joy, and Alice has loved having a little brother.

The last three years have held so many heartbreaks, nights where I've sat on the edge of the bathtub and sobbed till I felt utterly empty inside; days spent in hospital, as Alice adjusts to new limitations and medications; small, daily griefs as well as the huge gaping ones.

But we have also had so many surprising joys, the greatest being that Alice is still with us at all. At eight years old, she has no sight and limited speech, and for the last year and a half she's needed a motorised wheelchair to get around. She's still in school, thanks to the indomitable Miss Hamilton, who has championed her cause as the school's Special Education Needs Coordinator and won battles for us that we didn't even know we had to fight.

Matt and I have grieved every small loss of Alice's, even as we've celebrated the major milestones. Birthdays, Christmases, writing her name, being able to swim...these have all been hard-won triumphs. There have been challenges and frustrations, far too many, and the worst is when Alice experiences them herself, thinking she is stupid, hating her failing body and mind, railing against the way things are.

But we've worked through them, if not past them, drawing together in the midst of the sorrow, and we've found support in local groups, as well as the yearly international conference for families of children with Batten disease. We've travelled as far as Newcastle and Swansea to meet with other families in situations similar to ours; a year ago we even went to Disney World, in Florida, with a dozen other Batten families, for the most magical week of our lives. So many good things, amidst the sad and the hard and even the impossible.

A few months after Anna came back into our lives, the cancer finally claimed my mother; she was at peace at the end, which is all anyone can ask for. Since her death, my father has come by a lot more, spending many evenings and weekends with us, sharing in our lives.

As for Anna... I don't know what we'd do without her—and I don't know what she'd do without us. The last three years has had us entering a deeper friendship than anyone could have imagined, least of all me. Two and a half years ago, Alice was flower girl at Anna and Will's wedding, a highlight for all of us.

We are all a family, in the truest sense, and even Jack has become more involved, relocating back to the UK two years ago, and seeing Alice as often as he can. It's happened just as I once said I wanted it to, and yet in a way I never would have imagined or even tried to bring about. If I'd known what lay ahead when I first got pregnant, I think I would have faltered at the first step. But here we are, and despite everything, because of everything, it is good.

"Alice!" Toby slows on the swing as he points to his sister, coming through the play park's gates on her mobility scooter, Anna by her side. Every Saturday they have an ice cream date at

Swoon Gelato, just the two of them. It's the highlight of Alice's week, and undoubtedly of Anna's too, and I love seeing them both so happy.

Taking Toby's hand, I turn towards them. "How was the gelato? What flavour did you choose?"

"Chocolate brownie as usual for this kid," Anna says with a smile, touching Alice's golden hair. "Why mess with a good thing?"

"Why indeed." I glance at Alice, who has a smear of chocolate around her lips. She's been on purely pureed food for a year now, and a feeding tube is surely in her future. But today, she had ice cream, and that is enough.

"And for you?" I ask Anna. She has been working through Swoon's flavours for the last year, rating each one.

"Amarena Cherry Cheesecake. I told Alice it was six out of ten."

"Why only six?"

"Not enough cherries." She rests one hand on her barely-there bump for a second before bending down to give Toby a hug. "I saw you on the swing there, big boy."

"I did it by myself!"

"Amazing." And it *is* amazing, because Toby came to us from a background of abuse and neglect, cowering at the smallest thing, unwilling to try anything new or unknown. I gave up the idea of a perfect family, a newborn I could claim as my own, a long time ago. Toby belongs to me as much as Alice. They are my children. There is no *but*. Looking back at my own childhood, I don't think there ever was.

"Matt's barbecuing sausages," I say as I put one hand on Alice's shoulder, anchoring me to her. She is warm and solid and real. She is here, and we are happy. "Shall we go home?"

Anna and Toby both nod, and Alice gives me the kind of grin that reminds me of when she was a baby, when she was new.

Every day is new. Every day is a miracle of grace. Together we turn for home.

# A LETTER FROM KATE

Dear reader,

Thank you so much for taking the time to read *Not My Daughter*. I am so pleased that you did and I hope you enjoyed it.

If you did, and would like to be the first to hear about my new releases, just sign up at the following link. Your email address will never be shared and you can unsubscribe at any time.

*www.bookouture.com/kate-hewitt*

The idea for the book came to me when I was reading a newspaper article about the ethical complexities of modern fertility treatments, especially when more than two people are involved. I am fascinated by the ethics of parenthood in contemporary society, with so many scenarios occurring that we couldn't have envisioned even a generation ago, and the struggle we all have in navigating this new and ever-changing landscape.

Yet at its heart, *Not My Daughter* is not so much a story about ethics, as about the hidden grace we can find in sorrow and tragedy, and how the worst of circumstances can lead to surprising joy—something I truly believe and have lived out, in a smaller way, myself.

While researching the medical background for *Not My Daughter*, I learned so much about Batten disease, which is truly a heart-wrenching condition. You can learn more about it through the Batten Disease Family Association, at *www.bdfa-uk.org.uk*.

Thank you to those at the Association who answered my questions concerning diagnosis, genetics, and living with the disease.

If you enjoyed *Not My Daughter*, I would be so grateful if you could spare a couple of minutes to write a review. You can also get in touch via my Facebook page or Twitter account, or join my Facebook group Kate's Reads, where we discuss all sorts of books. I always am grateful to hear from readers, so please do reach out!

Thanks again for reading!

Best wishes
Kate

# ACKNOWLEDGMENTS

It takes a village to raise a child, and so it took with this book! Thank you to all the lovely team at Bookouture: my wonderful editor Isobel who gave me such invaluable feedback on the first very rough draft (!) as well everyone on the staff who has helped to launch my books into the world—Peta, Kim, Noelle, Emily, Alex, Alexandra, and Ellen, to name but a few.

Thank you to the medical professionals online and in real life who patiently answered my many questions, often asked in ignorance.

Also thanks to Margery Williams, whose beloved children's book *The Velveteen Rabbit* inspired part of this story.

Thank you also to my online writing friends who are always there to listen to me moan and then tell me I really can do it—the Savvies, the members of the Bookouture Author Lounge, and my dear friend Jenna.

Thank you also to my wonderful family who are so patient when I am absorbed in writing, and a special mention to my daughter Ellen, who reads my books out loud as I am writing, making me cringe—as much as I hate that habit, you definitely help make my books stronger! Love you!

# READING GROUP
# GUIDE

# DISCUSSION QUESTIONS

1. Should Anna have offered to donate an egg to Milly at the beginning of the book? Why or why not?

2. How did Anna and Milly's friendship change throughout the story? What were the reasons for the change?

3. How much of the tension between Anna and Milly was due to Milly's pregnancy, and how much to the history of their friendship, and especially what happened when Anna was eighteen?

4. Did you feel Anna was justified in considering applying for custody of Alice? Why or why not? Were Matt and Milly justified in their response? How could things have been handled differently?

5. How did Jack's involvement affect the rupture of Milly and Alice's friendship? Was he justified in his concerns?

6. How was Milly's relationship with her mother integral to her own view of motherhood? In what positive and negative ways did it affect her?

7. How did Alice's diagnosis change the dynamics between Anna and Milly? Why do you think that happened?

8. Why did Matt feel so guilty, and how did that affect his actions and attitude towards Anna?

9. Both Milly and Anna are able to find a certain level of peace and even joy amidst Alice's terminal condition. Do you think that is realistic? Have you ever experienced something similar, even in a small way?

VISIT **GCPClubCar.com** to sign up for the **GCP Club Car** newsletter, featuring exclusive promotions, info on other **Club Car** titles, and more.

 @grandcentralpub     @grandcentralpub     @grandcentralpub

# ABOUT THE AUTHOR

Kate Hewitt is a *USA Today* bestselling author. Her works include the Hartley-by-the-Sea series set in the Lake District, the Willoughby Close series set in the Cotswolds, and the Tales from Goswell series, written as Katharine Swartz.

She lives in a small market town in Wales with her husband and five young(ish) children, along with their two golden retrievers.

You can learn more at:
kate-hewitt.com
Twitter @katehewitt1
Facebook.com/KateHewittAuthor